W9-CKI-766

Carved
in
Stone

Books by Elizabeth Camden

THE BLACKSTONE LEGACY

Carved in Stone

HOPE AND GLORY SERIES

The Spice King
A Gilded Lady
The Prince of Spies

The Lady of Bolton Hill
The Rose of Winslow Street
Against the Tide
Into the Whirlwind
With Every Breath
Beyond All Dreams
Toward the Sunrise: An Until the Dawn *Novella*
Until the Dawn
Summer of Dreams: A From This Moment *Novella*
From This Moment
To the Farthest Shores
A Dangerous Legacy
A Daring Venture
A Desperate Hope

Carved
in
Stone

ELIZABETH
CAMDEN

BETHANYHOUSE
a division of Baker Publishing Group
Minneapolis, Minnesota

F
Camden
Elizabeth

© 2021 by Dorothy Mays

Published by Bethany House Publishers
11400 Hampshire Avenue South
Bloomington, Minnesota 55438
www.bethanyhouse.com

Bethany House Publishers is a division of
Baker Publishing Group, Grand Rapids, Michigan

Printed in the United States of America

                    Library of Congress Cataloging-in-Publication Data
Names: Camden, Elizabeth, author.
Title: Carved in stone / Elizabeth Camden.
Description: Bloomington, Minnesota : Bethany House Publishers, [2021] | Series:
    The Blackstone legacy ; 1
Identifiers: LCCN 2021015483 | ISBN 9780764238437 (trade paper) |
    ISBN 9780764239342 (casebound) | ISBN 9781493433735 (ebook)
Subjects: GSAFD: Mystery fiction. | Suspense fiction.
Classification: LCC PS3553.A429 C37 2021 | DDC 813/.54--dc23
LC record available at https://lccn.loc.gov/2021015483

This is a work of historical reconstruction; the appearances of certain historical figures are therefore inevitable. All other characters, however, are products of the author's imagination, and any resemblance to actual persons, living or dead, is coincidental.

Cover design by Jennifer Parker
Cover image of woman by Lee Avison / Arcangel

21 22 23 24 25 26 27   7 6 5 4 3 2 1

1

*H*ow could a man buy a new suit with a dozen eggs? Patrick O'Neill sighed, protecting the basket of eggs as he navigated through the crowd of pedestrians to the tailor's shop on Mulberry Street. He should have earned a bit of cash from drawing up Mrs. Donovan's last will and testament, but the old woman paid him with eggs instead. She'd come to this country during the Irish Potato Famine, and Patrick had a soft spot for folks like her, so he settled for the eggs.

Life would be cheaper if he could buy ready-made suits like most people, but broad-shouldered men who stood six feet four inches tall rarely had that option. Everything Patrick wore had to be made to order, and it got expensive. Still, the tailor owed him for staving off an eviction last month.

A bell above the shop door dinged as Patrick entered, and the tailor greeted him warmly.

"There's the Lower East Side's most famous lawyer," Mr. Collins said. "I figured we'd be seeing you." The tailor continued stacking bolts of cloth on the cramped shelving over the only sewing machine in the overstuffed shop.

"What makes you say that?" Patrick asked, his Irish accent a little thicker than normal. He left Ireland when he was fourteen, but his natural brogue came back strong when he was among his own.

"Your ma was bragging about the big case you've got coming up," Mr. Collins said. "What sort of man would battle the Blackstones in a rumpled old suit like the one you're wearing?"

Patrick tried not to wince. "Let's not go tossing that name around, okay? No one is supposed to know about this yet."

Even the Blackstones didn't know about it yet. They were the most powerful family in New York City, and they would come after him the instant they found out what was brewing. Surprise was one of the few advantages Patrick had, and he wanted to keep a lid on this case until the last possible moment.

"Fiona, come out here and take Mr. O'Neill's measurements," the tailor called toward the back of the shop.

Patrick braced himself. He'd hoped to escape this appointment without the tailor's daughter waiting on him. Fiona was a pretty nineteen-year-old who looked at him with hot eyes and a hungry expression. She approached him with a tape measure, and Mr. Collins brought out a few bolts of cloth for Patrick to choose from.

"Those people are going to make mincemeat of you, boy-o," Mr. Collins said in a worried tone. "They'll send you running straight back to the seminary."

"No!" Fiona tossed a measuring tape over Patrick's shoulders and ran her hands across his back to straighten the tape. "Nobody wanted to see you become Father What-a-Waste. Turning away from the priesthood is the best thing you ever did."

Last year Patrick had balked only two weeks shy of his vow to enter the priesthood, and guilt still plagued him. Father Doyle had paid for him to go to college and law school. They let him practice law the entire time he'd been in seminary because everyone assumed he would become a lawyer for the church. He owed them, but as his final vows loomed, so had his incessant, unquenchable longing for a family.

6

He wanted a wife. He wanted children of his own, not just the chance to minister to others. He wanted a huge, rollicking family with kids climbing all over him when he returned from work and a pretty wife waiting for him at home.

Patrick was thirty-four and still unmarried, which caused people in the neighborhood to hurl their daughters in his direction. At the moment, Fiona's hands were traveling in a dangerous direction as she measured the length of his inseam.

"Fi," he said, feeling his face flush, "a little decorum, please."

Mercifully, her father grabbed the tape measure and shooed Fiona to the other side of the shop.

Patrick nodded to the basket of eggs. "The eggs and my help with getting the landlord off your back last month will make us square for a new suit, won't it?"

Mr. Collins nodded as he continued taking measurements. "That it will. Now, tell me, boy, what germ of insanity prompted you to take on a seedy client like Mick Malone?"

Mick Malone was the most contemptible man Patrick had ever represented. Mick had escaped convictions for kidnapping and murder, but everyone knew he was guilty. Now he was hoping to cash in on his notoriety by penning a memoir, and the Blackstones' reaction was going to be savage.

"Mr. Malone is entitled to legal representation, same as any man," Patrick replied.

"You'd better take a bath after dealing with that one," Mr. Collins warned. "Your mother said Mick was drunk as a skunk when you met with him last week." The tailor spoke quietly, but news of Patrick's mother's gossiping was worrisome. They lived in the Five Points, a rowdy Irish slum where secrets spread like wildfire. Patrick needed to know exactly what his mother had blabbed all over the neighborhood.

"What else did Ma tell you?"

"Oh, you know, how proud she is of you. How she wishes you'd marry and start giving her grandbabies, now that the church won't get you. Don't blame your ma. She's bursting with pride whenever she talks about you, Patrick lad."

That might be, but she needed to stop running on about his clients. His typical cases battling evictions or bailing someone out of jail were as dull as watching paint dry. Not the Blackstone case. Defending Mick Malone against the Blackstones was the most important case of his career.

"Come for a fitting next week," Mr. Collins said. "You'll look as smart as any of those shifty Blackstone lawyers. You are Ireland's and America's finest!"

Patrick nodded, wishing he was half as confident as his tailor.

Patrick bought his mother a bouquet of daisies on the way home. The flowers would help soften her up before he read her the riot act over the way she was jabbering about his cases. Birdie O'Neill's greatest hobby in life was bragging about her son, and it had become a problem.

When Patrick first began practicing law, he'd asked her not to discuss his cases. She'd pinched his cheek and promised to behave, but inevitably he'd hear about her nattering whenever he visited the barbershop or a pub. It was usually harmless, but this case was different.

It had all started when Father Doyle showed up at their apartment two months ago, pleading for Patrick's help with the infamous Mick Malone case, and Birdie overheard everything. Patrick didn't want the case, but how could he turn down his old benefactor?

He walked up to the fourth-floor apartment he shared with his mother and let himself in. Birdie lay sprawled on the sofa at a strange angle, watching the pigeons feed on the lump of suet she set on the windowsill for them.

"You okay, Ma?" he asked.

Birdie turned her face toward him and sent him a smile. "Daisies! How nice."

She still made no move to rise. Patrick crossed to the other side of the room, where they kept a pitcher filled with water from the pump that served everyone in the building. On the way, he noticed the cake his mother had brought home from the bakery. It looked like a basket. The bottom half used interlocking strands of chocolate frosting to look like wicker, and real strawberries were mounded atop the cake. If he didn't know better, he'd have mistaken it for a genuine basket of strawberries.

"Those cakes sold out before I even finished them," she said with pride.

Birdie O'Neill's cakes made the Gerald Bakery famous. Crowds of people came to the bakery window each day to admire her whimsical creations. Sometimes they were towering layer cakes built to resemble city landmarks like Grand Central Station or St. Patrick's Cathedral. Other times she imitated the natural world, like this strawberry basket cake. Once or twice a week, she brought a cake home to share with the neighbors. It made them one of the most popular renters in the building.

"Nice cake," he said, picking out a ripe strawberry and popping it in his mouth.

Birdie still hadn't gotten up from the sofa, and there was nothing on the stove for dinner. That was odd. She usually took great pride as a housekeeper. Her day started at four o'clock each morning when she headed to the bakery to start the ovens, and she finished by early afternoon, which left her plenty of time to prepare dinner. Their apartment usually smelled like heaven when he arrived home.

"What's wrong?" he asked, since she wasn't the sort to complain.

"I fell while lugging in a sack of flour from the wagon this morning," she said. "It was dark, and I slipped on a loose brick."

He closed the distance between them and hunkered down before her. "And you worked the rest of the day?"

"Don't worry, it was nothing," she teased while pinching his cheek. He didn't complain. He'd finally persuaded her to stop pinching his cheek in public, but he didn't have the heart to ask her to quit at home. "The pain went away for a while, but now it's bad again." She had a bandage on her forearm too.

"Did that happen when you fell?" he asked with a nod at the bandage.

"I scraped the wagon wheel on my way down. It's nothing. Mr. Gerald patched it up as soon as I got inside."

"Mr. Gerald ought to lug his own sacks of flour."

"Don't be taking that tone," she said. "Mr. Gerald is a fine man who has always treated me well."

Maybe, but Birdie was too old for lugging heavy sacks and tending hot ovens before the crack of dawn. No man should have to worry about his mother collapsing under the weight of a thirty-pound sack of flour.

"You can quit, Ma. I'm making decent money these days."

"Please don't make me point out that Mr. Gerald always pays in cash."

Patrick looked away. When they'd first arrived from Ireland, they were so poor that Patrick had to beg on the streets. That sort of shame never fully went away, and depending on his mother for steady income was humiliating. He would start getting tougher with his clients. Some of them could afford to pay in cash, and he needed to start demanding it.

But first he needed to win the Mick Malone case.

"Ma, you've got to stop talking about my cases in public," he said. "Keep quiet about the Mick Malone case. It's important that his book gets published before the Blackstones find out about it."

"They'll get wind of it sooner or later," she pointed out.

"Let it be later. The book will hit the shelves in September. The closer we get to that date without anyone knowing about it, the better our chances."

No one in the city wanted to take on the Blackstones, but sometimes a man didn't have much choice.

2

*T*he Friday evening soirees at Gwen Blackstone Kellerman's home were famous. She originally started hosting them as a way for the professors at Blackstone College to relax and unwind after a week of classes, but over the years they had grown into much more. Artists and intellectuals from across the city vied for a chance to attend her soirees, which could last until dawn. The informal gatherings became a place where professors debated new ideas and artists mingled with academics. It was said that Mark Twain was inspired to write a short story based on a conversation he had with an aging English professor in the corner of Gwen's garden.

These weekly gatherings were Gwen's proudest accomplishment, since she would probably never become a botany professor like she'd once hoped. Dreams of a successful marriage and motherhood had also passed her by, but her soirees made Blackstone College a thriving intellectual community.

So far tonight she had consoled a professor whose latest experiment didn't pan out, listened to a musician play his new composition on her piano, and toasted the birth of a baby boy to a physics professor. It was a brilliant, moonlit summer evening . . . which was why the gloomy expression on the college president's face seemed so strange.

President Matthews had been appointed two years ago and

was still struggling to find his footing among this tight-knit community. He lived next door to Gwen on a tree-shaded street where most senior faculty lived. Not everyone on campus appreciated the new president, but Gwen understood the challenges he faced better than most and did her best to support him.

"Gwen, if it isn't too much trouble, I'd like to go next door for a brief discussion," he said.

She was in the middle of listening to a visiting professor from Japan discuss his research on undersea volcanic activity. "Can it wait a few minutes?" she asked, eager to hear more about how molten lava could occur underwater.

President Matthews shook his head. "It is a matter of some delicacy. I wouldn't ask if it weren't important."

Gwen nodded and headed across the crowded parlor toward the front door. There were sixty people here tonight. Most had spilled onto her terraced garden to enjoy the warm summer evening, but a group of the oldest professors had staked their claim to the upholstered furniture in her front room.

"Gwen, what is with this amazing tree?" a chemistry professor asked, holding up the dwarfed Himalayan cedar in its ceramic pot.

"It's called a bonsai tree," she said. "Professor Watanabe brought it to me as a hostess gift tonight. Isn't it darling?"

Over the years, people had brought her flowering shrubs, herbs, and bulbs from across the world, making the two-acre garden behind her house a showpiece. It was a green-scented world where science and beauty converged. Her happiest hours were spent in the calm oasis of her garden, and she loved sharing it with the people of Blackstone College each Friday evening.

Two more people tried to intercept her before she made it outside. The gentle hum of crickets sounded in the distance as she and President Matthews walked across the lawn to his house next door. A light on the front porch glowed as he led her inside.

"You added new wallpaper," Gwen said as she stepped into the foyer of the president's house.

"It was my wife's idea," he said. "I hope you don't mind the change."

"Of course not. It's your house now."

President Matthews still seemed ill at ease whenever he invited her inside because this had once been her father's home. Theodore Blackstone was the college's founder and had served as its president for twenty-eight years. Gwen had been born in this house and lived here until she married Jasper and moved next door.

Or perhaps the new president's deference to her was because of her maiden name. Everyone knew she was a Blackstone by birth, and the name tended to inspire awe, fear, and ghoulish curiosity.

"Tell me what I can do for you," she prompted once they were seated in his study. The windows were open, making it easy to hear laughter and the faint sound of the piano from her house next door.

"I received bad news this afternoon," President Matthews said. "Your uncle has made good on his threat to terminate funding for the college."

Gwen bowed her head. Uncle Oscar had been threatening the college's funding for years, but she hadn't believed he would ever end it. Her mind reeled, unable to imagine a world without Blackstone College in it.

She glanced outside toward the people mingling in her garden. None of them knew how close the college teetered on the edge of bankruptcy.

President Matthews continued outlining their situation. "I hoped my negotiations with the senior members of the Blackstone family would be successful without appealing to you for help," he said, his voice placating and cautious.

People on campus still treated her with kid gloves even though it had been two years since she lost both her father and her husband in the same week. She had fully recovered from both tragedies, but President Matthews still seemed worried about hurting her feelings.

"I'm afraid that without additional funding, I will be forced to close the physics department," he said.

Her shoulders sagged. "That department was very dear to my father."

"Other colleges in the city can take our students in physics should the worst occur. New York University has an excellent program in physics."

"I don't care about New York University," she said with a sigh. "I only care about the colleges founded by Vanderbilt and Carnegie, and you know why."

Cornelius Vanderbilt and Andrew Carnegie had both created colleges to enhance their reputations, and soon Blackstone College would be equally prestigious. If all went well, someday the name Blackstone would stand for scientific and medical progress rather than greed and exploitation.

"Yes, yes," President Matthews said. "Unfortunately, the physics department hasn't yet turned a profit. At least the biology and chemistry departments have patented some of their work, but overall, we have an atrocious record of—"

His sentence choked off, and Gwen smothered a laugh. "You can say it," she teased. "I know my father was terrible at managing money."

President Matthews looked grateful that she took his gaffe in stride. "Your father was a great man, but not the best steward of a budget. Gwen, I'm afraid the situation is dire. Eliminating departments is only a short-term solution. If your family does not reinstate their annual donations, the college will face bankruptcy within the next few years."

It was inconceivable. This college was her entire world. She grew up here, went to college here, got married here. She intended to spend the rest of her life on these forty acres of ivy-covered buildings and intellectual progress. For eight years she'd been the wife of the college's leading researcher, and she taught the introductory botany classes. She hosted faculty parties and cheered up students who sometimes flagged under the weight of demanding academic rigor. *This* sort of work was what she was born to do, not haggle over money or tangle with the bank.

"President Matthews, please understand that I have no influence over how my uncle and grandfather parcel out the Black-stone fortune."

The only reason her father could pressure the bank was be-cause everyone in the family felt sorry for him. The last bit of sympathy from her family's banking empire had died with him, and now the college was gasping for breath. Tuition revenue could never keep their research-intensive programs afloat.

"The only thing that will prove the college's worth to my family is if we develop some magnificent scientific discovery that will garner national attention and help blot out the . . . well, the other things my family has been associated with in the past."

It was an elegant way of alluding to child labor, unsafe business practices, and union busting. Such ugly words. But those were things of the past, and the Blackstone Bank had come a long way since the tragedy that nearly destroyed her father.

It hurt to see the anguish on President Matthews's face. He was still young, but the sprinkling of gray in his hair had increased in the past two years. He'd inherited a financial mess from her father, and it would take a while to repair.

"You're doing a wonderful job," she assured him. "You have my complete, unstinting support. Tell me how I can help."

He gave her a reluctant smile. "I know you dislike leaving campus and dealing with your uncle, but if you could appeal to him to reverse his decision, it would be a godsend."

Appealing to Uncle Oscar meant confronting the two things she disliked most in the world: lawyers and the snarl of down-town Manhattan. There was a reason she rarely left the college campus. This secluded haven in the Upper West Side was free of the congestion, noise, and skyscrapers that clogged downtown. Gwen would happily go through the rest of her life ignoring financial ledgers or the tedium of legal haggling if she could.

But if a woman loved something, she needed to fight for it.

"You can count on me," she told President Matthews.

His whooshing sigh of relief underscored how important it was that she succeed.

Gwen left the safety of Blackstone College to confront her uncle and grandfather first thing on Monday morning. Tension coiled tighter with each mile as the carriage rolled farther into the heart of Manhattan, with its chaotic mix of carriages, trams, and automobiles all vying for dominance on the congested city streets. She never liked it here. The towering buildings blotted out too much of the sky, and it didn't feel natural.

The carriage finally arrived at her family's bank on the intersection of Wall Street and Devon. She rarely came here anymore and braced herself for meeting with her uncle.

"We're here," she said to the two bullnecked men sitting on the carriage bench opposite her. Anytime she came to the bank, she brought bodyguards. Zeke and Lorenzo had been with her since childhood, but after her father died, she reassigned them to other positions at the college. She no longer wanted to live in a protected bubble, but life could be challenging for anyone whose last name was Blackstone. Six years ago, an anarchist tried to assassinate her uncle as he left the bank. No Blackstone felt entirely safe entering or leaving the bank since.

Lorenzo helped her alight from the carriage while Zeke scanned both sides of the hectic street. She craned her neck to look up at the marble columns of the Blackstone Bank, which had occupied this block of coveted Manhattan real estate for over fifty years. The neoclassical building had six columns on the front portico to symbolize the strength of corporate America.

Lorenzo walked beside her as they approached the bank, and Zeke followed behind. A uniformed doorman held the steel-studded copper door open for Gwen and her bodyguards as they passed into the cool hall of America's leading investment bank.

Her heels clicked on the marble floor and echoed off the coffered ceiling. This wasn't the sort of bank that did business with individual customers, so there were no tellers stationed behind counters. All the important business took place upstairs, where analysts made recommendations for funding the nation's infrastructure. Over the decades, the Blackstones had financed ports, canals, and railroads that crisscrossed the nation. They floated bonds to support cities, states, and foreign governments. It was said that France would have fallen to the Germans in 1871 if her grandfather hadn't propped up their army with an emergency loan.

A clerk rushed forward to meet her. "Good morning, Mrs. Kellerman. Your grandfather and uncle are expecting you. Would you like tea or refreshments before heading up to the fifth floor?"

She turned to her bodyguards. "Why don't you both relax and have something to drink?" Once inside the well-guarded confines of the bank, she had no fear of kidnappers, bombs, or blackmail.

Zeke and Lorenzo headed toward the lounge, while the clerk escorted her to the elevator. A uniformed attendant closed the gate on the elevator and cranked the brass dial to begin the lift. Even the elevator was grand, its marble floor inlaid with turquoise and jade. Her grandfather did nothing halfway.

The word *grandfather* usually conveyed a warmly paternal man fading into old age while occupying a rocking chair. Nothing could be further from the truth concerning Frederick Blackstone, who so disliked the implications of the word *grandfather* that he had ordered her to call him Frederick once she became an adult.

She pasted a serene smile on her face as she entered Frederick's office. Velvet draperies framed floor-to-ceiling windows with a perfect view of the New York Stock Exchange only two blocks away. Frederick sat at his desk while Uncle Oscar stood by the window, his pearl-handled walking stick at his side as he glowered at her through his one good eye. A black patch covered the other eye, ruined by the assassin's bomb six years earlier.

"Gwen," her uncle greeted her tersely. "Still wearing your Rapunzel look, I see."

She touched the long braid of blond hair draped over her

shoulder. Most women in Manhattan pinned their hair up in fussy styles, but Gwen preferred a more natural look and usually wore it down. Instead of torturing herself with tight corsets, she favored the loose gowns that were coming into fashion among the artistic set. She was a free-thinking woman and loved the softer silhouettes of the Art Nouveau movement, but her uncle was far more traditional.

Still, she didn't want to get distracted from her mission. She lifted her chin a notch and met her uncle's single good eye. "I've come seeking a reinstatement of the college's annual funding. The new president is doing amazing work, but he needs more time before he can run the college without a deficit."

Uncle Oscar approached her, leaning heavily on the cane as he drew near. The bomb that ruined the tendons in Oscar's right leg had also killed two innocent bystanders. The doctors had feared Oscar would never walk again, but her uncle's indomitable will came to the fore, and he'd trained his body to adapt to its shortcomings. He could now walk as quickly as anyone, albeit with a distinctive lurch.

"We founded that college as a sop to keep your father happy," he said. "It was supposed to add luster to the Blackstone name, but it's never performed as hoped."

"Not true," she insisted. "Just last month *Harper's Magazine* featured us on their cover. Our biochemistry department expects to have a treatment for tetanus within the next few years."

"And I expected the college to be financially self-sufficient by the last decade," Oscar said.

Her grandfather nodded in agreement. "When your father was president of the college, he wasted far too much money on expensive professors and overly ambitious research."

Gwen looked away. Her husband had been a perfect example of one of those idealistic professors who was brilliant but profligate with his research budget. "We always knew the college would initially lose money—"

"It's been thirty years!" Uncle Oscar interrupted. "The entire idea was a foolish endeavor to pacify Theodore. He had no business being a college president if he couldn't even balance a checkbook."

Gwen maintained her serene expression. "It wasn't to pacify my father, it was to turn around the reputation of a family name that had become synonymous with greed and avarice. We've spent decades improving our reputation, and now you want to throw it all away?"

Oscar lifted a book off the table and tossed it at her. Its pages splayed as it flew, but she caught it just before it hit the ground. She read the title on the cover and gasped.

The Flamboyant Life and Adventures
of Mick Malone: A Memoir

Mick Malone, the man who haunted her childhood nightmares. She didn't even realize he was still alive.

"That book will be released in September," Oscar said. "One of those seedy journalists from the *New York Sun* got an advance copy and wanted my opinion. It's slated to become a bestseller. Your fancy college has done nothing to dampen the public's appetite for sordid gossip."

Gwen's mouth went dry as she read the summary of the book, which promised the details of Mick Malone's colorful life of crime, including special insight into the Blackstone scandal and the injustice he endured at the hands of the most powerful family in America.

The irony was that Mick Malone wasn't a victim, but a criminal who had perpetrated a profound crime against her family. Everyone knew he was guilty of kidnapping and killing her three-year-old brother shortly before Gwen was born. Her father paid the ransom, but her brother was never returned. Days went by, then weeks, then years, but young William Blackstone was never found.

Her father hired an army of private investigators to hunt for the kidnappers. Within a week, they caught Malone, along with undeniable proof of his guilt. His apartment contained hundred-dollar bills with serial numbers matching those in the ransom payment and the typewriter with the flawed key that had typed the ransom note. Most chillingly, there was a single shoe belonging to little Willy Blackstone that was stained with blood.

Malone was put on trial for kidnapping and murder. It was a hanging offense, but a slippery defense attorney distracted the jury by putting the Blackstones' reputation on trial. At that time, the Blackstone name was synonymous with greed and exploitation. When the prosecutor objected, the defense attorney claimed the shameful details were essential to Mr. Malone's defense because the list of Blackstone enemies was endless. How could the laughing Irishman who loved his wife and went to church every Sunday be a villain who kidnapped children? Day after day, the defense attorney presented witnesses who testified to various Blackstone depredations and pointed to other suspects, such as union leaders, anarchists, and disgruntled businessmen who'd been driven into bankruptcy by the unforgiving policies of the Blackstone Bank. There were plenty of suspects who might have killed Willy Blackstone, and the jury wanted to send a message.

They found Mick Malone not guilty despite the overwhelming evidence against him.

Not guilty. The verdict practically killed her father but delighted the press. People hailed Mick Malone as a working-class hero, a man who challenged the hated Blackstones and lived to tell the tale. While everyone agreed it was a shame about the child, unsympathetic journalists touted the plight of other children who labored in Blackstone-financed coal mines and factories. Twelve men considered all the evidence and decided there wasn't enough proof to send Mick Malone to the gallows.

The verdict changed her father forever. Theodore suffered a nervous breakdown, and he began believing the hatred against his family was justified. In a desperate attempt to find meaning in his son's death, Theodore created Blackstone College, dedicated to education and curing the diseases of the poor. Her grandfather never liked the expensive venture that had yet to turn a profit, but he agreed because Theodore asked it of him.

The college had helped the Blackstones slowly rehabilitate their image, but all that goodwill would suffer if this revolting memoir stirred up old animosity against them.

She placed a trembling hand over the book. "I didn't even realize Mick Malone was still alive."

"He's a washed-up old drunk," her grandfather said. "I won't take this lying down. We've already filed paperwork with the court to halt publication. I'll sue them for libel and defamation of character."

Gwen instinctively recoiled from lawsuits, lawyers, and anything that smacked of conflict. Why couldn't people simply behave like decent human beings? She and her father had created a paradise on earth in their forty-acre campus where people respected and supported each other. It was as close to the Garden of Eden as could exist in a fallen world, and this awful book on her lap awakened old demons she believed were safely consigned to the past.

"I don't think so," she said, scrambling for ways to mitigate this disaster. "Suing Mick Malone will roll back decades of goodwill we have garnered from the college. We need to handle this with finesse."

"What do you recommend?" Oscar asked. In truth, her uncle wasn't a horrible man. He was smart and had suffered more than most from the hatred aimed at her family. Perhaps she could work with him to defeat a common enemy.

"Mick Malone is obviously in need of funds," she said. "I suggest we quietly pay him off. A thousand dollars ought to do it, and it will save us the headache of this memoir seeing the light of day."

"Absolutely not," Oscar snapped. "That man killed my nephew and destroyed my brother's spirit. I won't pay him a dime."

"Then look the other way while I do it," she said. It was galling, but her family's peace of mind was worth it.

Uncle Oscar began pacing. "Malone will never settle for a thousand dollars. He knows the book will earn far more."

"Agreed," Gwen said. "That's why we offer his lawyer the same deal to persuade him to settle."

Uncle Oscar's brow quirked in reluctant admiration, but he shouldn't be surprised. It was impossible to grow up in the Blackstone family without a bit of their cunning rubbing off on her.

"The lawyer will know that we have unlimited funds to stop this book," she continued. "We can drag this out, delay their profits, and cost Malone's publisher a fortune in legal fees. Or we can pay Malone's lawyer in hope that he will pressure Malone to come to terms."

Uncle Oscar wanted to keep arguing, but Frederick lifted a hand to call an end to the discussion. "An excellent suggestion," he said. "I'll have one of our lawyers begin the process."

"Let me do it," Gwen said. "I'm less threatening than a lawyer, and I'll get the job done quickly. And if I can scuttle Mick Malone's memoir, will you sign a document restoring the college's annual funding in perpetuity?"

Frederick's eyes narrowed. "I'd never guarantee anything in perpetuity," he said instantly. "Try again."

"Five years," she countered. "Continue the college's annual funding for the next five years, at which time the college must show the ability to generate enough revenue to cover our operating budget."

The corner of her grandfather's mouth turned down as he considered her proposal. It didn't take long for him to reach a decision.

"Our lawyers have already initiated a preliminary injunction to halt the publication of the book," he said. "I don't like calling attention to scandal better left in the past, so if you can prevent that public court case, I will authorize a five-year extension on the college's funding. I will commission a profile of Mick Malone's lawyer to discover his weaknesses and provide insight for your fight."

Her grandfather's terms were nonnegotiable, and Gwen felt compelled to accept. It wasn't what she'd hoped. She now had to deliver on this unsavory deal or her grandfather would never reverse Uncle Oscar's decision to yank the college's funding.

But she was not without hope. In her experience, lawyers would do anything for a quick payoff, and she suspected any man who aligned himself with Mick Malone would be no different.

3

*P*atrick poured more water over the pot of wilting marigolds on his office's window ledge. It hadn't looked this droopy when he bought it last week, and he'd been watering it daily in hope of a resurrection. His mother swore that talking to plants could perk them up, but Patrick couldn't bring himself to do it.

Besides, he had a meeting with a prospective client in a few minutes. He had no idea what Mrs. Gwen Kellerman wanted, but he hoped she could pay in cash instead of eggs or laundry service. The rent on his office was due in two weeks, and he needed the money.

It wasn't much of an office. No telephone, no electricity, and only a single window with a view of the brick wall across the alley. He kept the window and office door open to encourage a little breeze, even though it exposed him to noise from a leather-stamping shop below. It wasn't anyone's idea of an ideal office, but it came with a desk and a filing cabinet, which was all he needed. A scrap of paper folded into a tight square and placed beneath the leg of his rickety desk kept it steady, so all was perfectly fine.

Except for this miserable, wilting plant on the windowsill. "Come on, what is it you want?" he broke down and asked the plant.

ELIZABETH CAMDEN

"It wants a little air for its roots," a cool voice said behind him. "You're drowning that poor marigold."

Patrick almost dropped the plant when he spotted the woman standing in the open doorway of his office. *What a stunner!* She had pale green eyes and a long braid of honey-blond hair draped over her shoulder. She looked serene. It was the perfect word to describe that swanlike neck and gentle humor on her face. She wore a loose, flowing gown in a soft printed silk and was probably the prettiest woman he'd ever seen.

"Mrs. Kellerman?" he asked, holding his breath in silent prayer. She looked like someone who could pay in cash, and a client like this could pay his office rent for months.

"Indeed," she replied. "And you are Mr. O'Neill?"

"That I am," he said, stepping around the desk to tilt an office chair toward her. Too late, he noticed an ugly beetle squatting in the center of the seat and blanched, but she calmly picked it up before he could knock it away.

"Beetles are good luck," she said, cradling it in her palm as she carried it to the open window and set it on the ledge. "This one eats aphids, so you should count yourself fortunate."

He counted himself a prime idiot for making a terrible first impression, but she didn't seem upset as she returned to sit in the same chair that had so recently housed that beetle. He was about to apologize for it when he noticed two hulking men standing in the hall outside his office.

"Who are the toughies?" he asked, immediately on guard. The men exuded menacing suspicion despite their fine clothing.

"They accompanied me here," she replied. She glanced over her shoulder at the closest man. "It's all right, Zeke. I'll be fine if you'd like to wait downstairs."

"Begging your pardon, ma'am," Zeke said, "but we'll wait right here."

"Very well," Mrs. Kellerman said. She stood to close the door, but the shadowy outlines of the men were still apparent through the frosted glass. "I hope you don't mind," she said

25

to Patrick. "The Five Points has a rather alarming reputation, and I didn't feel comfortable coming alone."

It was understandable. The Five Points was named after the intersection of five streets in the middle of urban squalor and ramshackle tenements. It was the most notorious slum in the city, ruled by rough Irish street gangs when Patrick arrived almost two decades earlier. In recent years, reform-minded New Yorkers had torn down some of the worst tenements, renamed the streets, and tried to give the slum a new reputation, but he could understand that a woman like Mrs. Kellerman wouldn't feel comfortable coming to this part of the city.

"How can I be of service, Mrs. Kellerman?"

Instead of answering, she nodded to the plant on the windowsill. "You've been overwatering that marigold, which is a shame. Marigold leaves can be brewed into a wonderfully healing solution with astringent properties."

He leaned back in his seat, wishing she would keep talking. Her voice was so gentle. It was calming and joyful at the same time. Soothing. "How do you know so much about marigolds?"

"In my deepest heart, I once wished to become a specialist in botanical medicine," she said, a gorgeous shade of pink staining her high cheekbones. "I wanted to become the next Hildegard of Bingen, growing a monastic garden brimming with herbs and plants to cure the people who came to her hospital for hope."

Patrick knew all about the medieval Benedictine nun. After all, he had a Saint Hildegard medal around his neck at this very moment. He always wore it beneath his shirt because he didn't want people thinking he was a superstitious clodhopper, but he couldn't help himself. He tugged the medal out from his shirt to show her.

"Hildegard is my patron saint," he said. "I was born on her feast day, and I always liked the idea of a nun who could stand up to kings and popes." Mrs. Kellerman didn't seem the least put out by his saint's medal, but it was probably time to get down to business. He tucked the medal back under his shirt. "Now, what can I do for you, Mrs. Kellerman?"

The warmth in her face cooled. "I've come to ask why a respectable lawyer would lower himself to represent a murderer like Mick Malone."

It felt like a kick in the gut. Mick Malone was the seediest character he'd represented in his eight years as a lawyer, and he didn't like that she threw it in his face.

"The jury found him not guilty," he said simply.

"We both know that many factors went into that verdict, and none of them had anything to do with Mr. Malone's innocence. No reputable man would have anything to do with him."

Probably, but he wouldn't betray a client by gossiping about him with a complete stranger. "And what makes you think I'm a reputable man?"

"Because you were educated by the Franciscans at Saint Boniface College. I know that you were a hairsbreadth away from taking vows into the priesthood and have performed free legal services for the church ever since. I know you volunteer at a Salvation Army soup kitchen every Saturday and are universally trusted by the people of the Five Points."

"You've done your homework," he said, his discomfort growing. She'd obviously sought him out over the Malone affair, and he saw no point in wasting time beating around the bush. "But I'd much rather discuss what brings you here today than my sad and stifled history with the Franciscans."

"I'm disappointed you are representing Mr. Malone," she said. "I was hoping you might reconsider the situation."

"No."

"I wonder what Father Doyle would think of your affiliation with Mr. Malone."

"You know Father Doyle?" he asked in surprise. Father Doyle was his mentor at Saint Boniface and possibly the best man Patrick had ever known. The hardest thing about turning away from the priesthood was disappointing Father Doyle.

"Father Doyle showed me how to cultivate white willow bark and taught me its anti-inflammatory properties," she said. "He

27

is a saintly man, and I can't imagine he would approve of his former pupil taking on such a disagreeable client."

"It was Father Doyle who asked me to do it."

That got her attention. "No!" she exclaimed in an appalled voice.

He held his hand up in a helpless gesture. "Ask him if you don't believe me. I know the entire world thinks Mick Malone is guilty, but that trial happened long before you or I were old enough to know anything about it. He is entitled to tell his story, even if it wakes up the Blackstone sleeping dragon."

"It's already woken the sleeping dragon, which is why I am here to offer your client a thousand dollars to stop publication of his memoir and avoid a long and costly lawsuit."

He shook his head. "I doubt he'll take it."

"The Blackstones will pay Mr. Malone's attorney the same amount if his client accepts the offer."

Patrick leaned back in his chair, rubbing his jaw. This was a tactic he hadn't seen coming, but he couldn't even think about accepting the deal. Could he? A thousand dollars was more than he'd ever earned on a single case. It would mean his mother could quit working extra shifts at the bakery.

But it would be a betrayal of a client. It was suddenly warm in the office and perspiration prickled beneath his suit jacket. He couldn't do it.

"That seems like double-crossing my client, and I'm an upright man." Which was sometimes a shame. Mrs. Kellerman was a stunning woman, tall and willowy and fit. He wasn't free to pursue a married woman, but admiring her seemed fair game.

Her voice was cool as she kept up the pressure. "Frederick Blackstone will file a blizzard of lawsuits to stop publication of Malone's book," she said. "You can help your client avoid all that, and each of you can pocket a tidy sum. We can conclude this business by the close of business today."

"Who sent you here?" he asked her. "The Blackstones?"

She nodded.

He stood. "Let me tell you what I think of the Blackstones and their mercenary techniques for extracting every drop of blood from the working classes. They slap their name on charities and toss around a few dollars, hoping to disguise decades of ruthless exploitation, and assume all is forgiven."

"They toss around *millions* of dollars, and it must not have worked if you still have such a poor opinion of them."

Patrick had known from the day he accepted this case that the Blackstones would come after him. This morning he'd learned that they filed for a preliminary injunction to stop the memoir, but he hadn't expected a second salvo to come in the beguiling form of Mrs. Kellerman.

"Why did they send you?" he asked. "Why not a few of their high-powered lawyers?"

She laughed a little. "That was my grandfather's first impulse, but we decided to try honey before vinegar."

He froze. "We? You're related to them?"

"My maiden name is Blackstone," she said. "William Blackstone was my brother." She waved a hand toward the shadowy figures of the men outside his door. "I've always had bodyguards. My father lived in terror that history might repeat itself, and he kept me sheltered until the day he died. Losing my brother was a wound that never fully healed for either of us."

A deluge of embarrassment threatened to drown Patrick. "My pardon. I didn't realize your connection to the case. Of course you have every reason to resent Mick Malone. I hope you can understand. . . ."

He hoped she could understand that lawyers sometimes had to hold their noses and take unpopular clients. The justice system could never be fair unless everyone had access to a lawyer. *Everyone.* Even unsavory people like Mick Malone.

"I understand that money can do strange things to people who lack it," she said. "We can avoid the legal assault my family is prepared to throw against Mr. Malone and settle this quickly. All your client needs to do is sign an agreement never to publish a memoir."

She set the proposed contract on his desk. He snatched it up and quickly skimmed four pages of text that would effectively hogtie Malone from ever profiting off the 1870 crime.

It was probably a trap. The Blackstones wouldn't let Malone get away this easily.

He tossed the papers down on his desk. "I don't trust it."

She shrugged. "It doesn't matter what you think of our offer. You have a legal obligation to present it to your client, and if he takes the deal, you will be well compensated for your services."

She left the office in a swirl of silk and the scent of rose water. His mouth went dry, and his heart sped up. Gwen Kellerman was temptation personified, and it had nothing to do with the money she dangled before him. It was the alluring and unsettling effect she had on him as a man, and that alarmed him more than anything.

4

Patrick needed to convey Mrs. Kellerman's surprising offer to Mick Malone. The sale of the book would earn more in the long run, but Mick might take the quick payoff to avoid the legal hassles. Either way, Patrick wouldn't take her bribe. He liked his integrity too much to sacrifice it for a little quick cash.

Mick lived in a seedy rooming house just off Mulberry Street. The late-afternoon sun warmed the pavement and mingled with the stink from chimney stacks, salted cod, and rubbish collecting in the alleys. The air rumbled as an elevated train passed overhead. Peddlers hawked their wares, and children played in the alleys. It was a rough neighborhood without a blade of grass, just buckled concrete and hard-packed dirt.

The Five Points had horrified Patrick when he arrived as a fourteen-year-old immigrant. Ireland was poor, but it was a rural poverty that didn't feel so desperately bleak. The raucous squalor of the Five Points was alien to him. All he could see from the roof of his boardinghouse were endless streets of concrete, laundry lines, and chimney stacks. Women shouted from windows to their children below, roving gangs intimidated shopkeepers, and he'd been forced to grow up fast.

The Irish gangs were tough, but Patrick rubbed along okay with them. By the time he was sixteen, he'd learned to fight and was soon earning a pretty penny in the bare-knuckle boxing pens. It was a brutal way to earn a living, but he was big, fast, and tough. Were it not for Father Doyle, Patrick would have eventually become one of those Irish gangsters, but God had other plans for him.

The stairway in Mick's tenement was so cramped that Patrick had to duck as he climbed to the third-floor hallway. Water stains marred the plaster, and a single lightbulb provided dim illumination for the entire hall.

He knocked on Mick's door and waited. It cracked open to reveal the suspicious eyes of Mick's wife. Ruby Malone's face immediately brightened when she recognized him.

"Patrick, love!" Ruby exclaimed, reaching a hand through the narrow opening to cuff him on the shoulder. She had been named for her fiery-red hair, although it was now faded with age. Rumor had it she was the best pickpocket in the neighborhood and had only been imprisoned for it twice.

"Mrs. Malone," he said respectfully. "Can I come inside?"

The narrow gap closed an inch more. "I'm afraid I can't invite you in. What do you need, love?"

"To talk with Mick. Is he here?"

She rolled her eyes. "He's at the pub already. The one on Anthony Street."

"Can I come in? I'd like to speak to you as well."

The opening in the doorway narrowed even farther. "Oh, this isn't a sight for your saintly eyes. Good day to you, Patrick."

The door slammed in his face.

Was it possible Ruby had a man inside? Mick and Ruby were famous for their long, loud, and boisterous marriage of thirty years, but Mick had a roving eye, and maybe Ruby was balancing the scales. Or fencing stolen property. Whatever was going on in that room, he wasn't welcome inside, so he headed to Anthony Street in search of Mick.

He wasn't hard to find. A crowd had already gathered at the pub, and Mick was holding court in the middle of it. He was a gangly man with a swath of long, yellowy-white hair. He held a crowd spellbound, gesturing with his hands as he gazed into space, his Irish brogue thick as he spun his tales.

"Ireland is home of the proud, but it doesn't have the freedom that I've found in America," he said. "The Irishmen of the Five Points are grumbling, growling, strong, and loyal. We've grabbed our plot of this godforsaken city and made it our own. We may be poor, but we are *free men*!" he roared. "The days of crawling on our bellies are over. We bow to no one. We fear no one."

Some good-natured foot stomping and growls of approval rose from the crowd, but a voice from the back challenged him. "Not even the Blackstones?"

"Especially not the Blackstones," Mick said, warming to the topic. "Oh, they had me once," he conceded. "They locked me in a dungeon and tried to send me to the gallows, but they couldn't break me. No, sir! And my loyal Ruby visited me every day in that dank cell. She was a font of female compassion, a balm for any man's abused soul."

A few catcalls rang out, but Mick caught Patrick's gaze through the smoky interior.

"Well then, not-quite-Father Patrick," Mick called out. "What brings you into this den of iniquity?"

"We've got business to discuss."

Mick straightened a little. "You hear that, lads? I've got important business with the neighborhood's best lawyer. Let me have a beer first."

Patrick shook his head. "Sorry, Mick. I promised my mother I'd bring home dinner, and she's waiting. Let's go outside now."

Mick didn't look happy about it, but he followed Patrick out the pub's back door. Talking about Mrs. Kellerman's surprising offer on a public street wasn't ideal. There were people in this neighborhood who'd kill for a thousand dollars, but Ruby had made it plain Patrick wasn't welcome at their place.

"Well?" Mick asked as they shuffled into the grubby alley behind the pub. "How many copies of my book are they going to print? And when can I get paid for them?" His hand trembled as he lit a cigarette.

Mick would get fifteen percent of the book's profit, and Patrick would get two percent if he won the lawsuits the Blackstones were sure to launch. The money would be welcome, but the bigger prize would be publicity for Patrick's legal services. Winning a case against the Blackstones' intimidating phalanx of lawyers would catapult him to fame in the city, but first he was legally obligated to pass along Mrs. Kellerman's offer.

"I don't know when you'll see any money," Patrick said. "The publisher won't pay until the judge considers the pending injunction against the book. The Blackstones are already trying to block it, and I can't wait on payment forever."

"I've got an entire case of cigarettes you can have," Mick offered.

"I don't smoke."

"Well, I don't have any money. You know that."

"You've had an interesting proposition," Patrick said. "The Blackstones will pay you a thousand dollars for agreeing to drop the book permanently."

Mick leaned against a gritty brick wall as he drew hard on the cigarette, his eyes pensive. "I was hoping to make a lot more than that."

"But this is guaranteed money, payable immediately. If you gamble on the memoir, it could be years before the court lets the book go to press. I think you'll win, but there is no guarantee."

Mick's hand trembled even harder. Those tremors were a dead giveaway that Mick hadn't drunk enough yet tonight to calm the shakes. Up close, the ravages of age and alcohol were easier to see than when he'd been holding forth in the pub.

"The quick money is tempting," Mick finally said. "I'd pounce on it, but Ruby won't want to sell out. She has her heart set on buying a place in Brooklyn. A little flat with our own kitchen and maybe even a window. What would *you* do in my shoes?"

"I'd ask your wife how badly she wants that place in Brooklyn. She won't get it with a thousand dollars."

Mick nodded and tossed the butt of the cigarette on the

ground, grinding it out with his shabby boot. "Good idea. Let's go ask her."

Patrick's hand shot out to stop him. "I was there right before I came to the pub. It didn't seem like she wanted to be disturbed."

"Don't worry about it," Mick said as he started ambling down the alley. "She picked up some stuff from the printer that's a bit hot and probably didn't want your pious eyes seeing it."

Hot? That could mean any number of things, but as long as Ruby wasn't wrapped in the arms of an illicit lover, he wouldn't mind concluding this business today. Mrs. Kellerman's offer carried a stink on it, and he wanted to put it behind him.

Ruby was no more welcoming to him this time, even when Mick swaggered into the single room they shared and drew her into a hearty kiss and a tacky grope. She twisted out of her husband's embrace and tugged her blouse back into place.

"I wasn't expecting you so soon," she said to Mick. "I barely had a chance to throw a cloth over the mess I picked up from down the street."

The only thing with a cloth over it was a small crate at the end of a rumpled, unmade bed. The room reminded Patrick of the squalid place he'd lived when he first got off the boat. It had a table with two chairs, a chest, and a bed with a thin mattress. All washing and cooking took place in a communal room down the hall.

Mick took a seat on the cloth-covered crate and dragged Ruby onto his lap. "It looks like we're already making the Blackstones jumpy, love," he said, then told her about Mrs. Kellerman's offer.

Ruby seemed offended by the suggestion. "A thousand dollars? When those people live in palaces? Tell her to fling it in the sea."

"Are you sure?" Mick asked. "We could get the money right now. Think of it, love. A thousand dollars will buy you some new clothes and restock the pantry."

"You mean it would restock the wine cellar," she corrected.

"We didn't flee Ireland to be those people's lapdogs. You did eighteen months in jail waiting for that trial. A jury found you not guilty, and those people never even said they were sorry. Tell them to take their thousand dollars and stick it where the sun doesn't shine."

The words sparked something in Mick, and he stood, tossing Ruby to her feet. "That's my girl," he boomed and swept her up into a hug. He tried to twirl her, but his gangly frame couldn't manage it, and they both went crashing to the floor. They howled in a combination of pain and hilarity.

Patrick looked away. Mick and Ruby were both thoroughly disreputable, but he envied their closeness. Going through life alone was hard. He wanted what they had. He wanted a woman in his life, not the lonely existence of a bachelor still living with his mother.

In the ruckus, Mick's boot dragged the cloth from the crate, and Patrick's eyes widened as he stared at it.

Ruby was hiding something "hot," all right. It looked like a stack of incendiary broadsheets. He couldn't read much through the slats, but the words *Blackstone* and *Injustice* printed in large, bold-faced type were easy to see.

Mick peeled himself up from the floor and grinned as he saw where Patrick was looking. He popped the lid from the crate and handed him one of the flyers. "I thought I'd stoke up a little advanced publicity for my book," he said proudly.

It didn't take long to scan the page. This was going to be a problem. The ghostwriter who penned the memoir had carefully avoided outright slander, but this screed was a direct assault on the Blackstones, their bank, and the businesses they funded.

"Use these flyers for kindling, not publicity," Patrick warned Mick. "I worked with your writer to be sure the book had no outright lies that could get you convicted of libel, but this document is full of it." He read directly from the flyer. "'The Blackstones outlaw clocks in their coal mines so they can trick a man into thinking he's worked only ten hours when he's actually worked twelve.' You know that's not true. There is now a clock in every Blackstone mine, factory, and cafeteria. No one is being lied to about what hours they've worked."

"But they used to."

"Maybe, but not today, and this leaflet could get you convicted of libel."

Before he could say more, a pounding on the door interrupted him.

"Mickey!" Someone banged again and shouted from the hallway. "I've brought reinforcements from Mingo County."

Mick opened the door, and men started funneling inside, but Mick pushed them back. "Hey, Donahue. You're early. I've got my lawyer here."

Patrick eyed the half-dozen men standing in the hallway. Mingo County was a coal mining region in West Virginia, one of the areas that had given the Blackstones trouble over the years.

"What do you need a lawyer for?" Donahue asked. He was a wiry man with hard eyes and cheekbones like blades in his thin face.

Mick straightened his collar. "I don't know if you've heard, but I've got an important book coming out soon." Sarcasm dripped from his voice, and it didn't look like Donahue appreciated it.

"Aye, which is why I don't like a lawyer sniffing around. What's in that crate?" Donahue pushed into the room and grabbed a flyer. "What are you doing with this?"

Mick gave a smirk. "Since they're all over West Virginia, I figured I'd use some here in New York. They'll help sell my book."

"We're about more than selling books," Donahue said in a low tone. "If you think that book is going to do the trick, you're an even stupider old drunk than we thought."

"Who are you calling an old drunk?" Mick snarled, bumping his chest against the younger man's.

"Pipe down," Donahue ordered, easily brushing Mick aside. "We've got a lot to discuss, and it's time for the lawyer to leave."

Ruby grabbed Patrick by the arm. "Your ma will be waitin' dinner for you, love," she said, funneling him toward the door.

"Hey, Patrick," Mick called out, "tell them no deal, okay? I've got too many irons in the fire to settle for the Blackstones' scrawny deal."

Patrick had the answer he expected and nodded to Ruby before leaving the boardinghouse, but something was wrong here. Despite the ribbing he took from folks in the neighborhood, he was no wide-eyed innocent. His job brought him into a world of prostitutes, pickpockets, and grifters. He was even willing to represent Mick Malone, possibly the shadiest man in the Five Points, because Father Doyle asked it of him.

Patrick was honor-bound by his profession to work in the best interests of his client, but that same code of ethics meant he couldn't overlook a crime in progress, and Patrick sensed something shady. What motivated those men to come all the way from West Virginia and partner with Mick Malone against the Blackstones?

Patrick had no proof of wrongdoing, but he couldn't look the other way. The ethical obligations of a lawyer often collided with the integrity of an upright man, and sometimes it was hard to know what to do.

In this case, Patrick would rely on the one man who had never steered him wrong, and that meant a visit to Father Doyle the following morning.

Saint Boniface College was in the heart of Brooklyn, surrounded by factories, ironworks, and tenements. Elevated trains rumbled overhead, and a dozen different languages could be heard on any given street corner. There were no walls around the college, so Patrick had a good view of the German delicatessen across the street as the owner lugged a side of beef into the shop.

Father Doyle sat on the bench beside him as Patrick recounted the previous day's events at Mick's place. Dressed in all black except for his clerical collar, Father Doyle still looked exactly as he did sixteen years earlier when Patrick first spotted him heading toward a trolley stop in the Five Points. He had chased the old man down to ask what it took to become a priest. It was the moment that changed Patrick's life forever. Father Doyle had glanced at his black eye, split lip, scabbed-over knuckles, and drawn the right conclusion about how Patrick earned a living. There probably weren't a lot of boxers who aspired to the priesthood, but Father Doyle was generous with his time that afternoon and provided Patrick with a path to a new and better life. During those early years, Patrick believed the best way to prove his devotion to God was to aim for the highest rank, and that meant the priesthood. It was the purest form of commitment and came with lifelong responsibilities and sacrifices he was eager to assume. His vows would be joyfully offered and forever carved in stone.

It hadn't worked out that way, and he still carried the shame of bailing out on Father Doyle. The upside was that he could help the old priest by counseling people in the streets instead of in the pews. That meant venturing into the seedier side of life, and he still came to Father Doyle for advice.

"All I have is a hunch," he told the priest. "Mick claims he's only writing a book to earn a little money, but I think it's part of a bigger scheme. Those men from Mingo County didn't come all this way to help Mick sell his book."

"And what makes you think they're up to no good?" the priest asked. "Because of the way they look? Because the people of Mingo County have no love for the Blackstones?"

"I think they're here to stir up trouble," Patrick said. "I agreed to represent Mick for that book, but I didn't sign up for anything else, and I don't like being dragged into it."

Patrick had already read the memoir to be sure it contained nothing that libeled the Blackstones. The memoir seethed with resentment, but if all it did was assert Mick's opinions, the Blackstones had no legal cause to block its publication.

"The memoir is foul," he said. "Most of it is bellyaching about the indignities he's endured at the hands of the Blackstones. Not that the Blackstones are angels, mind you. There's something deeply tricky about that family. They sent a woman to bribe me into scuttling the book."

"What woman?" Father Doyle asked.

Memory of his irrational attraction to the Blackstone woman still plagued Patrick, and he sent a cautious glance toward the old priest. "Gwen Kellerman. She claimed to know you. Does she?"

"I'm well acquainted with Mrs. Kellerman," Father Doyle said in a warmly approving tone. "She is the sort of quiet, gentle light that makes the world a better place."

It wasn't what Patrick wanted to hear. It would be easier to dismiss his attraction if she'd been stamped in the same ruthless mold as the rest of her family. He shrugged off Mrs. Kellerman and shifted the conversation back to Malone.

"I know Malone kidnapped that child," he said. "If he was willing to confess and repent, I'd gladly help him make a clean breast of it. But no, he wants money so he can move to Brooklyn. He's slime, Father. Next time you kick a case my way, try to find someone who isn't up to his eyeballs in corruption."

"Already done," Father Doyle said agreeably. "The holy sisters who run the primary school are having trouble paying their water bill, and the city is threatening to cut them off. I was hoping you might volunteer your legal services."

Patrick nodded. "Whatever you need. You know that."

Father Doyle had funded Patrick's education, but the church rarely wanted men fresh out of school to assume the responsibilities of the priesthood. After college, Patrick began practicing law and got plenty of experience in the real world, then returned to the seminary once he was ready to proceed into the priesthood. He continued practicing law while studying theology, but two weeks before taking his final vows, he balked.

His gaze strayed to the delicatessen across the street. The owner had a young and shapely daughter named Bettina, and Patrick's willpower stumbled one autumn afternoon when he spent a forbidden few hours with her behind an abandoned rail station. He wasn't cut out to be a priest; he wanted a wife. He wanted a partner and a mother for his children. He wanted a big, rollicking family along with a woman he could kiss and hold until dawn. Trying to deny that longing was like asking his heart to stop beating.

He didn't want a quick, shameful tryst behind a rail station. He wanted the blessing of God and his community when he stepped out with a woman by his side. Patrick had been shaking in mortification when he confessed his forbidden encounter with Bettina to Father Doyle, but his mentor didn't seem surprised.

"The priesthood is a calling," he had said. *"We can't have reluctant warriors in our ranks, but there are plenty of other ways you can serve God in the world."*

Thousands of people never set foot in a church and instinctively recoiled from priests wearing that intimidating clerical collar, but they might listen to a former boxer with scars on his body and an accent like theirs. Patrick lived among the ordinary people—rich or poor, clean or struggling in the muck—and tried to teach by example.

As much as it hurt, turning away from the priesthood had been the right decision. He did good work on the street, helping keep kids out of the gangs and giving hope to the downtrodden . . . but he wanted a family. He even envied Mick and Ruby Malone. They were so crooked they couldn't walk a straight line if a pot of gold was waiting at the end of it, but they loved each other. They were never lonely.

God would send him the right woman when it was time. For now, he would seek out Mrs. Kellerman to decline her offer, and then he would forget about her.

5

The greatest disappointment of Gwen's eight-year marriage was that she failed to conceive a child, but she found solace in the company of the children who made their home at Blackstone College. President Matthews's two boys often climbed the fence separating their yards to play in Gwen's garden. Then there was little Mimi, whose mother worked in the accounting office. Mimi was eight and suffered a number of physical disabilities that prevented her from attending a normal school, so she spent her days on campus. She was a favorite among the students, who coddled and protected her.

This morning Gwen sat with all three children at her backyard koi pond, the centerpiece of her garden. A physics professor had installed the pump, and a group of students had helped her stack rocks to create levels within the pond so that water splashed down the tiers and attracted birds and butterflies. There was plenty of room to perch on the flat rocks surrounding the pond, and the children loved to feed the fish.

Naturally, the boys started pelting the food at the fish, but what could one expect from six- and eight-year-old boys?

"Be gentle," Mimi said from where she sat on a chair next to the pond. The iron braces on her legs made it impossible for her to clamber over the rocks like the boys. Life wasn't easy for Mimi, who already wore thick eyeglasses and depended on a rolling walker. Nevertheless, she lit up the entire campus with her bottomless good cheer, and Gwen had always been protective of her.

"This one is fat," the older boy said as he dangled a bit of lettuce just above the surface of the water. "I'll bet it's pregnant with a baby."

Gwen bit back a smile. "Koi don't have babies. They lay eggs."

Behind her glasses, Mimi's brown eyes grew wide. "When is she going to lay eggs? Can I watch? Will you let me name the babies?"

Before Gwen could answer, the older boy started climbing the oak tree, reaching for a tiny plant that had taken root in one of the deep chinks in the tree bark.

"Leave it alone," Gwen cautioned. "I don't know how much longer that bromeliad can survive in that spot, and I want to protect it."

"Why is it growing on a tree trunk instead of in the ground?" Mimi asked.

"The wind must have carried the seed there," Gwen answered. "They can lie dormant for years before a bit of water and heat awakens them. Seeds are hardy little things, and I admire that."

"I admire that too," Mimi said, looking at the bromeliad in its precarious perch.

"Ahem."

The man's voice startled her, and Gwen shot to her feet. Good heavens, that lawyer from the Five Points was at the gate of the garden fence, watching them. How long had he been standing there?

"My pardon," Mr. O'Neill said. "I knocked on the front door, but no one answered. I heard voices back here and followed."

Her mouth went dry. He was here about that awful memoir. The suffocating fear of losing the college had been looming over her for days, and now he was here with the answer.

"Dare I hope your client accepted my offer?" she asked.

"I'm afraid not. Malone turned it down."

She flinched and turned away. There would be no miraculous salvation for the college from writing a few bank checks. She braced a hand against the garden wall, gathering her thoughts. She had to try again. She had to try again *now*, because Uncle Oscar's decision simply could not stand.

She turned back to the children still clustered around the koi pond. "Time for you to head back to your house," she said to the boys, scooting them toward a low-hanging branch they used to climb over the fence separating their yards. She held the vine of wild jasmine aside so they wouldn't crush the blooms and helped them over.

Mimi reached for her walker. "Do I have to go too?"

"Yes, sweetie. I'll take you back to your mother." She glanced at Mr. O'Neill. "Will you walk with me to campus? You and I need to speak privately."

"I'm not sure what we have left to discuss," he said. "My client was firm in his decision."

She liked his voice. Gentle but firm and with a hint of an Irish accent. He wasn't particularly handsome but still enormously attractive. His face was rugged, as though carved by an axe. His hair looked like it couldn't decide if it wanted to be light brown or blond, and his nose had been broken at least once, but none of it lessened his appeal. He looked strong, like a protector, and all women secretly liked that in a man.

She led him and Mimi down the brick path to the front of the house and then on the one-block walk to the campus. Mimi's lumbering gait made for slow progress, but Mr. O'Neill seemed to enjoy craning his neck to admire the buildings and the natural beauty of campus. He even came inside the administration building when Gwen escorted Mimi to the office where her mother worked. The building's arched hallways and wood paneling made it feel like an old-world castle, and she squinted once they emerged back into the sunlight.

"Have you ever been to Blackstone College?" she asked. He

hadn't, so she pointed out the various buildings and the fountain splashing in the center of the quadrangle.

"What is your role on campus?" he asked. "Do you teach?"

Gwen's lifelong dream had been to become a professor here, but that was reserved for people with doctorates. She once contemplated enrolling at New York University to get her doctorate in botany but had balked at the prospect of living in downtown Manhattan, surrounded by towering skyscrapers, the noise, the traffic. Just . . . no. It wasn't possible.

"My husband was the head of the biology department," she said simply.

"Was?"

"He died two years ago."

"I'm sorry," he said. "You chose to stay on campus?"

"Oh yes, I'll never leave this place." Her reply was instinctive. This college was her home, and she had never even considered leaving it. "I teach a class on botany each semester, but mostly I enjoy tending the gardens and looking after the students. They get dreadfully homesick, even though they'd die before admitting it, and I like mothering them."

His gaze roamed across the ivy-covered buildings and manicured lawns. "This isn't anything like where I went to college. It's a good thing your family has money."

She sent him an amused half smile. "I'm afraid this college is the only investment our family made that reliably loses money every year."

"Maybe a little less money spent on fancy buildings would have been prudent."

Like many people, Patrick O'Neill didn't look beneath the trappings to see the miracles that were the true beating heart of this college.

She gestured to the building directly behind her, a four-story granite masterpiece with windows that sparkled in the sunlight. "Do you think the buildings are where our money goes?"

He looked at her blankly. "I'm sure they cost a pretty penny."

They could have been built with my father's pocket change, she silently thought. "Come with me, and I'll show you the college's real treasure," she said. "It has nothing to do with fancy buildings or pretty landscaping. The amount we spend on it dwarfs everything you can see with human eyes. Are you willing to open your mind and heart to learn about it?"

A glint of curiosity sparked behind Mr. O'Neill's big, strong face. "Lead the way."

Against his better judgment, Patrick was intrigued. Sparring with the Blackstones was a dangerous undertaking, and he was already powerfully attracted to this woman. Now that he knew she was a widow, he was even more intrigued.

"This is the jewel in our crown," Mrs. Kellerman said as she led him into the cool interior of the chemistry building, where their footsteps echoed in the hallway. "Our research focuses on diseases like botulism and tetanus. These are rare diseases that only afflict a few people each year, but the victims tend to be poor with little hope for a cure. Most colleges are researching treatments for the big diseases like tuberculosis where there's far more profit."

She stopped before the open door of a laboratory where several men and two women were bent over microscopes and lab books. The blackboard behind them was covered in what looked like hieroglyphics.

"My father's dream was to cure the diseases of the lame, the halt, and the blind," she said. "Every person who walks through the gates of Blackstone College feels the same, even though we know it's going to be a steep road. If finding a cure was easy, it would have already been done. So we chip away at the problem, year after year, decade after decade. We lose more battles than we win, but we don't give up, because each failure means we are one step closer to the finish line."

Next she took him to a room with a wall of refrigerated cases, briefly opening them to reveal test tubes of serums and samples.

"These are strains of cowpox, chicken pox, and smallpox,"

she explained. "We send professors and graduate students to India and China to collect additional strains of the diseases as they evolve, trying to stay one step ahead and mass produce vaccines that will treat these diseases anywhere in the world. The college has already vaccinated almost half a million people for smallpox in India."

She led him to the next room, which looked like a library, but instead of bookshelves it held rows of maps and floor globes. "This is where we track disease," she said, showing him how colored thumbtacks pushed into the maps indicated disease outbreaks.

He'd never heard of most of them. Beriberi, pellagra, yaws, and pertussis were all unfamiliar words to him, but apparently the college had teams of people working on each disease. Each year they spent a fortune sending their scientists abroad to gather samples and bring data home to analyze. They sponsored conferences and scientific journals to share information. They had an alert system to communicate news of outbreaks that might occur anywhere in the world. Chemists could swing into gear to mass-produce vaccines and then transport them to people in need.

"We are on the cusp of something wonderful," Mrs. Kellerman said. "The lame, the halt, and the blind can be cured. We can move the unmovable object. We're fighting against all odds to accomplish something that's never been done before. *This* is where our treasure lies. *This* is what I'm fighting for." The radiance in her face dimmed. "And when someone smears the Blackstone name, *this* is what they're smearing."

It felt like she'd struck him, and in a way she had. He was paving the way for a seedy memoir to pollute the air with old grievances against the Blackstone family. It wasn't something he could be proud of.

"For what it's worth, I wish Malone had taken your offer."

"I do too," she said softly. She looked around the strange library, filled with maps and globes that tracked human suffering around the world, then back at him. "I want you to remember this. What you see in this room is *hope*. It's hope for millions of forgotten people in the world who need someone to extend a hand of compassion. We are good people. When you use your time and skills to help a man like Mick Malone, you are working against this."

Before he could defend himself, she turned to walk away, leaving him at a loss. He'd never had such a humbling set-down before, even more effective because of her quiet grace.

Somehow he had to gain Gwen Kellerman's respect, but he had no idea how to do it without betraying a client.

6

*E*ach morning when Gwen awoke, she enjoyed a blissful few seconds of peace while listening to the meadowlarks in her garden.

Then she remembered the threat to the college, and the fear set in. She couldn't leave this place. She couldn't let the college fail. Her ploy with the lawyer had failed, so now her best hope was to convince her grandfather to override Uncle Oscar's decision.

Normally her uncle and grandfather moved in lockstep accord, but if she could get Frederick away from the office and into the scholarly oasis of the college, he might soften. Frederick was meeting her for tea this afternoon in the college's outdoor café, and Gwen prayed she could earn his support.

Her former bodyguard, Zeke Jankowski, now worked at the café that was surrounded by manicured box hedges to create a private haven from the rest of campus. Only a handful of students remained on campus during the summer, so the café was empty.

Except for a single woman nursing a cup of coffee in the far corner. She wore an immaculate white linen gown that ought to make her look washed out against her white-blond hair, but Vivian Chastain always looked magnificent.

"I didn't realize you were coming, or I wouldn't have let her in," Zeke said as Gwen arrived at the café. "You shouldn't have to put up with that woman."

Gwen squared her shoulders. A better person might let Zeke tactfully handle the matter, but she had been far too tactful over the years.

"I'll be all right," she said quietly to Zeke, then headed toward Vivian, who looked up in surprise. Gwen would sound dignified and ladylike if it killed her. "I'm meeting with my grandfather in a few minutes, and it would be best if he didn't see you. I think you should leave."

Vivian's tone was also coolly polite. "I'm not finished with my coffee."

Gwen lifted the cup and tipped its contents into the nearby planting bed. "Now you are." She set the cup down with barely a click, and Vivian wasn't so cool anymore.

"That coffee cost ten cents!"

"Are you expecting me to pay for it?" Gwen asked. "I won't."

Vivian stood, her eyes narrowed. "But you're so good at paying for things," she said, hostility beginning to crack her voice.

Zeke immediately stepped between them. "Let's settle down," he said. "Miss Chastain, it's true. Mr. Blackstone is on his way, so you ought to leave if you want to keep your job here."

Vivian's expression did not waver as she glared at Gwen. "Did you buy him too? Poor Gwen only has friends who are on her payroll. Maybe someday you can buy yourself another husband."

"Shut up," Gwen said. She managed to keep her tone quiet, but her fists instinctively clenched. "Shut up and leave."

Vivian turned away and collected her handbag. It was a pricey one, lavishly embellished with seed pearls and a gold clasp. It was surely a gift from Jasper. Before leaving, Vivian leaned in for a final barb.

"He loved me," she whispered. "He *always* loved me, even on the day he walked down the aisle with you."

Gwen remained motionless as Vivian departed, hoping Zeke didn't sense her mortification.

"I don't know why you tolerate that woman," Zeke said, holding out a chair for Gwen.

She sat. "We all have our crosses to bear. Mine is named Vivian Chastain."

"You could have her fired. The college doesn't even teach music anymore, but you found her a position in the accounting office."

It was the ultimate irony. Blackstone College had been established to pursue excellence in scientific research, but Jasper had always pushed for the addition of a music department, claiming there was an intersection between mathematics and music. Vivian was their first hire to teach classes in piano.

During those early years, Gwen had no idea Vivian was Jasper's mistress. How many times had she welcomed Vivian into her home for her Friday night soirees? Even after Gwen learned the truth, she still fought to maintain a façade of domestic harmony.

Then Jasper died, and the music department soon closed. It was never a good fit for Blackstone College, but Gwen found a position for Vivian in the accounting office. Did that woman even know what Gwen had done on her behalf? Would she be less nasty if she did?

"I don't want her fired," she said in a gloomy voice. "There is a child to consider."

Mimi was Jasper's only child. Life was going to be hard for Mimi, and Gwen intended to help the sweet girl who'd been born with such challenges. Mimi spent most of her time in the safe cocoon of Blackstone College and didn't yet understand how different she was. Gwen wanted that to continue for a few more years, which meant she had to tolerate the girl's mother.

"Here comes my grandfather," she said. "Please say nothing about Vivian. Her presence is an irritant to him, and he's been pestering to have her fired ever since . . . well, for a long time."

"I hear you, Mrs. Kellerman. You've got a bigger heart than me."

Not really. She hated doing the right thing where Vivian was concerned, but she had more important battles to fight. Her grandfather was heading her way, and funding for Blackstone College was on the line.

She stood as Frederick strode toward her with remarkable vigor for a man about to celebrate his seventy-eighth birthday. She'd always been mildly intimidated by her grandfather. Frederick's ramrod-straight posture, sharp eyes that missed nothing, and the iron mask of his expression that never showed emotion were intimidating.

"Have a seat," he ordered once he arrived at the table. "We have much to discuss. Have you read that vile memoir by Mick Malone yet?"

Gwen was taken aback. "I would rather weed the area around the college's septic tanks. It seems less distasteful."

"I gather your mission to dissuade the scoundrel's lawyer did not succeed."

"He turned down my first offer," she admitted. "I haven't given up hope, but are you truly going to let Uncle Oscar make good on his threat to cut our funding?"

"It doesn't matter what I want. Oscar commands more votes than me."

That was true. Frederick controlled thirty percent of the bank, while Oscar only held twenty percent, but Oscar commanded the allegiance of the other shareholders. Oscar had a proven track record of astounding financial success, and the remaining shareholders were intensely loyal to him.

"Could you try?" she asked. "If I can count on your thirty percent stake, perhaps some of the other shareholders would side with you."

"Or perhaps you can deliver on your promise to scuttle the memoir. If you can't, Oscar goes to court next week to argue for an injunction against it. It's only a court hearing, so there won't be many people there, but I don't like it."

One week didn't leave her much time, and her anxiety ratcheted higher. "What are his odds of winning?"

"Not good. What makes it even more galling is that the book

is a pack of lies." He took the slim advance copy of the memoir from his suit jacket and handed it to her. "I read it last night. Most of it is nothing more than Malone boasting about his life of crime, mixed with vitriol against our family. He still claims innocence and that the real kidnappers planted the bills from the ransom payment in his room. The only new information is that Malone finally admitted he is a thief and was planning a midnight heist of a jewelry store around the time William disappeared. What he writes in chapter five has a ring of truth to it. Start on the second paragraph."

Gwen didn't even want to touch the book, but she swallowed her distaste, opened it to the marked page, and began reading.

New York in February can be bitter, and the winds sweep through the city, sending sleet and misery straight into a man's soul. I remained at my post, hour after wretched hour, watching and learning the behavior of the night watchman who patrolled the streets around the jewelry store.

The time was ripe for a heist. It was a week after someone had kidnapped the Blackstone boy, and the police were distracted searching for him. That meant the night patrols were thin, and there would never be a better time for a late-night robbery. After a few more nights of careful observation, I would make my move, and my beloved Ruby would never need to work another day in her life.

I was half-frozen to death when I got back to my boardinghouse. In those days the rooms didn't have heat, but it was always warm in the boiler room. It was three o'clock in the morning, and I hobbled on frozen feet to the boiler room to thaw out. That was the plan, but a gang of tough-looking men were already in there. They had a little kid with them, about the same age as the missing Blackstone boy, held up close to the furnace.

The kid looked half-dead. His skin was pasty white and covered in sweat. His eyes stared off into space like they didn't see anything anymore. He was wheezing, and it sounded like death had already settled in his lungs. The men spoke in Italian, and I couldn't understand a word they said, but I knew that boy was in trouble. I also knew he was the Blackstone boy because he had those pale green eyes like all the reward notices wrote about. I risked my life by stepping forward and offering to fetch a doctor for the lad. It took the men by surprise. One of them dropped the kid, and another came at me swinging. I ducked, but someone clobbered me from behind, and it was lights out after that. When I came back around, I'd been hauled out into the alley like yesterday's trash and left to die in the cold. The men and the kid were gone. That was the last I saw of the Blackstone boy.

A crushing weight of sadness settled on Gwen's chest, and the book slipped from her fingers. Her grandfather was right. The passage in the boiler room felt real. It had been brutally cold the week her brother was taken. Maybe his kidnappers intended to return him, but when he sickened, it became too risky. They let her brother die rather than fetch a doctor.

Her father would have liked to have known this. For years her parents had held out hope that a miracle might happen. They used to look into the faces of children playing in the parks. They lit candles in churches. The mystery of William's disappearance left them forever wondering what had happened to their son.

Now at least Gwen knew. The cowards dared not come forward with his body, and he had probably been buried in a pauper's grave.

"There's not much else new in the book," Frederick said. "Malone claims he didn't report what he saw in the boiler room because he feared the Italians and if he squealed, they'd know it was him. They framed him, but even after he was arrested, Mick kept quiet for fear the Italians would go after his wife in revenge. So he kept his silence and put his faith in God during his trial."

The mental image of her brother, wheezing, pale, and dying in a grubby boiler room, gave Gwen a new mission. She didn't merely want this memoir stopped, she intended to solve the mystery of what had happened to her brother.

And she was going to use Patrick O'Neill to make that happen.

7

*L*ike every Saturday, Patrick served lunch at the Salvation Army soup kitchen, then cleaned up afterward. He was scouring the bottom of a stew kettle when a thick-necked man approached.

"Mrs. Kellerman would like to see you," he growled.

Patrick looked up, surprised to see one of Gwen Kellerman's bodyguards. He didn't appreciate being summoned like a servant. The Salvation Army had a tiny crew of overworked employees, and he would finish his duties before darting off to see what Mrs. Kellerman wanted. She had effectively torn his conscience to shreds last week by showing him her college's ambitious plans to cure the world's diseases. She'd been kind, gentle, and lethally effective in the way she did it. Unlike the rest of her family, she was a thoroughly decent person. She was womanly and earthy and kind.

And alluring. She sparked a raw, primitive desire to haul her behind one of those fancy college buildings and kiss her breathless.

Patrick scowled and went back to washing the pot. "Tell her I'll come when I'm done cleaning up."

The thick-necked bruiser retreated, and Patrick went back to scrubbing. He shouldn't feel guilty for noticing that Mrs. Kellerman was a looker. Any man with a pulse would notice.

She was Eve bearing the apple; Delilah tempting Samson. She was surely here to tempt him with something else to scuttle Mick's book, and he steeled himself against it.

He half expected her to be gone by the time he emerged an hour later onto the sweltering city street, but she sat alongside her two bodyguards at a sidewalk table outside the Italian deli across the street.

She didn't belong in this neighborhood. It was gritty and loud, and the smells . . . well, the fishmonger's shop two doors down couldn't be expected to smell like a garden. The tannery smelled even worse, and moldering trash littered the alleys. Her gown was a soft, filmy shade of white and her hair a glorious cascade spilling down her back. She looked like a long-stemmed rose among shabby weeds.

"Back again, Mrs. Kellerman?" he teased. "I'm beginning to think you've got a thing for dirt-poor lawyers." Flirting was second nature to him, and he was glad she didn't seem offended. He yanked out a chair and helped himself to a seat. "I hope you're not here asking for help to stop Mick's book. I'm all set to go before a judge next Friday, and your family doesn't have a prayer of winning an injunction."

It was almost impossible to block a book before publication. He'd been preparing for weeks, and the law was on his side.

"The injunction is my uncle's idea, not mine," she replied. "None of us want Mick Malone to benefit from his crime, but what I care about more than anything is learning what happened to my brother. Did you know my father once offered a $100,000 reward to whoever could solve the mystery of William's disappearance?"

Her voice was nonchalant, but she watched him intently. She was about to fire her first salvo.

"I did," he admitted. "Half the people in the Five Points searched every nook and cranny for him. They quit after the police arrested Mick."

"The reward is still available. Are you interested?"

He folded his arms across his chest as the pieces started to fit together. "What are you suggesting?"

"You have access to Mr. Malone. He trusts you, and in the process of preparing that memoir, perhaps you discovered something about how he pulled off the kidnapping. The law of double jeopardy means he can't be prosecuted again for murder, and the statute of limitations on his other crimes expired long ago. Mick Malone could shout his guilt in the public square and the law couldn't touch him, but I still want to know what happened to my brother. You can help. It won't be double-crossing a client. It will be solving a mystery and bringing peace of mind to a family who still mourns."

"And winning $100,000 dollars in the process."

She nodded. "Precisely."

Against his will, his heart started thudding. It was a figure so big he could scarcely get his mind around it. He and his ma could buy a proper house with four walls and a roof instead of sharing a tiny apartment. He could pay Father Doyle back for all those years of schooling he'd stiffed him on by not becoming a priest.

But he'd have to betray a client first.

Temptation was nothing new to Patrick. Girls had tempted him since he developed a healthy appreciation for anything in skirts when he was thirteen years old. He'd been tempted by a law firm in Boston that paid an actual salary instead of barter. He was tempted by rousing songs at the pub, freely flowing whiskey, and freshly baked blueberry scones. At the moment he was tempted by the alluring glint in Mrs. Kellerman's eyes and the long, slender curve of her neck as she challenged him. Life was full of temptation, and he was used to battling it.

"No thank you, ma'am," he said simply.

Then she hit him where it hurt.

"What if I gave the reward to your soup kitchen? I saw dozens of people get turned away. Most were mothers with hungry children. The reward money will keep this soup kitchen funded for years, and there'd be no more turning away hungry people who had the misfortune to be at the end of the line."

What she said was true. The ladies who ran the soup kitchen liked him because he had the muscle to keep order during the occasional rumpus that happened when they ran out of food.

"Whatever you tell me will be confidential," Mrs. Kellerman said. "All I want from you is the truth about Malone's role in kidnapping my brother, and I think you know how he did it."

He looked at the soup kitchen, where every Saturday he scraped the bottom of the kettle to eke out a final meal, then had to disappoint everyone else in the line. *Every Saturday*. He leaned forward to brace his forearms on the tops of his knees, twisting his hands and thinking.

He knew exactly how Mick had kidnapped that boy, because he'd personally scrubbed all the details out of the original manuscript, but Mick's drunken confession still seared in Patrick's mind. The Blackstones suffered the anguish of unanswered questions, and Mrs. Kellerman deserved to know the truth, but he couldn't betray a client.

"I wish there was a way I could help you," he said honestly. "I can't."

"Would it help if I doubled the reward?"

He shook his head. "It would only make it harder for me to turn you down. This isn't fun for me, ma'am. You have no idea."

She leaned across the table, her lemony perfume tempting him as she kept up the pressure. "With $100,000 you could get out of the Lower East Side," she said. "You could put your talent to work someplace worthy. Buy yourself a better office. Take a better class of clientele; people who deserve your time and talent."

He folded his arms across his chest in satisfaction, for she'd just made her first mistake. He wasn't ashamed to work here. He was proud of it.

"Take a look at where I live." He tilted away to gesture at the weeds growing in the cracked pavement, the trash collecting in the alley, and a drunkard slumped against a wall. "You look at a neighborhood like this and see a slum. I see the garden I was meant to tend."

Mrs. Kellerman's eyes widened. In admiration? He couldn't imagine a low-rent lawyer like him could impress her, but the signs were unmistakable. A gleam of respect lit her eyes, but it vanished quickly, replaced by a hint of steel.

"You know something," she said. "You know more than what Malone wrote in that book."

He did, which was why he wanted to avoid this conversation. He gave a dismissive shrug.

"Did you know that in the years after it happened, my parents used to look into the faces of children they saw in parks and in church pews? They never gave up hoping."

He glanced away, unable to imagine what her parents had endured. Mick was guilty down to the marrow of his bones, and his greed was about to victimize the people who loved Willy Blackstone all over again. Patrick struggled to find the words to mitigate the pain she felt.

"Both of your parents have passed on now," he said gently. "I can't do anything to help them, and learning the details of your brother's kidnapping and death will only plant images in your mind that are better left in the past."

She banged a fist on the table. "I want to know," she said in a voice that came from deep in her gut. "I grew up haunted by my brother's absence. I pretended that he was still alive, that he would someday come back and be the strong, protective older brother I should have had all along. That's impossible, but I owe it to William to uncover the truth about what happened to him."

"I can't help you, and I'm sorry for it," he answered honestly.

"Sorry enough to tell what you know?"

He shook his head. "I'll be in court on Friday morning, doing my best to see that Mick Malone gets the protection the Constitution affords him. No more, no less."

"I'll be there in the front row, waiting for you to make a mistake so I can pry the door of this case wide open."

It would be best if she stayed away from the hearing. The

family wasn't wrong for trying to stop Mick's book, but they were going to lose.

"Mrs. Kellerman, this memoir is going to be published," he said as kindly as possible. "Don't read it. Don't think about it. Mick's blatherings can't undo the honorable work you and your father created at that college. Don't let Mick drag you down into the muck with him."

His words didn't make a dent in her. The steely light of determination came back into her pale green eyes. "This will never be over for me," she said. "Even if you win your court case. Even if Mick Malone sells a million copies of that book, I will come after you again and again and again, because I think you know what happened to my brother."

He did, and that was what made this conversation so painful. He pushed away from the table and stood, unable to meet her eyes. "I'm sorry about what's going to happen in court. You seem like a decent woman, and I want you to know that defending Mick gives me no pleasure."

He began walking back to his office, but the pained expression on her face haunted him the entire way.

8

*P*atrick wore his new suit to the meeting with Mick's editor at the publishing company. On most days he wore simple shirtsleeves with suspenders because it made his clients feel more comfortable, but when he talked business with the publisher, it was best to look sharp.

And he'd need to look extra sharp for court tomorrow, when the hearing for Blackstone vs. Carstairs Publishing was the first case on the docket. Carstairs Publishing was not New York's finest imprint. Raymond Carstairs published a weekly tabloid filled with society gossip and crimes of lurid interest. Their books were dime-store westerns or seedy detective stories. The Mick Malone biography was going to be their crowning glory.

Raymond had asked to meet with Patrick at seven o'clock in the evening. It was an odd time for a business meeting, so Patrick assumed they would be going out for a meal.

"You said there wasn't anything libelous in Mick's book," Raymond challenged the moment Patrick walked into his office. With his slicked-back hair and thick mustache, Raymond looked like an angry bulldog.

Patrick held up his hand. "That memoir has plenty of libel in it, but it's presented as Mick's personal opinion and not a statement of fact. That gives him the pass he needs. We've got the freedom of the press on our side."

Raymond rubbed his palms together so hard that his knuckles started cracking. It seemed he enjoyed the prospect of a trial. "This'll be a lesson the Blackstones will never forget. They're going to lose and be humiliated by what I've got planned. Actually, what Mick has planned. This is all his idea."

The first hint of misgiving took root. "What's Mick's idea?"

"Follow me," Raymond said with an enigmatic smile as he left the office. "We're heading down to the brewery on Orange Street."

"A brewery?" Patrick asked in confusion.

Raymond nodded. "It's got a cellar big enough to hold everyone, and no windows. We don't need an audience for this sort of meeting. Mick's got a plan to whip up a little pretrial publicity."

The brewery was in an old brick building that was locked for the evening, but a thick-necked man in a bowler hat let them in through a side door.

Noise from a dense crowd rose from the basement, and Patrick's unease grew as he headed down a narrow, twisting staircase. Dank smells mingled with sawdust and the yeasty scent of hops. He ducked to avoid smacking into the low beams over the steps, but once he was downstairs, the space opened up to reveal a huge underground cellar. The ceiling was vaulted like the undercroft of a church, with domed archways and brick walls. Wooden barrels as large as a man covered most of the floor, but crammed in among them were hundreds of people.

"Lord have mercy," he muttered as he got a glimpse of the crowd. Most looked like plainly dressed workingmen, but there were plenty of women with babies and a handful of children in the mix. They were packed shoulder to shoulder around the wooden barrels. The rough-looking men from Mingo County were here, clustered near the back alongside men wearing coveralls and work boots.

"Quite a turnout," Raymond said with pleasure. "Some of these people came all the way from Ohio to join in the protest."

"What are they protesting?" Patrick asked, a sick feeling gathering in his stomach.

"For a start, the Blackstones' attempt to silence Mick Malone. They'll be in court tomorrow to help balance the scales. This is your army, Mr. O'Neill!"

This wasn't the sort of army he wanted to command. If they were angry enough to travel across the country to protest against the Blackstones, they would be hard to control. Rowdy, undisciplined, and seething with resentment, these weren't the sort of people who could influence a court hearing in a positive manner.

Mick Malone caught his eye and angled through the crowd, his face swathed in good cheer. "Quite a gathering, isn't it, Patrick my man! Let's get this meeting underway."

A pair of workers hoisted Mick onto the top of a barrel of beer. The crowd soon settled down, and Mick began speaking.

"Thank you for coming all this way to support a man's freedom of speech," Mick said. "A special tip of the hat to you folks from Carnegie Steel," he said with a nod to a silent group of men nearby. "And hello to my good friends from the Baltimore rail yards. Who else have we got here tonight?"

"Boilermakers from Dayton," someone bellowed.

"Six roustabouts from Allegheny Oil," another said.

"Four welders from the Philadelphia shipyard," a clarion voice called in a tone that sailed over the crowd.

Mick's humor evaporated. He straightened to look at the welder from Philadelphia, a tough-looking man with a scar splitting one brow.

"No one invited *you*, Liam," Mick said to the man, who lifted his chin at the cold welcome.

"I invited myself, Uncle Mick."

The men locked challenging stares, but Mick broke the tension by sending a wink and a salute to the younger man. "Welcome to my nephew Liam and the other welders from Philly," he said with a devilish gleam in his eye. Liam grinned and saluted back, and the introductions continued.

The range of workers here was astonishing: miners, iron-workers, men from shipyards, and women who worked in the woolen mills. All of them worked for companies financed by the Blackstone Bank, and all of them had a simmering resentment toward the Blackstone family. Most of them looked like they'd already been drinking.

Mick was enjoying himself as he stood atop the barrel and gave instructions to the crowd. "As my fine lawyer makes his case in court tomorrow, your job will be to voice approval when warranted and provide some good, healthy disagreement when things aren't going my way."

A clamor of stomping feet and a rumble of approval met Mick's announcement.

Patrick was appalled. Preliminary court hearings rarely had spectators, and if this crowd showed up, it would be a disaster. Courtrooms weren't the place for a labor rally.

He shouted a warning over the din. "The judge will throw you out of court if you misbehave."

"That's the plan," Mick said as he rubbed his hands together. "Let the authorities try to toss out the hardworking people who toil for the Blackstones, the Carnegies, and the Rockefellers. I want people who have dirt beneath their nails and sweat on their brows to be heard. We're the people who made America great, not Frederick Blackstone and his ilk. The people gathered in this cellar are the heart and soul and muscle of this country, and we will be heard!"

One of the boilermakers shook a bottle of beer and uncorked it, spraying foam over the crowd. Some laughed while others pushed and shoved to get out of the way.

"Settle down, now," Patrick warned, but his voice didn't carry over the boisterous gathering.

A gang of miners started chanting a labor song, riling up the crowd. A few of the women locked hands and began hopping in a circle dance. Spray from another bottle of beer arched over the crowd.

"Settle down," Patrick yelled again, but the commotion only got worse. A fight broke out near the back when a drunken man fell onto a child, prompting the boy's father to start swinging.

A piercing whistle split the air. Liam, the welder with the scar splitting one eyebrow, sprang on top of a chair, his face grim. "Quiet!" he bellowed, and within a few seconds, the crowd settled down. The brawny welder stood with his hands on his hips as he surveyed the assembly.

"For those of you who don't know me, my name is Liam Malone, nephew to Mick Malone, the man of the hour." He flashed a wink at Mick, who returned it, but Liam's face quickly settled into an expression of deadly earnest. His voice had the rough cant of the other workers but without a trace of an accent, Irish or otherwise.

"It's all fine and good if you want to carouse down here tonight, and even if you want to cause a little ruckus in the courtroom, but I won't tolerate it outside the courthouse tomorrow," he warned. "Go ahead and let the judge and the Blackstones have it in court, but as soon as a few of us get thrown out of the courtroom, I want more people to funnel in and stir things up again. The people waiting outside to take their places will be orderly and respectful. You will be well-dressed to blend in with the other spectators, or the courthouse guards won't let you in."

"And who's going to keep them in line?" a blaster from Mingo County taunted.

"I will," Liam said in the voice of command. "Everyone here will follow my orders, or I'll see you thrown out. My goal isn't to drum up publicity to sell Mick's book, it's to block Carnegie's plan to create U.S. Steel, the largest corporation this country has ever seen. That's why we came all this way, right?"

Patrick was vaguely aware of the impending merger the Blackstone Bank was financing. It would merge Carnegie Steel and ten other steel mills into one monstrous corporation that would control most of the steel production in the country. It would strangle competition and crush the rights of workers. Suddenly the crowd assembled in this cellar began to make sense. The steelworkers, iron miners, and men who built things with their hands had come to stop the creation of the U.S. Steel Corporation.

Patrick's unease ratcheted higher as Liam Malone continued speaking.

"If the government won't stop the creation of U.S. Steel, the working people will," Liam said. "If we fail, Carnegie and the Blackstones will have a monopoly on the steel industry. Try getting a metalworking job anywhere in this country if you get on the bad side of U.S. Steel."

The crowd was silent as the tough welder's words sank in.

"We start by flinging mud on the Blackstones," Liam continued. "By stirring up bad sentiments from years past, we'll make people take a second look at handing the Blackstones the reins of the world's biggest company. Then we'll go after Carnegie and J.P. Morgan. We are joined together in a common cause, struggling side by side to give dignity to the working people who built this country. We start that journey tomorrow by whipping up a little controlled chaos in the courtroom."

Patrick eyed this newcomer. Liam's battered duster jacket and calloused hands made him look as humble as everyone else here, but he carried an air of command that made him dangerous. He outlined plans for the next day with calm, clear precision. Patrick's fears about uncontrolled disorder began to ease, even as his misgivings about Liam Malone rose.

Mick came to stand alongside Patrick, a bottle of beer in his hand and alcohol on his breath. "That boy shouldn't have come. I told him to stay home, but he came anyway. He's a force, to be sure."

Patrick could already tell that Liam Malone was dangerous by the way he controlled the crowd tonight. Patrick could either risk the anger of the crowd by throwing Liam out . . . or he could join forces with him.

It was ten o'clock before the gathering dispersed. Patrick loitered against the grainy brick wall of the cellar as he watched Liam shake hands and swap stories with people from other states. He needed to speak with the welder privately. Tomorrow's hearing was going to be the most important case of his career. Having a little wind in his sails from a sympathetic audience would help, but he couldn't let it get out of hand.

Finally, the last of the workers began funneling upstairs, and Patrick followed closely behind Liam. As others dispersed on the darkened street, Patrick pulled Liam aside.

"I'm not going to let you turn tomorrow's hearing into a protest against U.S. Steel."

Liam's face tightened a little. "It already is," he said. "Two hundred people didn't leave their homes and families to help my uncle sell more books."

Patrick stepped in front of Liam, forcing the other man to stop walking. "You need your uncle Mick to sell those books. If this case dies tomorrow, the books get destroyed in a bonfire. Right now, no one outside of New York City even knows about this book. Go ahead and whip up a little steam among your followers, but let me steer it in the courtroom. If we win, copies of that book will make people all over the country think twice about letting the Blackstones get a controlling interest over the steel industry."

A gleam of respect lit Liam's pale green eyes, and he offered a calloused hand. "We have a deal."

Patrick shook Liam's hand and breathed a sigh of relief, because Liam Malone was not a man he wanted as an enemy.

9

*P*atrick arrived early at the courthouse to review his notes ahead of the most important hearing of his career. Judge Rothwell hadn't arrived yet, and the jury box was empty, for this wasn't a trial. It was only a hearing to see if the court would halt distribution of a book before publication, and Judge Rothwell would decide the verdict on his own.

The Blackstones' lawyer sat at the plaintiff's table, but Patrick was too nervous to sit. He paced before the gallery, eyeing the spectators who filled the seats, most of whom were Mick's crowd. They wore homespun clothes and carried lunch pails. They were better behaved than last night, but he could sense their excitement simmering just beneath the surface.

There were only a few Blackstones here. Gwen Kellerman sat beside an elderly man who was probably Frederick Blackstone. Patrick couldn't meet her eyes because he was about to defend Mick's slurs about her family, and the prospect gave him no joy. He was grateful for his spiffy new suit because there were a lot of eyes on him today, and he adjusted his freshly starched cuffs while pacing before a row of seats reserved for the journalists.

The law was on his side today, but he had plenty of strikes against him. His Irish accent tended to come on strong when he was nervous. The opposing counsel was Eugene Alden Fletcher, a Harvard-educated attorney who spoke with the clipped accent that upper-crust New Englanders had mastered generations ago.

The bailiff entered the courtroom. It was a good thing he had a hefty build that could stand up to a little rough-and-tumble, because it might get rowdy soon.

"All rise!" the bailiff intoned, and the crowd stood.

Judge Rothwell entered the room, his black robes swaying as he mounted the steps to the raised dais holding the judge's desk. He tapped his gavel and bid the crowd to sit.

Patrick took a seat beside Mick and his publisher at the defendant's table. The judge wasted no time in starting the proceedings.

"In the case of Blackstone vs. Carstairs Publishing, we are deciding if the plaintiffs have sufficient cause to prevent the publication of the defendant's memoir. The burden of proof lies with the Blackstones, and it is a high bar. Freedom of speech is one of this country's most cherished liberties. The plaintiffs are thereby required to prove serious and libelous intent in the memoir."

A low murmur rose up from Mick's crowd, but a single tap of Judge Rothwell's gavel caused it to fade. The rules of the court required an expert to testify on the plaintiff's behalf, and Oscar Blackstone had been chosen to explain the damage the memoir could cause the Blackstone Bank. He had a tough, battle-scarred appearance as he limped toward the witness stand. He leaned heavily on a cane and wore an eyepatch, all mementos of the hostility directed at the Blackstones.

The plaintiff's attorney made the most of his client's injuries. "Are you able to see me, sir?"

Oscar gave a curt nod. "As well as any one-eyed man can see."

"How is it you came to have only one eye?"

Patrick stood. "Objection. Former crimes against the Blackstone family have no bearing on the case today."

"Sustained," the judge said. "Please proceed, Mr. Fletcher."

The Blackstone attorney asked several questions regarding the importance of a bank's reputation in conducting business, and Oscar easily answered them. Mind-numbing testimony about financial details dragged on for over an hour as the witness outlined how his bank forged alliances to fund large-scale corporations. The nation's other largest bank, controlled by J.P. Morgan, would partner with the Blackstones to finance the creation of U.S. Steel, and that alliance could falter if the reputation of the Blackstones took a severe hit.

Patrick assumed a polite expression when it was his turn to cross-examine Oscar Blackstone. He rose and approached the witness box. "Mr. Blackstone, the success of your bank goes without question, but you have claimed that my client's book libeled *you*. I must ask for specific examples in which my client unfairly defamed your family."

Oscar raised his chin. "Page thirty-five, the second paragraph."

Patrick slipped on a pair of clear glass spectacles. He didn't need them, but they made him look smart. He opened the book, quickly spotted the insulting passage, and read it aloud for the court.

"'Frederick Blackstone is the spawn of the devil, and his son is his sulfur-breathing henchman. My sainted grandmother used to tell me tales of demons that haunted the hills of Ireland, devouring the innocent and spitting out their bones after sucking the blood and marrow from their lifeless bodies. That's who the Blackstones remind me of.'" He looked up at Oscar. "Is that the offending passage?"

"It is."

"And are you the sulfur-breathing henchman referred to in the first sentence?"

Muffled laughter rose from the gallery, but Oscar maintained his dignity. "I assume so, yes."

"This passage is Mr. Malone's opinion, is it not? He merely states that you remind him of a terrifying demon."

"It's insulting and an outright lie," Oscar said.

"A lie that you remind him of a blood-sucking demon? Others have gotten the same impression over the decades."

Another spurt of laughter and stamping of feet came from the audience. The judge banged his gavel, and once again the crowd settled down.

"That's why I'm here," Oscar responded. "To stop this sort of insulting press."

Patrick took a long and pointed look at the journalists in the front row. They were his best allies this morning. "Insulting press?" he asked. "Surely members of the press are entitled to their opinions, even if those opinions are unflattering."

"But not libelous," Oscar countered. "My bank is in the middle of the largest merger in this country's history, and a sterling reputation is essential."

Patrick turned to the judge. "Your Honor, I suggest that the passage I just read is only the opinion of the author and no intelligent reader could mistake it for a literal fact." He turned back to Oscar. "Are there any other examples of libel in my client's book?"

Oscar named the page, and Patrick once again flipped to the offending passage. His mouth twitched, but he fought back the laughter because Oscar had picked a rich one. He cleared his throat and read aloud.

"'The Blackstones treat their employees worse than the pharaoh treated the slaves of Egypt.' Is that the passage?"

"It is," Oscar said. "We don't know how the pharaoh treated his slaves, and Malone says we are worse than the pharaoh. We aren't."

"*Do* we know that?" Patrick asked. "Let's see. I wonder if the pharaoh offered his slaves an eight-hour workday and a full thirty minutes for lunch. Blackstone-financed factories rarely do. I wonder if the pharaoh deliberately neglected to check the birth certificates of his slaves so he couldn't be accused of exploiting underaged children. The companies you finance rarely confirm their youngest employees' ages. So my hunch is that you and the pharaoh are giving each other competition in terms of raw exploitation."

Laughter from the crowd prompted the judge to tap his gavel, but even Judge Rothwell was trying not to laugh.

The Blackstones' attorney stood to object. "Your Honor, the defendant's lawyer is making a mockery of the proceedings."

"Mr. O'Neill?" the judge asked.

"I am merely being literal," Patrick said. "If the plaintiffs use a literal interpretation of Mr. Malone's text, it's fair for me to use that same measure. In Exodus 1:14 we're told that the pharaoh made his slaves' lives bitter with hard service. I'll warrant we can find some people in Blackstone-financed factories who could say the same."

"Exodus says the pharaoh used his *slaves* harshly," the Blackstone attorney said. "None of the people working for the Blackstones are slaves. They are free to leave whenever they choose."

Patrick returned fire with good-natured aplomb. "While that may be true today, Mr. Malone's experience with the Blackstones dates to 1870, when workers often had contractual obligations making it impossible for them to simply walk away. Sir, may I suggest you don't want to debate about biblical interpretation with me?"

"You tell it to him, Father What-a-Waste!" someone yelled from the back row. A handful of people stood to clap and catcall.

Judge Rothwell banged his gavel. "Bailiff, escort those men in the back row out of the building. This is a courtroom! There will be no more such outbursts today."

The bailiff scowled as he headed toward the disorderly men, who stood and funneled out of the room, catcalling the entire way down the aisle and out the door.

Patrick caught a glimpse of Mrs. Kellerman sitting stone-faced beside her grandfather. He couldn't even send her a nod of compassion without risking the momentum of his attack.

"Continue," the judge ordered, and Patrick asked Oscar for another libelous passage, which he dispatched with similar wordplay. Projecting casual charm while briskly deflating

Oscar's arguments was harder than it looked, but he kept it up until lunchtime, when the judge banged his gavel.

"Court is in recess for one hour. We'll convene again at one o'clock."

Patrick hid a smile. This morning had been a victory, and he expected to do just as well after lunch.

10

The morning had been torture for Gwen. Watching her family become the target of mockery was awful, and having it come from the charming Patrick O'Neill made it even harder. She sat between her grandfather and her cousin Edwin during the morning proceedings.

Actually, Edwin was a second cousin, but he was one of her more interesting relatives, having made a living buying and selling antiques he collected during his world travels. He was only two years older than she was, so they naturally paired up during family gatherings. With his floppy blond hair and lazy elegance, Edwin had always been one of her favorite cousins.

"Oscar is getting his head handed to him," Edwin whispered to her during the hearing, and Gwen silently agreed. Wasn't it strange how humor could be such a lethal weapon? Time seemed to drag as she watched Patrick smile and tease and laugh as he eviscerated Uncle Oscar all morning, and she braced herself for more after lunch.

At least Judge Rothwell began the afternoon session with a stern warning to the spectators.

"I won't tolerate any more outbursts," he said. "I am willing to clear the courtroom and hold the rest of the hearing behind closed doors. You have been warned."

She could only pray the warning would have the desired effect as Uncle Oscar headed toward the stand and their attorney began questioning him about potential damages that could result from Malone's book. It was warm in the courtroom, and her eyes glazed over as he delved into tedious financial details. Her attention wandered over the spectators behind the defendant's table, who so far were better behaved this afternoon, but that probably wouldn't last.

One man caught her attention. Instead of watching the proceedings like the others, he was watching *her*. He was a good-looking man despite the scar splitting one eyebrow, but his stare was so disconcerting that she immediately turned her attention back to Mr. Fletcher as he continued guiding her uncle through his testimony.

"Has Mr. Carnegie pulled out of the deal?" their lawyer asked.

"No, Mr. Carnegie knows we are a bank of faultless reputation," Oscar said. "We are grateful for his support, but Carnegie Steel represents only a fraction of the proposed merger, and others could lose faith in the bank."

The questioning continued, and she peeked again at the scar-faced man across the aisle. He was still watching her. His scrutiny kept shifting between her and her grandfather.

The way he stared was rude, and she lifted her chin, refusing to let him bully her into looking away. He was handsome in a rough sort of way, with dark hair that needed a trim. He had pale green eyes and reminded her of someone, but she couldn't place him.

She elbowed her grandfather.

"What?" Frederick asked.

"There is a man in the third row on the opposite side," she whispered. "He's been staring at us."

Her grandfather turned to look, then sucked in a quick breath.

"Your father," he said. "That man looks like your father once did."

Even in Gwen's earliest memories, her father already looked

old, worn down by grief and stress, but she'd seen pictures of him as a young man in his prime, and the resemblance to the man on the other side of the courtroom was startling. It was hard to guess the stranger's age, but he looked about her age. William would be thirty-three if he had lived.

Her grandfather pulled on the knot of his tie. His hand shook, and his breathing was ragged.

"Are you all right?" she asked.

"I need air," he said, and she stood to help him rise. Edwin did too. It was worrisome how heavily Frederick leaned on her as she guided him toward the center aisle. Others on the bench pulled aside to let them pass as she helped him out of the muggy room.

The vestibule outside the courtroom was empty. She guided Frederick to a bench.

"We're probably imagining things," she said. Her grandfather's hand shook as he dragged out a handkerchief and blotted his face.

"Probably," he replied after a long pause. "It's been a stressful day, and this hearing has stirred up bad memories. That man is surely no one. He looks like an ordinary laborer, not a Blackstone."

But he *did* look like a Blackstone. Her parents had more than a dozen photographs of Willy, and she'd seen them all. He was a sturdy little boy, with an olive complexion and unusually pale eyes. It was impossible to guess what he would have looked like had he grown up.

"I didn't see him," Edwin said. "Describe him."

"He looks like Theodore," Frederick groused. "All except the rude stare. My son was a kind and gentle man, nothing like that ruffian."

A roar of laughter rose from the courtroom, followed by a banging of the gavel. The judge demanded order, then said something else so low she couldn't hear.

"Objection!" the Blackstone attorney shouted, but the judge overruled the objection and continued speaking.

"It doesn't sound like things are going well," Edwin said.

Gwen nodded and hurried to the courtroom doors, cocking her ear to listen. The judge said the Blackstones hadn't proven their case and there was no point in continuing the discussion about damages without a finding of libel.

A cheer rose from the crowd, complete with hooting, stomping, and jeering. The judge banged his gavel for order, but it didn't stop the commotion. Footsteps came pounding toward the door, and she backed away and returned to her grandfather.

"It sounds like we lost," she said. "Stay here. I'm going to find that man before he leaves."

The doors opened, and two hundred people came streaming out. She had to battle the crowd to keep moving toward the doors, determined to intercept the man with the pale eyes and the scar that split his eyebrow.

He wasn't hard to spot. He was a few inches taller than most of the triumphant and jeering spectators. She pushed through the crowd and managed to grab his elbow.

"Please," she said. "We need to talk to you."

He glanced at her through narrowed eyes. "Who is 'we'?" he asked in a challenging tone.

"My grandfather and I would like to speak to you."

Frederick was already by her side. Edwin stood a few yards away, watching from a distance. The crowd thinned as the courtroom emptied quickly, and they gestured for the man to follow them a few yards away where it wasn't so crowded.

"I'm Gwen Blackstone Kellerman, and this is my grandfather, Frederick Blackstone," she said. "May I ask your name?"

He stared at her grandfather. His demeanor was suspicious and hostile, without an ounce of the deferential respect people usually afforded her grandfather. "Liam," he finally said. "Liam Malone."

She sucked in a quick breath. "Are you related to Mick Malone?"

"Yeah, he's sort of an uncle."

"Sort of?"

"Yeah, sort of," he said impatiently. "Look, what's your business with me?"

Heavens above, what if Mick had snatched her brother and smuggled him away to be raised by someone in his family? William was so young when he was taken that he might have no memory of his early years. The possibility that she could be looking at her long-lost brother was too preposterous to believe, but she couldn't entirely dismiss it either.

"Exactly how are you related to Mick Malone?"

He narrowed his eyes. "It's none of your business, lady."

"You don't need to be so rude," she said. "All I did was ask a polite question."

The hint of a sneer darkened Liam Malone's face. "Blackstones aren't polite. You stand on the throat of the working people so you can slurp up ill-gotten gains." He glanced at the sapphire on her hand. "That pretty blue rock on your finger could choke a horse. How many children went hungry so you could walk around with that vulgar ring?"

"That's enough," Frederick warned. "You are to treat my granddaughter with respect."

"I'd respect her a lot more if she yanked that ring off her finger and dropped it in the nearest collection basket for the poor."

"This is my wedding ring," she defended, cradling it against her chest.

"And within a city block of this courthouse there are hungry kids without shoes." He bellowed the charge so loudly that it echoed down the marble corridors of the courthouse. "You think you're above criticism because you're a woman? My mother has burns on her hands from working in a glass factory. The girls in my town drop out of school at twelve to work in the mills. What have you ever done? In your entire life, what have you *ever* accomplished to earn that rock on your finger?"

Anger gathered and grew brighter. She didn't deserve this narrow-minded man's insults and impulsively tugged the ring off and thrust it at him. "Here! It's yours. Do what you like with it."

He blinked, staring at her without making any move to take the ring. Onlookers had gathered, and it felt hot and airless in here, but she couldn't back down. Reporters watched with curious eyes as Liam continued to glare at her without moving.

"Go ahead, take it," she prompted. "Sell it and give the money to an orphanage. And while you're at it, sell that union pin on your lapel. You don't get to issue challenges like that without giving up something of your own."

He kept his eyes locked on hers as emotions flashed across his face. He opened and closed his mouth as though uncertain how to answer her, but he soon found his voice.

"You probably like masquerading as Lady Bountiful, especially since there are a bunch of reporters here to witness it," he said. "One can always expect the Blackstones to paint themselves with a saintly brush. I'm surprised you weren't wearing a halo in the courtroom."

He grabbed the ring and shoved it in his pocket, then smirked at her before disappearing into the crowd heading out the door.

Every impulse urged her to run after him and get her ring back. What a vile man. She'd hire someone to watch him and see what he did with her ring. She'd let him sell it, but if a penny of the proceeds went into his own pocket instead of helping the poor, she'd trumpet the news and knock him off his self-righteous pedestal.

"He's not one of us," Frederick said in a low voice beside her. "He looks like Theodore, but that doesn't prove anything."

"Hush," she whispered, because reporters were still watching, but she and Edwin traded worried glances. It was impossible to know what sort of person Willy would have become if he grew up in the warped, shady custody of the Malones.

"We'll have to keep an eye on him," Edwin said, and Gwen nodded, even though in her heart she knew Frederick was probably right. Her father had doted on Willy, and she didn't want to believe the cheerful boy he described could turn into that hostile, smirking man.

Patrick emerged from the courtroom riding a wave of ex-hilaration. Mick's book would proceed to publication, and today's ruling would make it hard for the Blackstones to come after them again.

It took a while to finalize paperwork in the judge's chambers, but he practically danced on air as he left the courthouse. Mick and Ruby had commandeered the pub across the street to celebrate, and he headed over to join them. By the time Patrick arrived, the taps were flowing and Mick stood atop the bar, preaching to the rowdy crowd as he recounted his glory in the courtroom.

Patrick didn't care. Mick Malone and his drunken ramblings were no longer his concern, and he scanned the room, searching for somewhere he could relax with a mug of his own. The tables near the back were mostly empty except for Liam Malone, looking angry and sullen. Unlike the others, who mingled with foamy mugs of beer and sloppy grins on their faces, Liam sat alone, arms folded across his chest as he moodily watched Mick spout forth.

Patrick wended through the crowd and sat on the scarred wooden bench beside Liam. With their backs against the wall, they had a good view of the entire pub, with its brass railings and sawdust covering the old wooden floorboards.

"Not in the mood to celebrate?" Patrick asked.

Liam kept glowering at Mick but finally turned to look at Patrick. "You're a lawyer. You probably know a lot about money and stuff, right?"

Plenty. The church had trained him in finance and corporate law in hope of someday using him as a lawyer for the archdiocese of the church. He was curious what had made Liam so moody.

"I know about money and stuff," he confirmed. "What do you need to know?"

Liam scrounged in his pocket and came out with a ring. He

held it beneath the table so no one else could see it. "Do you know where I can fence this?"

Patrick's eyes widened. "That looks like the ring Mrs. Kellerman always wears."

"It's her wedding ring," Liam said. "Where can I sell it for the best price?"

Patrick stood, careful to give nothing away as he lazily moved to stand in front of Liam. The first thing a good boxer learned was not to telegraph his upcoming moves to an opponent. He turned and, with lightning-fast speed, grabbed Liam by the collar, hoisted him up, then slammed him against the back wall.

"And how did you come into possession of Mrs. Kellerman's wedding ring?" He kept his voice low and soft, which was usually more threatening than shouting.

Liam didn't flinch. "She gave it to me," he said, his eyes full of challenge. He planted the sole of his boot on Patrick's thigh and shoved him back.

Patrick stumbled but regained his balance quickly. "That's a story I'd like to hear," he said. "And be careful with it. I'm friendly with the lady and will know if you're lying."

"We had words in the courthouse," Liam admitted. "I shouted at her and said she didn't deserve to wear a ring like that when there were poor people working in Blackstone companies who couldn't feed their children."

"And she just gave it to you?"

"She did." His voice was pensive and confused, lending credence to his words. "I was minding my own business after the hearing, but she grabbed my arm and came at me, stirring up old rumors and such. I didn't like it."

Patrick straightened a chair he'd knocked over in the scuffle, then sat back on the bench, gesturing for Liam to do the same. They were both tense and cagey, but Liam resumed his position, slumped against the back of the bench with his arms crossed.

"What old rumors?" Patrick asked.

"There's always been rumors about me," Liam said. "I don't think they're true, and she should have left well enough alone."

"What sort of rumors?" he pressed.

Liam snorted. "That Uncle Mick found me under a toadstool. That he bought me from the gypsies, or that the fairies dropped me down a chimney. It's all hogwash. My mum swears it's a big lie, and that she suffered the agonies of the damned when she gave birth to a ten-pound baby." He gave a harsh scoff. "Don't ever get her started on the topic, because she won't stop bellyaching about the torture she endured giving birth to me, and I have to promise her pearls from the East to make up for it."

Patrick leaned closer. "And did the rumors say it was a three-year-old child Mick found under a toadstool?"

"Nope." Liam's face grew pensive as he stared into the distance. "I think I might have been born in Ireland. I remember being on a ship, feeling the wind on my face and the sun glinting on the water. I think maybe someone brought me over and gave me to the Malones. I don't look like either one of my parents."

"But you remember being at sea?"

Liam nodded. "I think it's my earliest memory. I remember standing beside a man and being very happy. I felt safe." He gave a harsh laugh. "Of course, if I came from Ireland, that means my parents aren't my parents, and nothing will set Janet Malone off faster than implying something like that. 'Ten pounds,' she'll holler, then cuff me on the head."

"Did you know Liam is the Irish name for William?"

"Yeah, I do." He held up his hand. The sapphire ring glittered on the top knuckle of his pinky finger. "I don't want this ring. She gave it away to shame me, to show how easily she could do it. I don't want anything to do with her or this ring."

"Then give it to me." Patrick held out his hand, and without hesitation, Liam yanked the ring from his finger and slapped it in Patrick's palm.

"I'm trusting you to do the right thing with it," Liam said.

Patrick nodded. "I will," he said, because suddenly he had a far bigger mystery to solve.

11

Gwen retreated to her grandfather's office on the top floor of the Blackstone Bank after the courtroom debacle. She resisted the urge to point out that she'd been right about the bad publicity that would come from challenging the memoir in court. By the time the reporters were done with the story, every bookstore in town would be swamped with advance orders for the memoir.

It was water under the bridge. What still haunted her was the strange encounter with Liam Malone.

"Giving your ring away was a foolhardy thing to do," her grandfather said, scowling at her from the opposite side of his desk. "What on earth possessed you?"

Her cousin Edwin and Uncle Oscar looked equally baffled as they waited for her answer. It had been an impulsive move sparked by an instinctive need to defend herself against that awful man's contempt. The odd thing was how easy it was to give her wedding ring away.

"I want to see what he does with it," she said. "It will tell us what sort of man he is."

Oscar sat in a chair near the window, rolling an unlit cigar in his hands. "If you want to know who he is, I'll commission a dozen Pinkerton detectives and have a complete report by the end of the week, but why do you care about this no-account laborer?"

Uncle Oscar had been on the witness stand most of the morning. He hadn't seen Liam and didn't understand their concern.

"He looks like Theodore," her grandfather said. "The same eyes. The same coloring, the same shape of his jaw."

Oscar set down his cigar, his expression hardening as he understood Frederick's reasoning. "Preposterous. Willy Blackstone is dead and gone. So is Theodore. Don't start imagining things."

"We can't bury our heads in the sand and pretend this doesn't exist," Edwin said.

"He's nobody," Oscar snapped.

"He's not nobody, he's got my wedding ring," she said, and Oscar whirled on her.

"For pity's sake, I'll buy you another ring, but you are to let me handle this from here on out, do you understand me?"

She flinched at his furious tone. She hated conflict, and it was too farfetched to believe that Willy could still be alive. Yes, there was a resemblance between Liam and her father, but that couldn't prove anything. And a sloppy drunk like Mick Malone couldn't have kept a secret like this all these years.

"Get your Pinkerton agents on him," Frederick ordered Oscar. "We need to learn everything possible about him."

For once, all of them were in complete accord.

Elation still zinged through Patrick's veins when he arrived home, eager to recount his victory in the courtroom for his mother. Birdie hadn't felt well all week, prompting him to pick up some sandwiches from a vendor on the way home.

"Hey, Ma," he said as he entered their apartment. "I brought pastrami sandwiches with extra—"

He froze, gaping at his mother sprawled on the floor.

He dropped the bag and rushed to her side. "Ma? What's wrong?"

She lay at a weird angle, stretched out with her head and shoulders twisted unnaturally.

"I can't get up," she said through clenched teeth. "My back started hurting so bad. I fell and have been stuck here for hours."

To his horror, she started crying.

"Not to worry, I'll help you up." He tried to lift her, but her back stayed frozen in that unnatural backward arc. Patrick quit trying to help her stand and scooped her up to carry her to the bed.

"I'm sorry to be such a bother," she said in a choked tone.

"Nonsense, you weigh less than a child."

The fall she'd taken at the bakery must have been worse than they thought. Even after he got her settled on her bed, she had that weird backward curve in her spine, like a bow pulled taut. It was abnormal.

"I'm going for a doctor," he said, prepared to shoot down all her arguments against the expense. She'd always boasted that the last time she'd seen a doctor was on the day she delivered him into the world.

"Yes, I think so," she said, which only made him worry more.

"I'll get Mrs. O'Shea from next door to come sit with you while I'm gone," he said, and once again she gave him no complaint.

Luckily, old Dr. Phalen lived only a block away in an apartment over the butcher's shop. Even so, Patrick was out of breath as he ran up the stairs and pounded on the doctor's door, begging him to come right away.

"Back pain?" Dr. Phalen said, pulling the wrinkles of his face into a frown. "Can it wait until morning? My wife just put a hot shepherd's pie on the table. A dram of whiskey is probably the best thing for your ma anyway."

Patrick shook his head. "Please come now. Something isn't right. Her back has been bothering her all week, but this is different." He explained how his mother fell while lugging a sack of flour that was too heavy for her.

"I'll come," the old doctor said with a sigh of resignation. Patrick sent an apologetic nod to Mrs. Phalen, still sitting at the dinner table with the feast laid out before her. This surely wasn't her first meal spoiled by an inconvenient call for a doctor.

Half an hour later, Patrick paced in his parlor, straining to hear what was being said behind Birdie's closed bedroom door while Mrs. O'Shea's knitting needles clicked in a reassuring rhythm. They'd both been booted out of the sickroom when Dr. Phalen arrived, but this was taking an awful long time simply to diagnose back pain.

At last the door opened, and they both stood. Dr. Phalen looked even older than usual as he approached them.

"I'm sorry, Patrick lad, but it looks like your ma has tetanus. Lockjaw has already set in, which is why she's having a hard time speaking. Muscle spasms are holding her back in that contorted shape. I'm afraid there is nothing that can be done."

"How long will it last?" he asked.

The doctor's eyes darkened with sympathy. "It's only going to get worse in the next few days. And then she will die, lad. I'm afraid there is no cure for this form of tetanus."

No. Patrick shook his head. No, he couldn't believe this.

Mrs. O'Shea crossed herself and collapsed onto a chair, but the doctor continued speaking.

"It's the cut on her arm that did her in," he said. "I took the bandages off and examined the wound. That's where the infection got in, and it takes a while to manifest. She said she fell against a rusty wheel when she lugged that sack of flour. I'm sorry, Patrick."

It was inconceivable that his mother would die because of a cut on her arm. It was only a scratch! He would find another doctor, someone who could give him some hope. He stared blankly ahead, his gaze catching on the cake Birdie had brought home today. She had been well enough to bake earlier today, and now Dr. Phalen said she was on her deathbed?

The doctor and Mrs. O'Shea continued talking about how to

make Birdie comfortable, but it sounded like their voices came from a hundred miles away.

"I think it would be best if you called for a priest," Dr. Phalen advised, and Mrs. O'Shea agreed.

Patrick collapsed on the sofa. His mother's cheerful light was going to be snuffed out because she had lugged a sack of flour too heavy for her. No hope. Was there anything worse than being robbed of hope?

"The lame, the halt, and the blind can be cured." He straightened as Gwen Kellerman's voice sounded in his head. Tetanus had been among the diseases Blackstone College was trying to cure.

He vaulted to his feet. Dr. Phalen had already left, but Patrick bounded after him. "Wait!" he shouted, his voice echoing down the hallway. "Blackstone College is working on a cure for tetanus. I heard about it."

The doctor shook his head. "They are decades away from a vaccine," he said. "I wish it were otherwise."

Was it a vaccine? He tried to remember exactly what he had seen in the laboratories of the college. Mrs. Kellerman said their serums to treat disease were still in the testing phase. *Serums*, not a vaccine.

He didn't care. Doing nothing was intolerable. Even if it was only a slim chance for a cure, he was going to reach for it.

Gwen considered canceling the Friday evening soiree after the catastrophe in court that day. News of the humiliating defeat was already spreading on campus, and she didn't want to discuss it with anyone.

But she quickly rejected the idea of canceling. She had hosted these gatherings every Friday evening for the past ten years. Even on the dreadful week when Jasper and her father died, the campus community gathered at her home to support her, and it had been one of the most affirming nights of her life. The professors had more respect than to gloat or gossip about Blackstone family problems. As she prepared for the soiree, her spirits began lifting, ready to engage with the lively and intelligent people who made these gatherings so rewarding.

The first cluster of professors arrived, along with a visiting paleontologist from the Smithsonian, who brought a dinosaur bone from an excavation in Nevada. Gwen marveled at the heft of the bone as they passed it from person to person. Others began a game of charades in the garden. Inside, a chemistry professor argued with an English professor about whether tea could be reheated without affecting the flavor.

Proceeding with tonight's soiree had been the right decision. That silly memoir didn't matter to the rest of the world. And the strange man she saw in the courtroom? It could be weeks before Uncle Oscar's detectives learned anything about him, but the odds were that Oscar was right. Her overactive imagination had probably gone too far.

She joined the debate about the wisdom of reheating tea. Some insisted no one could tell the difference, while others vehemently disagreed.

Dennis Conway, a young professor from the chemistry department, stood on the reheating side. "Reheating will not affect the molecular structure of plain black tea," he insisted.

Old Professor Snow disagreed. "I can always tell," he claimed, but Dennis wanted proof and turned to her in supplication.

"Gwen, may we invade your kitchen to conduct an experiment of fresh versus reheated tea? For the good of humanity, we must learn the truth."

This was why she loved these Friday soirees. She never knew how the evening would unfold, but they were always a delight. President Matthews offered to serve as an impartial observer to ensure the fresh tea and reheated tea were fairly presented to the taste testers.

She and Dennis had retreated to the kitchen to set out teacups when the incessant ringing of the doorbell cut through the dull roar of the soiree noise. Someone answered the door, and Gwen went back to preparing a new pot of tea but was soon interrupted.

"Mrs. Kellerman, I need your help."

She blinked, not quite believing that Patrick O'Neill was standing in her kitchen doorway, panic on his face. He was a disheveled mess, his sandy hair windblown and his collar askew.

"Good heavens, what's wrong?"

"The doctor said my mother has tetanus. He says there's no cure, but I think your college is working on a remedy. Some kind of serum."

She clasped a hand to her throat. Tetanus was a horrible disease, and Dr. Haas was working on it, but he wasn't here this evening.

"How long has she been showing symptoms?" Dennis asked.

"They started today," Patrick said. "She cut herself ten days ago, but she only started having the muscle seizures today. I remember Mrs. Kellerman saying the college has a treatment for it."

Gwen fidgeted. "We do, but it's only been tested on humans a few times."

"And those people died," President Matthews said.

Dennis shook his head. "Two died, two survived."

"That's better odds than the doctor gave my mother," Patrick said. "How can I get it to her?"

That was the problem. The laboratory with the serum was in Queens, and the ferries would stop running soon. It would take hours to get the serum here, but she would try.

"I'll get you the serum," she began, and Mr. O'Neill let out a mighty breath and sagged against the kitchen wall. This was no easy cure, and she needed to be sure he understood. She grabbed both his shoulders and forced him to meet her gaze. "Mr. O'Neill, please understand, this is a long shot. The serum may not save your mother's life, and it might even make things worse. We simply don't know enough yet."

He looked like he wanted to weep. "I understand, ma'am. I know you can't work miracles, but there's nothing worse than having no hope."

She nodded, but it would take a herculean feat to gather all the people necessary to administer the treatment, and she didn't know if they had enough time to make it happen. The treatment was new and risky. They failed as often as they succeeded, but they would try.

"Go back to your mother," she said, "and start praying, because the next few hours are going to be harder than you can imagine."

12

By the time Patrick arrived home, the apartment was crowded with a priest, a pair of nuns, and the O'Shea family waiting in the front room.

"Any change?" he asked Mrs. O'Shea.

"She's asleep," the older woman said. "Have you got the medicine?"

He shook his head. "The doctor and his assistants are on their way, but the serum is in Queens. I was told if we can get it to her before sunrise, she'll have a fighting chance."

But no guarantee. He slumped on the couch and listened to the O'Sheas gab with the priest, but he couldn't join in. It was hard not to watch the clock, but every few minutes his eyes strayed over to it. Ten o'clock. Then eleven. Soon it was midnight, and still no sign of Mrs. Kellerman and her serum. Was it only snake oil? Had he been getting his hopes up over a pipe dream?

A little before one o'clock, the clomping of hooves sounded in the lane below. He stuck his head out the window and spotted a carriage with four horses galloping through the deserted streets towards their building. Mrs. Kellerman sat beside the driver on the front buckboard.

"Up here!" he hollered from the open window, heedless of

the late hour. Who cared about sleep when his mother's life was on the line?

A few minutes later Mrs. Kellerman and a stocky man with a graying mustache and a bald pate came bustling into the apartment. Two younger men edged inside as well.

"I am Dr. Haas," the old man said in a thick German accent. "I've brought a pair of research students who are helping me with the study. This is Hiram Schuller from Brooklyn and Jake Gold from Oklahoma."

Patrick nodded to the men. "Good. My mother is in the back room."

"Not so fast," Dr. Haas said. "I need you to understand that this serum is experimental. It may help your mother, but it is just as likely to cause her symptoms to worsen. We must monitor the entire process."

"I understand," he said, gesturing toward the bedroom, but Mrs. Kellerman laid a hand on his arm.

"What Dr. Haas is saying is that your mother will become a test subject. He will measure and document her symptoms. He will need to take photographs too. I know it seems like a terrible invasion of her privacy, but it's necessary to help us develop the serum."

One of the young men held a bulky camera, and Patrick cringed at the idea of photographs. Birdie wouldn't like being seen by strangers the way she looked. The muscles in her face had seized to draw her mouth into a grotesque smile she couldn't move.

"I'll be sure she understands," Patrick said.

"The procedure is painful," Dr. Haas said. "We will need to inject the serum directly into her spinal column."

A wave of dizziness overcame Patrick, and he nearly fainted. "Lord above, is there nowhere else you can give it to her?"

"The other alternative is a direct injection into the brain, which would involve drilling a hole in the patient's skull, and that adds to the risk."

"Let's go for the spine," Patrick said, praying this wasn't

all a terrible mistake that would cause his mother even more suffering on her way to the other side.

He led Dr. Haas into the bedroom, then knelt beside the bed, wincing at Birdie's hideous grin that starkly contrasted the fear in her eyes. She lay on her side because her twisted spine made lying any other way impossible.

"These are the specialists I told you about, Ma. They'll need to examine you before they can use that special medicine. Maybe take a couple of photographs. Don't be embarrassed. They know more about this disease than anyone in the world, and someday this is going to help a lot of people. Will that be okay?"

She couldn't speak, only nod.

"Excellent," Dr. Haas said, then proceeded to take his mother's temperature and pulse and used a weird-looking device to measure the bend in her spine.

The younger research assistant set the camera near Birdie's face to take her picture. She couldn't even change her expression, but Patrick knew she'd be horrified to be photographed like this. She closed her eyes, and a tear leaked out. He grabbed a section of the sheet to blot it.

"Okay, Ma. The picture-taking is over. Now comes the hard part."

Thank the Lord for Gwen Kellerman. She explained the procedure with a softer approach than the blunt German professor and described how the serum contained antibodies that would fight the tetanus bacteria. In order to get the life-saving serum where it needed to go, they would inject it into Birdie's spinal cord.

Patrick held his mother's hand as the knowledge sank in. Once again, there was no change in her expression but terror in her eyes. She began panting and more tears fell, but when Mrs. Kellerman asked for permission to proceed, Birdie nodded.

Dr. Haas and both his students moved to the other side of the bed while the professor prepared a syringe. Patrick was thankful Birdie couldn't see the size of the needle or the large bottle of cloudy, amber-colored fluid. The professor pulled *a lot* of fluid into the syringe, and knowing where it was going to go . . . another wave of dizziness hit Patrick, and he struggled to stay calm.

"Mr. O'Neill, would you be more comfortable outside?" Mrs. Kellerman asked.

As much as he'd rather be anywhere else, Birdie's look of panic made his answer easy. He pulled up a stool and sat beside her bed, reaching down to hold her hand.

"I'm not going anywhere, Ma. I'll be with you the whole time."

Dr. Haas said the procedure would take about five minutes, which was plenty of time to say a bit of the rosary. Patrick grabbed the olive-wood rosary draped over the bedpost and laid it across his mother's hands. One of the research assistants took his position at her shoulders, and the other at her knees. They were holding her in place, because this was going to be bad.

"Are you ready, Ma?"

She squeezed his hand and dipped her chin. It was all the permission Patrick needed. He looked at Dr. Haas and nodded.

Thank heavens for the strong men. They held Birdie braced against the mattress, but she screamed when Dr. Haas inserted the needle, and the keening wail cut straight to Patrick's heart. He started praying over the scream, hoping his voice might cut through her pain and give her something to focus on. He pressed the rosary into her hand.

"Hail Mary, full of grace, the Lord is with thee," he said. "Blessed art thou among women, and blessed is the fruit of thy womb, Jesus. Holy Mary, Mother of God, pray for us sinners now and at the hour of our death. Amen."

His mother's garbled *amen* almost made him weep at her effort. He moved her fingers to the next bead on the rosary and recited the prayer again. Birdie still whimpered in pain but did her best to stumble through the prayer with him. Now that the needle was in, Dr. Haas was slowly injecting the serum.

"You're doing well, Mrs. O'Neill," the doctor said.

His words didn't make a dent on his mother's stricken face, so Patrick kept praying the rosary. After ten Hail Marys, they recited the Lord's Prayer, then began the next round of Hail Marys.

"Halfway through," Dr. Haas said, and Patrick continued reciting the rosary. They got nowhere close to completing the next decade of the rosary before Dr. Haas mercifully declared the infusion complete.

"All over," the doctor said. Birdie let out another wail as he withdrew the needle. Then he cleaned the injection site and applied pressure.

Was this going to work? It was in the Lord's hands now, and Patrick could only pray his mother's misery would be worth it.

They hadn't reached the end of the rosary, but Patrick needed to hear the final words, and Birdie did too. He moved her fingers to the crucifix dangling at the end of the rosary.

"Glory be to the Father, and to the Son, and to the Holy Spirit. As it was in the beginning, is now, and ever shall be, world without end. Amen."

Peace settled on him. The horrifying procedure might only serve to make his mother's final hours even more painful, but people had been born, suffered, rejoiced, and died for millennia. He and Birdie were no different. Come what may, God's will would prevail.

13

Gwen felt limp as she left the sickroom. Dr. Haas had given something to Mrs. O'Neill to help her sleep, but they would be monitoring her condition closely in the coming hours.

Patrick shuffled forward and dropped onto the parlor sofa. She wasn't used to seeing such a physically strong man flop down like that, but he seemed completely drained as he braced his head in his hands and stared at the floor.

"I know death is a normal part of life," he said. "A better Christian wouldn't be so afraid of it."

Her heart ached, and she reached for words to offer comfort. "All Christians are human, and it's normal to fear the unknown."

There wasn't much room in this tiny apartment for Dr. Haas and his assistants, but they would move in for several days to monitor the patient's progress. A neighbor offered to bring over some blankets and pillows to make pallets on the floor for the two medical students, and Dr. Haas would stay in Patrick's bedroom.

Gwen feared Patrick's room might reflect a bachelor's slovenliness, but instead it had a puritanical tidiness. The bed was neatly made, and there was no clutter or knickknacks on the chest of drawers. The only hint of personality was a rosary just like his mother's, also draped on the bedpost. There wasn't a single thing she needed to do to tidy it for the professor.

There wasn't much food in the kitchen other than a startlingly beautiful cake under a glass cover. It looked like the Taj Mahal, with a dome and spires, all covered with vanilla icing and little candies for the finials.

"My mom is a baker," Patrick said from the other side of the room. "That's what she made today before she got so sick."

"She's quite an artist," Gwen said.

Hiram, the medical assistant from Brooklyn, hovered close to look. "She's a Michelangelo!" he said, but their words of praise only seemed to upset Patrick, who remained on the sofa, staring at the cake while he twisted his hands.

His voice was full of regret when he spoke. "I'd offer you a slice, but I dare not touch it. If she dies, that cake will be her last great creation."

Her heart ached at the anguish in his voice. If his mother died, he'd probably keep this cake untouched beneath its glass dome for weeks. "Nonsense," she said. "*You* are her last great creation, and you know that she would agree with me on that."

A reluctant hint of a smile tugged the side of his mouth, then vanished. An awkward silence stretched in the apartment, and then Hiram's stomach let out a mighty growl. He clamped his hand over his middle in dismay, but it served to break the spell on Patrick, who stood.

"Oh, let's cut into that cake. It's going to be a long night, and Ma would want you to have it."

He lifted the glass dome, and the scent of vanilla filled the room. Patrick found a knife, and Hiram brought plates down from the shelf. Patrick stood before the cake, staring at it, his face tragic.

"Would you like me to cut it?" she asked gently.

He passed her the knife. "Thanks," he said simply, but the moment she began cutting, he flinched and turned away.

"I need some air," he said and headed toward the window

to lift the sash. To her surprise, he squatted down, stuck a leg out, then crawled through the opening and onto a fire escape bolted to the brick exterior of the building.

Every instinct urged her to go and comfort him. They were supposed to be enemies, especially after the debacle in the courtroom, but he was in pain, and she couldn't ignore it.

"I'll go see to him," she said, passing the knife to Jake.

In her entire life she had never crawled through a window, but she could do this. She hiked up her skirts and twisted low to fit beneath the window frame, then got a leg through. She expected the fire escape platform to be right there, but she dangled her foot in vain.

"Whoa there, ma'am," Patrick said. "Can I help you out?"

She extended her hand, and he took it. Her spine scraped the bottom of the window frame, but she got through the window with the grace of an ungainly cow.

"You can call me Gwen," she said once she finally had both feet beneath her. Steel grating clanged beneath her shoes, and she shook her skirts back into place.

"I'm not the sort to call a fine lady like you by her given name," he said, and she was sorry for it.

"I wanted to be sure you are all right."

He sagged as he braced his hands on the railing and looked out at the dark lane illuminated by only a few streetlamps. "No need to fear I'll fling myself over. I'm sorry I'm such a lousy sport, but I'm not good company right now. I'm mostly just tired and scared straight down to my bones."

"It's all right to be afraid," she said.

He merely shrugged. "I've never lost anyone before. My father died before I can remember. You've got a lot more experience with this than me."

"I'm no expert on dying or grief," she said. "I'm sure what you are feeling is perfectly normal."

"You're young for a widow. You're probably not even thirty-five or forty years old."

"I'm twenty-nine."

He blanched and turned away. "Oh Lord, now I've really dug a hole and dived into it headfirst."

He looked so mortified that she had to choke back a laugh. Men were atrocious at estimating women's age, which was why so few of them dared try.

"It's okay," she said, still battling a laugh.

"It's not okay." He looked to the heavens for relief, and it was time to put him out of his misery.

"Knock it off, Patrick. We both have bigger things to worry about."

He bowed his head, then sent her a grateful look. "You're quite a woman, Mrs. K. I'll confess, I didn't expect you to be so nice."

"Why not?" She stepped up beside him and curled her hands around the cold metal railing.

He shrugged. "I was rough on you folks in the courtroom today. I'm embarrassed to admit it, but I've never thought much about the real people living behind the imposing Blackstone name." His face darkened, and he straightened, digging around in his pocket.

"Here," he said a little gruffly. "I think this is yours."

Lamplight glinted on her sapphire wedding ring, and she could scarcely believe her eyes. "Where did you get that?"

"Maybe you saw a tough bloke in the courtroom today. Dark hair, angry scowl, split eyebrow?"

"I know who you're talking about."

"He said you gave him the ring. True?"

"True."

"Why did you do it?"

She took the ring back and slipped it onto her finger. "I don't know," she said truthfully.

The strange man had triggered ominous emotions, and she couldn't let him walk away while unanswered questions clawed at her. Giving him the ring had been an impulsive move to learn more about him.

He had passed the test. That didn't mean he might be her

missing brother. In all likelihood, it was the stress of the past week causing her imagination to run wild.

Her gaze strayed over the lane. Laundry lines cluttered the space between the buildings, and discarded crates were stacked behind the pub across the street. There were probably worse neighborhoods, but this was the grittiest she'd ever been in, and she hugged her arms around herself. She didn't like it here.

One of the research assistants stuck his head through the window opening. "The carriage driver wants to head back to the college. Are you going with him?"

"I'm coming," she said, then glanced back at Patrick, sending him a brief nod of farewell before climbing back through the window.

She thought about him the entire carriage ride back to campus. The past few hours had torn down the barrier between them, and he didn't feel like an enemy anymore. He felt like a powerfully attractive man, and that was even more dangerous.

14

wen worried about Patrick and his mother throughout the following day, even though one of the research assistants had telephoned to report that Mrs. O'Neill was doing well.

It wasn't enough for her. Late in the afternoon, she returned to Patrick's apartment, drawn as if by a lodestone and needing to know more about how *both* O'Neills fared. She brought Lorenzo because the Five Points was a frightening place and looked even worse in the daylight. Its streets were a chaotic tangle of shouting vendors, honking horns, and barking dogs. Her carriage lurched over potholes, and the cramped, tightly packed buildings felt oppressive. The building where Patrick lived was clean, but the walls were dingy from smoke stains and so thin that the noise from outside leaked in.

She knocked on Patrick's door, and Hiram answered. "How is Mrs. O'Neill?" she asked.

"Holding her own," the research assistant said, stepping aside to let her and Lorenzo enter. "She's sleeping, and so is Patrick."

The front room looked like a tornado had blown through, with bedding, dirty dishes, and remnants of lunch littering the space. Gwen instinctively began tidying up. It was hard, since there was no running water in the apartment, but she folded the bedding and stacked the dishes. Dr. Haas helped and provided her with a full report about Mrs. O'Neill's progress.

There was almost nothing left in the apartment to eat. She'd seen dozens of vendor carts on the street below, hawking sausages, kippers, boiled ham, and catfish pie. None of it sounded appetizing, but she sent Lorenzo down to buy enough for everyone's dinner. She eyed the dirty dishes but wasn't sure how to wash them without a sink.

"There's a pump down the hall," Hiram said. "I'll go fill a pitcher." Before he could leave, an abrupt banging on the door startled them both.

"O'Neill, you in there?" a gruff voice demanded.

Gwen hurried to the door so the obnoxious knocking wouldn't wake Patrick or his mother.

"Hush!" she scolded the gangly old man on the other side of the door. "There's a sick woman in this apartment, and that rude pounding is entirely unnecessary."

"Rude pounding?" the man repeated. "I'll give you a rude pounding if you don't tell me where O'Neill is. He missed our appointment this morning, and I'm his most important client."

She stilled, recognizing the man from the courtroom yesterday. "Are you Mick Malone?"

"That's me. Is O'Neill here or not? He missed our meeting."

Gwen scrambled for a way to take advantage of this situation. Standing aside, she gestured Mick into the apartment, struggling to maintain a calm expression. "Please keep your voice low, as people are sleeping after having been up all night. I gather you have a memoir about to be released?"

Mick stood straighter and preened. "That's right. I'm about to be famous all over again."

A chill raced down her spine. This man had killed her brother and thrown a grenade into the center of her family from which they never fully recovered.

"Congratulations," she managed to say without her revulsion showing. "You must be very proud. Are there any new and earth-shattering tidbits in the memoir?"

Malone loved the attention and started boasting about how he got a glimpse of "young William" in the boiler room. He sat on the sofa, spreading his legs and arms wide as he painted the picture in colorful terms. Hiram and Dr. Haas looked appalled on her behalf, but Gwen sent them a quick shake of her head, warning them to say nothing. If Mick Malone didn't know who she was, he might slip and mention a detail she could latch on to.

"Now, mind you, I didn't have anything to do with that boy going missing," Malone said, wagging a skinny finger at her. "I'm as pure as the driven snow when it comes to what happened to that poor child."

His hands trembled, and he was sweating even though it wasn't hot in here. They were classic symptoms of an alcoholic abstaining from drink. So was irritability and difficulty thinking clearly. A better person might feel guilty for exploiting his weaknesses, but Gwen pressed forward, hoping to trip him up.

"Why did you need a lawyer? If you're telling the truth, you've got nothing to hide."

"Because I'm a smart man, miss. That's why I need a lawyer."

"And was Mr. O'Neill a good one? Did he catch any details he thought better for you to withhold from your book?"

Malone's smile was devilish as he rubbed his hands together. "There were plenty of good parts he wanted scrubbed from the book. I'd bet you'd love to know what they were, wouldn't you!"

She matched his smile and leaned forward. "I would indeed."

"Maybe if the book sells enough, I'll come out with a sequel. After all, they can't prosecute me for anything anymore. I was found not guilty by a jury of my peers. I could spill everything and still get away with it."

She clenched her fists but kept her voice calm. "A sequel won't sell unless you've got a good story. What else have you got to tell?"

Mick glanced at Hiram and Dr. Haas. "What about the pair of you? Would you be willing to shell out a dollar for insight into the bottomless well of Blackstone family corruption?"

Dr. Haas still looked puzzled but answered as she hoped. "I suppose."

Malone clapped his hands and hooted. "Exactly what I wanted to hear," he roared.

"Shh," Gwen soothed. If Patrick woke up, he'd come out and end this conversation. "Don't get ahead of yourself. Tell me what kind of details would be in a second book. I have a keen eye for spotting what would sell."

"I don't scatter my gems around for free," he said. "What's it worth to you?"

Before she could answer, the sound she dreaded happened. The bedroom door opened, and a bleary-eyed Patrick emerged.

"Mick? What are you doing here?"

Mick stood and took a step toward Patrick, shaking a finger. "We had a meeting this morning, and you missed it, boy-o."

Patrick glanced around the room. Dark circles shadowed his eyes, and he looked exhausted but still alert enough to take stock of the situation. He opened his mouth to speak, but she stood and interrupted him.

"Mr. Malone was about to tell me an interesting story. Let him talk."

"Don't say anything, Mick." Patrick took a step forward, blocking her view of the old drunkard. "This is Gwen Kellerman. She was a Blackstone before she got married. William Blackstone was her brother."

Mick reeled back so quickly he almost toppled over. He let out a stream of curses. "You tried to trick me, woman!"

Gwen glared at Patrick. "You didn't have to tell him that."

"Yeah, I did." Patrick dragged a hand through his disheveled hair. "I'm sorry, Mrs. K, but it's my job to protect his legal rights."

Anger rippled through her. After she'd saved his mother's life, his loyalty to her only enemy in the world was infuriating.

"This is how you pay us back for what we've done for you?" she snapped. Patrick flinched and looked away, but she wasn't in the mood to be kind. "Why couldn't you have looked the other way while I pried the truth out of him? We all know he's guilty." She turned to confront Mick. "You did it, didn't you?" she accused, stepping closer to him, her palms itching to slap him. "Look me in the face and tell me you had nothing to do with my brother being snatched from his own backyard."

Mick gathered himself up, chest out, jaw thrust forward. "I didn't have anything to do with it," he sneered. "It was the Italians who took that boy, and I paid the price for it. Now you waltz in with your fancy Blackstone manners and act like you own the place. You don't belong here, missy. This is the Five Points. Go back to your fancy mansions and—"

"That's enough," Patrick said. "You're not the victim here, Mick."

The old drunkard wheeled toward Patrick, his eyes narrowed in suspicion. "What's she doing here, anyway? Are you working for the enemy, boy-o?"

"Don't take that tone with me," Patrick answered. "I've had to hold my nose while working for you, and you ought to be grateful—"

"Shhh!" Hiram said. "Mrs. O'Neill needs her rest."

It was as though a bucket of ice water was thrown over them. Patrick cast a worried glance at his mother's closed bedroom door, but Gwen wanted to scream in frustration as her chance to get information out of Malone dwindled away.

The front door flung open. "Fried catfish and biscuits!" Lorenzo announced as he entered the apartment. The way he held the greasy paper sacks aloft made him look like a conquering hero returning from the wilds. The elation on his face faded as he scanned the grim crowd. "Is Mrs. O'Neill okay?"

"She's all right, but I'd like to throw this one out the window," Gwen said with a glare at Mick Malone.

"And I'd like to rub that snotty look off your face," Mick taunted.

Once again, Patrick stepped between them. "Mick, I'm canceling our meeting today, and it would be best for you to leave now." He grabbed the sack of fried catfish. "Mrs. Kellerman,

I'm sorry this happened. You didn't deserve to be on the receiving end of that, but you're welcome to join us for dinner."

Patrick wouldn't have been able to swallow even a bite of the greasy catfish, so he retreated to his mother's bedroom while the others ate. Anything to escape the accusation on Gwen's face. She deserved more than what he'd been able to do for her.

In hindsight, he wished he hadn't interrupted when he overheard Mick boasting. If Gwen learned the truth about her brother's kidnapping from Mick, it would save Patrick from the moral dilemma of betraying a client's confidence.

After helping his mother drink some warmed milk, he headed out to the front room, where Gwen and the others sat at the table, the remainders of dinner scattered before them. They had the relaxed look of the well-fed, all except Gwen, whose face was as cold as sculpted marble.

"Can I speak with you?" he asked with caution.

To his relief, she gave a stiff nod and stood. The fire escape was the only place they could have privacy, and Gwen navigated through the window with more grace this time, hiking her skirt, lowering her head, and moving through the opening easily. He followed using the same ducking posture.

"You're getting better at this," he said, closing the window with a lighthearted smile.

She didn't return it. He couldn't expect her to, really.

"Gwen, I'm sorry," he said. "To the bottom of my soul, I'm sorry."

"He was just getting ready to spill something important when you came out."

The pain on her face made him look away. "Mick Malone is a world-class liar," he said. "I once saw him keep an entire pub fascinated by his tale of smuggling a piece of the true cross out of the Vatican while the Swiss guards chased him across Christendom for a solid year. You can't believe anything he says."

"Then why didn't you let him talk?"

It was a fair question, and Patrick struggled with how to respond. When did his obligation to the client end and his duty to be a decent man begin?

"I can usually tell when Mick is lying," he said. "He brags and struts and waves his arms, commanding attention like an actor on the stage, but once he blabbed a story to me when he was sloppy drunk. We were alone in his boardinghouse. He sat slumped in the corner with his head lowered in shame."

God help him, he was going to tell her. She deserved to know. The law could never punish Mick, and Gwen deserved peace of mind for the foul crime Mick had perpetrated against her family.

It was the night after they submitted the manuscript of Mick's book to the publisher. Mick had insisted on buying a bottle of cognac to share with Ruby, but when they arrived at his home, Ruby had gone to visit her mother in Brooklyn. Mick wanted to share a dram, and Patrick saw no harm in it, even though Mick's room was a hovel with only a single kerosene lamp to illuminate the grubby interior. The stink of dirty laundry was strong, and Patrick took only a few sips of the cognac, but Mick bolted it down, one dram after another, until half the bottle was gone.

And that was when the true story came out. Patrick remembered every detail as though it were yesterday.

"He was a cute little kid," Mick had said, the light of the kerosene lamp carving deep hollows into his sorrowful face. "I'd been watching him play in the backyard of that mansion for weeks, learning his schedule and biding my time. Every day he took his dog outside to run around on the lawn and do its business. His nanny usually came out with him, but sometimes she stayed inside because it was cold that winter."

The cognac soured in Patrick's belly, but he dared not interrupt, and Mick kept talking.

"There was a big old pear tree in the yard next door, and I hid in its branches to watch the boy bring his dog out after lunch each day. It was an English bulldog, which is a completely useless animal. No good as a guard dog, no good for hunting, and lazy as the day is long."

Patrick didn't want to hear this. It seemed too real, too tragic, but he kept listening, revolted and entranced.

Mick took another swig of cognac, then continued. "All kids like puppies, and I started bringing one with me when I staked out the house. One day after the nanny went back inside, I slipped into the yard. The boy didn't seem to mind, but his dog sensed the puppy I had hidden in my coat, and it came lumbering over. I showed the puppy to the boy, and he asked if he could play with it. I put a finger over my lips to shush him and said we would need to go into the yard next door if he wanted to play with the puppy. He was happy to agree. After I had him in the neighboring yard, I conked him over the head. And that was that."

Mick's story came to a halt, but Patrick needed to keep pushing. "How did the Italians get him?"

Mick shrugged and refused to answer.

"How did the Italians get him, Mick?" Patrick demanded.

Mick started weeping, moaning that he was surely going to hell because of how that child suffered, and it was all his fault. He sobbed until he got sick in the chamber pot.

When Patrick pressed again for more details, Mick unleashed a string of curses and threw the bottle of cognac at Patrick's head. Patrick ducked, and the bottle smashed against the wall.

"I didn't mean for anything bad to happen to the kid, I swear it!" Mick whimpered. "I should have taken better care of him. I should have gotten him a doctor."

"So he died, right?"

Mick nodded, weeping. "That sweet little kid is gone forever. He never had a chance."

That was the last that Mick revealed. Patrick risked a look at Gwen. Her face was stark with anguish, and he covered her hand with his.

"I'm breaking every rule in the book by telling you this, but Mick can't be prosecuted for it anymore, and you deserve to know what happened. He told the truth about how he snatched your brother."

Gwen squeezed his hand. "The man in the courtroom, the one who had my wedding ring—he claimed to be related to Mick, but he looks like my father, not Mick Malone."

Patrick's gaze flew to hers. Apparently, Gwen had the same suspicion he did, but the possibility that Willy Blackstone had survived was minuscule.

"There was a $100,000 reward for information about your brother," he said. "There's no way someone wouldn't have come forward to claim it. I think William died from pneumonia, but I don't know the circumstances. The only thing I know for sure is that Mick can't be tried a second time. He got away with it, and the government can never come back for a second bite at the apple."

With each word he spoke, Gwen's shoulders slumped a little more. "Is he at least sorry?" she asked, her voice tissue-paper thin.

"I believe so. It's been thirty years, and it's tormenting him still. If he were a practicing Catholic, I'd tell him to go to confession and make a clean breast of it. He never will, but I think he regrets what he did."

"So do I," Gwen said. "So did my parents. To their dying day, they always wondered what happened to my brother." She turned her eyes to him. "You are far too good for Mick Malone."

"That's not a very high bar," he said, trying to ignore the surge of feeling from the simple way she held his hand. Then she let it go and turned around to tug the window back open. He helped, and she crossed back into the apartment, leaving him feeling irrationally bereft.

"The carriage is here to take you back uptown," he heard Hiram tell her.

Gwen would return to her world. That was probably for the best, but he would never forget what she had been for him during these past twenty-four hours.

109

15

Over the next week, Gwen tried to keep the whirlwind of painful memories at bay by lavishing attention on her house and garden. She pruned herbs and crossbred roses in her backyard sanctuary. In the evenings, she embroidered new wall hangings for the dining room. Her home was nothing like the cold marble mansions where the rest of the Blackstones lived. Gwen always felt out of place in the vacant grandeur of those palaces, and had chosen to live in a warm, cozy home of hand-carved wood, soothing colors, and a splendid garden that felt like paradise.

Perhaps if she had been blessed with children, this house wouldn't matter so much, but she loved every board, shingle, and windowpane of this home she'd designed and decorated from the ground up. Each room reflected her taste, from the trailing ivy vines carved on the fireplace mantel to the iron hardware inspired by medieval knotwork. Gwen had embroidered the coverings on the seat cushions from her own design of a rose trellis. Rugs loomed by local weavers covered the floors, and tiles from an artisan's kiln surrounded the fireplace.

Everything in this comfortable home was exactly how she wanted it, which was why she would fight hard to keep it, especially since her husband's mistress intended to take it away.

It was right after dinner when Vivian arrived on Gwen's doorstep. Gwen reluctantly allowed her inside, since she didn't want the neighbors to witness this embarrassing confrontation.

"Jasper would have moved heaven and earth to protect his daughter," Vivian said as she paced in the parlor. "I think you're being very selfish by denying Mimi a proper roof over her head and the protection of his name. Those were the only things he wrote in his will. His *only* dying requests."

Gwen remained seated at her dining table with the bonsai tree before her, pretending a calm she did not feel as she clipped the miniature tree to maintain its dwarfed shape.

"If Jasper wanted Mimi to have his name, he could have divorced me and married you," Gwen said. "He didn't."

"He couldn't afford to," Vivian snapped. "We all know why he stayed married to you."

The taunt hurt because it was true.

Vivian continued pacing, her gaze traveling over the parlor with covetous eyes. "Are you so selfish that even after he's dead, you can't give Jasper his last request? His wishes were clear. The doctor and three other men watched him write that will."

Gwen hadn't. In the final days before Jasper died, she'd cleared out of the home they shared and allowed Vivian to move in. It was Vivian who was at his bedside when Jasper died. Gwen didn't doubt the validity of the handwritten will, for it was perfectly in keeping with Jasper's desire to give everything he had to the woman and child he loved so desperately.

But Jasper didn't have the authority to give this house away. He might have given his heart to Vivian, but he couldn't give her Gwen's house. Gwen had written Vivian a large settlement check in recognition of Jasper's intention to see her cared for but had kept the house.

Gwen's mistake was that she'd done it without benefit of a lawyer. Her husband's extravagant love for another woman was an embarrassment she didn't want aired before attorneys, and she assumed the fat settlement would be enough to make Vivian go away.

She was wrong. There was no signed agreement that by

accepting the money, Vivian would disavow ownership of the house. Three months ago Vivian had started making demands, claiming that the settlement money was for Vivian, but that Jasper had wanted Mimi to have the house.

"Under no circumstances will I ever leave this house," Gwen said.

"I'll take you to court," Vivian replied. "The will is valid. What kind of mother would I be if I didn't fight in Mimi's best interest?"

"And I'll fight you back," Gwen said with far more confidence than she felt. The house was titled in her name, but the laws of marital property were a bit of a mystery. Would a sympathetic judge side with Vivian because of the child? She didn't know, and the prospect of a lawsuit frightened her. She continued twisting a wire around the limb of the bonsai tree, gently bending it into place as she pondered the problem.

"So typical," Vivian sneered. "You can't even let that poor tree grow naturally. You clip and groom and twist it into shape, just like you tried to do with Jasper."

Gwen would not sink to Vivian's level. "You can throw as many barbs as you like, but you're not getting this house."

"I'll get a lawyer," Vivian threatened. "As a good mother, I will fight for the rights of Jasper's child. This house *will* go to Mimi if it's the last thing I do."

The door slammed behind Vivian when she left, and Gwen dropped the pruning shears, her fingers shaking too hard to keep working.

Vivian was wrong about one thing. Gwen never could force Jasper to her will. After she learned about his affair, she'd desperately sought to please him. She quit spending so much time in the garden and tried to improve her appearance. She got manicures to soften her hands. Instead of wearing her hair in its normal braid over her shoulder, she bought heating tongs to style it in spiraling waves down her back, just as Vivian wore hers. Instead of her loosely flowing gowns, she bought tight corsets and tailored clothes—again, like Vivian wore.

Nothing worked. In hindsight, it was humiliating how hard she'd tried to win her husband's affection, but Gwen would never surrender to his mistress again.

The problem was that Vivian had the will in her possession, and Gwen couldn't remember exactly what it said. She should have hired a lawyer from the beginning. It would have been humiliating, but she wouldn't be in this position if she had a lawyer from the outset.

The harsh clang of the telephone broke the silence of the evening.

The telephone was the only thing she disliked about this house. It was like an invader in her home, making her jump at all hours. She sighed and walked to the dim hallway outside the kitchen where the telephone was mounted on the wall. Gwen had tried to liven up the hallway by adding a line of glass tiles from the Tiffany studio at shoulder height. She'd hoped the whimsical tiles in iridescent gold and emerald would be a cheerful sight while dealing with the annoying intrusion of telephone calls.

She lifted the earpiece and spoke into the mouthpiece. "Hello?"

"Is that you, Mrs. K?"

Patrick's Irish lilt was an immediate balm to her frazzled nerves. How endlessly good-natured he was, and how welcome his voice after the nastiness of dealing with Vivian.

"It's me." It had been a week since his mother had the serum injection, and she was out of the danger zone, but Dr. Haas continued documenting her recovery by the hour.

"Dr. Haas sent me down to the pharmacy to call you. He wants to know if you can send some of the medicinal tea leaves from your garden with one of the research students tomorrow."

"Yes, I can do that."

"Excellent."

"Don't hang up yet," she impulsively said. Patrick was trustworthy and good down to the marrow of his bones. Perhaps he could help. "I have a hypothetical legal question for you."

"Let's hear it," he said agreeably.

"If a person's last will and testament gave away something that he didn't own—for example, if a man wanted to leave a house to someone, but the house was titled in his wife's name—would the wife have a legal obligation to honor the will?"

"Ouch. That sounds ugly."

"Indeed." She traced a finger along the tiles. She couldn't lose this house. She couldn't.

"A person can't give away something he doesn't own," Patrick said. "If he could, I'd like to give the Brooklyn Bridge to my ma, but the courts won't honor it."

Relief crashed down on her, releasing a flood of tension. It was exactly what she wanted to hear. She bent her head as tears threatened. It shouldn't matter so much, but this house was the only paradise she ever wanted. A ragged breath escaped despite her best efforts.

"Mrs. K? Are you all right?"

She sniffled. "I'm all right."

"Are we still speaking hypothetically?"

"Yes," she managed to get out.

"And are you hypothetically crying?"

"Right again," she said, this time with a little laughter mingled in. "There is a bit of stickiness around the ownership of my house, and it's been weighing on me." Her voice started shaking. "Quite badly, in fact."

"Stay right there," Patrick said. "I'm coming over. I can pick up the tea while I'm at it."

She hung up the earpiece, feeling outlandishly happy at the thought of Patrick O'Neill's impending arrival.

Mrs. O'Shea was with his mother, giving Patrick the freedom to see what was bothering Gwen. He couldn't ignore the anguish in her voice. He would slay every dragon in her world if it would make her feel better.

It was dark by the time he arrived at her house. It was a nice one, but no fancier than the other houses on this tree-lined street bordering the campus of Blackstone College. The house was lit up both inside and out. It seemed foolish to waste electricity on a porch light, but rich people were odd.

He knocked on the front door, and Gwen answered. "You didn't have to rush across town on my behalf," she said.

"Yes, I did. You sounded upset, and I can't have that."

A lamp with a stained-glass shade of green and amber glowed on the foyer table. She led him down the hallway and into the parlor, where the windows were framed by tapestry panels that looked like they came out of a medieval cloister. The interior of the house was a feast for the eyes, with dark wood and leaded-glass windows. He could see why she didn't want to lose this place.

"You really do like the medieval world." He stepped closer to the window to admire the tapestry panels woven with a riot of vines, berries, and tiny little creatures.

"None of it is authentically medieval," Gwen said. "The tapestries are a William Morris design, and the tiles are from a local designer."

The entire house felt like a glorious work of art. "I feel like I've just stepped into the Book of Kells."

She sucked in a quick breath. "Have you seen the Book of Kells?"

"I saw it when I was a kid."

Sometimes even the poor got to see great art. His mother had taken him to see the famous Bible on display at Trinity College, where the illuminated pages with intricate scrollwork in gilt paint dazzled him. His mother had been just as impressed.

"After we saw that Bible, my mother started cutting scrollwork into her shortbread cookies. I think it was what inspired her to become an artist in her baking." He shook the memories away and got down to business. "Now, then, Mrs. K. How about you tell me who hypothetically wants to steal your house?"

She maintained that perfect poise, but a flush of color stained her cheeks. "My husband scrawled a will on his deathbed. He left this house to a child he had out of wedlock. His mistress is coming after me for it."

Patrick's eyes widened. He'd heard that rich men sometimes felt entitled to women on the side, but that wasn't the sort of world Patrick ever wanted to live in.

"Was the house titled in his name?" he asked.

She shook her head. "It was in my father's name because he paid for it. When he died, my father left everything to me. He died five days before my husband."

"So on the day your husband died, you had already inherited this house?"

She nodded. "The assets hadn't been distributed, but my father's will was very specific. He had recently learned about Jasper's . . . indiscretions. It infuriated him, and he drafted an amendment to his will leaving everything to me alone and specifically disinheriting Jasper. Have a seat, and I'll tell you everything."

They sat at the dining table, which was lit by the glow of a stained-glass lamp overhead, and she began speaking. The story didn't take long. Her husband had scribbled a handwritten will that was properly witnessed, but Gwen ignored it. Instead of giving her the house, Gwen wrote a substantial check to the mistress to encourage her to go away.

He couldn't quite believe it. "In my world, if a wife learns her husband is stepping out on her, she sets his belongings on fire and gives his horse away. She doesn't write the mistress a bank check."

"I just wanted the problem to go away," Gwen said. "Giving her this house would have been unthinkable. It's the only place I truly love."

He wanted to tear his hair out in frustration but gentled his voice anyway. "Gwen, why didn't you get a lawyer to help with this?"

She twisted the sapphire ring on her finger, rotating the stone in a quick, practiced motion. "Lawyers mean headaches and conflict and persnickety haggling." A little humor glinted in her eyes. "Present company excluded."

116

If everything was as she described, the will had no legal weight because Jasper Kellerman didn't own the property he sought to give away. The mistress had the power to embarrass Gwen, but that was all.

"Gwen, if you ever need a lawyer, come to me. I'll keep your confidence, and I'm a good listener. You can tell me anything, and I won't judge."

Her eyes softened, and she looked at him curiously. "Why didn't you become a priest? Father Doyle said you were one of his most promising students."

It was a personal question, but Patrick didn't hesitate to answer.

"There were lots of reasons, I suppose. When I was a young man, I felt myself going down a dangerous road, and I reached out to the church for salvation. The further I got into the seminary, the more I realized it was the wrong path for me. I'm best at helping the kind of people who never set foot in a church. The ones who've been beaten up by life and think they're lost beyond redemption. I can help them navigate the legal system so they can start over with a clean slate. Sometimes their biggest problem is just believing they're worthy of a second chance. Or a tenth or twentieth chance. Jesus never put a limit on the number of times a sinner can ask for forgiveness. Sometimes when a ne'er-do-well hears it coming from a person like me, they're more likely to believe it than when it comes from the pulpit."

"And you didn't get in trouble for leaving the seminary?"

He shook his head. "The church doesn't want a priest who isn't a good fit. I'm only sorry it took me so long to figure out. I want to get married someday, but I'll wait until I know it's right, because there won't be any going back on those vows. They will be carved in stone to last for all time."

He loved the way she watched him with a mix of curiosity and admiration in her expression. Who could have imagined a Blackstone would ever look at him with admiration? He liked being worthy of her respect. She was so alluring that it made his blood pump faster, and he glanced around the room to distract himself. The colors were warm, woodland shades of maroon, sage, and brown, but they suited her.

Only one thing looked out of place. A framed print over the dining room sideboard looked like it had come from a child's book. He stood to examine a picture from the Hansel and Gretel fairy tale that showed an older boy with his arm sheltering Gretel as he led her out of the darkened forest.

"Jasper and I fought endless battles over that picture," Gwen said. "It was always my favorite picture when I was growing up, but he thought I needed to outgrow it. He said it reflected my unhealthy obsession with having an older brother. Maybe it does, but I don't care. I wasn't even born when Willy died, but I loved the idea of an older brother. Someone who would always look out for me."

The longing in her voice hurt. Maybe this explained why she'd been so eager to believe Mick's rabble-rousing nephew might be her long-lost brother. Patrick would give anything if he could deliver William Blackstone back to her, but that boy had been in a pauper's grave for thirty years.

She placed a hand on his arm, her touch as light as a butterfly's wing. "I'm sorry I dragged you out here so late in the evening." Her voice was gently feminine, and he wanted to drown in it.

"You needed someone to lean on. I'm glad it could be me."

The amber light overhead illuminated her face with a warm glow. The way she gazed up at him triggered all sorts of inappropriate cravings.

"You would have been a wonderful priest," she said. The admiration in her gaze made him feel ten feet tall.

He leaned forward, lowering his head until his nose almost touched hers. "Mrs. K . . . I would have been a terrible priest." Priests shouldn't have this overwhelming attraction to a woman in need of comfort.

With the tip of his fingers, he tucked a stray lock of her silky hair behind the shell of her ear. It was a shocking intimacy, but she didn't pull away. She leaned into his hand, and it was all the permission he needed.

He lowered his head and kissed her. She kissed him in return, and soon her arms entwined behind his back. It went on and on until he needed to come up for air.

"Well, this is a bit of a surprise," he said.

"Not to me."

Raw hunger overcame him, and he swooped down to kiss her again. She met him measure for measure. He hadn't expected this—the buzz, the spark, the intensity that flared to life as he held her.

"Don't go," she whispered, low, soft, and velvety. "Stay until the last streetcar."

He glanced at the clock on the mantel. They had an hour until the streetcars stopped running for the night. He closed his eyes and savored the way she leaned against him for support. "I'm not going anywhere, Mrs. K."

He wanted her to be the one. It felt right. A tiny piece of him shouted that she was too far above him and this could only lead to trouble, but he silenced the voice. They were a match, and he'd be a fool to deny it.

16

To Patrick's amazement, Gwen started visiting his apartment each evening. At first, she used the excuse that she wanted to observe his mother's progress, but soon she simply came to spend time with him.

He looked forward to her visits all day. Each time she arrived at his apartment, she got a quick update on his mother's health, and then they hurried out onto the fire escape to be alone. In between kisses, they talked about everything. They debated whether Charles Dickens was better than Mark Twain. He explained why Catholics say the rosary, and she talked about her hope of one day becoming a professor of botany if she could ever tear herself away from home long enough to earn a doctorate.

"I even know what I'd like to study," she said one evening while watching the sunset from the fire escape. "I have a theory that old seeds can still sprout under the right conditions, and I'd like to see if I can accomplish it. There is a monastery in Spain that found seeds from an extinct date palm that are at least three hundred years old. I've asked them to send me some, but so far they have refused." She glanced at him, curiosity in her face. "I don't suppose you have any special pull, do you?"

He swallowed back a laugh. After abandoning his priestly vocation, he was the last person likely to have sway with those

120

Spanish monks. "I've got no connections. Have you tried buying them?"

"I've offered them a king's ransom, and they said no. That was last year. This year I asked a biology professor to appeal to them on humanitarian reasons. Healers have used date palms since antiquity for their medicinal properties. The seeds the monks have are from an extinct palm, so we might glean new medicines from them. I expect to hear back from them soon."

The mention of the college's medical research prompted him to ask what was in the lifesaving serum given to his mother.

"Do you know what white blood cells are?" Gwen asked.

"There are only two kinds of blood in the world," he replied. "Red like mine and blue like yours."

There was a time when pointing out their disparity in wealth was a touchy subject, but not anymore. They'd grown so close over the past few weeks that he teased her without restraint.

"Blood has different types of cells," she explained. "Most are red, but about one percent of our blood cells are white. They are part of our immune system and fight infection. The serum is developed from the white blood cells of horses that have been exposed to a mild form of tetanus."

He was aghast. "You gave my mother horse blood?"

She nodded and told him how the college owned a research lab and a stable of horses in Queens. The horses were given a tiny injection of tetanus bacteria, and in time their blood developed antibodies to the disease. The blood was then harvested, spun to separate the white blood cells, and then developed into a serum. It sounded like a mad scientific experiment, but Patrick thanked God for it and would add those horses to the list of things he prayed for each night.

The only niggling detail of this dazzling relationship with Gwen that bothered him was where they met each evening. Huddling on the fire escape wasn't the proper place to court a woman, making him wonder if she was ashamed of him. She had yet to step out in public with him where others could see them together. There were going to be snooty people who slammed their doors in Gwen's face if they learned she was consorting with an Irishman, and he needed to know if she was up for that. He was searching for a wife and couldn't lay his heart on the line if this was no more than a fling for her.

They'd been out on the fire escape for almost an hour, and Patrick had been trying to work up the courage to ask her to go with him to a baseball game, but it was hard. If she said no, they'd have to stop these daily meetings, and he didn't want to give them up.

A breeze whipped down the narrow lane, loosening tendrils of her hair. He loved the way she tucked them behind her ear. The simple gesture seemed so timeless and feminine.

"There's a baseball game coming up," he finally said. "Boston will be in town, and last month they trounced our guys pretty bad, so New York will want revenge."

Gwen rolled her eyes. "Baseball," she muttered.

"What's wrong with baseball?"

"President Matthews wants Blackstone College to form a team, and it sends chills down my spine."

"And why is that, Mrs. K?" He loved the way she became so animated speaking about the college.

It was a breezy evening, and a gust of wind sent a handkerchief from Mrs. O'Shea's laundry line flying toward them. Gwen snatched it out of the air before it could sail down the street.

"Lookie there," he teased. "You've got the makings of a fine outfielder."

He impulsively clasped her around the waist and lifted her into the air. She was so tiny compared to him that it was easy to hoist her up. She laughingly clung to his shoulders, and he demanded a kiss before setting her down.

A metallic *pop* sounded from the fire escape next to them, and Mrs. O'Shea's laundry line tore loose, dropping away from the building and dangling in the air as sheets, trousers, and blouses slipped off and flapped in the wind. A few kids cheered as they scrambled after the clothes tumbling through the lane.

"Those scamps are going to steal Mrs. O'Shea's laundry," he said.

"Are you sure?" Gwen asked. "Maybe they're collecting it for her."

There wasn't time to respond to her naivete. Mrs. O'Shea couldn't afford to lose those clothes, and more than half her laundry was now blowing down the street.

"Come on, let's go round that stuff up." He vaulted down the fire escape steps, loud metallic clangs sounding with each footstep. She was right behind him. They reached the street only moments later.

"Give me back those bloomers, kid," he roared at a youngster who couldn't be older than eight or ten.

The brat stuck his tongue out at him. "Make me!"

Patrick scooped him up and tossed him over his shoulder in one swift move. The kid howled in outrage, but other street urchins chased after the rest of Mrs. O'Shea's laundry, and an example needed to be set.

"Grab the bloomers from him, Gwen."

She must have done so, because the kid thrashed and cursed like a sailor, demanding them back.

He dumped the kid back on his feet. "Be glad I don't send you to the reformatory," he shouted, then went running after a girl who dragged a bedsheet behind her. He snatched the sheet before she could disappear down an alley. Patrick balled it up and threw it at Gwen. "Hold these, I'm going after more."

Now the kids were scrambling in earnest. Pillowcases, blouses, and undergarments were scattered on the cobblestones. Gwen gathered up what she could while he chased after the street urchins.

Most of the kids didn't fight too hard. They weren't too keen on someone else's underthings, but the laundry was easy pickings, and anything was a prize to kids who lived close to the bone.

A rickety old vegetable crate lay abandoned in the lane. Patrick flipped it upright and dumped the laundry inside. By the time he'd scooped up the last pillowcase, they were both winded and exhilarated.

"That was kind of fun," Gwen confessed.

"Kind of like running after baseballs."

She burst into laughter. "If you say that word one more time, I'm going to have to leave."

"Well, we can't have that," he said, slinging an arm around her shoulders. "You pick a place for us to go. Somewhere public."

She pulled back to look at him in confusion. "Why so earnest?"

This was it. He turned her shoulders to face him squarely. "I want to keep seeing you, but out in the open. We've rubbed along pretty well over the past few weeks. I like you."

He knew she liked him back, but he didn't know if she was embarrassed to be seen with him. He'd never know as long as they kept huddling on the fire escape. Heat prickled across his skin, and his heart kicked up to an uncomfortable pace.

"I like the idea of you and me," he continued. "I know we seem so different on the outside, but I'd be a happy man if you wanted to step out in public with me. Officially, that is." His face flushed. "If you're game."

"I'm game," she said. "Wherever you want, I'll go with you."

"Come here." He grinned, tugging her into his embrace. A couple of the street kids saw them and let out rude catcalls, but he didn't care. The fact that Gwendolyn Blackstone Kellerman looked up at him with admiration shining in her pretty green eyes sent him over the moon.

It looked like they might have a future after all.

17

Patrick's mother was sullen as she sat in the corner of her bedroom, watching him change the linen on her bed. She was still too weak to help, and he assumed her moodiness was born of frustration at the length of her recovery. He was wrong.

"When are you planning to tell me about that woman?" she asked, disapproval heavy in her voice. "I know she shows up every evening after I've gone to bed and the pair of you sneak out onto the fire escape."

Patrick blinked in surprise. "Mrs. Kellerman?"

"Aye. Never in a million years would I have suspected you of running around with another man's wife."

"She's a widow, Ma," he said, mildly amused that his mother had been stewing herself into a snit over nothing.

Birdie's eyes widened into two huge circles of embarrassed surprise. "Well, that puts a whole new spin on things, doesn't it?"

He grinned and finished making the bed, wanting the room to be tidy before Dr. Haas arrived. Her medical appointments were coming to an end, which meant Patrick needed to settle up on the bill. He'd pulled two hundred dollars together, but it would probably cost more than that. It shouldn't take him too long to pay, since his victory in the Blackstone case had already brought him new clients. The owner of a canning factory wanted his help with a zoning issue, and three people wanted wills. All would pay in cash.

Birdie pestered him for details about Gwen, but he was reluctant to discuss her yet. The feelings he had for Gwen were too raw and primitive. He wanted to chop down a tree for firewood to warm her house. Build her a castle. He wanted to haul home a side of beef to feed their family, the dozen children they would have together. He wanted to plant her on top of a pedestal and be a hero for her.

"I like her," he said simply, hoping Birdie would settle for that answer.

She'd have to, since Dr. Haas had arrived. Patrick stood off to the side and watched the examination in approval as his mother was able to stand, bend, and raise her arms on command.

A sense of well-being flooded him, and he impulsively bowed his head, praying silently. *Dear Lord, you saw fit to take my father before Birdie had the big family she always wanted. Please, please let her live long enough to welcome grandchildren who will love her as I have done.*

"It looks as if all your motor skills are working as hoped, Mrs. O'Neill," the doctor said as he concluded his examination. "Start getting up on your feet for five or ten minutes at a time. Aim for a little more each day."

Patrick closed the door to his mother's bedroom before walking the doctor to the front room because he didn't want her worrying about money.

"I need to know what I owe for my mother's treatment."

Dr. Haas looked surprised. "That's not necessary. Everything is paid for by the college."

Patrick shook his head. "A man should pay his own way in this world, but I don't know how much that special serum costs."

"Each dose costs around fifteen thousand dollars."

Patrick choked on his own breath. He cleared his throat a few times while gathering his thoughts. "That's a little steeper than I thought," he managed to get out. It was more than he had earned in his entire life. He could go to his grave still owing on that bill.

"That's why we don't expect anyone to pay for it," Dr. Haas said with a good-natured clap on Patrick's shoulder. He went on to relay how expensive it was to maintain a stable of horses, a team of medical assistants, the laboratories, and the years of research that had gone into the production of the experimental serum. "Don't worry about the money," the doctor assured him. "We're still in the testing stages, and we gained valuable insight from your mother's treatment. Besides, the college treats this as a charity case. No need to worry about payment."

Patrick felt sick. He didn't like being beholden to anyone, but especially not Gwen. He didn't want to be seen as a charity case. He needed to make good on this bill, or it would eat away at him and taint the purity of what he and Gwen had together.

And that he couldn't bear.

Patrick still worried about that staggering debt as he headed out for his stint at the soup kitchen. How could a man stand proud and tall with liability like that on his soul? He tried to put the debt out of his mind as he arrived at the soup kitchen to lug water, wash tables, and swap out pots.

He hefted a five-gallon pot of chicken stew to the serving counter where old Mrs. Magill was scraping out the last of the day's first batch. She stood aside so he could swap her empty kettle for the new one, prompting the crusty old man she had just served to complain.

"How come I got the dregs?" he growled around the butt of a cigar still clamped in his teeth. "I want another bowl."

Mrs. Magill cowered a bit. She was too kindhearted for a gritty neighborhood like this, but Patrick didn't mind standing up to a bully.

"Take the cigar out of your mouth when you address a lady, eat what you've been given, then go to the back of the line. If there's anything left, you can have another bowl."

"There's never anything left!" the old man groused.

"Fancy that! Be grateful for what you got, then." Patrick lifted the empty pot but wouldn't take it to the kitchen until he was certain the cigar-chomper wouldn't cause more grief for Mrs. Magill. He followed the old man through the tables to one of the few vacant spots left. It was always crowded in here, and Patrick cleared some abandoned bowls from the table, putting them in the empty kettle to carry back to the kitchen.

That was when he noticed Liam Malone leaning against the back wall of the room, watching him.

Patrick instinctively knew the hard-eyed welder wasn't here for a bowl of stew, but he asked anyway. "Hungry?"

Liam shook his head. "My uncle said you work here on Saturdays. I need to talk."

Everything about Liam's stance, from his worried gaze to his bobbing Adam's apple, indicated he was nervous. After Mick's victory in court, the troublemakers who came to the city to whip up resentment against the U.S. Steel deal had gone home, including Liam and the other welders from Philly.

Now Liam was in New York again, and Patrick wanted to know why.

"Come on back to the kitchen. You can help me scrub pots." Patrick led the way, and Liam followed.

It was sweltering in the kitchen, with the stoves and ovens working at full blast, but Liam rolled up his sleeves without complaint and lowered the empty pot into the sink filled with wash water.

Patrick grabbed a rag to begin drying bowls. "Out with it, then."

"I need a lawyer," Liam said.

"You came a long way, and I don't practice law in Pennsylvania. I'm afraid you've wasted your time."

Liam glanced at one of the ladies preparing a vat of coffee, then back at him. "It's a New York problem and not something I want overheard."

Patrick nodded. "Help me finish the lunch duty, and we can talk when we're done."

128

The cleanup didn't take long because Liam worked hard. He scrubbed, dunked, rinsed, and dried. He was clearly no stranger to work, as he cleared dishes, swept the floors, and wiped down the tables. Patrick finished the chores an hour earlier than he could manage when working on his own.

"We can talk in the alley behind the kitchen," he suggested.

Liam nodded and followed. Empty crates and dented trash cans cluttered the narrow brick alley. There was nobody else back here, but Liam glanced nervously up and down the street before speaking in a low voice.

"I don't know who to trust," he finally said. "Uncle Mick said you were a decent lawyer and you promised not to tell any of his secrets. Something about the rules of being a lawyer."

"That's right."

Liam fidgeted, continually shifting his weight. "Yeah, well, the only lawyers I've met are shysters who work for the owners of the steel mills. You're nothing like them. You seem like one of us, like I might be able to trust you."

"Trust me to do what?"

Liam looked him straight in the eye, his face intent. "You know the rumors about me, that me and that Blackstone kid might be one and the same. I don't know if they're true, but I have eyes in my head. I saw a picture of Theodore Blackstone, and we look alike. I wouldn't put it past Mick to play mean and dirty. My dad had a long and healthy hatred for the Blackstones. He's been dead for ten years, so there's no asking him, but he played dirty too. Crocket Malone was a brute, and I left home as soon as I could get away from him. I've been working in the Philly shipyards ever since."

"And your mother? The one who bemoans delivering a ten-pound child? Is she lying too?"

"Maybe," Liam said. "She still lives in Pittsburgh and has a big box of legal papers under her bed. I've tried looking through it to find a birth certificate or something else to prove who I am, but I can't make much sense of all those papers."

"Why not?" Patrick asked. "It shouldn't be hard to spot a birth certificate."

Liam stared moodily down the alley. "I'm not much for reading," he admitted. "I need help going through that box."

"Can you read at all?" Patrick didn't want to embarrass Liam, but he needed to know.

"Not really," Liam said. "I can sign my name but not a whole lot more, and there's no one I can trust to help me with those papers."

The prospect of traveling all the way to Pittsburgh to help a virtual stranger look for a birth certificate was absurd. Patrick had a stack of new clients, and his mother still needed him.

"Take the box to the nearest Catholic school and ask the nuns to help," he said. "They'll keep your confidence."

Liam's shoulders slumped, but only for a moment before straightening back up. "Yeah, I figured you'd say something like that. Hey, thanks anyway. You did a good job for my uncle, and I'm grateful."

Liam headed down the alley, hands stuffed in his pockets.

Unbidden, the drawing of Hansel and Gretel in Gwen's dining room rose in Patrick's mind. It had been thirty years since her brother's kidnapping, and it still nagged at her. If Patrick could prove who Liam Malone was, one way or the other, Gwen would want to know. He could never repay her for the serum that saved his mother's life, but maybe he could grant her deepest wish by finding out what happened to Willy Blackstone.

"Wait!" he shouted down the alley, but Liam had already disappeared into a sea of pedestrians and lumbering wagons on Mulberry Street. Patrick ran a few blocks, constantly scanning the crowds until he spotted Liam heading toward the streetcar stop.

"Liam, wait!" he shouted again, for Liam was about to board the streetcar, and Patrick doubled his speed. He was breathless by the time he got to Liam's side. "I changed my mind. Let's leave for Pittsburgh as soon as we can."

This might be the only thing he could ever do for Gwen, and he wouldn't hesitate again.

Gwen was writing invitations for Friday's soiree when the perfect thought struck. She would invite Patrick! She hadn't realized he was so sensitive about how they'd been meeting on his fire escape, and having him attend one of her weekly gatherings would let him know that she was proud to be seen with him.

She'd always assumed she would someday marry another Blackstone College professor. It wasn't that she objected to men in other lines of work. She simply thought it would be easiest to marry someone who already belonged here.

That was before she met Patrick. An involuntary thrill triggered inside her when she thought of his face, rough with affection as he gazed at her. Patrick was everything a woman could want in a man. Kind and giving and intelligent, but also a man of raw strength and a rock-solid foundation. She remembered the first night they'd kissed, when he spoke of the vows he would someday make to his wife. *"They will be carved in stone to last for all time,"* he had said.

The doorbell interrupted the quiet of the evening. When she opened the front door to see Patrick standing on her front porch, it felt like her dreams had magically brought him to her.

"Hello, Mrs. K."

She beamed in reply. "Good evening, Patrick."

"Can I come inside? I had an interesting conversation with Liam Malone today."

The haze of infatuation vanished, and her hand tightened around the doorknob. In the past few weeks, she'd managed to consign the disquieting man to the back of her mind. Uncle Oscar's detectives hadn't finished their report on Liam Malone, but she had already decided his physical resemblance to her father was a mere coincidence.

She sat on the padded chair beside the fireplace while Patrick sat on the hearth, only inches away, cradling her hand as he spoke. She felt sick as he relayed the conversation he had with Liam Malone, who claimed there were rumors and unanswered questions about his early years that might point to the chance that he could be Willy Blackstone.

Her gaze strayed to the Hansel and Gretel painting in the dining nook. Liam Malone was so crass and aggressive. Boorish. Not at all like she expected her older brother to be.

But she had to know.

"I'm going to Pittsburgh with him to search for proof," Patrick said. "It may take a few days, but if he's your brother, I'll find out."

Her heart swelled in her chest. "You would really do that for me?"

"I would do anything in the world for you."

The breath left her lungs in a rush. How long had it been since she could lean on a man she could implicitly trust?

"I think I'm falling in love with you," Patrick continued, without shame or embarrassment. "That means there's no mountain I won't climb. No wall I'm not willing to blast through on your behalf."

A spark of pure joy burst to life. "Oh, Patrick . . . I feel the same. I know there may be a few stumbling blocks ahead for us—"

He stopped her with a kiss, then grinned at her. "You're tiny enough for me to pick up and carry over them."

She laughed in delight as he stood and lifted her from the chair, twirling her as effortlessly as though she were a loaf of bread. *This* was what she'd always wanted in a man. A protector. A man she could trust with her deepest secrets, her heart, her soul.

He set her on the ground, and she clung to him tightly. "God bless you, Patrick. You're taking a piece of my heart with you to Pittsburgh, but I've never felt so safe trusting it to anyone before."

He clasped her so tightly that she felt the pounding of his heart. He would come through for her. Finally, *finally* she had a man she could lean on.

18

When Gwen received a summons to join her family on Uncle Oscar's yacht for a Sunday afternoon sail, she decided to decline. She wanted to spend that time with Patrick before he headed off for Pittsburgh. But when she called Oscar's house to decline the invitation, she got her marching orders.

"I insist the entire family attend," Oscar said. "We will be discussing bank business, and your presence is mandatory."

Nothing in the world was more tedious than bank business, but Oscar was adamant, and since the college's funding still teetered on the edge of destruction, Gwen dared not disobey.

The sun was shining as she arrived at the marina. Everything felt brighter this morning. She was young and in love. The sky was a cloudless blue. Patrick was going to Pittsburgh to find her an answer about Liam Malone, one way or the other.

Gwen climbed the steeply angled gangway to board the *Black Rose,* her uncle's grand yacht that had a staff of eight deckhands, four stewards, two cooks, and a captain. The crew kept the teakwood deck polished to a high shine, and the brass fittings gleamed in the sunlight. Belowdecks were staterooms for eighteen people, a cardroom, a dining room, and a bowling alley.

Once aboard, Gwen surveyed the family already assembled

on deck. A few of her cousins played shuffleboard on the rear deck, and Oscar's wife sat in a deck chair like it was a throne. Poppy Blackstone was Oscar's second wife and younger than Gwen. Having a male child was desperately important to her uncle. When his first wife died after thirty years of marriage, having given birth to only a single daughter, Oscar wasted no time seeking out a young and healthy bride. Rumor had it that before he married her, he ordered Poppy to visit a specialist to ensure she was capable of bearing children. Poppy had conceived seven months ago, and now she swanned around like she was carrying the child of Zeus, constantly cradling her expanding waistline.

Gwen took the seat beside her. "Do you know why we've all been summoned?" Aside from funding the college, she had no interest in bank business, and ordering the entire family to a meeting was odd.

"I have no idea," Poppy said, slowly waving a fan before her face. Her blond curls were artfully arranged beneath a jaunty hat perched on her head. "It can't be too important, since Natalia isn't here."

That was a surprise. Natalia was Oscar's daughter from his first marriage, and he always wanted her nearby when discussing bank business.

"Where is she?" Gwen asked.

"At the bank." Poppy rolled her eyes. "Some excuse about building a railroad through Siberia. Apparently, the funding for supplies simply can't wait until Monday." Poppy leaned in a little closer. "Russians," she muttered, not bothering to hide her disdain. Oscar's first wife had been Russian, and Poppy instinctively competed with the dead woman's memory.

Oscar strolled over, his cane tapping on the decking. "Natalia is transmitting payments for supplies to the Trans-Siberian Railway because construction will grind to a halt without food and fuel. We are both very proud of Natalia, aren't we, Poppy."

It was a statement, not a question, and Poppy wisely sat up a little straighter and brightened her tone. "Heavens, yes. You should see her at the bank, Gwen. Natalia sits right beside the telegraph operator to arrange the negotiations because he doesn't understand Russian, but she speaks it like a native. It's very impressive."

Oscar would probably have made Natalia his successor at the bank if the operating trust permitted it, but the rules were clear. Only men could inherit power at the bank. Gwen had never minded that, but Natalia did.

Oscar tapped the leg of Gwen's chair with his cane. "Natalia told me that one of your college professors cured a woman with tetanus. Is it true?"

"It appears so."

Uncle Oscar nodded in approval. "Good. When can the serum be monetized?"

"That's a question for Dr. Haas, not me."

Oscar raised his hand and snapped his fingers, summoning his personal secretary. "Contact Dr. Haas at the college. Get him to lock down a patent on that serum, and be sure it's owned by the college, not the man."

Even on a yacht party, Uncle Oscar was all about business, but Gwen was busy strategizing ways to introduce Patrick to her family. Some of them would hold his connection to Mick Malone against him, but she would set them straight about what a wonderful man he was. Despite Patrick's worries, her family weren't snobs.

Well, Poppy was a snob, but the rest of them were mostly decent people. After long years of anguish over her disastrous marriage to Jasper, it felt like her world was unfolding as it should.

By one o'clock, all twenty-four family members who lived in Manhattan had arrived, and the *Black Rose* was ready to sail. The chief officer stationed at the bow of the ship gave the signal, and the winches rumbled as the chains rolled in. The long blast of a whistle signaled their departure from the pier. A string quartet played Mozart, and stewards circulated with trays of elegant tea sandwiches.

As usual, most of her family socialized by generation. Her grandfather had five sisters, all of whom had married men of leisure and produced numerous children. The explosion of women in Frederick's generation accounted for the lopsided distribution of power in her family. The operating agreement that governed Blackstone Bank prohibited women from inheriting shares. Only the male descendants of Frederick and those five elderly aunts inherited voting shares, and few showed much interest in the bank. They usually trusted Uncle Oscar to vote their shares according to his judgment.

Frederick and his sisters sat clustered beneath a canopy that shaded them from the sun, while their children, all of whom were well into middle age, inspected the delicacies laid out on a banquet table.

Gwen migrated toward members of the third generation, who were nearer her own age and terrifically fun. Her cousin Chester, who owned some of the finest racehorses in New York, was talking to her cousin Edwin, and she decided to join them. Edwin always provided excellent conversation.

"What happened to you?" she asked Edwin. The last time she'd seen him was three weeks ago in the courtroom, when he was hale and hearty. Today he lounged on a chair with his leg in a plaster cast.

"I broke my leg last week hiking in the Adirondacks. Miserable business. But, Gwen, I saw a farm with two hundred peacocks strutting about the property like they were the emperors of India. You can't imagine the cacophony. I'm not sure which hurt more, my leg or my ears. Say, do you know why we've been summoned here? I've heard Oscar is still trying to buy Carnegie Steel."

The last thing Gwen wanted to think about was the impending steel merger, which was why protestors had flooded the courtroom that awful morning.

"Oscar's plan is bigger than just Carnegie Steel," Chester said. "He wants to swallow up a bunch of other steel companies so he can corner the market. The new corporation will be called U.S. Steel, and it's destined to make us all richer than Midas."

He continued talking, but Gwen's attention always wandered during tedious bank discussions. She was about to stroll over to join her grandfather's elderly sisters beneath the canopy when Oscar interrupted.

"Gwendolyn, a moment, please," her uncle said, gesturing her toward the port side of the yacht.

She drew alongside him, and Oscar glanced around to be certain they were alone before speaking.

"I heard back from the detectives I sent after that man you saw in the courtroom."

Her heart skipped a beat. "Yes?"

"He's nothing more than a malcontent steelworker. He's originally from Pittsburgh, but now he's in Philadelphia, where he leads the welders' union in the shipyards. He loves stirring up trouble in the press. Here's an example."

He handed her a newspaper folded open to an article about the merger that would create U.S. Steel. An underlined passage quoted Mr. Liam Malone of the local union.

It's bad enough having a bloodsucker like Andrew Carnegie controlling the nation's biggest steel company, but if the Blackstones buy him out to create U.S. Steel, we won't just have Andrew Carnegie bleeding people dry in Pittsburgh. There will be a hydra-headed monster strangling the workingman all over the country. I intend to fight this unholy alliance with every breath in my body.

Gwen turned her attention back to Oscar. "We already knew he was a union man. What else have you got?"

"His father was Crocket Malone," Oscar said. "Crocket was a felon who brought his son up to follow in his disreputable footsteps. When Liam was twelve, the police caught him and his father setting fire to a steel mill in Pittsburgh. Two months later, they were arrested for throwing rocks through the mill foreman's window, and a baby was hurt. Like father, like son. He's not one of us."

"But is that proof that he couldn't be my brother?" she pressed.

"No, but there's plenty of other evidence. The steel union in Pittsburgh awarded Crocket Malone a stipend in 1866 for the birth of a child. That's about when Liam Malone would have been born, and he doesn't have any brothers and sisters. He is Crocket Malone's first and only child."

Gwen's heart sank. She wasn't sure if she wanted Liam Malone to miraculously be her long-lost brother or not. It would be horrible if Willy had been raised to become someone who set fires and attacked people in their own homes. She wished Patrick was still in town so she could tell him not to waste his time in Pittsburgh, but he'd left an hour ago.

"Thank you for investigating," she said to Oscar. "It wasn't what I hoped to hear, but I'm grateful for your help."

Oscar nodded. "Just forget about him, okay? I also wanted you to know that I've had a change of heart about the college. Since our reputation is going to take a beating over that vile memoir, it's the wrong time to cut off funding. Natalia has a soft spot for the college and asked me to grant a one-year extension on your funding."

A jolt of happiness shot through Gwen. A one-year extension wasn't much, but having the axe lifted off the back of her neck was at least a temporary reprieve. "Thank you!" she said. "And please thank Natalia as well."

"Let's join the others," Oscar said. "I have an important announcement to make, but you needn't concern yourself with it. It's only bank business."

She took a seat alongside her cousins. Soon the entire family gathered in the open area near the bow of the ship. Oscar began talking about the corporate merger in which he would partner with J.P. Morgan to buy Carnegie Steel. Ten other steel companies would be bought at the same time, and Oscar explained exactly what that would mean for their family.

"Once this deal is complete, the new corporation will control seventy percent of the steel production in the United States, and as their banker, this will make us a very wealthy family."

Gwen couldn't see what all the fuss was about, because they were already obscenely wealthy, but Oscar went on to explain that this deal had the potential to be the largest business merger in history.

"The partners of Blackstone Bank will meet in July to have a formal vote endorsing the deal." Uncle Oscar paused, looking unusually stern as he scanned the assembled family members on the deck. "I only need a simple majority among the share-holders for the merger to succeed, but I want a unanimous vote among the Blackstones endorsing this merger. All the men here have shares in the bank. Between Father and myself, we already have a fifty-percent share of the vote, so we have an automatic majority, but I want our partners to see that we are unified in this decision. As a sign of good faith, I want every man here to promise you will vote in support of the merger."

"What will you do if they don't?" Gwen teased. "Make them walk the plank?"

A couple of her cousins giggled, but Oscar didn't. His glare was fierce as he answered.

"We must present a united front. The press and labor unions hate this deal, and the government may try to block it. Still, this deal is good for business, the consumers, and the people in this country. I won't stand for your bleeding-heart liberal sympathies, Gwendolyn."

"I haven't uttered a word against the deal," she defended. Her knowledge of high finance couldn't fill a thimble, but her opinion didn't matter. Only the men had a vote in the bank. Most of her male cousins and uncles spent their days in idle leisure, but each of them had one or two percent of the bank vote. All together they controlled twenty-five percent of the voting shares, although it was an academic issue. They always followed Oscar's lead.

"I want all the men on board to sign a statement turning over their voting authority to me," Oscar said. "My secretary will acquire the signatures."

All of her cousins agreed, and Oscar's secretary brought a

tray with the legally binding proxy forms for each man in the family to sign. It meant that Oscar now controlled a strong majority of the votes in Blackstone Bank.

Not everyone who held shares in the bank was a Blackstone. John D. Rockefeller owned a five-percent stake, and a group of French investors owned another six. Smaller shares were owned by rich people scattered all over Europe and America, but the Blackstones controlled the rest.

Once the proxies were signed, Oscar had a final announcement. "Our family has been blessed with wealth and prestige. In the coming months, it is going to be tested as this steel merger gathers momentum, but when it is accomplished, we will be wealthier than any Medici prince."

He gave a curt nod to the waiters, who began distributing the champagne glasses. Corks popped, people cheered, and they raised toasts. Gwen celebrated alongside them. She was in love, and the college had another year of funding.

All was right in her world.

19

The trip to Pittsburgh in a sweltering third-class train compartment was a miserable experience, but Patrick was eager to prove himself to Gwen. He could never drape her in jewels or be a world-famous researcher like her first husband, but he could give her what she wanted deepest in her heart. He would climb whatever mountain was necessary to make that happen, and for today, that meant going to Pittsburgh to unravel a mystery.

By late afternoon he and Liam were drawing near the outskirts of Pittsburgh, where sooty clouds hovered over the horizon. The train approached from the north, moving through the wealthier neighborhoods where rich industrialists built their homes to escape the ever-present smoke.

"The blast furnaces burn day and night," Liam said from the bench beside him. "Rich people moved out here to get away from the smokestacks, but soot now reaches the fancy parts of town too." He gloated as he said it.

Soon the wide lawns and fine houses gave way to office buildings and warehouses that stored petroleum, gas, and coal to fuel the industrial metropolis. They passed glass and leather factories, steel mills, and oil refineries. Soot left its shadow on the sidewalks, the lampposts, even the trunks of the trees.

After leaving the train, they took a streetcar to the neighborhood where Liam had grown up. Its bleakness was unsettling, and the air had a taste to it. It might have been Patrick's imagination, but the children tossing a ball in the street had an ashen look.

Liam grew up in a row house that adjoined fifteen other identical units, all leased to steelworkers from the nearby mill. It was impossible to tell the original color of the brick because of the soot.

"We've got at least an hour to poke around before my mom gets back from work," Liam said. Janet Malone worked at a nearby glass factory, but his father had died from lung disease ten years earlier.

Liam vaulted up the front steps to unlock the door, triggering the eager bark of a dog inside.

"That's just my dog, Frankie," Liam said with pride.

The lock was sticky and demanded some jiggling, but the moment Liam was inside, he dropped to his knees to greet a fat, ugly bulldog that waddled up to him.

"Who's a good dog?" Liam growled, grabbing a handful of wrinkly fur and giving the dog a vigorous rub. "Give me a kiss, you old slobber-bucket."

Patrick watched in appalled wonder as Liam lay flat on his back, letting the dog plant its paws on his chest and lick his face. The dog emitted a nonstop stream of grunts, snuffles, and little yelping barks. Liam finally rolled upright and lifted the dog to carry it like a baby.

"This is Frank," Liam said, tilting the dog's wrinkly, mashed-in snout toward Patrick. "He usually lives with me in Philly, but Mom's been watching him since I went to New York."

A glance around the room showed a clean but humble home. Patched furniture stood atop a worn braided rug, and a row of dishes was proudly displayed on a plate rack, the only ornamentation in the house.

"So you like English bulldogs," Patrick said, and Liam nodded.

"I've always liked bulldogs. Frank is my third."

Willy Blackstone had an English bulldog. They were an expensive breed and useless for hunting, guarding, or anything except lumbering a few paces and collapsing for a nap. Willy Blackstone had been out with his bulldog when Mick tempted him over the backyard fence. Liam's affinity for bulldogs couldn't prove anything, but it was an interesting detail.

Patrick was eager to get started, and Liam brought the mysterious box hidden beneath his mother's bed into the main room. It was a battered old shipping box, tattered on the edges and carrying a musty smell. Inside was an explosion of papers and documents.

It was soon apparent why Liam hadn't been able to make much sense of them. Most were legal forms from Crocket Malone's various arrests and court appearances, but there were family papers too. Liam had two older brothers, both of whom had died within a week of being born, and the box contained plenty of evidence for both boys. There were birth certificates from a hospital and baptismal certificates from the church. The local union had paid a stipend for the birth of both boys. The baptism certificates were clipped together with a Saint Philomena prayer card, the patron saint for infants and newborns.

"Were you ever baptized?" Patrick asked.

Liam looked momentarily taken aback. "Probably. My mother always made me go to church."

"There's no certificate of baptism for you, but both your brothers were baptized."

"That's because they were blue babies and a priest showed up the day they were born to get the job done. Not me. According to Mom, I had lungs that could shake the rafters, and they didn't need to drag a priest out of bed for a rush job."

Patrick continued sorting the papers. The largest stack was lawsuits filed by Crocket Malone suing neighbors, his employers, and even the local newspaper that wrote articles critical of his labor union. The second-largest stack was Crocket's arrests.

Patrick held up a legal filing for when Crocket was charged with smashing windows at a mill.

"How come your dad got arrested so much?"

Liam snorted. "Because Crocket Malone liked busting heads and causing trouble." He nodded to the document with a grin. "I was with him that day. It was kind of fun, until a swarm of cops showed up and beat us both into a bloody pulp, but we probably deserved it."

Patrick looked at the date on the paper. "You must have only been a kid."

"I was fifteen, and the mill was owned by Andrew Carnegie. My dad said that Andrew Carnegie was the devil and all Four Horsemen of the Apocalypse rolled up into one person, and he deserved whatever trouble we gave him. Besides, if I didn't help, my dad would have busted my head in."

Patrick asked the question that had been plaguing him for days. "There was a $100,000 reward for the return of the Blackstone child. Did your dad hate the Blackstones enough to forgo a reward that big just to seek revenge?"

A muscle bunched in Liam's jaw, and his eyes were dark as he considered the question. "Yeah. He hated them that much."

A vicious man might take twisted satisfaction in raising the kidnapped child of his enemy in the world created by the Blackstones' avarice. According to Liam, Crocket took him out of school in the eighth grade and put him to work as a stove-tender, shoveling coal into an open furnace. Liam went to union meetings, where he learned to hate the owners of the steel mills. While normal parents read their children bedtime stories, Crocket showed Liam autopsy photographs of people killed in factory accidents. Someone who would do that to a child might gladly turn away from the reward to carry out his perverse revenge.

They spent two hours examining every piece of paper in the box but found nothing documenting Liam's life before the age of five. It was frustrating, because the lack of evidence couldn't prove anything.

But at six o'clock Janet Malone returned home, and then the real battle for proof began.

Liam's mother was a tiny, birdlike woman with calloused hands, a narrow face, and faded auburn hair rolled into a bun. Liam took the lead in the uncomfortable interrogation. The grilling went on for over an hour, and Janet never budged from her insistence that she was Liam's natural mother.

"I want the truth," Liam said, pacing the worn rug before his mother, who sat stonily at the kitchen table with an untouched cup of tea before her. "Why did you baptize Michael and Connor, but not me? Why isn't there a birth certificate for me?"

"Maybe because I had just delivered a ten-pound baby and didn't have the strength to pop out of bed and run all over town collecting paperwork," Janet retorted.

Patrick's initial instinct had been to protect Janet from Liam's aggressive tone, but she was a tough, scrappy woman who proved capable of defending herself.

"You took pictures of the other babies, but not me," Liam said. "Why not?"

"Because the doctor said Connor wouldn't survive the week, and Michael had already died when we got his picture made," Janet defended. "There was no fear of you dying. You squalled loud enough to wake the neighbors."

"I was six years old before you got around to having my picture made," Liam said. "Why so long?"

Janet folded her arms across her chest. "You don't know anything about how demanding a baby can be. If you would get married like any decent son your age, you'd have a passel of your own and wouldn't wonder why I didn't have the time to take you to a photographer's studio. Why don't you settle down with Nora Cunningham? Her ma told me that girl is getting tired of waiting for you."

"I'm not going to marry Nora Cunningham," Liam growled.

"Why not? The only chance I have for grandchildren is standing here being stubborn and disrespectful. You need to settle down and start having babies of your own. Then I could—"

A loud banging on the front door interrupted Janet.

"Anyone home?" a man's voice called from outside. "I need help. Please! I need help."

Liam seemed eager for the distraction and bounded to the front door in three steps. "I'm not marrying Nora, and that's the end of it," he tossed over his shoulder, then yanked the door open.

A wiry man who looked ill and panicked stood on the front stoop. A couple of other men clustered behind him, but Patrick stared at the man in front, who had wiry red hair and the longest nose he'd ever seen.

"Are you Liam Malone?" the redheaded man asked.

"I am. What do you need?"

A knife flashed before plunging straight into Liam's abdomen. Liam yelled and doubled over, grabbing at the knife before it could plunge again. The other men shoved through the front door, one hefting a sledgehammer above Liam's head.

Janet screamed, and Patrick vaulted forward to wrench the sledgehammer away, then used it to clobber the invader, who dropped to the ground.

Liam and the redheaded man rolled on the floor. Blood was everywhere, and the knife was raised for another plunge, but Liam held his attacker by the wrist. Before Patrick could help, someone punched him in the head, and he went down.

Pain nearly blinded him, but he'd taken punches before. He sprang up. He couldn't see straight but unleashed a fierce round of blows at the blurry form of his attacker. Janet's screams mingled with agonized yells from Liam wrestling for control of the knife.

Patrick slipped on the blood. He couldn't meet his end in a grubby tenement. Not when his mother still needed him. Fear mingled with panic as he scrambled upright. He focused all his power into his right arm, driving his fist into the nose of the man before him. The man went down and didn't move.

Liam's attacker had him pinned to the floor, and Patrick

hauled him off and threw him aside, then kicked him in the gut to keep him down. The knife skittered across the floor, and Janet grabbed it.

Two men were down, and the redheaded man looked at them in panic before staggering out the front door and escaping into the night.

There was no time to waste. Liam lay in a pool of blood, and he wasn't moving anymore.

"Go get help!" Patrick ordered Janet. She ran out into the street, her scream echoing off the row houses. People were already heading their way, and Patrick balled up a handkerchief and pressed it to the gut wound. Liam's yell of pain was deafening, and soon there were half a dozen people in the room.

"A doctor," Patrick managed to stammer. "Is there a doctor?"

"Milly is calling for one now," someone said. "The police too. They'll be here soon."

Patrick nodded, his head still throbbing. He'd been in dozens of ugly boxing matches but never feared for his life before, and it wasn't over yet. Warm blood pulsed from Liam's abdomen, soaking through the handkerchief.

"Move aside," a man said. He stuffed one of Janet's hand-crocheted pillows against Liam's gut, pressing it tight and causing another anguished yell.

Patrick stood and stepped away as a wave of exhaustion overcame him. The man who'd brought the sledgehammer was trying to twist away from a pair of brawny neighbors who held him pinned down, but the third man, whom Patrick had knocked out, lay motionless on the floor.

"Better watch that one," he warned one of the neighbors. "He's strong and fast."

"No need," the neighbor said. "He's stone dead."

A horse-drawn ambulance arrived to take Liam to the nearest hospital, and Janet went with them. She'd been sobbing like a banshee but stopped when the hospital orderly said she couldn't ride in the ambulance unless she controlled herself.

Patrick stayed at the scene, wondering who had a motive to kill Liam Malone. If Liam was the missing heir, it would thrill some of the Blackstones, but others might have a tremendous financial interest in keeping him away.

The house swarmed with neighbors and police officers. The invader who'd wielded the sledgehammer was arrested on the spot, but the dead man still lay on the floor where he'd fallen almost an hour ago. Patrick knew exactly what had happened. A direct blow could break a nose, sending a sliver of bone up into the brain and killing a man.

Patrick cradled his right hand against his sternum as he paced. A couple of his fingers felt broken, but he wasn't dead like the man on the floor. A photographer from the police department finally arrived to take pictures of the dead man and the rest of the crime scene. The police said Patrick couldn't leave yet, which meant he had to remain in the same room as the dead man until someone from the morgue arrived to take the body away.

He wished he had a rosary. Saying the rote prayers would help focus his scattered thoughts, because he was too agitated to pray right now. He'd killed a man. He hadn't meant to, and he'd do it again if necessary, but he was sick over it. That man had a mother. Maybe he had a wife and even children. With a single punch, Patrick had changed their world forever.

He had punched hard. Fear had driven him to pull his fist back and shoot it forward with all his might. Life would never be quite the same after tonight, because a man was dead and it was his doing.

Forgive us our trespasses as we forgive those who trespass against us. He had already forgiven the dead man, but he worried about the mother and wife and children who didn't yet know the man they loved was dead.

A pair of police officers finally approached him. The younger one spoke first. "You're the man who punched that guy to kingdom come?"

Patrick winced. "It was me," he said, no pride in his voice.

"Let's go somewhere we can talk," the older officer said in a thick German accent. What was it about a German accent that made people sound so angry? His badge identified him as Sergeant Dittmer, and Patrick followed him through the front door and into the night.

Clusters of neighbors still loitered in the street, gaping through the open doorway at the bloody scene inside.

"What happened?" Sergeant Dittmer asked once they were a few yards from the onlookers. The younger policeman took out a notepad, pencil at the ready.

Patrick's legal instincts kicked in. What happened tonight was a straightforward case of self-defense, but it was possible the Blackstones had played a role in it, and they might try to twist this.

"I was with Liam and his mother all evening. We were minding our own business when someone came pounding on the door. Liam answered and got stabbed about two seconds later. Two others barged in to finish the job, and I stopped them. I've never seen them before."

"And Liam? Did he know them?"

Patrick shrugged. "You'll have to ask him that."

"Does Liam Malone have any enemies?" Sergeant Dittmer asked.

Any leader of a labor union had plenty of enemies, but Patrick doubted this had anything to do with the union. He nodded to the dozens of neighbors loitering in the street. "They could probably answer that better than me. I only met him a few weeks ago." Had it only been three weeks? It seemed forever now.

"And what is your relationship with Mr. Malone?"

He thought carefully before answering. He had offered Liam a little legal advice, but he wasn't officially his lawyer. If he identified himself as such, it would get back to the Blackstones, and something warned Patrick against that.

"Just a friend," he said.

"You must come to the station to file a formal report of what happened here tonight," Sergeant Dittmer ordered.

The brusque tone worried Patrick. "Am I a suspect?"

"No, but we need a formal statement," Sergeant Dittmer said.

Patrick glanced pointedly at the officer with the notepad. "I just gave you one. I'm heading to the hospital to check on my friend. His mother may need help."

He walked around the officer taking notes and headed toward the house. The blanket-covered corpse was being carried out on a stretcher, and Patrick instinctively paused to cross himself. He hated what he'd done tonight, but if he hadn't been here, Liam would be dead.

"Do you have someone on the force who can stand guard at the hospital?" he asked Sergeant Dittmer. "Whoever ordered this attack on Liam might try again."

Sergeant Dittmer scoffed. "We don't have spare men to serve as a private police force."

That wasn't a surprise, but Liam was still in danger. If he survived tonight's attack, he would be frail and defenseless for weeks.

Patrick scanned the bystanders loitering in the street. He recognized some of them as people who'd come to New York for the hearing. They were strong men from the steel mills and factories. *They* would be his private police force.

He stepped forward. "I could use some people to help stand guard at the hospital."

Five minutes later he had his volunteers, and now his job was no longer solving the mystery of Liam's birth, but simply to keep him alive.

20

Gwen had become increasingly confident that she wanted Patrick O'Neill to become a part of her life. He was strong and kind and funny. Thoroughly good. He had gone all the way to Pittsburgh just to help her solve the mystery of Liam Malone. The last, lingering vestiges of her resentment over his representation of Mick Malone evaporated in the face of Patrick's unstinting generosity. What other man would so selflessly give of himself?

She didn't give a fig about their class differences, but some of her relatives might look down their noses at him. She couldn't bear it if they treated Patrick shabbily, and that meant she needed to recruit Uncle Oscar's wife, the Blackstones' reigning social maven, to her side. Poppy was the most virulent snob in the family, but Gwen would try to soften her.

Poppy had invited a number of the Blackstone ladies to admire her newly decorated nursery. It would be the perfect opportunity for Gwen to announce that after two years of lonely widowhood, she was ready to begin a formal courtship.

Poppy and Oscar lived in a marble monstrosity on Fifth Avenue. Oscar's daughter from his first marriage lived there as well, but Gwen didn't expect Natalia to join the party. The animosity between Poppy and Natalia was palpable, but Gwen had always liked Natalia, even though they couldn't be more different. While Gwen chose a bohemian life among artists and intellectuals, Natalia was a buttoned-down woman who inherited her father's skills as a business analyst.

A pair of her aunts arrived at the same time as Gwen, and they exchanged greetings outside the house. Gwen reached out to embrace her favorite aunt. Technically, Martha was her great-aunt, the youngest of her grandfather's five sisters.

"I'm so glad Poppy could lure you away from campus," Aunt Martha said. "I know you don't care for the city."

"I couldn't resist the chance to see Poppy's nursery," Gwen said, feeling only a twinge of jealousy. She'd always wanted children, but Jasper's disinterest in her made it almost impossible to conceive. Maybe she would soon have children of her own. Patrick would be a wonderful father. Perhaps she was getting ahead of herself, but the longing to have Patrick's dependable strength and humor in her world was becoming increasingly hard to deny.

Oscar's home was made of white marble, gilt furniture, and had murals painted on every soaring ceiling. To her surprise, Natalia waited for them in the hallway. It was a Monday, and Natalia had dressed for work in a tailored indigo suit with a nipped-in jacket and wore her dark hair coiled into a sleek chignon.

Gwen kissed Natalia's cheek in greeting. "I gather I have you to thank for your father's decision to extend funding on the college for another year."

"My father's heart is deeply buried, but I know where to find it."

Aunt Helen moved in, her pin curls bobbing as she scrutinized Natalia. "I didn't think you'd want to attend Poppy's little tea party."

Natalia smiled tightly. "Father has asked me to make an effort to appease Poppy. I'll have a little tea, then go to the bank. I'm excited about a new proposal to develop the Russian turpentine industry."

Was there anything duller than the turpentine industry? It

was hard to know if Natalia was genuinely excited about the topic or merely wanted to escape Poppy's tea party. A little of both, probably.

Natalia led them into the breakfast room, where Poppy was already entertaining the other elderly aunts. Aunt Helen leaned heavily on her cane as she limped toward the tea table, but Poppy interrupted before she could sit.

"No, no, don't sit," Poppy said. "We can't have tea until you've seen the nursery. I know you've all been bursting with curiosity."

Aunt Helen exchanged an annoyed glance with her sisters, but they dutifully followed Poppy down the hallways of white marble and gilded mirrors. Gwen expected the baby's room to have similar princely grandeur, so she was stunned when she stepped inside the nursery. Everything was black, bronze, and scarlet.

The aunts looked baffled, but Poppy brimmed with pride. "It's Japanese," she said, running her hands along the black lacquered crib. "This sort of décor is all the rage in Europe. I've heard that the Prince of Wales is redesigning his own rooms in the Japanese style."

The crib, changing table, and rocking chair were all made of black lacquered wood. Hammered bronze covered the chest of drawers sitting in front of a wall painted in deep red tones. Normally Gwen loved the fresh simplicity of the Japanese style, but instead of the soft muted hues usually associated with it, Poppy had opted for the drama of scarlet and black. Panels of rice paper covered the windows, and a folding screen painted with cherry blossoms was the only hint of joyfulness in the child's nursery.

"It's very artistic," Aunt Martha managed to stammer, and the other aunts nodded in vigorous agreement.

"Yes," Aunt Helen said, clutching her cane as she scrambled for something nice to add. "It's very, *very* artistic."

Gwen leaned over the crib to pick up a doll dressed in a silk kimono. "This is darling," she said.

She passed the doll to Martha so the kindest of her aunts could enthuse about the beautifully embroidered kimono. Martha murmured polite comments, then passed the doll to Helen, who looked at Poppy in dismay.

"Dearest, I'm afraid I can't see it very well in this dim light," she said. "My eyes aren't what they used to be."

"Yes, it's quite dark in here," Martha said. "Might we go to the breakfast room, where we can admire this charming kimono properly?"

Poppy seemed annoyed that the old ladies didn't want to linger in the oppressive nursery, but they were already filing out of the room. The mood brightened once everyone was in the sunlit breakfast room, where a proper tea graced the table and the aunts made a suitable fuss about Poppy's baby, due to arrive in two months.

After ten minutes discussing the baby, Natalia set down her teacup. "It's eleven o'clock and past time for me to be at the bank."

Poppy's expression cooled. "Then, by all means, run along. It's certainly no surprise where your priorities are."

Natalia kept a serene expression on her face as she gave each aunt a quick hug in farewell, then departed. An awkward silence filled the room until Aunt Martha filled it.

"I imagine Oscar is so excited about the baby," she said. "Have you picked a name?"

Poppy nodded. "We have decided on Alexander. I wanted to name him Frederick Samuel after our fathers, but Oscar wanted something entirely new."

"What if it is a girl?" Aunt Helen asked, and Poppy looked taken aback. Everyone knew Oscar insisted on having a son. If Poppy dared to produce a girl, she would probably find herself expecting again by the next full moon.

"We expect that it will be a boy," Poppy replied, effectively shutting down the conversation. She cradled her swelling belly, constantly stroking it with slow, deliberate circles. "Of course, Natalia is going to be very jealous. She's always fancied herself her father's pride and joy. She won't like being supplanted by my son, but perhaps it will be for the best. It's unnatural for a woman of Natalia's age to still be single."

Poppy's assertions seemed cruel to Gwen, but the aunts agreed. All the Blackstone women had married before the age of twenty, so for Natalia to be twenty-eight and still single was unusual. Gwen probably would have chosen a different sort of man had she waited until she was a little older instead of rushing to the altar with Jasper when she was only eighteen. Instead of a handsome face and academic prestige, she would have chosen strength and integrity and a sense of humor. Status didn't matter. She wanted a strong, confident man who was a protector by nature. Her gaze trailed out the window as she contemplated Patrick's raw-boned charisma. He would be a wonderful father, and if they married, it probably wouldn't take long for her to conceive, would it?

"Gwendolyn! Are you blushing?"

She startled. Aunt Martha had been prodding her, and all the aunts stared.

"I think she's been woolgathering over a man," Helen said. "Tell us everything!"

Gwen hadn't expected to broach the matter so early in the day, but Aunt Helen had just provided a perfect opening. Everyone in her family had been urging her to remarry, and the aunts would surely be delighted, even if Patrick was a little outside their class.

"Yes, I may have found someone," she said, and all the women leaned forward. Even Poppy seemed curious enough to stop rubbing her belly. "His name is Patrick O'Neill. I met him—"

"That sounds Irish," Poppy interrupted.

"He is. Patrick came to New York when he was fourteen."

Poppy's face froze, and the aunts traded quick looks but remained neutral. "Yes?" Aunt Martha prompted. "Tell us more."

"He is a lawyer and very clever. I'm afraid he had a run-in with Oscar over that awful memoir, but I hope that can be water under the bridge. I know Patrick and I seem like opposites. . . ." So much depended on these next few minutes. If she could get the aunts on her side, they would smooth the way for Patrick. These women had stepped in to help raise her after her own mother died. They seemed hopeful on her behalf as they waited to hear more about Patrick. "I know we seem like opposites, but Patrick is everything that is strong and courageous in a man, and I can't wait for you all to meet him."

Poppy lifted her chin. "Oscar told me about him. He's Irish. And Catholic. I'm reluctant to say it, but I hear he is quite uncouth."

"Don't be so snooty," Aunt Martha said dismissively, but Poppy was quick to defend herself.

"I'm not snooty, I'm merely pointing out an obvious fact. It's one thing for Gwen to flaunt her bohemian ways on campus because people expect that sort of thing among college people. But no one appreciates lowbrow Irish lawyers on Wall Street. It's a very different world."

Aunt Martha came to Gwen's rescue. "Pay her no mind, Gwendolyn. My own Milton is a man with a profession."

She beamed in gratitude at Aunt Martha, whose husband earned his money from running a shoelace factory. Poppy might hold her nose at such a workaday trade, but Milton was a fine, upstanding man who had been warmly accepted into the Blackstone fold. Patrick would find a kindred spirit in the self-made Uncle Milton.

"I don't know if Patrick and I have a future yet," she admitted. "It's still very new, and our families are so different. He's devoted his life to defending the poor, and his job might be taken amiss by some in the family."

"But if you married him, he won't need to keep working," one of the aunts pointed out.

He wouldn't, but Gwen suspected he would want to. "Patrick is very proud. I think he will want to keep working. If things continue to progress, I hope everyone in the family will accept him as warmly as they did Uncle Milton."

Aunt Helen smiled, but her voice was still cautious. "Of course we will accept him, my dear . . . but will he accept *us*?"

The question took Gwen aback. It had never occurred to her that Patrick would reject the people in her family. After all, snobbery tended to be a one-way sentiment.

"Patrick is the most open-minded man I've ever met. Of course he will accept us." She looked at Poppy. "Except for you, Poppy," she teased. "You're a tough nut for anyone to accept."

The aunts laughed uproariously, and Poppy pretended to as well. Gwen hugged herself, a little spurt of glee blossoming inside, for she was well on her way to lowering the bars between her and Patrick's worlds.

21

Patrick sought out the nearest Catholic church the morning after the attack on Liam, desperate to ease the crippling ache of having killed a man. He fell to his knees in the tiny box of the confessional booth but couldn't even clasp his hands in prayer because of the splint on his right hand. His broken fingers were a constant reminder of the moment he threw that punch.

God, did I do the right thing last night? He desperately prayed for understanding and why God had sent him into the horror of last night or what sense could be found in it.

After a few moments, the panel covering the latticed screen slid open to reveal the silhouette of the priest on the opposite side of the confessional.

"Bless me, Father, for I have sinned," Patrick said. "My last confession was three months ago." It felt like another lifetime. Three months ago, he didn't know how it felt when a man's nose fatally crunched beneath his fist. It was a sensation he could never forget.

"And what brings you here today?" the priest asked.

"I killed a man in self-defense." Even from the other side of the screen, Patrick heard the priest's startled breath. He rushed to explain how a defenseless man was assaulted by three strangers and how he intervened. He hadn't meant to kill anyone, but good intentions counted for little when a man was dead.

"I will forever wonder if I could have handled it differently. I'm a strong man, and there might have been another way."

"Were you driven by anger or hatred when you struck that blow?"

"No, it was fear." Patrick's heart pounded again at the memory of those few, fleeting seconds. "That man was a sinner, but all life is precious, even the sinners, and I hate what I did."

"We have a duty to help those in distress," the priest said. "That was what you did, and it clearly wasn't your day to become a martyr."

"I still feel guilty."

The priest coaxed Patrick to delve deeper into his turbulent emotions, and over the next ten minutes, his heart rate slowed to a normal pace. Some people struggled in the confessional, but Patrick felt at ease here, and it was at times like these when he regretted leaving the seminary. He and the priest discussed how God didn't demand perfection of them, and Patrick had done the best he could with the few seconds he had to defend himself. They recited their final prayers, and then the priest said the words Patrick had been waiting to hear.

"Your sins are forgiven. Go in peace."

Patrick crossed himself and stood. "Thanks be to God."

When he stepped outside into the sunlight, he looked up at the cloudless blue sky, marveling at the immensity of creation. *God, thank you for the blessing of being alive today, and for leading me out of the darkness of last night. Please guide my steps to do your will. The path ahead is not clear for me, but I will listen for the signs and use the blessings you've given me to make this world a better place. Please be with the family of the man who died last night. They are suffering, and I pray that you and Jesus and Mary hear their anguish and comfort them. I pray for them all.*

The last of his restlessness faded away, and he was in a better frame of mind when he arrived at the hospital. The men's ward was a long room with twelve beds on each wall, divided by a wide aisle. Metal chairs separated each bed, and there was no privacy. Ailments ranged from broken bones and blood disorders to a case of shingles.

Liam was the only stabbing victim. His liver had been badly sliced, requiring some internal stitches, plus thirty stitches on his abdomen to patch him back up. The loss of blood made him weak, and the nurses had been bringing him glasses of beef juice mixed with bone marrow to restore his blood.

Liam looked ashen and ghastly as Patrick pulled up a chair and sat. "How are you feeling?"

"Like a dead man," Liam said weakly, and his gaze flicked to Patrick's splinted hand. "You?"

"I've been better," he admitted. "It looks like we're both going to survive."

If possible, Liam wilted even further against the sheets as his eyes drifted closed. "Yeah," he finally said. "Thanks for what you did. I'm grateful."

Liam's tone was weak and despondent, and Patrick didn't have any words of comfort because they both understood the implications of what had happened last night. Someone wanted Liam dead, and last night's attack was probably just the beginning.

Over the coming days, the police investigation into the attack failed to make progress, even though they had the abandoned knife used to attack Liam. It was a hunting knife with a carving of deer antlers on the handle, but no one in Pittsburgh recognized the make of the knife or where it might have been purchased.

A man named Lenny Phelps was the only assailant who'd been captured alive, and he cracked under questioning. He said the ringleader of the group was the redheaded man who got away. Phelps claimed he and his dead friend had been hired only an hour before the attack and had been promised a thousand dollars to carry out the deed. The only other thing Phelps knew about the ringleader was that he'd been hired by someone in New York City, because the three of them were supposed to go to Manhattan to collect payment after the deed was done. Unless they could catch that redheaded man, they had no way of knowing who ordered the attack or if they would try again.

That meant Liam had to be guarded around the clock. The chairs on either side of his bed were constantly filled. Janet sat in one, and brawny men from the steelworks rotated shifts in the other. At first the hospital tried to enforce visiting hours, but someone from the local union paid a visit to the hospital administrator to make him think better of it.

The following week in Pittsburgh could have been torture as Patrick felt his new clients in New York dwindle away, but it turned out to be a blessing. After his two-hour shift at Liam's bedside each morning, Patrick headed straight back to the church.

Father Murry, the man who heard Patrick's confession, was building a school on the back of the property and always needed free labor. Patrick worked alongside other volunteers to mix concrete and lay bricks. On the days it was too rainy to build, Patrick helped Father Murry set up a system to keep his school accounts separate from the church ledger. After all, Patrick had gone to law school with the intention of managing church real estate and investments. It felt good to sink back into church work again.

In the evenings, he dined with Father Murry. He confided everything to the old priest, including his guilt for having taken a college education and three years of seminary training, then failing to follow through into the priesthood.

"Do you regret leaving?" the old priest asked.

Patrick shook his head. "I want to marry. I want to be a husband and a father so badly it keeps me awake at night. When I finally sleep, I dream of a family. They are nameless and faceless . . . but the desire to love and be loved is strong. No, I don't regret leaving."

"Is there a woman in particular?"

Gwen Kellerman seemed perfect. Each time they were together on the fire escape, it felt like he'd met the perfect match for his soul, but a marriage meant more than two people. It meant the joining of families and communities, and in that area, he didn't know if they could survive the firestorm.

"I don't know," he admitted. "There's a woman I care for, but she's far above me."

"The ground is always level at the foot of the cross," Father Murry said, but Patrick merely grunted. He could accept that they were all equal in the eyes of God, but it was the eyes of the world that worried him.

"I owe her for an expensive medical procedure, and not being able to pay eats at me. A man should pay his debts."

Father Murry gestured to the half-finished school outside the rectory. "I'm taking from you. You've been donating your labor to the school and haven't asked for a dime in compensation."

"That's different."

"Indeed it is. When you figure out the perfect way to balance the scale of debts and obligations, I hope you'll let me know. And, Patrick, a word of friendly advice: don't let your pride blind you to the blessings God has dropped in your path."

Nine days after the assault, Patrick helped Liam walk out of the hospital and into a carriage to take him home. So far, he hadn't told Gwen anything about the attack. He didn't want to alarm her until he could be sure about Liam's parentage, and that meant it was time to pin Janet down about the truth.

The journey exhausted Liam, who sat on the sofa in the home where he grew up. Pillows kept him propped in place, and Frank the dog lay sprawled on the floor, useless for anything but comfort. Liam was too weak to argue, so Patrick did the questioning.

"Who do you think has a motive to kill Liam?" he asked.

"It was probably some sort of labor dispute," Janet said, her knitting needles flying like mad, but she wouldn't meet his eyes.

Patrick scoffed. "The ringleader came from New York, and whoever ordered the hit has deep pockets. The odds are good they will come after Liam again, and we need to know why."

"I don't know why!" Janet said, her needles clicking faster. Patrick had been questioning her for an hour, and she was getting more and more agitated.

"Please tell the truth, Ma," Liam said. "I'll love you no matter what."

Janet's face crumpled, her eyes squeezing shut and her lower lip wobbling, but her knitting didn't slow. Janet Malone knew the truth. She either gave birth to Liam or took him in as a three-year-old, and Patrick sensed she wasn't telling him the truth. He tried a different angle.

"How old was Liam when you first saw him?" he asked.

The needles finally stopped, and her hands dropped to her lap. Her head was low, and she didn't look at him.

"I don't know," she whispered. "He was sick. Dying."

Liam stiffened, his expression tense and alert. His mother kept talking.

"I was terrified," she said. "Mick was on the run, and he gave the boy to my husband, swearing us both to secrecy. We knew who he was, but my husband said it felt good to have a little revenge on the Blackstones, and I was never much for standing up to Crocket Malone."

The tension drained out of Liam, and he sagged, staring into the distance. His expression was impossible to read. Anger? Relief? It seemed to frighten Janet, and she rushed to continue her story.

"We didn't think you would live," she said. "You were so sick. Your lungs were full of fluid, and I was the only one who could soothe you. When I rocked you on my lap, you were so grateful. You cried when I had to step away. You were so needy, and I loved being needed. My own baby had only been in his grave for three months, and I was still grieving."

Liam turned his face away but thumped on the cushion beside him. Hearing the command, Frankie lumbered to his feet and laid his big head on the sofa cushions. Liam mindlessly stroked the dog's head. His hand trembled.

"Why did you lie all these years?" Liam finally asked.

"I wanted a son," she said. "When you finally got better, it was too late to give you back without getting into trouble ourselves. We left New York and moved to Pittsburgh, where no one knew us. We figured that if Mick got convicted, he would roll over and confess, but he got away with it. The day I heard the news, I fell to my knees and wept because you'd been with us for almost two years and I couldn't bear to give you back."

Patrick curled his hands into fists but tried to block any other emotion from his face. Janet Malone had perpetrated a horrible crime. The grief of losing her own babies could not excuse stealing another woman's child. He watched Liam carefully, searching for any sign of emotion, but the welder simply looked drained.

"If you want to go back to them, I'd understand," Janet whispered.

"I don't want anything to do with those people," Liam said weakly. "Even if it meant I'd inherit a little money, that's not who I am or who I want to be."

"It's more than a little money," Patrick said.

"A lot of money, then." A range of emotions crossed Liam's face as he stared at a spot in the corner of the room. "I've always prided myself on earning my own way. I get up in the morning, even when my bones are still tired from the day before, and make my way to the shipyard. I do good work. Sometimes, when the steel is still hot, I take a file and press my initials into the metal. I always do it in a spot where no one will ever notice, but I'm proud of my work. All over the world, there are ships that have my initials hidden on them. Sometimes I see one of them sail back into the Philly harbor, and I secretly think, *I built that ship.*"

The passion on his face drained away, slowly replaced by disdain. "I could never be someone who takes a fistful of money for nothing. Where's the pride in that? I'm a man. I earn my own way. The Blackstones can keep their sparkly jewelry and fancy houses."

Patrick shifted uneasily. Not many people would walk away from a fortune to continue living in a row house, but even if Liam stuck by his decision, that wouldn't be the end of it. If the Blackstones were trying to kill him, they would come after him again and again until they succeeded. Liam probably wouldn't survive the year.

"Some of that money would be welcome," Janet said. "I don't know how we're going to pay that hospital bill without it."

Liam sounded exhausted when he replied. "I'll figure something out. I kind of wish I had that woman's sapphire ring back."

"She's your sister, you know."

Liam snorted. "We come from different worlds."

"Nonsense," Patrick replied. "We are all created in God's image. Gwen Kellerman is no better or worse than the people in this room."

There was only one thing Patrick was sure about: Gwen didn't have anything to do with the assault on Liam. Her house was nice but nothing like the gilded palaces where the rest of her family lived. All she seemed to care about was the college, and she wouldn't put it at risk to murder her own brother.

"Liam, I think you need to either change your name and disappear out West or go to New York and settle things with the Blackstones. If an ordinary welder from Philly gets killed in a back-alley brawl, no one will raise a stink about it. If you can get recognized as William Blackstone, you'll be much harder to take down. It will be your best protection against another hit."

Liam was pensive as he digested the news. The shadows beneath his eyes were dark smudges against the deathlike pallor of his face. He was barely strong enough to stand on his own two feet, but he was going to have to walk back into New York City and fight for recognition from one of the most powerful families in America.

"I know you're right, but I don't know how to begin," Liam said weakly.

Patrick didn't either, but Gwen would. "I think our next move is to go to your sister," he said, praying that Gwen would be prepared to accept Liam into her world.

22

*wen considered the feast she had prepared for Patrick's
return. He had called from the train station to tell
her he'd arrived back in the city and that she should
expect a visit this evening. It gave her enough time to run
to the Irish bakery a few blocks from campus and buy plenty of
food because Patrick had been traveling all day and would be
hungry. She spread an Irish lace tablecloth over the table, then
filled the sideboard with a platter of corned beef sandwiches,
cranberry scones, and a jar of clotted cream. She didn't know
if he would prefer the spiced apple cake or the almond cake, so
she'd bought both. She arranged a few peony blossoms snipped
from her garden to complete the table. Maybe it was a little
much, but she wanted Patrick to know that she would celebrate
his Irish heritage.

She had barely finished arranging the flowers when he
knocked on her front door, and she hurried to let him in.

The shapes of two men were visible through the cut-glass
leaded window in the door, and one of them was Patrick.
The smile fled her face when she recognized the other. Liam
Malone stood beside Patrick on the front stoop, looking like
death warmed over.

"You look awful," she said.

Liam's mouth twisted. "Thanks. Can we come in?"

She glanced at Patrick, whose face was uneasy, but he met her eyes squarely and nodded. She clenched the doorknob as the implications of Liam's presence sank in. Patrick wouldn't have brought Liam here unless it portended something big.

She led the way to the parlor. "Are you hungry?" she asked, even though she suddenly felt too ill to eat a single morsel.

Patrick shook his head, and Liam plodded slowly into her parlor, where he lowered himself into the wingback chair without being invited. Patrick took the chair beside him and gestured for her to sit on the sofa across from them.

She remained standing. Anxiety made it impossible to sit. Liam was big and intimidating and seemed out of place in her parlor. His pallor made him look ill but didn't diminish his toughness, and he frightened her.

"Tell me what you've learned," she managed to ask Patrick in a calm tone.

"There's no easy way to say this," Patrick said. "Somebody attacked Liam last week. There were three of them, and they stabbed him in the gut. They meant to kill him."

She sucked in a startled breath. "How do you know? Were you there?"

He held up his right hand. "I broke two fingers during the brawl. Yes, I was there, and it was an unprovoked attack. The ringleader came from New York and was promised a small fortune to take him out."

Her gaze flew to Liam. Someone like him surely had a lot of enemies. The report submitted by Oscar's detectives contained a long history of rabble-rousing likely to provoke resentment.

Liam hadn't moved a muscle from where he sat, but he'd been watching her intently from the moment he walked inside. "I'm sorry we got off on the wrong foot the other day," he said to her. "I gave your ring back to Patrick. I shouldn't have shamed you out of it." He glanced at her bare hand. "Where is it?"

She covered her hand. The decision to stop wearing her wedding ring was a deeply personal choice she refused to discuss with a stranger. But Liam probably wasn't a stranger, and the prospect made her queasy. He looked so much like her father it was scary.

The silence lengthened as Patrick looked between her and Liam.

Finally, Liam spoke. "My mother confessed that Mick Malone brought me to her when I was three years old. That makes me your brother."

The news was not entirely unexpected but still drove the breath from her lungs. "Oh," she said.

It was such a puny word and couldn't begin to encompass the whirlwind of emotions triggered inside. This rough, hard-eyed man with a bitter heart wasn't who she'd imagined her brother would be.

She clasped her hands to stop them from trembling. She couldn't assume anything, and they'd always had a plan to identify her brother should someone come forward to assume his identity. They'd never told the police or the newspapers. They needed to keep this tiny detail private so it could never be faked. It was time to use it.

"Take off your right shoe," she said.

"What?"

"Your shoe. If you're really my brother, I'll be able to tell."

She eyed his shoes. They were battered and worn at the heel, the leather so scuffed it was beginning to split. He didn't lean over, merely used his left foot to nudge the right shoe off.

"And the sock," she said.

He gingerly leaned over to insert a finger into the top of his sock and tug it off. His foot looked shockingly white compared to his bronzed face, but he was a man who worked in the sun and had the weathered skin to prove it. His foot looked as pale as her own.

She pushed a footstool toward him. "Put your foot up on the footstool, please."

He did, and she knelt to examine the bottom of his foot. According to her father, he'd taken Willy to the river to teach him to swim shortly before the kidnapping. The boy had been running along the shoreline and stepped on an oyster shell that cut the bottom of his foot so deeply it required ten stitches.

She held a lantern close. A silvery scar ran along the arch of Liam's foot. It was an old scar, about three inches long, and impossible to fake.

Should she be delighted or terrified? A tremor began deep inside, and she put the lantern on the floor for safety.

She couldn't look at him. Tears blurred her eyes because her father had gone to his grave never learning that his son had survived. *He had survived!* Liam Malone was nothing like who they'd imagined Willy would grow up to become, but her father would have rejoiced no matter what.

"I wish my father could be here to see this." She still couldn't look at Liam. If she saw mockery or triumph in his face, she would snap.

"I wish so too." Liam's voice was a little rough but not unkind. "My own dad wasn't someone I'd wish on anyone."

She rose on legs that felt like water. What was she supposed to do now? Liam Malone wasn't what she expected or wanted. She'd harbored an irrational dream all her life that her big brother might someday miraculously reappear, so why wasn't she happier?

She must not let her emotions show. Too many conflicting feelings warred inside, clawing their way to the surface and beyond her control. It was cramped and stifling in here, too many eyes on her.

"Excuse me for a moment." She rushed for the door to the garden, slamming it shut the moment she was outside. The night air was damp and humid, and she sucked in a deep breath, willing her heartbeat to slow.

Behind her, the door opened.

"Gwen?"

It was Patrick. The good-natured epitome of sainthood was probably ashamed and embarrassed by her. She didn't want him seeing her like this.

"I'm alright. I just needed some air."

Footsteps sounded as he drew up alongside her, staring out into the moonlit garden. "I understand this must be a shock for you. Perhaps not an entirely welcome one."

There was no point in hiding; he could see right through to this small, unworthy part of her.

"I expected him to be different," she whispered.

Patrick rested a hand on her shoulder, and it felt like strength and understanding flowed from his palm into her. She leaned her cheek against his hand for a moment before standing straight again.

"He's not a bad man," Patrick said. "I've seen much to admire in him. The two of you are very different, but people of good character can disagree and still be admirable."

She nodded, knowing it was true, but a tangle of emotions still warred inside her. "It doesn't seem fair. My parents suffered so much. I don't understand why God put them through such suffering only to bring Willy back after they're dead. It's pointlessly cruel."

Patrick's face was carved with compassionate understanding. "I've had more time to come to terms with this than you," he said. "What happened to your parents was a tragedy, but I think that sometimes the Lord sends us into the valley for a reason, even if we don't understand why. Would your father have torn himself free of the bank and created the college were it not for the loss of his son? We'll never know, but the Lord was with your father throughout all the sorrow and the pain. And good came out of it. Do you believe that, Mrs. K? Because I do. That's the meaning of faith."

Gwen bowed her head. The college wouldn't have been formed but for what happened to Willy. Patrick's mother and countless others had been saved because of the college, but what happened to her parents was still hard to accept.

And there were more challenges ahead. Liam was going to be trouble. Her father would have moved heaven and earth to bring William back into the fold of the family, but now it was her job, and it must begin tonight. She would give Liam the same welcome her father would have lavished on his long-lost son. It was the last gift she could give to the generous man who gave so much of himself to the world.

She reached for Patrick's hand and kissed the back of it. Once again, he had come through for her in her moment of doubt. "I still think you would have been a good priest, Patrick."

"It's a good thing I'm not," he said with a wink at her.

She swallowed hard and led the way back inside. Liam hadn't moved from the wingback chair, and she took the seat opposite him. The fireplace hearth stretched between them, and Patrick sat on it, almost like a mediator between the two of them.

"Someone attacked you?" she asked, opening the awkward topic.

Liam nodded. "I think one of the Blackstones was behind it."

"That's ridiculous," she snapped. "Our family spent a fortune looking for you. They wouldn't do anything to harm you."

Patrick set a calming hand on her knee. "I think it's possible," he said gently. "It seems to me your uncle and your grandfather both stand to lose a lot if William Blackstone shows up alive and well."

"They won't lose a dime," she said. "My father left everything he owned to me. *I'm* the only one who stands to lose anything. Half of everything I own, to be precise."

Liam glanced nervously at Patrick, as though seeking advice. "I don't need half," he stammered. "I've got a big hospital bill hanging over my head, though, and I'd be grateful for help with it."

His voice trailed off as he clenched and unclenched his fists, and she noticed his fingernails were badly bitten, gnawed down to the quick. They hadn't been that way when he confronted her outside the courtroom. A tiny bit of sympathy awakened.

"I will make suitable financial arrangements," she said primly. Her father would expect her to give Liam half of everything she'd inherited, and she would. She'd never cared about money or power. Not like—

She froze as dark thoughts cascaded in, overwhelming in their implications. Uncle Oscar had tremendous sway at the bank, in part because he'd inherited her father's voting shares, but those shares should have gone to *Liam*. If Liam could prove himself to be her father's son, he would get half of Oscar's shares in the bank, and that ten percent stake might indeed be worth killing for.

Sweat prickled on her skin. She didn't want to consider it, but Uncle Oscar had plenty of reasons to fear a reappearance of William Blackstone.

"Gwen?" Patrick asked. "What's wrong?"

She couldn't meet his eyes. Patrick was so good, and shame washed through her for even thinking Uncle Oscar might be capable of murder. But the more she thought about it, the more serious the implications became. Liam could wreak havoc on the bank if he chose.

"When my father died, his nearest male relative inherited his partnership shares in the bank," she said. "Since William was presumed dead, my father's ten percent went to my uncle. Oscar now has a twenty-percent stake in the bank. Add that to my grandfather's thirty percent, and the two of them can rule the bank without opposition." She swallowed hard, watching Patrick's face transform as he understood.

"You're saying that if Liam can prove his identity, your uncle will lose the votes he inherited from your father. Liam could throw a wrench into anything your uncle and grandfather have planned for the bank."

All she could do was nod, dazed at the prospect. Liam watched with curiosity, but not quite enough. He didn't understand the implications of what she was saying.

She met his eyes and spoke frankly. "If you controlled a ten-percent vote in Blackstone Bank, you would have a shot at scuttling the U.S. Steel merger."

It clicked. Liam lifted his chin, and his eyes brightened. "How do I get my hands on those shares? And when is the vote?"

Patrick held up his hand. "Don't get ahead of yourself. The

more important issue is trying to keep you alive, because we've just spotted a very good reason someone might want you dead."

As quickly as Gwen's fears were raised, she realized how foolish it was. Uncle Oscar commanded the loyalty of the Blackstones and most of the other bank partners scattered across the world. Oscar already had the signatures of the other male relatives assigning him their votes for the merger.

"I can't imagine anyone in my family is trying to kill Liam," she said. "Last week my uncle locked up seventy-five percent of the vote in favor of the U.S. Steel merger, and all he needs is a simple majority. Even if Liam gets the ten percent back ahead of the vote, he can't scuttle the merger. He can embarrass my uncle by exposing a rift in the family, but that's the extent of it."

The other twenty-five percent of the bank was owned by various investors all over the world, and most of them would probably vote in support of the merger as well.

Frankly, Gwen didn't care about bank business. Right now, she only cared about how she could ease Liam back into the family. And the perfect opportunity was coming up. Every June her grandfather held a family reunion at his summer cottage. The gathering at the spacious, sprawling estate on a pristine island would be the perfect opportunity for Liam to meet everyone, but when she told Liam about it, he was skeptical.

"It sounds like a perfect opportunity for me to get snuffed out," he said darkly.

"Liam, no one in my family is trying to kill you." Frankly, she was embarrassed she had even considered the possibility. "And if you want to control my father's votes at the July meeting, you must be at that reunion. The rules for the bank are very firm, and one month ahead of the vote, everyone who is authorized to vote must have their names submitted to the board for recognition. If you want those shares, you're going to have to show up in person and get my grandfather to recognize you."

"When's the reunion?" Liam asked.

"Three weeks. We have a lot of ground to cover before you'll be ready to meet everyone."

He would need decent clothes, a haircut, and a lesson in basic manners. Once she helped Liam smooth down his rough edges, he could eventually fit into her family. He might even become the sort of older brother she'd always longed for.

She would *not* hold his upbringing against him. Her father would have rejoiced and killed the fatted calf to welcome Liam back into the fold. She would do the same. A seed of hope took root. It was time to extend the olive branch and begin afresh, for she had her older brother back.

"Help yourself to something to eat while I get my album of photographs so you can start getting to know our family," she said. "Oh, Liam, this is going to be fun!"

Patrick couldn't believe Gwen's naïveté. All evening she had been chattering as she shoved countless photographs beneath Liam's nose, trying to get him to learn the faces of all his cousins, uncles, and aunts.

Learning people's names and faces wasn't what Liam needed. Liam needed an intensive course in finance and contract law. The biggest industrial merger in history was unfolding, and Liam was about to be plunged into the middle of it. He couldn't read, he harbored a grudge against corporate America, and he had a fresh three-inch wound in his abdomen. Liam was about to walk into a nest of scorpions, and Gwen wanted to show him family photos.

Her excitement dimmed a little when she turned another page. "That's our mother," she said, and for once Liam seemed truly interested.

Patrick was too, and he leaned over to admire the photograph of a woman standing on a beach, shading her eyes from the sun as she looked directly into the camera. Now he knew where Gwen got her blond hair and serene countenance.

"How did she die?" Liam asked.

"She caught meningitis when I was six years old. I don't have many memories of her, but they are all good." Her smile was wistful as she studied the old photograph. "She loved letting me cuddle with her, and she wore orange blossom perfume. To this day, when I smell orange blossoms, I feel very happy. Content." She slipped the photograph free of the page and handed it to Liam. "You keep it."

Patrick held his breath, hoping Liam wouldn't do anything stupid, but he held it in his big, scarred hands as if it were a holy relic.

Gwen turned another page and kept talking. "You see how dapper our cousin Edwin looks in that summer suit?" she asked, pointing to a photograph. "We can order one just like it for you to wear at the family reunion. Perhaps we can visit the tailor tomorrow."

Patrick frowned. "Gwen, we can't stay here. If word gets around that your brother has returned, he won't be safe."

She was still skeptical that the attack on Liam originated from her family, but she agreed to take Liam elsewhere while she taught him what he needed to know about her family. Blackstone College had a second campus where they raised horses and students learned how to manufacture various antitoxin serums.

"It's summer, so the dormitory will be empty," Gwen said. "We can be alone out there while we work with Liam on all aspects of the family and bank business."

"Where is this other campus?" Patrick asked with a sinking heart. Back home, his mother was still too weak to return to work, and his rent was due in six days. It was time to return to the obligations of his normal life, but Gwen clearly expected his help mentoring Liam.

"It's in Queens," she said. "Remember? It's the place where we make the tetanus serums."

Guilt gnawed at him. If it hadn't been for Gwen and that serum, his mother would be dead right now, and he hadn't been able to pay a dime toward her treatment.

"It is agreed, then?" she asked. "We can take the nine-o'clock train to Queens tomorrow morning and stay at the student dormitory."

Liam wore a bewildered expression as he met Patrick's gaze. "What do you think?"

Liam had been acting strangely all evening. The confident swagger and headstrong opinions were gone. Now he was out of his depth and uncertain, constantly leaning on Patrick for advice. For better or for worse, Patrick was the only person Liam trusted in this new and unfamiliar world.

But Liam would need to start trusting Gwen. She could get him spiffed up before meeting his family, because there was no way Liam Malone would have credibility with the Blackstones in his current rough state.

"I think retreating to Queens is a good plan for you," he said to Liam.

"Excellent!" Gwen said. "We can leave in the morning."

Liam nodded, and Patrick had to help him stand. It took him a while to get Liam settled in one of the bedrooms, but when Patrick returned to the parlor, Gwen was waiting for him.

"Can I speak with you for a moment?" he asked her.

Her eyes softened as she stepped closer to him. "Of course."

Even her voice sounded softer, and he dreaded what was about to happen.

"Patrick?" she asked, touching his arm. "What is it? You can tell me anything."

It was impossible to meet her eyes as he spoke. "I can't go with you tomorrow. I need to get back to the Lower East Side and my other clients."

"But we need you." She sounded hurt. "I don't think Liam even understands what an investment bank *is*. How can he earn my grandfather's confidence if he is completely ignorant of finance and corporate law? You can tutor him."

"Aren't there any professors at the college who can teach him what he needs to know?"

She shook her head. "We have scientists and physicians, not modern-day warriors who do battle with banks and the corporate world. That's you! You're the perfect person to teach Liam what he needs to know."

Patrick hated this, but he needed to be blunt since she didn't seem to understand. "Gwen, I can't afford to help you."

"Is it money you need?" She seemed surprised, which only underscored the gulf between them. Someone in her situation probably never worried about making rent or scrounging to pay for a bottle of medicine, but he couldn't afford to ignore it.

"I'm not a greedy person, but I can't go weeks without an income. I've already lost too much time in Pittsburgh, and I need to get back to work." It was humiliating, but he'd probably have to borrow from Mrs. O'Shea to pay his rent next week.

"Money won't be a problem," Gwen said. "I'll pay whatever rate you typically charge. A thousand dollars a week?"

"I need my dignity, Gwen. The going rate for a lawyer like me is $250 a week."

"Then I'll pay you $250 a week," she said, reaching out to grasp his forearms. "Patrick, I'm floundering and I need help. I need *you*."

The plea wormed its way beneath all his defenses. He *wanted* her to need him, but his bigger worry was that Gwen didn't seem to realize the danger Liam was in. She might believe only sweetness and light about her family, but he suspected one of them wanted Liam dead. And if Gwen was with Liam when a second attempt on his life happened . . . well, it was unthinkable. He needed to be nearby to protect them both. Taking money from her would be galling, but he couldn't afford to turn it down.

"All right, I'll take $250 a week, and I'm afraid I need an advance on it so I can pay the rent." He couldn't even meet her eyes and instead stared at a spot on the floor. Until this moment, he'd always felt like an equal with Gwen. Now he was a supplicant, and he hated it.

But he loved her enough to endure it. This was probably only the first of many times his pride was going to be tested by daring to fall in love with a Blackstone.

23

By noon the following day, they were aboard a first-class compartment on a train carrying them to Queens. Gwen watched Liam's expression as he took in the polished cherrywood paneling and the burgundy velvet covering the seats. Patrick and Liam sat on one side of the table while she faced them from the opposite bench.

Retreating to the empty dormitory on the Queens campus would give her the time she needed to teach Liam gentlemanly comportment and provide insight into their family history. She wanted to get along with him, but he made it tough. As soon as the train started moving, he bombarded her with rude questions.

"How come you dress like that?" he asked, gesturing to her loose-fitting silk duster that matched the saffron gown underneath.

"This is a very fashionable ensemble," she defended.

"It looks too big. Same with the getup you wore yesterday. Why don't you buy clothes that fit?"

Patience. Liam wasn't very worldly or he would know that loose, artistic gowns were the height of fashion among liberated women. "This is how many women in my circle dress," she said. "All the pre-Raphaelite models in Europe wear gowns like this."

Liam snorted. "You'd think fancy models could afford to buy clothes that fit. It looks like you've got a bun in the oven."

She quirked an annoyed brow. "I gather you are implying I appear to be in an expectant state?"

"That's one way of putting it," Liam said. "My uncle Mick would say you look 'a wee bit knocked up.'"

Patrick struggled not to laugh, which bothered her even more. Whose side was he on? Liam needed to learn he couldn't go about insulting a woman's appearance.

"The free-flowing gowns I wear are comfortable and the height of fashion among the artistic set. And I'd like to suggest that your uncle Mick isn't the best role model for you."

Everything from Liam's clothes to his deportment and blunt manner of speaking were a disaster. The stewards and porters on the train all dressed and behaved with more refinement than Liam. They blended seamlessly into this sophisticated world, but Liam didn't. His hair was too long, he didn't remove his cap inside buildings, and didn't know the rules of polite dining.

That became evident when a porter wheeled a slim cart to their compartment to deliver a light breakfast. Liam reached over to help the porter unload the cart, grabbing a pair of teacups.

"I can do that, sir," the porter said, looking uncomfortable as Liam reached for a basket of bread and handed it to Patrick.

"Let the man do his job," Patrick said quietly.

Liam froze for a moment, then nodded, his face flushed with embarrassment as the porter efficiently set silverware, folded cloth napkins, and a tea service on the table. The porter gave a slight bow of his head, which seemed to make Liam intensely uncomfortable, before sliding the panel shut with a whisper-smooth glide of the door.

Gwen draped the cloth napkin on her lap, but Liam tucked it into the collar of his shirt. Patrick also placed his napkin on his lap. Would Liam notice? He didn't appear to as he reached for a slice of bread and began buttering it.

"Patrick, will you lead us in a blessing?" she asked.

"Certainly." Patrick bowed his head and said a few words.

Liam paused but didn't put his buttered knife down during the blessing.

Gwen led an unconventional life, but at least she knew where the boundaries were. Liam didn't. He cursed like a sailor, ate with the gusto of a starved dog, and had no qualms about insulting people. She needed to use this time in Queens to transform him into a gentleman who could hold his own among her family.

She waited until everyone had tea before beginning her first lesson. "You need to understand the structure of the bank and the Blackstone finances."

Liam set his cup down with a *clank*. "Shoot," he said.

"Our grandfather founded the Blackstone Bank, and both his sons helped manage the investments. Uncle Oscar took to it like a duck to water, but my father never did. He wanted to do something good with the family fortune. Eventually, my father created—"

"*Our* father," Liam corrected.

She nodded. "*Our* father created Blackstone College. His initial investment wasn't enough to sustain the college, and our grandfather agreed to support the college until it could turn a profit. My father chose to invest most of our revenue into additional scientific research, which means we aren't yet self-sufficient and still depend on those annual gifts."

Liam appeared disinterested as he kept wolfing down tea biscuits. "Why don't you pay for it? You're rich."

She was, but even if she donated her entire fortune, the college would burn through it within three years. Their overseas research initiatives and laboratories were shockingly expensive, and they wouldn't be able to balance their budget until they patented their serums and vaccines, which might take decades.

In the meantime, the bank continued supporting them, and she did her best to help the college trim its expenses. She taught botany classes and managed the greenhouse for free. She hosted charity auctions and sold rare plants from the greenhouse. It helped, but it was only a drop in the huge, voracious hole in the college's balance sheet.

"I don't have enough money to keep the college afloat," she said simply.

"How much did you inherit when our father died?" Liam asked with his mouth full.

"A lot, but not enough to run the college. I need my uncle to reverse his decision to stop funding the college, and you can help with that."

Liam leaned back on the bench and met her gaze. "Cut to the chase. I want to know how much you inherited and what part I'll get."

Well, that was blunt. She wasn't accustomed to such frank speaking, but he had a right to know. "Twelve million," she said, watching Liam's jaw drop. "You might get half."

He recovered quickly. "Might? What's stopping me from getting half?"

"Me."

It was time to fight for the college, and she would be as blunt and aggressive as Liam. He still didn't understand the realities of his legal situation, so she would spell it out.

"Our father had two huge assets: his partnership in the bank and his personal estate. The bank's operating agreement dictated that his shares could only go to the nearest living male relative, so they went to Uncle Oscar. His personal estate was another matter. He had complete freedom to dispose of his estate however he chose, and he left every dime of it to me. He left no provision for you."

Liam's eyes narrowed, and he lifted his chin. "And you're cutting me out of it."

"I haven't said so." Her father would have wanted her to split the estate with Liam, and she would, but she refused to show all her cards at once. Liam was about to become a very powerful man, and they needed to cooperate with each other. "I know what Father would have wanted. He was a great man and would want me to give you half . . . provided that you use your shares in the bank to support the college."

Liam studied her as silence stretched between them. "So that's how it's going to be. You scratch my back, and I'll scratch yours."

"That's one way of putting it. I'd rather suggest that we help each other. You will encounter difficult businessmen at the bank, and I can teach you the best way to negotiate with them."

Liam snorted. "I learned about businessmen when I dropped out of school in the eighth grade and joined a union. Come at them hard, fast, and don't take no for an answer. Your fancy college means nothing to me. Any power I claw away from the Blackstones will be used on behalf of the workingmen of this world."

She silently cringed. Everything about Liam, from his brash manners to the pride he took in his eighth-grade education, was destined to be a catastrophe in the Blackstone boardroom.

She swiveled her eyes to Patrick, silently begging for help. He needed no prompting.

"You are about to walk into a den of snakes," Patrick said, making no effort to mask his Irish brogue. "These people don't fight with fists or words but with alliances and legal technicalities. I'll have your back and so will your sister, but nothing in this world comes for free. She's going to expect you to come through for her, and she's not wrong in asking for it."

Then Patrick directed his strong, Irish brogue toward her. "Gwen, you can't expect Liam to walk away from a crusade he's fought all his life. It would drain him of the fire that's made him the survivor he is. Like it or not, you two are going to have to get along with each other."

She rocked back in her bench. Liam was the one who needed fixing, not her.

Suddenly, her optimism about their three-week retreat to the Queens campus seemed far less certain.

24

efending Gwen from Liam's wisecracks was trying Patrick's patience, but he hoped the situation
would improve once they were no longer trapped
in a train compartment. They would each have their own bedroom at the dormitory in Queens, and the extra breathing room
would be welcome.

Patrick liked the Queens campus even though it was only
a single building located next to a horse stable and a fenced
grazing area. They were in the heart of the city, surrounded by
a tobacco shop, a pencil factory, and a delicatessen. This plain
brick building would be their home for the next three weeks
while they tried to smooth Liam's rough edges and teach him
the basics of how to function in refined society.

The first floor of the building contained a research laboratory, classrooms, and a large common area with tables for both
dining and studying. Dormitory rooms filled the two floors
above. A couple of stable hands lived on the top floor to look
after the horses, but the entire second floor was empty because
there weren't students here during the summer.

The dormitory rooms each had a single bed, a chest of drawers, and a desk. Patrick insisted Gwen have the only room with
a view of the horse pasture. He could sense how uneasy she
was in this noisy urban environment, but he and Liam loved

it. Frankly, the dormitory was newer and nicer than any place either of them had ever lived.

He was helping Liam unpack when Gwen tapped on the open door of his room.

"I've brought herbal sachets for everyone," she said, holding out several little lace-covered packets.

"What's a sachet?" Liam asked.

She set a couple on his pillow. "They are pouches of scented herbs to make things smell nice. I made these with lemon balm and lavender from my garden. They'll make your dormitory feel a little more like home."

Liam snorted. "I don't need that sort of girly stuff."

"Are you sure?" she asked. "The sheets smell like bleach, and a sachet will make them so nice when you slip into bed tonight."

"Bleach means the sheets are clean," Liam said, trying to give the lacy sachets back.

But Gwen was having none of it and tucked them back beneath Liam's sheets. "When dealing with polite company, you should graciously accept whatever is offered, even if it doesn't seem important to you. This may not seem natural to you, but you need to learn these little niceties."

Her voice had a whiff of schoolmarm to it that Liam didn't appreciate, but Patrick sent him a warning glare to stifle whatever rude comment he was about to make. Gwen had put up with a lot from Liam in the past few hours, and Patrick didn't like seeing her hurt.

The dormitory had a communal washroom at the end of the hall they would all need to share. Patrick thought the shiny white tiles looked nice, but Gwen's nose wrinkled at the sight of the urinals. Stalls provided privacy for the toilets, but the washroom was crude compared to what she had in her home.

"Hot water!" Liam said with approval, twisting the tap on one of the sinks. Hot water was an unheard-of luxury in the neighborhoods where Patrick and Liam lived, and the thought of a piping hot shower tonight was appealing.

Gwen fidgeted, and Patrick finally asked her what was wrong.

She nodded to the toilet stall. "I need to use the facilities. Can you both step outside?"

Liam was still fiddling with the hot water. "What's your problem? The toilets have doors."

"I would prefer a little more privacy," Gwen said delicately.

"Don't worry," Liam snickered. "Go ahead and let one rip if you want. I won't tell anyone."

Gwen's face turned bright red, and she stepped forward to jab a finger in Liam's face. "That's exactly the sort of tacky thing you can't say in polite company. I really shouldn't have to explain this to you, Liam."

"Look, Mother Superior, I'm a normal man, and this is how normal people talk."

"It's not how Blackstones talk."

Patrick didn't want to be the mediator between these two, but it appeared to be his role. "Liam, out," he ordered. "From now on, Gwen gets to use the washroom by herself, and you need to knock before entering."

Liam made quite a production as he turned off the taps and took forever to dry his hands, but he left, and Patrick followed him out.

"That woman drives me nuts," Liam grumbled as the door slammed behind them. "She nitpicks everything I do and acts like she walks on water when she's no better than the rest of us."

Liam continued to list Gwen's flaws as they walked down the hall. He complained about *everything*. The fussiness of her house, the way she dressed, the way she covered her nose with a handkerchief in the train station. When he insulted the way she didn't show her teeth when she smiled, Patrick had heard enough. He grabbed both of Liam's shoulders and shoved him up against the wall, pinning him in place.

"She sometimes drives me nuts too," he admitted. "Her compassion. Her valor. Her willingness to bend over backward to do what's right, even when it isn't easy. And, Liam, nothing about dealing with you has been easy. I adore that woman. Do you hear me? Get it through your thick skull that I'm not going to stand back while you keep lobbing insults at the woman I adore. Got it?"

Liam looked appalled as understanding sank in. "You and *her?*" he choked out.

"Yeah, me and her. You think you've got it tough having to learn a few table manners? When the world learns who you are, they will throw rose petals in your path and treat you like a long-lost hero. When they learn that I put my grubby hands on Gwendolyn Blackstone Kellerman, they'll spit on me."

He cringed even thinking about it, but he'd be a fool to think otherwise.

Gwen left to buy something for dinner as an excuse to get away from Liam, who was getting on her last nerve. She had never liked the Queens campus. Smack in the center of the city, it didn't seem like a college campus to her, but it would be a good place to keep Liam out of sight until he shed his atrocious manners. Nobody could actually be as stupidly crass as Liam Malone, could they? Thank heaven Patrick was here to play the peacemaker, because he seemed to be the only person Liam respected.

Things didn't get any better when they sat down for dinner in the common room. During the academic year, students used this room for dining, group lectures, and studying. It was an interior room with no windows and was furnished only with two large tables, a single stove, and a couple of shelves for dishes.

Gwen brewed a pot of tea, and Patrick set out the crusty Italian sandwiches she'd bought at the deli next door.

"You must grasp a teacup by its handle," she instructed after Liam palmed the bowl of the cup. "Tip the cup rather than throwing your entire head back like a sea gull guzzling down a fish."

"You people have rules for how a man should swallow?" Liam challenged.

"We have rules for *everything.*" She pretended not to notice when Liam rolled his eyes, but she couldn't ignore the way he hunkered down to eat his sandwich. "Sit up straight and bring your food to your face, not your face down to the food," she said politely.

Liam ignored her until Patrick kicked him under the table, and Liam reluctantly sat up straighter.

She kept her face serene as she continued speaking. "Tomorrow we'll go shopping for new clothes because looking like a gentleman requires a suitable wardrobe."

She could only pray that once properly attired, Liam might start behaving better. Something about a starched collar and a fine waistcoat seemed to instill a certain level of decorum in men.

The following morning, she took Liam and Patrick to the finest haberdashery in Queens. Wooden shelves stacked with bolts of fabric reached all the way to the ceiling, while glass cases displayed silk ties, enameled cufflinks, and imported buttons. Liam needed an entirely new wardrobe: custom trousers, broadcloth shirts, at least two frock coats, waistcoats, a morning coat, a cutaway jacket, and a double-breasted wool coat for when the weather turned cold. He needed a white suit for summer and a tuxedo for evenings.

A nattily dressed tailor took Liam's measurements for the custom suits, but Gwen bought him a ready-made suit as well. It lacked the sharp tailoring the others would have, but Liam needed to become accustomed to wearing a vest, tie, and starched collar as soon as possible. He had never worn a tie in his life, and Patrick had to show him how to knot it.

"It feels like a noose," Liam groused once it was tied. "It's too tight and it doesn't fit."

The tailor cleared his throat. "It fits perfectly, sir."

"You'll get used to it," she assured him, then looked at Patrick. "You need a new suit too."

Patrick blanched at the suggestion. "I just bought a new suit last month."

She'd seen that suit in the courtroom, and it was completely inadequate. The tailoring was rudimentary, and the cheap wool lacked the drape a quality suit should have. She scrambled for the softest way to make her point. "It's fine for daily wear, but if you ever meet with the board of Blackstone Bank, it's not up to snuff." She glanced at the haberdasher. "Please take Patrick's measurements for a top-of-the-line suit as well."

Patrick looked like he'd rather have a tooth pulled, but he submitted to the measurements. When she tried to add the suit to her bill, he rebelled.

"I can pay for my own suit," he said, but she overruled him. After all, she was the one who'd put him in a situation where he'd be meeting with Wall Street executives, so it was only right she foot the bill.

Liam wore his new suit out of the shop, and they headed to a custom shoemaker, where Gwen had Liam fitted for two black oxfords, a pair of brown derby shoes, and dress boots. The shoemaker brought out a pair of ready-made cordovan leather wingtips that already fit him perfectly. The classic leather shoes had a contoured sole with padding sewn into the footbed. At last she'd found something Liam wholeheartedly approved of.

"I'm never taking these off," he said in wonder. "These things are comfortable enough to wear to bed."

He tossed his shabby work boots into the trash before heading on to their last stop, a barbershop, to get Liam a haircut and a proper shave. Women weren't welcome in the barbershop, so she stepped outside to wait for them. It was a relief to get away from Liam's bawdy humor and relentless criticism of her. She bought a pretzel to feed the pigeons and tried to count her blessings.

Twenty minutes later, Liam and Patrick emerged from the barber. Gwen turned away from the pigeons to assess the results, and her heart nearly stopped.

With his new clothes and neatly groomed hair, Liam looked so much like her father that a bittersweet ache bloomed in her chest. What sort of man would Liam have become if Mick Malone hadn't snatched him as a child and turned him into a barbarian? If Crocket Malone hadn't raised him to be full of bile and resentment? What happened to Liam wasn't fair, and she needed to be more patient with his boorishness. No matter what it took, she would honor her father's memory by ensuring that Liam had a decent shot at the world.

The friendship Patrick had formed with Liam didn't preclude him from occasionally wanting to strangle the man, and it was entirely because of the atrocious way Liam treated Gwen.

They'd been on the Queens campus for almost a week, during which Gwen was consistently patient and compassionate toward her brother, yet Liam went out of his way to goad her, constantly needling her or rolling his eyes when she tried to help him.

His behavior baffled Gwen, but Patrick understood. Liam's pride was stung as he was forced to shed every aspect of his former life like an old snakeskin while trying to ape the manners of a world he held in contempt—but one that also secretly intimidated him.

With each of Liam's digs, Gwen wilted a little more. During Patrick's long afternoons tutoring Liam on business and investments, Gwen scrambled to find an excuse to escape the tension indoors and had decided to breathe new life into the scraggly horse pasture alongside the stable. Leave it to Gwen to see a patch of land and want to beautify it. She'd gone to a hardware store to buy supplies, and now she hoed, weeded, and worked on resurrecting the patch of Kentucky bluegrass.

Liam behaved differently whenever Gwen left the room. He was hungry for information and latched on to everything Patrick could teach him. The first order of business was to improve Liam's ability to read. He had dropped out of school twenty years ago and hadn't looked at a book since. At first Liam couldn't read more than a line or two, but he got better with practice. They put the financial section of the daily newspaper on the table before them, and Patrick read a sentence aloud while Liam's eyes followed along each line of text. Then Liam had to read the same sentence with Patrick ready to help.

Liam's ability to read came back quickly, but he could barely write. Patrick asked him to write a short summary of each article they read. Liam's spelling was an embarrassment and his handwriting was atrocious, but he never tired. No matter how long they practiced, Liam was eager to learn and peppered Patrick with questions about contracts, interest rates, and investments.

Then Gwen returned, and Liam was once again contentious and difficult. A perfect example was the day it was too rainy to work outdoors, so Gwen settled in with an embroidery hoop while Patrick taught Liam the difference between a stock and a commodity.

"Stocks are shares in a specific company, but commodities are raw goods like wheat, corn, or copper," he explained. "Depending on the supply of the commodities, the price rises or falls."

Liam jabbed a finger at the headline. "People are celebrating the lousy wheat harvest. It's coldhearted."

"It's not that they're celebrating, but the price of wheat is going up because of the floods in the Midwest. That means people who invested in wheat futures will—"

"Will get rich off hungry people," Liam said and glared at Gwen. "Do you people profit off these high-flying wheat prices?"

Gwen remained calm. "And by 'you people' are you referring to our family?"

"*Your* family," Liam said. "Your family lives in a palace and gets rich while everyone else is paying inflated prices for bread."

"Knock it off, Liam," Patrick warned. "Gwen and I are trying to cram enough business insight into your head so that Frederick Blackstone will assign your father's voting shares back to you. That's your best shot to help the working people of this country."

He didn't need to ask a second time. Liam straightened and

went back to painfully writing out his summary of the article, and Gwen sent Patrick a look of gratitude.

Thank you, she silently mouthed, and he beamed back at her. As much as he resented being torn away from home to play peacemaker between these two, Gwen needed his help, and that meant the world to him.

25

It had been a difficult two weeks, and Gwen spent most of it working in the pasture. She had already pulled out the pigweed and nutsedge, but the overgrazed patches of land needed heavy raking to break up the clods before she could amend the soil and scatter new seed.

"Why don't you hire someone to do that?" Liam called out from the porch swing set up beneath the eaves of the building. The oppressive heat had driven Liam and Patrick to have their study session outside, and Liam continually nitpicked at her efforts to restore the pasture.

She straightened and twisted her spine, rubbing the abused muscles that ached from two hours of hoeing. There was nothing beautiful about this urban bit of pasture, but she was proud of her efforts to improve it. There would be no sense of satisfaction if she hired someone else to do the work.

"I enjoy the challenge," she said. "Growing things and tending them has always been a hobby for me."

"They say Marie Antoinette milked cows as a hobby," Patrick said. "Rich people have strange hobbies."

"All rich people had better find a challenge in life, or their mind will shrivel," she said. "We can afford to be idle, and that can turn dangerous."

Liam wasn't impressed. "I've been working six days a week

since I left school at thirteen. I'd like the chance to suffer from these diseases of the idle rich."

For once Liam didn't sound angry or jeering, just a little . . . teasing? There was a glint of humor in his expression, and with relief she realized that, yes, he was teasing her. So was Patrick. The two of them rocked in tandem on the porch swing with stacks of books and newspapers beside them, but there were so many things Liam needed to learn that couldn't be found in books. Liam had no understanding of the seductive dangers that came from a life of vast wealth, but they were real, and she had a duty to warn him.

Gwen swiped at a gnat swirling near her face. "Do you have anyone special back home? A girl?"

"Nope. Why?"

The gentle creak of the porch swing continued as she contemplated the best way to frame her response. "You are a handsome man of marriageable age," she pointed out. "Soon you will possess a fortune. Plenty of women will find that very attractive."

"So you think the fortune hunters will be out to get me?"

"I *know* they'll be out to get you."

Liam shrugged and continued the rock of the swing. "Don't worry. I'm too smart to fall for that sort of girl."

How much should she tell him? Discussing her marriage to Jasper wasn't easy. Patrick already knew some of the details, but not everything. No matter how embarrassing it was, if sharing her story could help Liam avoid the mistakes she'd made, it would be worth it.

"I thought I was smart too," she said. "I was eighteen when I fell in love with my husband. Jasper was a biology professor at the college, and I thought he was the most brilliant scientist on earth."

She'd been flattered when he showed interest in her. The difference in their backgrounds didn't matter. Neither did the fact that she was an heiress and he a college professor fifteen years her senior.

The creak of the porch swing slowed, and she suddenly had the full attention of both men. Discussing her deepest humiliation wasn't easy, but she wanted them to know.

"Jasper published his research in prestigious journals and traveled all over the world to speak at conferences. He was our most celebrated professor. He earned a respectable salary and had no vices like gambling or drink. What I didn't understand was his ambition. He wanted to start his *own* academic journal and host his *own* conferences."

She leaned over to tug a few more weeds—anything rather than look at Patrick as she recounted these painful memories. "He married me for my money," she continued. "My father warned me that Jasper's ambition outpaced his resources, but I didn't care. I was honored that he wanted me to be his wife. I had no idea there was another woman in his life. Vivian was always the woman of his heart, and on the day Jasper married me, he betrayed us both."

Talking about this exhausted her, and the gentle compassion on Patrick's face was painful to see. She wandered to the fence to lean her forearms on the top rail.

"Jasper was clever in keeping Vivian nearby. He got her hired at the college to teach music, and I welcomed her into my home. I had no idea who she was to him, even after she became pregnant. Many people on campus thought she should be fired, especially after she refused to name the father of her child. It split the campus down the middle, but several professors rallied in her support. Jasper and I both did." A bitter laugh rose inside her. How naïve she had been. She'd helped Vivian furnish a nursery and scolded the faculty wives who wanted to ostracize her.

"I eventually learned the nature of her relationship with Jasper," she said. "I tried so hard to win him back from her. I bought curling tongs so I could style my hair like her. I bought cosmetics and painted my face, just as she always did. The last straw was when I found out he bought a house for her and their child, and that was where he'd been spending countless hours when I thought he was working late at the laboratory. I broke down and went running to my father for counsel."

The day she told her father about the affair was the only time she saw him roar in anger, throwing a vase across the room and vowing to cut Jasper out of his will. Her father had a heart attack a few days later and died before the end of the week.

She raised pained eyes to Liam. "Everything got worse after he died because the affair became public knowledge on campus. Vivian announced she would leave town, and Jasper panicked. He went running to her, but she wouldn't let him inside her house. He planted himself on her front porch, refusing to leave. It was February, and he spent the entire night there. He had pneumonia the following morning."

To this day it was hard to believe how quickly her life had unraveled. She tried to nurse Jasper through the illness, but she wasn't who he needed. None of the physicians who examined him offered any hope, so in those final few days, Gwen left her home and allowed Vivian and Mimi to move in.

Patrick looked dumbstruck, and she rushed to explain. "Despite all his flaws, I still cared for Jasper, and it was the only gift I could give him."

"What happened to the other woman?" Liam asked.

"She's still at the college."

Liam shot to his feet. "You shouldn't have to put up with that. Tell me who she is, and I'll go clear her out."

Liam's brute gallantry broke the tension. Imagining how he might unceremoniously dump Vivian off campus caused laughter to bubble up, but she soon sobered.

"I learned plenty from the sorry affair. After trying to make myself over into someone else to win Jasper's affection, I gave up and vowed to be true to myself." She held out her arms, facing them. Strands of hair escaped the messy bun at her nape. She was grubby from working outdoors and without a hint of cosmetics. "This is who I am. This is the real me."

"It's exactly how God made you," Patrick said with gentle

affection. "You're beautiful. You look like something out of the Garden of Eden."

His words were a balm to her battered spirit. Trying to make herself prettier for Jasper had been humiliating and futile, but the gentle heat in Patrick's eyes blasted that inadequacy to pieces.

"You're pretty enough," Liam conceded. "Except for that floaty dress you're wearing. It makes you look like you've got a pea in the pod."

She threw a clump of pigweed at him, and he caught it with a grin. For a moment Liam had been the protective older brother she'd always longed for. It had been nice for the ten seconds it lasted.

She stooped to pick up the hoe. "I'm telling you my sorry tale so you don't walk down the same path. Fortune hunters are everywhere. They can be hard to spot. Many people tried to warn me about Jasper because when an impoverished college professor marries an heiress, tongues wag. Jasper created a respected scientific journal, but jealous people claimed it was only because I paid for it."

"Did you?" Liam asked, and she wanted to explode in frustration.

"Yes, but that shouldn't have mattered! Why should anyone care who funded it? It was an excellent journal that advanced scientific understanding all over the world."

Patrick abruptly stood. A book fell off his lap and splatted on the ground, but he didn't pick it up. "I have some errands I need to run. If you'll excuse me."

Odd. He didn't smile or meet her eyes as he strode away. He headed toward the main street, his back stiff.

"Patrick?" she called after him. "Did I say something wrong?"

He held up a hand to acknowledge that he'd heard but didn't break his pace as he walked away. She looked at Liam, baffled by Patrick's odd behavior.

Liam frowned. "For a smart woman, sometimes you can be dumber than a stump."

"What's that supposed to mean?" she demanded. After baring her soul, leave it to Liam to start acting like a lout again.

"Patrick is street-smart and book-smart, but he's soft when it comes to you," Liam said. "He swallows his pride and lets you lord it over everyone. Hey, don't look at me like that. You probably can't help being an uptight Mother Superior, but go easy on him, okay?"

"Was it because I talked about Jasper?" It couldn't be. Patrick already knew about how badly her marriage had failed and why.

"It's because you talked about how Jasper was your dolly boy, and Patrick doesn't want to be your next one."

"Dolly boy?" she gasped. She'd never heard that expression but could guess what it meant. "I don't think that way about Patrick. He's my hero. I dream about him at night. He knows that."

Liam held up his hand. "I don't want to hear your seedy dreams about Patrick. All I'm saying is that he's been a true friend to me, and I won't stand aside if you toy with him. They say that blood is thicker than water, but it's not. If push comes to shove, I'd side with Patrick over you and the rest of the Blackstones any day of the week."

Her mouth went dry, and it felt like the ground was crumbling beneath her feet. There was no time to waste. If she had somehow offended Patrick, she didn't want another minute to pass before she tried to set it right.

Patrick strode down the street, eyes straight ahead as he plowed through the crowds of people on the sidewalk. It was late in the afternoon, and he needed to get to the tailor's before they closed. He ought to feel guilty for the way people parted to let him pass, but he was too angry. The story of Gwen's fortune-hunting husband was seared on his mind. Were they to marry, that would be the assumption everyone made about Patrick too. No matter what he accomplished in life, no matter how true their feelings for each other, people would brand him a fortune hunter until the day he died.

He needed to cancel the order on the suit she'd bought for him. He never should have let her buy it in the first place. The suit he bought last month was fine. Better than fine! It was custom-made to his size, and anyone who looked down their nose at it could take a flying leap into the sea.

"Patrick!"

Gwen's shout came from a block or two away. He didn't want to see her and quickened his steps.

"Patrick, wait!"

Her pleading tone scorched him. He hated hurting her, but unless she gave him the breathing room to be his own man, their relationship was doomed. He paused in front of a millinery shop and waited for her to catch up. She was breathless as she grabbed onto his arm.

"What's wrong?" she asked. "What did I do wrong?"

It was humiliating to even explain it to her, but she deserved the truth. Having this out on a busy street corner wasn't ideal, but he didn't want to go back to the dorm, where Liam might overhear.

"I shouldn't have let you buy me that suit," he said. "I'm heading over to cancel the order."

"Don't be ridiculous," she said. "I've already paid for it."

"Then I need to pay you back. A man has to have some pride, Gwen. I don't like taking money from you any more than Jasper did."

She flinched and stepped back a little. "I hardly think you're an expert on Jasper."

"I know you bought him that scientific journal and he resented the way it made him look to the rest of the world."

He walked over to the bench on the edge of the sidewalk, bracing his hands against the back of it. She didn't understand. Someone like her probably never could, but he had to try. His anger drained away, and he spoke without heat.

"My dad died before I can remember, so we were always

poor," he said. "When we lived in Ireland, all my clothes came out of the charity bin. I hated going to school, because other kids knew I was wearing their castoffs. The taunting got so bad that I'd walk a couple of miles to a neighboring village and rummage through their poor bin, because there might be a shirt or a pair of shoes with a little more life, and then the kids at school wouldn't know where they came from. That isn't something a man forgets. I won't ever be reduced to begging again."

Gwen looked stricken. "But I think only the best of you! Your generosity, your bravery. Patrick, I love you."

He looked away, unable to say the words in return. As much as he cared for her, they were going too fast. He'd underestimated the chasm dividing their worlds. Everything had been easy when they were alone on a fire escape, but in the real world, there were daily reminders of how far beneath her he was.

"I think the world of you, Gwen," he stammered, hating to see the hope fade from her face. She was trying so hard to be brave, but the hurt was impossible to miss.

"What's changed?" she asked. "I'm the same person I've always been."

"Your family won't accept a man like me."

She shook her head. "They're good people. Some are a little snobby, but that's true in any family, isn't it? Don't let my bad experience with Jasper mean we can't have a future. Please don't abandon me. I need you. Liam needs you."

"I'm not going to bail out, Gwen. I'll go to the island and help Liam as best I can." But he didn't know if he had a future with her after that, and it hurt.

He grabbed her shoulders and kissed her on the mouth, long and deep. She was everything that was good and pure and optimistic. His kiss was full of desperation, but he forced himself to withdraw.

"I adore you, but I don't know if we can weather the storm ahead of us."

"Whatever happens, we'll face it together, Patrick." She reached up to embrace him, and he returned it, holding her tightly and wishing he could believe her. Over her shoulder, he saw a *Help Wanted* sign in the millinery shop window, carrying the familiar phrase *No Irish Need Apply*.

Gwen was an open-minded woman, but he doubted her family would be any more eager to accept an Irishman than the shopkeeper who put that horrible sign in the window, and he feared the storm ahead was going to be bad.

26

*P*atrick tried to go on as before, but everything got more difficult after the afternoon in front of the millinery shop. He canceled the order for the new suit, but it didn't help the awkwardness he felt with Gwen. His inability to return her declaration of love hung like a black cloud shadowing every conversation.

Gwen pretended the awkwardness didn't exist, forcing a smile on her face each time he entered a room. He tried to meet her halfway, listening politely as she rambled about her wonderful family, but it was in Gwen's nature to see the best in everyone.

Today she sat beside Liam in the common room with the album of photographs open on the table before them. She pointed to a picture of an old man standing in the surf, casting a line into the water. "That's Uncle Milton," she said. "He's an avid fisherman. You should see the collection of rods and nets he brings to every family gathering. If there's any sort of seafood you like, just tell Milton, and he'll catch it for you."

She turned to look at Liam. "We should go over seafood forks before we get to the island, because we celebrate with an annual lobster bake on our grandfather's birthday. It's always been my favorite day of the entire summer. We dig a trench, fill it with seaweed, then add lobsters and mussels and clams. The entire family joins in, and it's tremendous fun. You'll love it."

Liam's grunt was skeptical, and Gwen noticed.

"Liam, the Blackstones are good people. I guarantee that our great-aunt Martha is the kindest woman you will ever meet. During the Civil War she volunteered in hospitals for imprisoned Confederate soldiers because few people wanted to tend to them. She did it until she caught cholera, then went straight back on duty once she recovered."

Although she spoke to Liam, Patrick sensed the praise she heaped on Great-Aunt Martha was intended for him.

Liam seemed doubtful too. "And what will our great-aunt Martha think of a man who has calluses on his hands and can barely read?"

Gwen didn't hesitate. "She will mourn what happened to Theodore's son and welcome him home with open arms." She twisted so she could look at Patrick, her face nearly bursting with hope. "You too," she said. "Aunt Martha knows about my struggles with Jasper and will be thrilled that I've found such a strong, decent man. You will both be welcome."

"I hope you're right, Mrs. K," he said. He wanted to believe her but couldn't disguise the suspicion in his tone.

It didn't make a dent in her sunny disposition. "I told my aunts about you, and they are all excited. Aunt Helen's biggest fear is that *you* won't accept *them*," she said with a laugh, then leaned forward to press a kiss to his lips.

The telephone rang, and Liam pounced on the opportunity to get away from them. "I'm averting my eyes," he called over his shoulder as he went to answer the telephone down the hall.

Gwen turned to show Patrick another photograph of Uncle Milton holding aloft a pair of crab traps in preparation for the famed annual lobster bake. Liam's voice soon interrupted her.

"Yo, Patrick. There's a priest on the telephone for you."

Patrick stood, wondering why Father Doyle would be contacting him here. He hurried down the hallway to take the receiver from Liam's hands.

"Yes, Father?"

It wasn't Father Doyle, but Father Murry from Pittsburgh, the one who heard Patrick's confession.

"I'm afraid there was a break-in at the church rectory after you left the city," Father Murry said. "Somebody stole a hundred dollars from the school fund, and the police got an anonymous complaint accusing you of doing the deed right before you skipped town."

"That's a lie!" Patrick's voice echoed down the empty brick corridor. Outrage mingled with embarrassment as the old priest continued talking.

"I tried telling that to the police, but they seem convinced you and that fellow who was laid up in the hospital were in cahoots together. They've already issued a warrant for both your arrests. All this happened last week, but it took me a while to find you."

Patrick's hands curled into fists. Whoever attacked Liam was now launching another assault, and it had been going on while they were mindlessly hiding out in Queens. The police had been after him for a week. Even now they could be closing in on them.

There was no time to waste. If Father Murry could track him down in Queens, so could the Pittsburgh police. Normally the police wouldn't cross state lines to track down a charge of petty theft, but nothing about this case was normal.

Patrick's mind still reeled as he headed back to alert the others. It hurt to see the innocent happiness on Gwen's face as she sat beside Liam, laughing about another photograph in her picture album, but she needed to know about the ugliness swirling around them. He explained what Father Murry had relayed to him, knowing this marked the end of their brief interlude here in Queens.

"It sounds like someone is trying to frame us," Liam said.

Patrick nodded. Framing Liam for theft would effectively stop him from ever being allowed to serve on the board of a bank, and it would ruin Patrick's legal career forever.

Even worse, if Liam landed in prison, whoever was after him might arrange a swift and brutal murder behind prison walls. Patrick needed to get Liam to safety as quickly as possible.

"We can go to my grandfather," Gwen said. "We'll be safe on the island, and the faster we can get Frederick to acknowledge you as Theodore's son, the safer you will be."

For once, they were all in agreement.

Gwen sent a carefully worded telegram to her grandfather's summer home on Cormorant Island, alerting him of their arrival the following day. Frederick didn't yet know she had confirmed Liam's identity, and she didn't want news of it going through a series of telegraph operators. She simply closed the telegram with a hint about why she was coming:

I am bringing Liam Malone with me. The two of you need to meet as soon as possible.

Cormorant Island lay off the coast of New York. The only way to reach it was by a ferry that made a single trip each morning. Sea spray misted Gwen's face as the ferry drew closer to the island.

"That's the town of Windhaven," she said, pointing it out to Patrick and Liam, who stood beside her at the railing of the ferry.

Windhaven wasn't much of a town, just some homes and shops nestled on the south side of the island, where four hundred people made their living from the sea. Frederick owned the entire north end of the island, which made his estate feel like a private kingdom.

Frederick's summer home perched high on a bluff overlooking the sea. Several acres of terraced lawns and gardens led down to the shore, where a cove of boulders protected her grandfather's private boathouse and dock.

They were the only passengers on the ferry this morning, so

Gwen tipped the skipper to deliver them straight to the boathouse on her grandfather's side of the island. The boathouse was easy to spot, with its two bays, a wraparound balcony, and a slate roof with a cupola on top.

"That boathouse is fancier than anywhere I've ever lived," she overheard Patrick whisper to Liam as the ferry drew alongside it.

A butler from the estate awaited them on the dock. "Your grandfather would like you to meet him for tea in the gathering room," he said once they had disembarked.

She sent Patrick and Liam a reassuring smile. "My grandfather can be intimidating, but I think you'll find him far more approachable here on the island than when he's in Manhattan."

Liam squared his shoulders and adjusted the jacket of his new suit. "I'm ready," he said, but his face looked like he was about to face a firing squad.

Stonemasons had built a staircase into the side of the cliff and up to the house. There were thirty steps, and she climbed them slowly, mindful of Liam's still-healing injury. Once at the top of the stairs, she tugged on the lapels of Liam's coat to straighten it.

"There," she said, smoothing the fabric across his shoulders. "Don't be intimidated, but please don't trot out any needless Marxist sentiments this morning, okay? The faster you can win my grandfather's blessing, the sooner he can start transferring my father's voting shares to you."

The house was straight ahead of them. It was a sprawling white mansion with gabled dormers, a widow's walk, and plenty of windows facing the sea. Gwen led them to the side entrance, where the screened doorway made its familiar creak as she opened it. She led both men down a hallway to a long room with white wainscoting and a bank of windows overlooking the ocean. The gathering room was a comfortable space with upholstered furniture and exposed wood-beam ceilings.

In contrast to the casual décor, Frederick stood at the far end of the room before the stone fireplace, formally attired in a black morning coat, vest, and tie. His back was straight as a bayonet, and his face was cold as he watched her approach.

"You can dismiss the servants," he said with a flick of his head toward Patrick and Liam.

It felt like a slap in the face, and surely the insult was even worse for Patrick and Liam. They both froze, and Gwen stopped as well. She wouldn't move an inch farther into the room without them.

"Patrick isn't a servant. He's a lawyer."

"Precisely. A servant."

Patrick leaned in. "Gwen, this is a family matter. Perhaps I should go."

"Stay," Liam said.

"And that man definitely isn't welcome," Frederick said with a pointed glance at Liam. "I won't welcome a union trouble-maker in my home."

Liam's eyes glinted with challenge. "How about welcoming me into your boardroom?"

"Liam, stop," she warned. When Liam was nervous, he turned belligerent, which wasn't the right way to deal with her grandfather.

"Let him talk," Frederick ordered, stepping closer and watching Liam carefully. "Exactly what are you saying?"

"I'm saying that I am entitled to a ten-percent voting share in the Blackstone Bank."

Her grandfather was impossible to read as he folded his arms across his chest. "And why is that?" he asked softly.

"I could take off my shoe and show you the bottom of my right foot. Gwen said that would mean something to you."

Frederick glanced at her, his face still inscrutable. "True?" he asked, the single word containing an ocean of hope.

"True."

A smile tugged one side of Frederick's mouth but vanished quickly. He looked at Liam and pointed to a chair. "Show me."

Frederick was once again a hard man of business as he walked to the fireplace, bracing a hand against the mantel, but he lowered his head and closed his eyes as if in prayer.

Liam wiggled out of his new oxford shoe and reached down to tug off the sock, then presented his bare foot on the coffee table.

Frederick crossed the distance to stand on the opposite side of the coffee table. His face was inscrutable as he inspected the old scar on the bottom of Liam's foot.

The examination didn't take long. After five seconds, he straightened, crossed to a chair, and lowered himself into it. His hands were shaking. "Well, well, well," he said, showing neither dismay nor delight. "This changes things."

Liam lowered his foot and tugged his sock back on. "I agree."

"I trust this marks the end of your flirtation with revolutionary nonsense," Frederick said. "We have no use for unions or anarchists in this home. But I would welcome Theodore's son."

Liam still looked hesitant. "You'll accept me, then?"

"As my grandson? Yes." Frederick turned to stare out at the sea, taking a few ragged breaths as a range of emotions flashed across his face, but when he turned to Liam again, he was entirely composed. "As for accepting you as a partner in the boardroom, that remains to be seen. Now, tell me about yourself."

Gwen held her breath. Liam could be such a wild card, but for once he comported himself with restraint. Over the next hour he recounted how he came to be a part of the Malone family, then followed in Crocket Malone's footsteps to become a welder and then a union leader in the steel industry.

"This is going to shake things up," Frederick said once Liam finished his story. "I suppose you will want half of everything."

"All I really want are my father's voting shares," Liam said.

"For now, that is out of the question. Only men fluent in corporate finance and the leveraging of investments can attain a position on the board."

"Gwen said the trust awards bank shares to the oldest male heir."

"It does," Frederick said. "And if that male heir was an infant, do you think we would invite him to the table? Of course

208

not. It won't happen until he has a college education and years of tutelage in the banking industry. Right now you are something of an embarrassment to the family."

She stood. "That's not fair."

"But it's the truth. Look at him, Gwen! His entire life has been spent working with his hands, not his brain. He has no understanding of the banking industry, no connections in the world of finance, and he speaks like a vulgarian."

Liam sat motionless in his chair, appearing to shrink beneath the barrage of insults, and her grandfather's tone softened a bit.

"I'll hire a tutor for you. Go to San Francisco or Toronto or London . . . anywhere but here. I'll find you a position in a West Coast bank where you can learn the ropes in anonymity. In five or ten years, you might be ready to join the board at Blackstone."

"And will the U.S. Steel vote wait five or ten years until I'm on the board?"

Frederick shook his head. "That deal is going to be finalized in July."

"Then I want to be on the board in July. I don't want Oscar Blackstone having control over what's rightfully mine. The fate of twenty thousand workers hangs in the balance, and I want the power to vote in their best interests."

Frederick began pacing the floor, his face drawn in concentration, but with a hint of secret delight too. "Your arrival will put a burr under Oscar's saddle, but that might be a good thing. Nothing inspires a man to fight more than a little competition, and I think you can give it to him, but you'll need to control it. Funnel your passion toward the workers if you want. Perhaps in a few years we can put you on the board."

Gwen stood. "But for today, will you welcome Liam into the family as your grandson?"

"I will. Some of the others might not."

Relief trickled through her. Frederick's acknowledgment was Liam's best protection against a future attack. Few people paid attention if an anonymous steelworker met with foul play, but such wouldn't be the case for a Blackstone.

"Liam is frail," she said to her grandfather. "Three weeks ago, a trio of men showed up at his house and stabbed him in the belly. If Patrick hadn't been there, they would have killed him."

She watched her grandfather carefully. She wasn't skilled at sniffing out deception, but Frederick's complexion turned pale, and he seemed genuinely shocked. He stopped pacing to take a seat.

"Last week someone tried to frame Liam and Patrick for theft from a church," she continued. "We suspect someone knows who Liam is, and they are trying to eliminate him before he gets any closer to our family."

"And if they can't kill Liam, they will ruin his reputation," Patrick said. "They can take me down in the process. I can't be a lawyer if I'm convicted of theft."

"There's a warrant out for our arrest," Liam added. "Whoever sent those thugs after me hasn't given up, and the odds are that person's last name is Blackstone."

Gwen cringed at the blunt accusation, but Frederick was impassive as he digested the news. His gaze flitted between Patrick and Liam, sizing up each man in his cold, methodical way.

"We saw the resemblance between Liam and Theodore when we were in the courtroom," Frederick said. "We commissioned private detectives to look into his past. I know about his history of brawling." He turned his attention to Liam. "I know you were arrested for a fistfight with the son of a mill owner."

"The guy insulted my mother," Liam said with a shrug.

Frederick continued. "I know you bet on baseball games and that you once got rough with someone who failed to pay what he owed. You are not a man without enemies."

"There's a big difference between swinging a fist and swinging a knife," Liam said. "Oscar Blackstone is the person who stands to lose the most if I show up on the scene."

Frederick shook his head. "Oscar doesn't need your shares to control the bank. I've got thirty percent, and he has twenty percent. Even if you take half of that, the other partners are loyal to Oscar. They move in lockstep behind him. He has more influence than anyone else, including me. If someone in our family tried to take Liam out of succession, it wasn't Oscar."

Frederick stood. "We mustn't get overly concerned about something that is probably rooted in old Pittsburgh rivalries. We are well protected on this island, and I won't permit anyone I don't personally know onto the estate. Everyone will be gathering next week for the annual reunion and lobster bake, and I will use the gathering to welcome my grandson back into the family."

Gwen beamed at her grandfather, then at Patrick.

"You see?" she said. Maybe it wouldn't be easy, but in time, the rest of her family would be as welcoming to Liam and Patrick as her grandfather had been.

27

*D*inner was a casual affair on the flagstone patio of Frederick Blackstone's island mansion, but Patrick didn't think any meal served by uniformed servants was casual. At least Frederick had shed his formal vest and coat in favor of a simple white shirt as they dined. The old man seemed relaxed as he asked Liam a series of congenial questions, nodding in warm approval and allowing Liam plenty of time to answer.

It wasn't until the last course that Patrick realized Frederick had been neatly and efficiently cutting Liam down to size throughout dinner. Frederick was so elegant as he did it that Liam didn't even realize what was happening. The young welder was simply too forthright to spot Frederick's manipulation.

"Tell me about your work in the Philadelphia shipyards," Frederick said as he stirred cream into his coffee. "I believe that's where Vanderbilt's latest steamship with the new screw-propulsion system was built. Did you take part in that?"

"I did!" Liam said proudly. "It was a monster of a job, and the engineers were looking over our shoulder during the entire installation, but it was a thing of beauty."

Patrick had difficulty following the conversation as Liam spoke of how a steamship was welded together, using terms like bearing systems, impeller blades, and plenty of other shipbuilding jargon. He and Gwen both sat in silence during the discussion, but Frederick easily kept apace, and Liam loved every moment.

"Last year I worked on a triple-expansion steam engine," he said. "I hear it's the fastest thing on the water, and rumor among the crew is that there will be a quadruple engine soon."

"Don't bet on it," Frederick said. "The British launched a new turbine design last year with the HMS *Viper*. It's got four steam shafts and two propellers. It's the fastest warship ever built, and it marks a revolution in steamship design. Things will get interesting in the next few years, which is why Vanderbilt is slowing production of his current design."

Liam stared at Frederick in reluctant admiration. "How do you know all this stuff?"

"It's my business to know," the old man said. "I invest millions in ship construction every year. Before investing in a new ship, I must understand the design of the ship and all its competitors. I have to be conversant in every aspect of shipbuilding, but my bank also invests in railroads, port construction, skyscrapers, and the mining industry. Each project requires intimate knowledge of the industry before I can make an informed decision. Do you understand what I'm saying?"

"Yeah," Liam said. "It means you spend a lot of time hitting the books."

Frederick shook his head. "I have investment analysts who hit the books for me, but I must understand each report they submit to me. After reading their analysis, I tour the factories, meet with the company owners, and study the current market economy. Then I decide if our limited capital is better invested in Vanderbilt's latest ship or in Rockefeller's new oil wells in Texas."

"Or buying up Carnegie Steel," Liam added.

"Precisely," Frederick said. "Right now, you are obsessed with how the steel merger will impact the workers. Your concern is not misplaced, but it's narrow. You don't have the perspective to exercise your voting shares. Most of our shareholders assign their votes to Oscar or myself because acquiring this level of industry knowledge is a daunting task. I want you to be able to converse as easily about railroads or cotton mills as you just did about ship building. I want you to be able to speak about foreign wars, international tariffs, and how the weather patterns affect crop revenues. Until you can do that, you have no business controlling voting shares."

Patrick folded his arms across his chest. This all sounded like a clever strategy to keep Liam off the board forever.

"I can learn," Liam said, but he looked uncertain as he shifted in his chair.

"Don't be discouraged," Frederick said. "I can arrange for you to start training with our business analysts on the third floor. Spend a few months in each department. Read the newspapers every day. In the meantime, work on your croquet. It's likely to be the primary activity once the rest of the family arrives. Watch out for Oscar's wife. Poppy takes her croquet more seriously than the Duke of Wellington staring down Napoleon at Waterloo."

Gwen chimed in with a funny story about an epic croquet game from last summer, but Patrick was too distracted to pay attention. Frederick had been masterful in undermining Liam's confidence and setting the stage to make it impossible for Liam to vote on banking affairs for years to come.

That meant the steel merger would face no opposition. And that Blackstone College wouldn't have any allies on the board. Oscar's one-year extension on their funding needed to be made permanent, which meant Patrick needed to help Liam get his voting shares. Banks were governed by operating agreements that were as binding as any public law. It would be a roadmap for how to get Liam on the board.

The evening air grew chilly, and servants began clearing the table. Gwen and Liam retreated inside, but Patrick followed Frederick into the garden.

"Can I have a word, sir?"

The older man hesitated for only a moment before gesturing

to a crushed-oyster-shell path heading toward the rose garden. "I could use a smoke," Frederick said, drawing a cigar from his suit pocket. "You?"

"No, thank you."

The scratch of the match and the quick scent of sulfur prickled Patrick's nose as he waited for Frederick to light his cigar, and then they set off for the rose garden.

There was no point in beating around the bush. "I would like to see the operating agreement that governs the bank," Patrick said.

Frederick blew a puff of smoke into the air. "It makes for dull reading. Ask me what you want to know, and I'll tell you."

"I would like to know every word in that agreement," Patrick replied. "A copy of the document would be the most efficient means of getting it."

"Are you acting as Liam's attorney?"

"For the time being. When can I see the operating agreement?"

"There is no hope of elevating an uneducated and politically radical man onto the board before next month's meeting. It's going to take years before he will be ready to exercise his voting rights, so why the urgency?"

Patrick deliberately emulated Frederick's congenial tone. "The good friars at Saint Boniface taught me to pay attention to the letter of the law, and that operating agreement is the Holy Bible of the Blackstone Bank."

Frederick smiled and nodded. "And what would the good friars say about a man who was repeatedly seen on a fire escape, embracing my granddaughter under the cover of darkness?"

It was a salvo Patrick hadn't expected, but it only derailed him for a moment. "They would say not to let your opponent change the subject. Liam is Theodore Blackstone's only male heir, meaning he is entitled to see the official operating agreement for Blackstone Bank."

"I shall arrange for a copy to be delivered immediately," Frederick said simply. "Now, about Gwen. I want your assurance that the incidents on the fire escape are a thing of the past."

Heat engulfed every limb of Patrick's body. He was used to parents throwing their daughters at him, not warning him away. Then again, he'd never reached above his station before. A pedigreed man like Frederick Blackstone was probably appalled that an Irish bogtrotter had dared touch his granddaughter. Gwen was a twenty-nine-year-old widow, not a green schoolgirl needing protection.

"What Gwen and I have is very special. I know the gulf between us is bigger than the Grand Canyon, but I will never do anything to hurt her."

"She will be hurt if she openly associates with a man like you."

The anger simmering inside Patrick burned brighter, but he tamped it down because Frederick was correct.

The older man continued talking. "Next week, dozens of relatives will descend on this house to welcome William back into the fold. There will be maiden aunts, nieces, nephews, and second cousins. Most of them spend their lives swanning around town to amuse themselves with empty pleasures and idle gossip. There are a few sharks among them, but most are mere plankton. My son Oscar is a shark, but don't overlook the plankton. They can poison the water if they choose and mustn't be underestimated."

Patrick nodded. "Aside from Oscar, do any of these people have voting shares?"

"The men related to me by blood each have one or two percent. All combined, it adds up to twenty-five percent, but they let Oscar vote their shares. They have no experience in banking and know he acts in a way to earn the most money."

"Who owns the rest?"

Frederick waved his hands. "People scattered all over the world. A monastery in Spain, a count in Russia. A few other people. They either telegraph their votes to us or authorize Oscar to vote their shares by proxy."

That remaining twenty-five percent was powerful, and perhaps Patrick could find a way to use it to save Gwen's college.

Patrick shared a bedroom with Liam on the top floor of the island mansion. It was painted in shades of pale gray and white, with a window overlooking the ocean. He woke to the sound of the surf rolling ashore and a cry of gulls in the distance.

He rolled over to see Liam silhouetted before the window, looking out to sea with a dismal expression. Outside, a haze of fog hovered over the ocean and blanketed the sky, the swirling white mists blurring the sunlight that tried to break through.

Patrick shrugged into a shirt and padded across the wooden floor to see what held Liam's attention down on the beach and was surprised to see that Gwen was already outside. Her bare feet left prints in the sand as she walked alone on the shore.

"Do you think she's really going to give me the money?" Liam asked. His voice was soft and worried, but there was no doubt in Patrick's mind about Gwen's intentions.

"She will."

Liam sagged a little. "Good," he whispered. "I could use it."

The statement was a surprise. So far Liam had seemed interested only in the power that came with the Blackstone name, not the money. "Why?"

Instead of answering, Liam drifted to a chair tucked beneath the eaves. He looked sick and exhausted as he lowered himself into it, staring out at the fog.

When he spoke, his voice was as bleak as the hazy sky. "Do you promise not to tell anyone? Not to breathe a word of it to a single soul?"

Patrick was trained as a priest and a lawyer. He knew how to keep a secret. "I won't tell anyone."

For a while Liam didn't say anything. He just kept clenching and unclenching his fists. "I don't know what to do about my ma. I told her that I'd love her no matter what, but the more I think about what she did . . ." His voice trailed off, and his face darkened as he rubbed his jaw. "When I was a kid, I never went a week without getting punched. My dad once knocked out two of my molars, and he thought it was funny. My ma was there for all of it. She sometimes tried to make things better, but she was usually too afraid to do anything. She could have gotten me out of there. She could have told someone who I was. The more I think about what she did, the more I hate her for it. I feel guilty, but there it is."

Liam glanced out the window, where Gwen was heading back to the house. "I'm jealous of her," he said. "When she thinks of her mother, she remembers soft hugs and orange blossoms." He gave a twisted laugh but looked almost ready to weep. "Can you believe it? Orange blossoms! My memories of being a kid are full of slamming doors and swinging fists and the taste of blood in my mouth."

The whispery sound of water rolling ashore was in stark contrast to Liam's ragged breathing. It would be best for his wounds to be lanced and purged, so Patrick said nothing and waited as Liam struggled with a lifetime of bitter memories.

"At least when Mick was around, things weren't so bad," Liam finally said. "Mick was always kind of funny and could talk Crocket out of a bad mood, but Ma couldn't stand up to either one of them. She let me grow up in that house even though she knew the truth."

Liam looked around, gesturing to the elegant furnishings and vaulted ceiling of the spacious bedroom. "And now I've wandered into all this. Money and power and a cozy life. How am I supposed to sleep at night, knowing my mother is still in that grubby row house with a leaky roof? I love her, but I'm mad at her too. I want to buy her a decent house, give her the key, and then walk out of her life forever. The thought of seeing her again and pretending that everything is forgiven is more than I can stand, and I hate, hate, *hate* feeling this way."

Patrick thought carefully before responding. Liam wouldn't be normal if he wasn't struggling with anger and betrayal in light of everything that had happened to him.

"It's not a sin to be angry. It's how you respond to it that matters," he said. "Liam, you just learned the truth three weeks ago. Take some time to come to grips with things before you cut your mother out of your life. She had to live with the same monster who terrorized you. Buy her a house if it will make you feel better—I can help with the legal part of that—but quit beating yourself up because you're angry. You've got a right to be mad, but I want you to know that God was with you through it all, even when you couldn't see him. And he's here now, so don't do anything stupid like vowing to cut your mother out of your life because she had human failings, okay?"

Liam gave a short, bitter laugh, but when he spoke again, there was a note of humor in his voice. "How come you always know the right things to say?"

"It's a gift," Patrick said casually. "You should listen to me more often."

Liam scrubbed a hand across his face as though to banish the old memories, and a spark of energy lit his eyes. "Yeah, okay. Let's head downstairs and figure out how we're going to claw my ten percent back from Oscar Blackstone."

Patrick nodded but silently prayed Liam had heard his counsel, because the sort of bitterness he'd expressed this morning could rise up to strangle a man if he didn't learn to master it.

28

Over the next week, Gwen watched as Liam's confidence rose and fell with breathtaking speed. One moment he seemed brash and ready to confront the world, and the next Frederick cleanly cut him down to size, reminding Liam of all the ways he was inexperienced in the world. During those times, Liam's confidence evaporated, and he retreated inside himself, biting his nails and refusing to look anyone in the eye.

The real pressure wouldn't begin until the rest of the family arrived next week. Frederick sent messages to everyone, confirming that the long-lost William Blackstone had been found. As patriarch of the family, Frederick insisted that everyone attend the annual summer gathering to officially welcome his grandson back into the fold.

The night before the family was due to arrive, Frederick coached Liam in the finer points of croquet. The Blackstones were zealous about croquet, and if Liam could participate, it would help ease his entry into the family.

Gwen had hoped Patrick would join them, but a lengthy document from town had arrived this afternoon, and he retreated to his bedroom to read it. Apparently, it was the bank's operating agreement, which contained the roadmap for how to get Liam appointed to the board.

She couldn't imagine anything more tedious than reading

forty pages of small-print legal verbiage and remained outside in the cool of the summer evening. The front lawn was kept meticulously clipped and groomed in order to host croquet matches, and she settled onto the porch swing to watch Frederick teach Liam.

It wasn't going well.

"You're not concentrating," Frederick groused as Liam rushed a shot and the ball skipped into the air and landed off the green.

"That's because I'd rather work on banking lessons instead of rich-people games," Liam said. "The July vote is coming up, and I want to be ready."

Frederick eyed the green before tapping his ball through the wicket. "Why do you so desperately want to be at that vote?"

"To vote against the U.S. Steel merger."

"Even though you have no chance of stopping it?"

"Even though," Liam affirmed. "I may not win, but I intend to go down fighting. There's valor in fighting all the way to the end."

Frederick straightened, casually leaning on the croquet mallet as he eyed Liam. All Gwen's senses went on alert. When her grandfather struck a deliberately casual pose like that, he was preparing to strike.

"And what if I told you I intend to use my thirty-percent stake to vote against the merger?"

Gwen's jaw dropped, but Liam looked guarded and suspicious. "Why would you do that?"

Frederick walked over to his ball, positioned himself, and tapped it toward the next wicket.

"Perhaps because I know how big a risk it is. Steel is a valuable commodity, but what if the market turns? Even a bank as large as ours is not impervious to the whims of the market, and investing most of our capital in a single corporation is risky. Natalia is leery of the deal, and so am I."

A door gently closed behind her, and Patrick joined her on the porch with a thick legal document in his hand. His expression was alert with tentative hope.

"Good news?" she asked.

"I don't know," he whispered. "Maybe." He turned his attention to Frederick as her grandfather continued speaking.

"Oscar believes this is the most profitable business deal of the century, and he may be right." Frederick moved his ball through the course with ease as he tapped it with a gentle *snick*. "Then again, maybe not. The unions are hostile, which adds another element of risk."

"You got that right," Liam said. "I've talked to hundreds of men, and not one of them—"

Frederick straightened and sent Liam a swift warning glare. "Another rule to follow, my boy. When you sense an opponent is swaying in your direction, it is best to shut up and listen. Understood?"

Liam immediately conceded. "Yes, sir."

Gwen could scarcely believe her ears. Was Frederick reconsidering his vote? She didn't care about steel one way or the other, but if her grandfather was willing to split with Oscar on this, perhaps he'd reconsider funding for the college as well. Beside her, Patrick reached for her hand and squeezed. They both held their breaths, listening to the conversation on the lawn.

"I am not as heartless as the world believes," Frederick continued. "I care about the people who work in Blackstone-financed mills and factories. I'm not convinced their rights can be safeguarded in a massive corporate conglomeration headquartered a thousand miles from the mills where people work." He straightened and met Liam's gaze. "Your father would have voted against this merger. I am skeptical about investing too much of our capital into a single corporation, but your father would have objected for humanitarian reasons. How can a company protect a far-off workforce the management never looks in the face? Theodore was a compassionate man, far too gentle for the world of finance. I will vote against the merger in his honor."

Liam dropped his croquet mallet and let out a mighty whoop of joy, but Frederick hadn't stopped speaking.

"Don't get overly excited," Frederick cautioned. "Switching

my vote is purely symbolic. Oscar has unanimity among the other shareholders, and they will endorse the merger. The vote will be seventy to thirty to support the merger."

"Not necessarily," Patrick said, heading down the porch stairs and holding up the legal document. "I've reviewed the operating agreement. You have the power to assign Theodore's shares to Liam immediately. It doesn't require a shareholder majority to agree. As senior partner, you can do it right now."

Liam looked thunderstruck. He wandered to a garden bench and sat, staring in amazement at Frederick. "Is that true?" he asked, a world of hope in his voice.

Frederick didn't break Patrick's gaze, but he nodded in concession. "Congratulations on finding that codicil. I didn't think you'd be able to spot it."

"Scrappy lawyers are good at digging," Patrick said. "And if we add Liam's ten percent to yours, the vote is sixty to forty."

"Which isn't enough to stop the merger," Frederick pointed out.

"Who says?" Liam demanded. "It shouldn't be hard to scrounge up a few people who want to side with the workers of the world."

Frederick's smile was equal parts cynical and condescending. "No one else in this family will vote against Oscar. Their livelihoods depend on him, and they will vote as he instructs them. The shareholders will earn healthy dividends as soon as the company is formed."

Liam still looked exhilarated. "I don't give up easily."

"Good," Frederick said. "You're going to need that fire in the coming years."

"I'm going to need that fire in the coming *weeks*," Liam corrected. "I intend to scrounge up another ten percent of the votes to stop the merger."

A calculating look came over Frederick's face. He walked with slow, careful steps to the cluster of chairs near Liam and took a seat. He retrieved a cigar from his breast pocket, lit it, and took a long and deliberate puff, all the while studying Liam.

"I can't figure out who you are," he said. "Have you inherited your father's overly emotional streak, or do you take after Oscar's calculating gamesmanship? Are you a person who is best suited to welding steel, or should you be directing the steel mill? It will be interesting to watch. The entire family will gather here tomorrow. Most of the men have a share or two to their name. Try to persuade them to your side if you wish. I will enjoy watching. But take my advice and don't let anyone know I have switched sides. The first rule of gamesmanship is to keep your cards close to your chest."

"I'd like to see Liam do that while walking around with a ten-percent stake of his own," Patrick said.

"You're dreaming." Frederick's tone was dismissive, but Patrick was not daunted.

"You have a potential new ally," he said with a nod toward Liam. "Oscar has been gathering allies to his side for years. You are the most powerful man in the bank, but you still need Oscar's cooperation for everything since the other shareholders all believe he has the magic touch. By transferring Theodore's ten percent back to Liam, the two of you will be a force to be reckoned with."

Frederick fired back with his own arguments against assigning the shares to Liam, but Patrick neatly countered every one, and Gwen loved watching him in action. His intensity, his confidence. The way he diced, parried, and sparred reminded Gwen of a warrior, but one who fought with words instead of brawn.

The sun began to set. Servants lit torches and brought food, but Patrick never tired as he fought on Liam's behalf. Each time Frederick scored a point, Patrick shifted and parried again. Pride bloomed in her heart, because her grandfather was seeing Patrick at his finest.

And in the end, Frederick agreed to authorize the transfer of voting shares to Liam.

They moved indoors to sign the paperwork. There was no electricity on the island, and dozens of candles flickered in the gathering room as Patrick drafted an agreement. Her heart swelled with pride as she watched him write out the document, his face tense with concentration, his penmanship precise and sure as he wrote. Even the scratching of his pen sounded like strength and confidence as he crafted the words that would change Liam's life forever.

"I shall send my butler back to the city with the agreement tomorrow morning," Frederick said as he leaned down to sign the papers.

Patrick looked up to catch Gwen's eye, his face flushed with pleasure as she stepped to his side. When his hand closed around hers, it felt like there was nothing in the world they couldn't accomplish.

Patrick was too wound up to sleep after finalizing the agreement. Gwen had looked at him as though he were a hero out of a storybook, and it could keep him fueled for weeks.

Long after the rest of the household turned in for bed, he and Gwen slipped down to the boathouse, where they could be alone. He wanted to savor the sensation of earning her respect and being worthy of her. He held her sheltered against his body as they gazed out at the darkened sea, hints of foamy white crests on the waves as they rolled ashore.

He had to admit that Gwen had been right about coming here. After a few bumpy days, her grandfather had seen beyond Patrick's Irish accent and humble roots and had begun to treat him well. Perhaps not as an equal, but as a man of consequence, and it was enough. Hope surged. There might be a future for him and Gwen after all. For years he'd been struggling to figure out what God wanted of him. He'd rushed toward the church to prove himself, but the priesthood had never been a natural fit. His calling was to serve others through the law, and hopefully through building a large, boisterous, and happy family of his own. He was ready to imagine such a family with Gwen.

"We could live in my house," she said as she snuggled within his arms. "Your mother could have the corner bedroom on the second floor. It has a window overlooking the garden."

"You won't mind having my mother live with us?"

As if reading his mind, Gwen immediately solved the problem of a lack of privacy. "We can build a fire escape on the side of the house where we can be alone."

He smiled against her hair. If he lived to be a hundred, the memories of their stolen hours on his fire escape would remain carved on his soul. Gwen rotated in his arms to kiss him, her arms snaking up high on his shoulders to draw him closer. Temptation for more clawed at him, so he lifted his head to gaze out at the sea. A few lights winked far off on the horizon, catching his interest.

"Is that the ferry coming back?"

Gwen turned to look, then shook her head. "That's the *Black Rose*, my uncle's yacht."

He eyed the yacht looming in the distance. Gwen explained that the *Black Rose* was too big to dock in the boathouse, so Oscar's family would spend the night on the yacht and come ashore tomorrow morning in a small tender boat once there was enough light to navigate.

They both watched the *Black Rose* looming on the horizon, and something deep in Patrick rebelled. Members of Gwen's family would soon descend on the island, and the real test would begin. He doubted the rest of Gwen's family would be as open-minded as Frederick.

"It used to be mine," Gwen said softly, still staring out to sea.

"What used to be yours?"

"The *Black Rose*."

He pulled away, dumbfounded. "You owned that yacht?"

"I inherited it from my father. I held on to it for a while, but Oscar had always wanted it, so I gave it to him."

"Gave? Or sold?" What Gwen did with her fortune wasn't any of his business, but she shrugged and confirmed that she simply gave the yacht to her uncle.

"The expenses are high," she said. "It requires berthing fees and a full-time staff. I was happy to give it to him."

Patrick couldn't afford to keep a yacht like that afloat for a single day, much less casually give it away like a pair of old shoes. It underscored the chasm between her world and his. He prayed they could find a way to bridge that chasm, for the next week would put it to the ultimate test.

29

*G*wen took care in setting up a lovely breakfast on the outdoor terrace. She asked the cook to prepare Uncle Oscar's favorite blueberry muffins and to squeeze plenty of grapefruit juice in deference to Poppy's well-known dislike of orange juice. By midmorning Oscar's family still hadn't arrived from the *Black Rose*, so the men sat down for breakfast without them. Liam put away an impressive amount of scrambled eggs and four of the blueberry muffins, but Patrick seemed ill at ease. He barely touched his breakfast and wouldn't meet her eyes. He'd been unsettled all morning, and it worried her.

They were just finishing breakfast when the others arrived. Poppy led the way, both her hands proudly resting on her large belly. Everybody stood to welcome them, Liam adjusting the cuffs on his new suit. Gwen sent him a reassuring smile for good luck.

"Did you start breakfast without us?" Poppy asked, sounding wounded as she surveyed the table.

"It's ten o'clock, Poppy," Natalia said dryly, but she stared at Liam with open curiosity.

Uncle Oscar was also riveted on Liam as he scrutinized him through his one good eye. "Gwen? I gather introductions are in order."

"Uncle Oscar, Poppy, Natalia . . . this is Liam Malone of Philadelphia. We have confirmed he is indeed William and have accepted him into the family."

"Have we, indeed?" Oscar said skeptically, still peering at Liam.

"Just look at him," Frederick said. "It's like looking at Theodore all over again. He's even got the same cowlick in his hair."

"A little macassar oil will smooth that down," Poppy said.

Liam shook his head. "I tried macassar oil once. I didn't like feeling like an oiled-down seal."

"I shall loan you Oscar's bottle before the rest of the family arrives and mistakes you for a ragamuffin," Poppy said. "Not everyone will be as understanding as we are."

Natalia was the only one to step forward. She brushed Liam's outstretched hand aside and pressed a quick kiss to his cheek. "Welcome back, cousin," she said. "You are very brave to join us for the annual lobster bake and croquet contests. The competition is always fierce."

Uncle Oscar maintained a steely gaze. "If you are indeed William Blackstone, why didn't you come forward years ago?"

Liam didn't back down from Oscar's challenging tone. "Did anyone ever snatch you from your parents when you were a little tyke and hide you in a windowless room where you didn't recognize a single soul? Then call you by a different name while you halfway died from pneumonia? And when you finally started feeling better, the only people you saw were two strangers you were supposed to call Ma and Pa if you wanted to be fed? Did that ever happen to you?"

"No," Oscar said silkily. "That never happened to me."

"It did to me. After a while, I believed them."

Poppy had already seated herself at the table and was filling her plate. "That doesn't make any sense. I remember my childhood perfectly. My earliest memory is when I crawled over the rim of my crib to play with my brother's croquet mallet."

Gwen sensed Liam beginning to bristle and rushed to avoid conflict. Smoothing a welcoming expression on her face, she took Patrick's arm. "Poppy, this is the man I was telling you about the day you showed us the nursery."

Oscar looked suspicious as she performed the introductions, but Patrick behaved perfectly, offering a generous smile, a handshake, and even a friendly wink at Natalia.

"So you're the man who has finally coaxed Gwen out of lonely widowhood," Poppy said. "She always has such an open mind when it comes to standards."

Her tone was gracious, but everyone heard the insult. If Gwen didn't snip Poppy's rudeness quickly, it would run rampant. She kept a serene smile but met Poppy's gaze squarely. "Darling, my open mind is the only way I've been able to tolerate you all these years."

Natalia stifled a laugh, but Oscar changed the subject as he joined his wife at the breakfast table.

"Enough pointless chatter," he said, swiveling his attention to Liam. "Tell me about yourself. I gather you've had an interesting life."

Liam shook his head. "Not until lately. I was just an ordinary welder until last month when someone stabbed me in the gut and turned my life upside down."

"Stabbed?" Poppy gasped. "Like with a knife?"

"Like with a knife," Liam confirmed. "We still haven't figured out who did it, but I'm on the lookout, because you never know what sort of scoundrels are lurking nearby."

"Who on earth would do such a thing?" Poppy asked, her voice filled with appalled wonder.

Liam swiveled his gaze to Oscar. "I don't know. The only enemy I've ever had was Ira Horowitz. I stole his girl in the eighth grade, and he put tacks on my chair to get back at me. That was twenty years ago. Then last month, three guys show up at my door and try to slice up my liver. Weird."

Gwen held her breath, watching Oscar carefully. He showed no sign of a guilty conscience as he adjusted the patch over his eye. "I had someone lob a bomb at me when I was leaving the bank one evening," he said calmly. "Powerful men often make enemies."

"Except last month I wasn't a powerful man, I was just an ordinary welder from Philly."

Then Oscar calmly said the last thing Gwen expected. "Gwen is the only one who'd stand to gain by your death," he said casually. "Gwen, did you have anything to do with the shameful assault on Mr. Malone?"

"I did not!"

"It must have been the eighth-grade romantic rival," Oscar said, but Liam wouldn't let the topic drop.

"I think you're wrong about Gwen being the only one who'd lose anything by my showing back up on the scene. Something about half your voting shares being up for grabs? And it might affect the merger with Carnegie Steel?"

Natalia choked on her muffin. It took a few moments to clear her throat, and she took a long drink of water before slamming her glass down to glare at her grandfather. "Are you going to let him have those shares?" she demanded. "A man who shows up out of the blue? We don't know the first thing about Liam Malone other than that he is a *man*. At least I would know what to do with those votes. I've earned the right to have a say in the bank."

"That's not how the game is played," Frederick said.

"Yes, I know," Natalia snapped. "If Poppy produces the golden male child, the newborn will leapfrog right past me into a top place at the bank."

"He won't leapfrog past *me*," Liam said. "Half of Oscar's shares came from my father, and I want them back."

"Liam, have you learned nothing since you've been here?" Frederick said from the head of the table. "You're getting ahead of yourself."

"Indeed," Oscar said. "Even if you got those shares, it won't make any difference. I will have unanimous consent from the rest of the shareholders to support the merger, so your ten percent won't matter."

Natalia still seemed annoyed. Gwen had never had any interest in the bank, but Natalia loved it. Watching Liam or a newborn child have the doors opened to them just because they were male must be galling.

Natalia looked at Frederick. "Is he right? Are you still firm in your decision to support the steel merger?"

Tension mounted as Frederick met her question with a gleam in his eye that seemed unnervingly ominous. "The chess pieces are moving," he said. "The world is changing. Power is shifting. I will be very interested to see what happens next."

Patrick sat on the back porch of the house with Gwen and Liam, watching more members of the Blackstone family disembark from various yachts and ferries all afternoon. Liam held a pair of binoculars to his face while Gwen provided insight into each group of people heading up from the boathouse.

"That's Bertie," she said, nodding to a portly man with a huge walrus mustache. "Don't mention golf, or he will talk your ear off, but he is hysterically funny. He can burp 'The Star-Spangled Banner.'"

"Does he have a job?" Patrick asked.

Gwen thought for a moment. "I don't think so. Neither does his son, Chester, who spends most of his time at the horse races."

The sea breeze carried laughter up the cliffside, making Patrick uneasy. He had nothing in common with these well-heeled people of leisure. Ladies with parasols strolled across the lawn while clusters of men smoked cigars. They were all dressed in white! Patrick had never owned a white suit in his life. Such an impractical garment wasn't part of a working-man's wardrobe.

This was awful. He was underdressed and out of place. Everything was so much easier when he and Gwen were on the fire escape, but if they were to have a future, this was the family he would join. He needed to see if he could get along with them. He returned to listening to Gwen point out the new arrivals as they disembarked from the ferry.

"The little girl in the pink dress is Penelope-Arabella. She plays the harp and has a pet turtle. And there's my cousin Edwin!" Gwen pointed to a slim young man wearing a white suit and a straw boater hat. He stood out from the others because of the cast on one leg, but he hobbled along with the help of a cane. Gwen proclaimed Edwin the most interesting of all her cousins, a man who traveled the world collecting rare antiques.

"After Edwin's last trip, he showed me a jade funeral urn," she said. "It's two thousand years old and very rare."

It was hard to keep these family members straight, especially all the elderly women. Frederick had five sisters, which accounted for the fragmentation of shares among their sons and grandsons, while Frederick's only direct male heir, Oscar, had accumulated a disproportionate share.

"I guess there's no more avoiding it," Liam muttered as he stood, looking overly formal in the dark suit Gwen had insisted on buying him. He looked like he'd rather have a tooth pulled than meet the people heading toward them, but Gwen was serene as she performed the introductions.

"Look who has decided to join us for the lobster bake this year," she teased, causing some polite laughter to ripple through the crowd.

Gwen stuck close to Liam as she introduced him to family members, all of them bursting with curiosity about the return of the missing heir. Some appeared fascinated, others skeptical. All were polite because of Frederick's acceptance of Liam as his grandson, and no one was ready to mount an outright challenge this early in the game.

Patrick stood a few yards away, hands fisted at his sides as he scrutinized the family members. Despite Frederick's skepticism, one of these people might be responsible for the assault on Liam. Patrick doubted anyone would try something in this public gathering, but he was on edge.

The gaggle of great-aunts were impossible to tell apart. They all wore white gowns and had their gray hair in identical buns mounded atop their heads. All had wrinkled faces and a complete lack of decorum as they swooped down on Liam.

"Good heavens, he does look like poor Theo, doesn't he, Blanche?"

Aunt Martha, the one Gwen adored, chimed in next. "You used to drool like a spigot," she told Liam. "Your poor mother needed to carry a second set of clothes for you. It looks like you've finally managed to contain it." She reached up to pinch Liam's cheek.

Aunt Helen was even worse. "Do you remember the time you escaped from your bath and came tearing outside during the annual picnic for the bank employees?" she asked with a cackling laugh. "You were buck naked, streaking through the front lawn in front of everyone. Do you remember that?"

"No, ma'am," Liam said.

"We do," Aunt Helen roared. "What about the time you jammed a snail up your nose? Your poor mother! She had to summon the doctor to get it out."

All these relatives vied to dominate Liam's attention, and he wasn't a skilled conversationalist. Gwen was tireless as she stood beside him, providing introductions and smoothing awkward lulls in the conversation.

Someone tugged on Patrick's elbow, and he looked down to see a young girl in a pink dress. She couldn't be more than eight or nine years old.

"Can you get me an ice cream cone?" she asked.

She'd probably mistaken him for a servant because he wasn't dressed like the other men. Patrick smiled anyway and hunkered down so he could be on eye-level with her. "I don't know if there's any ice cream. What's your name?"

"Penelope-Arabella."

"That's a pretty name. Do people call you Penny?"

Her face soured, and her voice brimmed with scorn. "I'm named after a woman who sewed two hundred scarves for soldiers during the American Revolution. I don't think asking someone to say my complete name is asking too much."

Gwen overheard the comment and rushed to the rescue. "Darling, the cook made strawberry shortcake for the children and set it on the back terrace. Would you like some?"

Penelope-Arabella dropped the snotty attitude and tore across the lawn to join the other children who swarmed around the dessert table. Gwen sent Patrick an apologetic glance for the girl's tone, then continued chatting with the elderly aunts.

Heat pounded down, and Patrick's attention wandered over the dozens of people on the terrace. The well-dressed people of leisure mingled with soft laughter and genteel greetings. Maybe the way they ignored him was to be expected. They hadn't seen each other in a while and might not have noticed the stranger in their midst.

There were two tiers of flagstone terraces built into the cliff-side that descended toward the shore. An elegant white gazebo stood on the far side of the upper terrace where the headwaiter conferred with Uncle Oscar, their heads together as they spoke. Oscar's face was grim, his mouth a hard line as he listened to whatever the waiter told him.

Oscar looked up and caught Patrick staring. The older man's eyes hardened as he began stalking straight toward them, his face darkened in anger.

"Good heavens, Oscar," Aunt Helen said. "You look like you just swallowed a wasp."

Oscar ignored the older woman and glared at Liam. "What's this I hear about Frederick's butler carrying a legal agreement to the bank this morning?"

"That's right," Liam said, but Patrick intervened, hoping to stop the younger man from saying anything more. Why couldn't Liam ever control himself?

"Perhaps we can speak about it later in private," Patrick suggested to Oscar, but Liam cut him off.

"Everyone is going to learn about it eventually." Liam turned back to Oscar. "You may as well know that Frederick has assigned Theodore's votes in the bank's business back to me."

An audible gasp could be heard from the aunts and other

assorted cousins gathered around. Natalia looked furious, but Oscar's face showed no emotion other than the clenching of his jaw.

"Why on earth would Frederick do such a thing?" one of the aunts asked.

"Because those votes are rightfully mine," Liam said. "Patrick found the rule buried in the bank's operating agreement that lets me have those votes back, and Frederick agreed."

Oscar's contempt was ferocious. "He's doing it because he's *using* you. He'll have you in his back pocket, which means he's managed to increase his control in the bank from thirty to forty percent."

Patrick stepped in before Liam could retaliate. Liam's impulses could flash into a conflagration if not controlled. Patrick strove for a calm voice. "Your father transferred the shares in a legal fashion. Liam is under no obligation to parrot Frederick's vote."

Oscar turned his ire on Patrick. "Liam is my father's pawn, but you're worse. You're just a paid lackey. If Frederick ordered you to go polish his shoes, you'd scurry to do so."

Patrick blanched, but before he could respond, Liam drew his fist back to throw a punch at Oscar's jaw.

With a lightning-fast reflex, Patrick stuck his hand out to intercept the punch. Pain shot up his arm because Liam's fist had hit his bad hand and barely healed fingers. He howled, dizzy with pain, and curled over his hand.

"You broke my fingers again, Liam," he managed to choke out.

The old aunts clucked in horror, and Liam looked aghast.

Gwen swooped in to hover over him. "Should we send for a doctor?" she asked in a panicked voice.

Patrick's vision cleared, and the pain began fading. He had to hold this together. He'd taken punches before and knew how to handle pain. Liam's punch had landed in the center of his palm, and despite the quick rush of agony, his fingers would probably be okay. He managed to straighten his spine and cast a surly look at Oscar, who had the grace to look mortified after being saved from a well-deserved decking by a man he despised.

"I'm okay," he said, still glaring at Oscar.

Liam looked ready to keel over in regret. "I'm sorry, Patrick! I don't mind if you want to punch my lights out for that."

Patrick swallowed back a sigh. "Let's all lower the temperature, okay?"

Oscar's insult was forgotten as a servant went to get ice for his hand and the old aunts started fussing over him. One of them guided him to a wicker chair, and Bertie praised his quick reflexes. Oscar suddenly decided to fetch a glass of punch on the lower terrace.

Patrick watched him go, silently stewing. He'd known he would have to endure some slings and arrows on his road to winning Gwen, but Oscar's unprovoked insult was a surprise. He thought about it all during the preparations for lunch as servants set the picnic tables and brought trays of food down for the family.

Oscar's ridicule was badly done on a number of fronts. It stirred sympathy among the aunts, but most importantly, it strengthened Patrick's resolve to get Liam on the board of the bank to give Oscar some real competition.

Gwen had been mortified by Oscar's attack on Patrick. Most of her cousins hadn't witnessed the incident, but word spread quickly. They cast furtive glances at Patrick and Liam during lunch, but few offered to join them at the table.

It was obvious Gwen needed to do a better job preparing the ground among her family. They didn't need to fall over themselves with love for Patrick, but she wouldn't tolerate outright rudeness.

After lunch, most of the third generation went down to the beach for a round of horseshoes. After settling Liam and Patrick in with her aunt Martha, Gwen headed down to join the cousins. Wind pulled at her hair, and she hiked up her skirt with a single hand while trekking down the steep hillside to the beach.

Her cousin Joshua, a lanky, athletic man who was studying art at Yale, had teamed up with Natalia, while Cousin Mildred instructed her daughter Penelope-Arabella on the proper way to toss the horseshoe. A trio of other cousins awaited their turn, but everyone stopped the moment Gwen approached.

"Gwen, are you *sure* that man is really poor Willy?" Mildred asked. "I imagine there are hundreds of men who have a scar on the bottom of their foot. It shouldn't mean anything."

"He's a dead ringer for Theodore," Natalia pointed out.

"Theodore never scowled like that man does," Mildred said with a critical glance at the upper terrace, where Liam still sat with the aunts. "I can't put my finger on it. He seems so crude. Raw. I don't like the way he walks."

Gwen raised a brow. "With one foot in front of the other?"

"Yes, but he does it crudely. He lumbers, like he is in a hurry. I should think a man of good breeding would walk in a refined manner. He would glide."

"I know how to glide," Penelope-Arabella interjected, but Mildred shot a glare to silence her daughter.

Despite Gwen's intentions to defend Patrick, it seemed Liam was the only person they wanted to discuss.

"How are we going to explain him to the rest of the world?" Mildred asked. "Are we supposed to actually *socialize* with him?"

"I will take the lead in introducing Liam to society," Gwen said. "And I will do so proudly."

"What about the ten percent of the voting shares?" Edwin asked. "Is Frederick really going to let Liam have them? *Ten percent?*"

Joshua shifted in discomfort. "It doesn't seem fair. I've been a member of this family for twenty-one years, and all I've got is one percent."

"Cry me a river of tears," Natalia said. "You dabble in watercolors, but I've been working at the bank for the past ten years, and I don't get a single share."

"Art is every bit as hard as your finance work," Joshua shot back. "Watercolors are the most unforgiving medium in the entire art world. Everyone knows that. And I still don't think it's fair that Liam gets ten percent right off the bat."

"That man is a *welder*," Mildred said in a horrified whisper. "A welder!" She clutched the horseshoe before her chest as though it were armor to protect her from the distasteful word.

Gwen had heard enough and met Mildred's gaze squarely. "Yes, Liam is a welder. He is probably the only person on this island with the know-how to forge that horseshoe you're holding. He and Patrick are both fine, hardworking people who get out of bed every day to earn the clothes on their back. Get used to them."

Her voice had started to shake. A scolding tone wasn't the way to persuade these people, and she drew a breath to steady herself before speaking again.

"In three days, we will have our annual lobster bake. You can ignore those not born into wealth and leisure, or you can open your heart to people who work with their hands and minds to make this world a better place. People who make horseshoes so you can play a game on the beach. People who get up in the middle of the night to bail strangers out of jail. You get to pick who is good enough to socialize with and who you'd rather snub, but I suggest you think carefully and choose wisely."

She whirled away to head back up the cliffside, wondering if she'd helped matters or only dug a deeper hole for Liam and Patrick.

30

The entire family was invited onto Oscar's yacht for a sunset sail. The outing would feature light hors d'oeuvres, fine wines, and a fireworks display from the shore after the sun went down. The yacht was too large to dock in the boathouse, so a small tender boat carried people in groups of twelve to the yacht.

Patrick dreaded it. Gwen might be dismissive of who had commissioned the hit on Liam, but Patrick still believed one of these people might be out to destroy the prodigal Blackstone. What if Liam "fell over" the side of the yacht? Once the sun went down, he could be knocked unconscious and dumped overboard without anyone noticing. A convenient drowning would be the answer to an assassin's prayers.

Two dozen people congregated at the boathouse, awaiting their ride to the *Black Rose*. Patrick stuck close to Liam's side. "Can you swim?" he asked, and Liam nodded.

"Anyone who works in a shipyard knows how to swim."

They boarded the tender and ten minutes later were aboard the *Black Rose*. Patrick gazed about in wonder. The *Black Rose* was two hundred and thirty feet long, with a shiny black hull and a slim gold line painted just above the waterline. It was powered by both sail and steam, and belowdecks had all the amusements to keep a rich man entertained: a player piano, a bowling alley, and a card room.

Liam seemed equally entranced as he admired the rigging, masts, and booms. The teak deck was coated with a sheen of marine spar, and every few yards a brass deck lamp provided a warm glow of illumination in the gathering twilight.

"This feels familiar," Liam said, running his hands along the metal rivets on the gunwale. "The smell of the varnish. The sound my feet make on the wood. I remember being on a boat like this with the wind in my face and feeling very happy."

Gwen's face ached with poignancy. "Our father used to take you out on this very yacht," she said. "He loved sailing and often took you. I wonder if that's what you remember."

The only experience Patrick had with sailing was the cramped third-class cabin he'd shared with nine other immigrants from Ireland. Sunset parties on a yacht were alien to him, and it was hard to know what to do. How was he supposed to make conversation with people who had never worked a day in their lives? A grown man named Wally played cards in the winter and "summered" in Newport. Who used *summered* as a verb?

Patrick snagged a flute of champagne from a passing waiter simply to have something to do with his hands, and Liam did the same. Gwen must have sensed their discomfort.

"Let's go talk to my cousin Edwin," she prompted. "He's the one who travels all over the world to buy and sell antiques. You'll like him."

She performed the introductions, and Edwin proved to be congenial and polite. He even tried to make conversation with Liam, but it was hard, since Edwin didn't even know what *welding* meant.

"It's something like making steel, correct?"

"Not really," Liam said. "I help assemble parts of a ship by welding the steel pieces together."

"Like a carpenter?" Edwin asked.

"Close enough," Liam replied.

The conversation stumbled to an awkward lull, but Edwin soon jumped in to fill the void.

"Say, do either of you like to shoot? There's not much worth hunting on the island, but Frederick has a decent launcher for shooting clay pigeons. We could have a match."

Patrick had never handled a gun in his life, and neither had Liam. Shooting clay pigeons was a pricey sport of rich people, and Patrick had to decline the offer.

Edwin turned his attention to Gwen. "Still at the college?"

"Of course," she said. "I intend to live the rest of my life there, unless Oscar gets fussy with the budget and closes us down."

Edwin looked skeptical. "He wouldn't do that. Poppy loves swanning around campus. So does Oscar."

"He likes earning money more," Gwen replied. "The college costs a lot to operate, and it isn't turning a profit yet."

"That seems a crying shame," Edwin said, although he didn't appear to be at all broken up about it. He glanced around the deck, then waved at another cousin who had just filled his plate at the banquet table. He was one of the third-generation cousins, the art student from Yale. "Joshua, have you heard anything about Oscar yanking funding for the college?"

Joshua popped a caviar-laden cracker into his mouth, then nodded. "Yup," he answered after swallowing. "The college has been a losing proposition for decades. My guess is that the college administrators are either lazy or incompetent. Good riddance, I say." He ate another cracker and headed toward a waiter who had just emerged from the galley with more champagne.

Edwin had the grace to look embarrassed by his cousin, and Patrick took the opportunity to advance the cause of the college.

"What are the odds of anyone here voting to keep Blackstone College alive? Maybe if enough people think it is important, they can make it happen even if Oscar disagrees."

Edwin shook his head. "That's a hopeless cause. Even if you

get Frederick and every other Blackstone to break ranks, you'll never be able to peel off the outside investors."

And those non-family shareholders controlled a quarter of the bank, too much to take for granted. "What can you tell me about the outside investors?" Patrick asked.

"There are a couple of banks in France who together own six percent. Oscar has been keeping the French army afloat with a massive infusion of cash and has their undying loyalty. They'd follow him over a cliff, if need be. Then there is a Russian count who owns four percent, and a Spanish monastery that owns three percent. I think Louise Carnegie owns around seven percent."

Patrick was stunned to learn that a woman had voting shares. "Is she related to Andrew Carnegie?"

"She's his wife," Edwin said. "He gave her the shares as a wedding present, and I think she still owns them. Very odd arrangement, that one."

"How so?"

Edwin seemed pleased to relay the story of how Mrs. Carnegie was decades younger than her husband, who was one of the world's richest men when he married her. She had signed a prenuptial agreement acknowledging his intention to donate his fortune to charity upon his death. The legal agreement set out a number of provisions to ensure she would be well provided for, and a seven-percent stake in the Blackstone Bank was part of that settlement.

Patrick was dumbfounded. "I thought women were precluded from partnership."

"Yeah, tell that to Andrew Carnegie when he wanted to give his wife a nice wedding present," Edwin said. "I think she is required by the operating agreement to let a male partner vote her shares."

Patrick met Gwen's eyes across the deck, and she seemed as surprised as he was. The palms of his hands tingled. He'd read the operating agreement but couldn't remember seeing any such provision. Could he have overlooked it? He'd paid careful attention to the voting requirements and couldn't remember any requirement for a partner to sign away their votes.

Which meant there was a possibility that Mrs. Carnegie and her seven-percent stake might be in play.

Gwen wandered away from the men. News that Mrs. Carnegie had somehow earned a place on the board was strangely painful. If it was possible for a woman to participate in managing the bank, why hadn't the opportunity been offered to Natalia?

Gwen glanced around the deck but didn't see Natalia among the people clustered at the refreshment table or at the shuffleboard game. Natalia rarely socialized with the others, and Gwen finally spotted her curled up on a bench near the stern, absently twirling a long strand of glossy dark hair while engrossed in a book.

Did Natalia know about Mrs. Carnegie? If any woman deserved a place in the boardroom, it was Natalia, who'd spent her childhood at her father's knee, soaking up stories of foreign investments like other children sought candies or toys.

Gwen and Natalia had never been close. There was no particular reason other than a complete and total lack of common interests. Perhaps chatting about the book that had her so engrossed could be a touchstone.

"What are you reading?" Gwen asked as she drew near.

Natalia glanced up from the book. "The history of the Rothschild bank and its influence on the secondary insurance market. It gets better each time I read it."

"Oh." Well, that brought the conversation to a crashing halt.

A hint of amusement lit Natalia's eyes as she clutched the book to her chest. "Did you think I was serious?"

"I did, actually."

"I'm not *that* dull," Natalia teased. "I've only read it once before. It's a slog, but an important work that can't be ignored. Sit down and tell me what I can do for you. You've got a pinched look."

Gwen sat. Actually, she and Natalia did have something in common. They were both women who had been precluded from leadership at the bank from the moment they drew their first breath of air.

"Do you know about Mrs. Carnegie?"

Natalia stiffened. It was barely noticeable other than the way her fingers curled around the rim of the book. "Louise Carnegie? Owner of a seven-percent stake in the Blackstone Bank?"

"You knew about it?"

Natalia nodded. "Andrew Carnegie has a gentleman's agreement with Grandfather. The operating agreement precluding women from the vote is ironclad, but Louise is allowed to assign her votes to whatever partner she chooses to vote on her behalf. So far, she's always given them to my father."

Which meant if Louise could be persuaded to assign them to Liam, they'd be seven percent closer to the magic number to save the college or grant Liam's dearest wish of preventing the creation of U.S. Steel.

"Is there any hope of persuading Mrs. Carnegie to vote against the steel merger?"

Natalia rolled her eyes. "Forget it. The steel merger is her idea."

That was a surprise. Gwen listened as Natalia filled her in on the gossip behind the Carnegie marriage. Andrew Carnegie was much older than his wife, who nagged him incessantly to retire so they could enjoy his remaining years together in Scotland. That couldn't happen unless Andrew cut ties with Carnegie Steel, which was why Louise was so adamant that the company be sold.

But Gwen knew Mrs. Carnegie was an advocate for female education, so she might be persuaded to assign Liam her votes to support the college. If that happened, Gwen still needed to find an additional three percent.

"What can you tell me about a Russian count who owns four percent?" she asked Natalia.

"Count Sokolov. He's completely insane." Natalia said it with a hint of amused frustration, and Gwen suspected she might be teasing again. Strange. She'd never thought of Natalia as someone with a sense of humor.

"Genuinely insane?" she asked.

"More or less. He's irrational and impossible to deal with. He lives somewhere in Siberia, and I've never met him. I think the rural isolation has done him in."

"How does he learn about the issues that are being voted on at the bank?"

"He generally votes as I suggest." She winked at Gwen. "It's almost as though I've got a four-percent stake myself."

"And could you be persuaded to use your influence with the Russian count to vote in favor of continued funding for the college?"

Natalia shook her head. "It's hopeless. My father is ready to stop funding the college after next year, and you'll never be able to gather enough votes to override him."

Gwen glanced pointedly at Liam, who stood on the far side of the deck playing shuffleboard with some of the other men, then back at Natalia.

Natalia set down her book, her face painfully sad. "So Liam is already breaking ranks and voting with Frederick. It doesn't seem fair."

"I agree," Gwen agreed. "The only way you or I can influence the bank is to lean on the men to vote the way we want. I would like your help getting the Russian count to vote in favor of extending the funding for the college. Blackstone College admits women. From the day it opened, we never had antiquated rules that kept women in the kitchen or told them they had no place in a boardroom. Natalia, we need your help keeping the college alive."

Natalia's eyes darkened as she stared at the men on the far side of the yacht. She looked fierce, angry, and determined.

"I think I can get you four percent from the Russian count," she said, and Gwen's heart soared.

Against all odds, she suddenly saw a path to win permanent funding for the college.

31

Long after the others had returned to the house for dinner, Gwen huddled with Patrick, Liam, and Natalia in the boathouse. It was the only place they were guaranteed not to be overheard by the rest of the family.

"It's nine o'clock here, which means it's the crack of dawn in Siberia," Natalia said. "We can contact him right now. Unless we can get his vote, there's no point in trying to recruit Mrs. Carnegie to our side."

"But you think we can really get his vote?" Gwen asked, a world of hope beginning to bloom inside.

Natalia snapped her watch shut. "I told you. He is completely insane, so we can't take anything for granted, and negotiations with him usually drag on for hours. We'd better get moving."

Gwen borrowed her grandfather's wagon to drive the four of them to the tiny fishing village on the other end of the island. It was ten o'clock before they arrived at Smitty's General Store, where the town's only telegraph machine was located. Mr. Smitty lived above the shop and came downstairs to facilitate the message in exchange for a few dollars.

The store smelled of coffee and tobacco. There were a few shelves of canned food, some larger barrels of oats and flour, and a service counter with three stools and a soda fountain.

"Where is the message going?" Mr. Smitty asked as he pulled the cover from the telegraph machine. With his wire spectacles and shiny bald head, he looked too old to still be working, but Gwen was grateful for his ability to operate the telegraph.

"Khabarovsk, Siberia," Natalia said.

Mr. Smitty's eyes widened, and he scratched his head in confusion. "I don't know the operating codes for a place like that."

"I have them." Natalia confidently rattled off a string of numbers. Apparently, she was in frequent enough contact with the count to have memorized the station. Gwen sat on a stool alongside Patrick and Liam as Natalia settled in beside Mr. Smitty on the other side of the counter.

"You'll want to make yourselves comfortable," Natalia said. "By the time Count Sokolov gets to the telegraph station, he likes to chat for a while before agreeing to do business. We're in for a long night."

Natalia dictated the first message to Mr. Smitty, requesting that the count be summoned to the train station office for a business transaction. Gwen purchased bottles of Coca-Cola for everyone, along with a sack of salted peanuts. While they awaited Count Sokolov's return message, Natalia explained how she'd been working with Count Sokolov on the construction of the massive Trans-Siberian Railway. The bank supplied funding for their steel, coal, and food supplies, and the count was in charge of a railroad segment through rural Siberia, meaning he was lonely, isolated, and bored out of his mind.

With the kerosene lanterns turned on high, the interior of the general store felt warm and surprisingly cozy as they waited for the count's response. Liam was completely engrossed in talking baseball with Natalia and Mr. Smitty, a subject guaranteed to bore Gwen into oblivion.

What would Patrick do if she slid her foot along the outside of his ankle? She kicked her shoe off to lift the hem of his trousers with her toe and slide it inside.

Patrick jerked upright but kept staring straight ahead. He pretended not to notice her wandering toes, but a flush quickly stained his cheekbones. She battled a smile as she slid her foot higher. How deliciously fun it was to flirt with her feet as the tedious baseball discussion dragged on.

Count Sokolov must have arrived at the train station to respond to their message, because the telegraph machine suddenly clattered to life with a message from the other side of the world. The message seemed to ramble on and on.

"Is he always this verbose?" Mr. Smitty asked as the ticker tape continued spitting out of the machine.

"Always," Natalia confirmed.

It took ten minutes for Mr. Smitty to translate the rambling string of Morse code and hand it over to Natalia. Her eyes traveled over the message, and then she read it aloud for the others.

Dearest Natalia. Tragic news. I fear I am about to die, for the beds at this outpost are little better than devices of torture. This morning I awoke in agony from a cramp in my neck. I must chop off my head to ease the misery. It is the only solution. I bid you the fondest of farewells. Dimitri.

Natalia looked at Gwen. "You see what I mean? This is typical, and I'm afraid we will need to exchange several such messages before he is willing to get down to business, but I'll try to get him on track quickly."

She dictated her response to Mr. Smitty:

Sir. Please delay the beheading until after I have your vote for the July bank meeting.

It was the first of many exchanges. Count Sokolov's messages were long-winded and deliberately avoided discussions of "tedious business," as he phrased it. He complained of the cold and how difficult it was to keep his violin tuned in the semi-arctic climate. When Natalia asked for his authorization to continue funding Blackstone College, the count wanted to know if the college taught poetry and if they agreed with him that Russian poetry was superior to the bland pablum written by American poets. Then he veered off into a discussion of the fragrant juniper berries he'd found, wondering if he should try his hand at distilling perfume.

Natalia glanced at Gwen. "Can juniper berries be used for perfume?"

"Will it move the conversation along if I provide a recipe for him?"

"He will be over the moon."

The store owner passed his notebook over, and Gwen scribbled a basic procedure for how to distill the essence of the berries and then combine the oil with an infusion of alcohol. Natalia sent the perfume recipe, giving complete credit to her cousin Gwen. She finished the message by trying to veer the conversation back on track.

Please consider it a gesture of goodwill in exchange for your vote to continue funding the college.

Instead of agreeing, Count Sokolov's return message was disheartening.

Gwen. Is that short for Gwendolyn?

When Natalia replied that it was, the telegraph nearly exploded with a cascade of clicks that took Mr. Smitty several minutes to decode. When he finished, Mr. Smitty cleared his throat and looked nervously at Natalia. "I don't think this message is relevant. Perhaps I should throw it away."

He started balling up the scrap of paper, but Patrick grabbed it. "I need to know exactly what Count Sokolov said. Legal negotiations depend on precise wording, even if it seems irrelevant."

Gwen watched Patrick as he read the message, his face darkening. He was scowling when he finally looked up.

"Mr. Smitty is correct," he said, not meeting anyone's eyes. "This is rambling silliness and should be thrown away."

Natalia disagreed and snatched the message to read it aloud.

Natalia. Please tell your cousin that I disapprove of her nickname. Gwendolyn is a beautiful name that is feminine, poetic, and charming. Gwen is a savagely blunt syllable that is devoid of the lyricism of her true name. Why do American women do this? Life is too short to opt for crude practicality over beauty and elegance. Please advise your cousin to reconsider how she presents herself to the world.

Liam snickered. "If the count is worried about how Gwen presents herself, I wonder what he'd think of those shapeless gowns she wears."

"They're not shapeless," Gwen defended. "These gowns are very fashionable in Europe."

"They make you look like you should be eating for two," Liam said.

Gwen looked heavenward. "Imagine . . . all these years I missed having an older brother to torment me." She turned her attention back to Natalia. "Is that man ever going to let us discuss the vote?"

"Eventually," Natalia said. "I warned you that he always does this before he lets me get down to business. I think he's just terribly lonely."

Minutes stretched into hours as the message exchange continued. It was almost midnight before they got the message they had been waiting for.

You know I trust your judgment, Natalia. Of course you may vote my bank shares however you wish.

"Glory hallelujah," Patrick said in exhaustion, but Natalia threw a bucket of cold water on their jubilation.

"We can't proceed until I pry the password out of him in order to vote by proxy," she warned. "The count supplies the bank's auditor with a unique password for each shareholder vote, and I can't register his vote without that password."

It took four more exchanges in which the count wanted Natalia's opinion on French cooking and to complain about the food served at his outpost. Only then did the count send his password for the September vote, which was *Stradivarius*.

"That's all we need," Natalia said. "Please forgive him for his quirks. I knew we would get there in the end, but these exchanges must be managed delicately. His feelings can be hurt so easily."

They thanked Mr. Smitty for his patience, and Gwen provided a generous tip on top of the staggering fees Count Sokolov's verbose messages cost to transmit and receive. Just before they left, the telegraph sprang to life one more time. It was a short message.

Tell your cousin that when I have perfected my juniper perfume, I shall name it Gwendolyn in her honor.

32

atrick tried to sleep late the morning after the epic telegraph session, but it was impossible. Thirty-eight people were crammed into the house, and even before dawn there were footsteps thudding on the staircase, doors slamming, and the shrieks of children romping outdoors.

On the neighboring bed, Liam groaned and pulled the blanket over his eyes. "Could someone please go shoot those kids?"

"Let's hold off on that while I make nice with Gwen's family," Patrick said while clipping his suspenders into place. He liked Natalia and Aunt Martha. He hadn't seen much to admire in the rest of them, but perhaps there was still hope. It wasn't fair to hold Gwen's family against her, and it might be possible to establish a modicum of mutual respect with some of them.

Because he wanted Gwen. Quite badly. She was perfect for him, as if God had designed the ideal woman to light up his life. Where she was weak, he was strong. She brought a softness to his world he didn't even know was missing until she came into it with her warm, gentle humor.

The only stumbling block was centuries of class differences between them. Would he be able to crack the door into her world? Would her family permit it?

He headed outside to make an attempt.

Dozens of people were already gathered on the upper terrace overlooking the shore, but Gwen was not among them. He scanned the adults, looking for someone with whom he might strike up a cordial conversation. Most of the men sat on lawn chairs facing the sea. A couple of them nodded a greeting when Patrick approached, but most ignored him. Only the stout man with the walrus mustache stood to welcome him.

"Bertie Abernathy," he said as he reached out to shake Patrick's hand. "It's probably a challenge to keep us all straight. Remind me again who you are?"

"Patrick O'Neill. I'm handling some legal work for Liam."

The jovial look in Bertie's eyes cooled a bit. "Oh yes, the lawyer. Say, if you're going to be staying for a while, would you like to borrow a dinner jacket? Old Frederick would never breathe a word, but he likes everyone decked out appropriately at meals."

"No, thank you," Patrick said, feeling every eye on him.

The men turned back to a discussion about breeding horses, and Patrick struggled to find common ground as he scanned the estate.

Then he spotted Gwen down on the beach with some children. She wore a white cotton dress with a crown of flowers in her hair. Children clustered around as she showed them how to make crowns of their own from sea oats and hawthorn berries. The sound of her laughter carried up to him, making his heart ache. She seemed so natural here, like she belonged.

He didn't, but he owed it to her to try. He wandered over to join a group of the younger cousins seated around a picnic table and reached for a chair to join them.

"Don't touch it!" Edwin shouted.

Patrick's hand froze. He had no idea what he'd done wrong, but every man stared in rapt attention at a loaf of bread and wedge of cheese on the table. Oddly, there were several ten-dollar bills weighed down beneath a plate. All four men held their breath as they stared at the center of the table.

One of the cousins leaned over to whisper what was going

on. "Edwin bet us all ten dollars that the beetle will go for the cheese instead of the bread."

Patrick looked again. Sure enough, a tiny green beetle was inching toward the center of the table. Everyone watched the beetle's clumsy progress with breathless anticipation.

These were the people Gwen thought were so wonderful? He crossed his arms and withdrew a few steps to watch the beetle's slow journey. Maybe he shouldn't be so judgmental. Ten dollars meant nothing to people this wealthy, so the gamble was probably harmless. Sixty seconds later, the outcome of the bet was determined when the beetle hauled itself onto the bread plate to a chorus of cheers. Money started changing hands, but Edwin was annoyed to have lost and smashed the beetle with his fist before brushing it away.

Patrick remembered the first moment he laid eyes on Gwen in his office. There had been a beetle squatting on her chair. She had cradled it in her palm, then carried it to the window and set it free.

He swallowed back his annoyance. Gwen managed to rub along okay in the Five Points even though it wasn't natural for her, and he would try to do the same here.

He wandered toward Joshua, the young college student from Yale, and invited him for a stroll along the beach. Joshua looked momentarily puzzled but agreed.

They walked on a path through the sea oats. They were close enough to the water to feel the spray from the surf as it rolled onto the beach, and sea gulls wheeled overhead.

Patrick scrambled for common ground. "I'm curious why you decided to go to Yale instead of Blackstone College," he asked the younger man.

"Blackstone College still has the reek of new money," Joshua said.

Patrick quirked a brow. "Really? I think it reeks of science and hope for the future."

"You sound like Gwen," Joshua said with a note of humor.

"There's nothing wrong with that, is there?"

Joshua glanced at Gwen, who was scavenging on the shore amidst a cluster of children. Now she wore a seaweed necklace in addition to her crown of flowers, and Patrick thought she'd never looked prettier.

"She's always been a bit of an odd duck," Joshua said. "And that husband of hers—everyone knew he was after her money. We all felt sorry for her. Bertie tried to warn her about Jasper before the wedding, but there was no talking to her. Like I said, she's an odd duck."

Patrick said nothing. Gwen had more decency in her pinky finger than any of these men of leisure who lounged on the seashore while the rest of the world worked.

"What sort of plans do you have for after college?" he asked.

"I don't want anything to do with the bank, that's for sure," Joshua said. "I like art. I spent last summer studying landscape painting in France and won third prize at an exhibition. Did you see the watercolor of the estate that's hanging in the common room?"

Patrick nodded. It was a nice painting of the house and the cliffside, but nothing special.

"I painted that," Joshua said in satisfaction. "I'd like to open an art gallery someday. Uncle Oscar said he would stake me in the business, but lately he's been less free with the wallet. Poppy spends money by the fistful, and he won't rein her in. Personally, I think it's embarrassing for a man to be so besotted over a woman half his age, but he works hard to keep dumping money all over her."

A group of younger cousins came meandering toward them, asking Joshua to join in a game of poker. "Edwin brought the poker chips, and we need a fourth player."

"Right," Joshua readily agreed.

They didn't ask Patrick to join, which was fine. He had no interest in playing games with grown men dressed entirely in white. Only men who never sweat, got dirty, or did real work wasted money on white clothes.

He headed back toward the lounge chairs, where most of

256

the older relatives were gathered with Poppy and Liam in the center. The annoying little girl was there too, and it looked like an argument was underway. Liam's expression was stormy as Poppy spoke with great passion, jabbing an index finger directly in Liam's face. Patrick quickened his steps to join them, and they all went silent as he approached.

Bertie turned to him. "Say, Poppy's heard some unflattering things about you. What's this about a warrant for your arrest over robbing a church?"

Patrick rocked back in disbelief. "I didn't rob anyone," he said tightly. "That was a trumped-up charge, and we told Frederick about it the day we arrived."

"That's what I've been telling them," Liam said. "If Frederick believed it, we'd have been kicked out the moment we set foot on this island."

Poppy lifted her chin to look at Patrick with disdain. "Liam can't help his background and we have to tolerate him, but we don't have to put up with *you*. I think you've overstayed your welcome."

"If he goes, I go," Liam said.

"What a wonderful idea," Poppy replied.

Aunt Martha raised her palsied hand in an appeal for peace. "I think we should all calm down. I trust Frederick's judgment, and, Poppy, you shouldn't be spreading unfounded rumors."

"I think stealing from a church is disgusting," Penelope-Arabella said. "You should know better than to steal from a priest, Patrick."

"And you should know better than to address a grown-up by his first name," he snapped, causing the girl to burst into tears and run to her mother on the beach, wailing about the man who was mean to her.

Poppy shot him a look that was the perfect blend of school-marm and malice. "We have an example to set for the children, and Gwen shouldn't have brought such trash to a family gathering."

Liam wasn't taking it anymore. "Poppy, beneath all those

snooty airs, I'm pretty sure you're the biggest wad of trash on this island. I grew up on the streets and can spot grifters a mile away."

The old aunts looked appalled, but Poppy's eyes gleamed with aggression as she flung insults back at Liam. Mudslinging wasn't getting them anywhere, so Patrick stepped forward to intervene.

"Where did you hear about this supposed theft?" he asked.

Poppy's tirade came to a halt. She gave him a withering glare as she reached into a canvas tote to produce a newspaper folded open to an article covering the Pittsburgh police blotter. A two-paragraph story mentioned the church burglary and named Patrick O'Neill and Liam Malone as suspects currently on the run.

"I intend to speak with my husband about this," she said. "We shouldn't have to tolerate a thief in our midst."

Poppy clasped a hand over her expanding belly as though feeling weak and let a pair of the elderly aunts support her as they guided her up to the house, but Patrick thought Poppy Blackstone might be the strongest and most dangerous person on this island.

Telling Gwen about the confrontation on the lawn was going to be hard. Patrick and Liam took her to the meadow behind the boathouse to discuss it in private. With her crown of flowers and flowing white gown, she looked like the personification of natural innocence. Her face transformed from radiant happiness to disillusionment and then anger as Liam recounted the delight Poppy took in spreading slander about them.

It made Patrick resent the Blackstones even more. They were contemptible. Thank heavens Gwen's father had the wisdom to raise her at the college, where she wasn't tainted by the decadence of her family.

She raised pain-filled eyes to his. "They aren't usually like this," she said in an aching voice, then turned to touch Liam on his arm. "Please don't hate them. It will only take a little time."

"Yeah, well, we don't have time," Liam said. "I wanted to scrounge up some people here to side with me against the U.S. Steel merger, but now everyone thinks Patrick and I are shysters."

"Someone has been watching us," Patrick said. "They've managed to poison the water here, but we can still go after Mrs. Carnegie and her seven percent of the vote. She's the only way we can get to fifty-one percent to save the college's funding."

Liam unleashed a streak of foul language. "Who cares about Mrs. Carnegie? She'll never vote against the steel merger."

Patrick moved in close. "But she might vote for the college, and that's just as important."

"Bull hockey," Liam growled.

"Watch your language around your sister."

Gwen stepped between them. "Liam, clean it up. Patrick, calm down. If we leave immediately, we can be in Manhattan before nightfall. We'll stay at Frederick's house, since it's empty right now and directly across the street from the Carnegies. I'll request a meeting with Mrs. Carnegie as soon as possible."

And if they could sway Mrs. Carnegie to their side, they could save the college.

33

*P*atrick loathed everything about the Fifth Avenue mansion owned by Frederick Blackstone. The main parlor was an opulent showpiece of cold marble so white it hurt his eyes. The chandeliers dripped with crystal, and the spindly chairs looked too delicate to sit on.

"I can see why your grandfather prefers living out at the island," he said as Gwen showed them into the parlor. He set down his traveling bag. He'd always been proud of this leather bag. It was the first quality item he bought once he started practicing law, but in this grand setting, he noticed its cheap clasp and faded leather. Gwen probably saw it too.

"I'll send for tea," Gwen said. "The servants didn't know we were coming, so don't expect anything fancy, but my grandfather always keeps an impressive collection of imported cheeses on hand. Would that be all right?"

"A cheese sandwich sounds good," Patrick said. "Liam?"

Liam wasn't paying attention. He was too busy running a finger along the wall. "Is this cloth or wallpaper?"

"Silk wallpaper," Gwen replied. "Please don't touch. It's antique and quite fragile. Make yourselves at home while I arrange for something to eat and place a telephone call to request a meeting with Mrs. Carnegie. Hopefully she'll be able to see us tomorrow."

Gwen disappeared down a hallway, leaving Patrick and Liam to stand uncomfortably in the gilded monstrosity of a room.

"This place gives me the willies," Liam said.

Patrick silently agreed, but Gwen's voice echoed down the hallway. "I heard that! You'd better get used to it, because Mrs. Carnegie's home is even fancier."

Liam sighed and plopped onto a chair. The delicate legs didn't collapse, so Patrick joined him on a nearby chair that looked like a throne. Suddenly everything felt very real.

"Don't let a little fancy decorating throw you off your mission," he said to Liam. "We're only *six votes* away from saving the college. I can almost taste it."

"I don't care about saving the college. I want to stop the steel merger. I'm only six votes away from that too."

Patrick sent him a warning look. "Louise Carnegie will never side with you, and if you alienate her, we lose our best shot at saving the college. You need to choose which battle to fight."

"I came here to fight for the workingman, not a bunch of rich college students."

Patrick vaulted off his chair, trying to hold his temper in check. He was on the verge of winning this for Gwen. "Who do you think benefits from the medicine Blackstone College makes? My mother has worked all her life in a hot kitchen, getting up before dawn to make bread for the people of this city. *She* is who the college helped. With a little funding and God's blessing, the next time a steelworker comes down with tetanus, the serum will be there for him too."

Liam glowered at him from the chair. "Andrew Carnegie has been the face of everything I've despised all my life. My father burned his hand while slaving at Carnegie Steel, and he never got a dime in compensation. All we got were threats of eviction because my dad was out of work for two weeks and couldn't make rent. And then there was the time—"

Patrick cut him off. "Andrew Carnegie doesn't even know who you are. Right now we need his wife's cooperation. If you lecture her on the wickedness of her husband, we'll walk away from this with *nothing*. We need to fight smart. Fight hard. I'll be with you the entire way, but don't you dare embarrass your sister by showing contempt for the Carnegies."

Now Liam was equally angry. He stood and started bellowing union platitudes, his voice echoing in the mostly empty mansion.

Gwen's voice broke the rant. "I step away for a few minutes, and the two of you are at each other's throats?" She stood in the open doorway, looking aghast as she held a tray of sandwiches.

Patrick closed the space between them and took the tray from her. "Never mind us. Did you get through to Mrs. Carnegie?"

Gwen nodded. "I spoke with her butler, and he said we can call on her tomorrow. Apparently, rumor of William Blackstone's resurrection from the dead is already making the rounds in the city, so I think she'll be willing to receive us. We should practice tea etiquette before heading over to see her."

Gwen went on to say that Mrs. Carnegie was a delightful woman but that they would still need to comport themselves with the utmost formality.

"I have already sent for your new suits to be delivered from Queens by tomorrow morning," she said to Liam. "And the macassar oil would be a good idea. I know you don't like it, but it would be best to have you properly turned out."

Patrick should probably swing back to the Five Points and get his own suit, because everything he had was grubby after traveling for the past two weeks.

They polished off the sandwiches, and when a maid pushed the tea cart into the room, Gwen coached Liam once again. "Back straight. Bring the teacup to your mouth, and don't slurp."

They finished the first pot, and Gwen had just ordered another when the doorbell rang.

Patrick instinctively stood to answer it, but Gwen pulled him back down. "Let the butler do it."

"Yeah, Patrick, let the butler do it," Liam teased.

A bit of laughter bubbled out of Gwen. "You seem to be settling into this new life with ease."

"Is that how it looks?" Liam quipped.

"Ahem." At the entrance to the parlor, the butler cleared his throat. "Mrs. Carnegie is here to see you, ma'am."

Patrick whirled to gape at the butler. Sure enough, a frighteningly grim middle-aged woman stood in the doorway. He scrambled to his feet and sent a warning glare at Liam, who finally stood as well, a sullen look on his face as he glowered at Mrs. Carnegie.

Louise Carnegie didn't look anything like Patrick expected. She was only forty-three but looked much older, with a dowdy face and matronly gown. She had a boxy attaché case and a scowling expression. In comparison, Gwen looked like a work of art in her flowery, floating silk gown.

"What a delightful surprise," Gwen said as she glided forward to greet Mrs. Carnegie.

It was a lie. Now that Patrick knew Gwen better, he could tell when she was terrified, and this was it. Her formal demeanor and carefully modulated tone were dead giveaways.

Mrs. Carnegie barely acknowledged Gwen. She simply stared at Liam. "You are William Blackstone?" she barked.

Liam nodded. "Yes, ma'am."

"You look like your father," Mrs. Carnegie said without a hint of warmth. "I came the moment I heard you had arrived in town. I am aware of your history with various steel unions, and I want your unconditional assurance that you will make no attempt to disrupt the impending creation of U.S. Steel."

Mrs. Carnegie had not even entered the room. She stood in the doorway and tossed the gauntlet down at Liam's feet. Liam did not bend.

"Not interested," he said bluntly.

Gwen raced to intervene. "We actually came for a number of reasons, not just the steel—"

"I'm here over the steel deal," Liam interrupted. "The creation of U.S. Steel is a monstrosity that can't be allowed to happen. I've got a seat at the Blackstone Bank, and I intend to use it to block the merger."

"You won't succeed," Mrs. Carnegie said.

Gwen fanned herself. "My, the temperature rose so quickly," she said with a nervous laugh. "Let's all sit down and have a nice cup of tea, shall we?"

"Tea isn't going to solve anything," Liam said.

Patrick had to save this situation before Liam threw a bomb into his future business partnerships that could never be called back.

"Tea is the beverage over which empires and alliances have been forged for centuries," he said calmly. Actually, strong drink and cigars probably facilitated more of those deals, but Mrs. Carnegie was calling the shots, and tea was probably her thing.

Gwen gestured to the table nestled in the alcove of a bay window. They sat, everyone so stiff that the air practically crackled. An uncomfortable silence filled the room as Gwen poured tea and passed cups to each person at the table. Every clink of china sounded harsh.

Mrs. Carnegie left her tea untouched but looked directly at Liam. "I will waste no time on polite conversation when the well-being of my family is at stake," she said. "My husband has an unhealthy obsession with the steel company he founded, but it is past time for him to retire and enjoy his golden years. That will only happen if he sells the company, and I intend to be sure it happens."

Gwen passed a bowl of sugar cubes to Mrs. Carnegie. "A commendable wish. My father gave all his waking hours to Blackstone College. He died in his desk chair. When a man loves something that much, it can be hard for him to step away."

Patrick watched the two women carefully. Gwen would probably give her eyeteeth to rip the discussion away from U.S. Steel, but her gentle attempt to steer the conversation back to the college did not work. Mrs. Carnegie kept her stare fixed on Liam.

"You don't have the power to block the merger, but I don't want any Blackstone polluting the air with hostility against it," Mrs. Carnegie said. "In the last week alone there has been picketing by union miners all the way from West Virginia to bellyache against this deal."

Liam snickered. "I figured the Mingo County guys would show up again. All we've ever wanted from Carnegie Steel is a fair shake for the workers, and you won't give it to us."

Mrs. Carnegie leaned down to unbuckle the straps on the attaché case. There was only a single item inside, a fat stack of pages held together with a metal fastener. She set it in front of Liam. "Please see page 82, section 12."

Liam shifted uneasily. "Um, I've got my lawyer here to help with this."

Patrick grabbed the document and flipped to the designated section. It was a dense and complicated contract. He'd never heard of some of these terms before, so he read the passage several times, trying to parse the words because they sounded too good for him to trust.

He glanced up at Mrs. Carnegie. "What does *profit-sharing* mean?"

Mrs. Carnegie's expression was calculating and knowing. "Exactly as it sounds. Any employee of U.S. Steel who is loyal and works hard can earn stock in the company."

"Loyal?" Liam scoffed. "That sounds like a code word for no unions."

"The document does not preclude unions," Mrs. Carnegie said. "It merely demands that workers who wish to earn ownership shares in the company live up to their contracted agreements with the owners. If they do, they will be rewarded. Those who propose innovative solutions or exceed production goals will be doubly rewarded."

Liam folded his arms across his chest. "Yeah, well, I don't trust it."

Patrick hunkered over the document and shut out the prattle from Liam to concentrate on the dense legal contract. Stock subscription plans, bonuses, work incentives—all of it voluntary. Mrs. Carnegie didn't *need* Liam's vote, but he could rock the boat, and she knew it. The guys from Mingo County were already back in town. Newspapers could promote Liam and his incendiary views on their front pages all over the country, fomenting hostility toward the new steel company.

Patrick looked up from the document. "Ma'am, might I have a moment alone with my client?" he asked.

"By all means, please take him away," Mrs. Carnegie said dismissively as she lifted her teacup.

Patrick dragged Liam into a darkened room off the corridor. The only light was from the lampposts on Fifth Avenue, which cast a glow of illumination from the window.

"The profit-sharing plan is generous," he said. "It gives workers a stake in the game. I've never seen anything like it." He leaned in close and whispered, barely able to contain the bubbling, joyous sense of urgency. "We can *win*. We can get a fair shake for the workers and save the college too. Cut a deal with Mrs. Carnegie. Say you won't raise a stink in exchange for her vote on the college."

Liam's shoulders were hunched, his arms clutched across his chest. "I don't know what to think. Is there any way to lock down that profit-sharing deal? Make it so they can't go back on their word?"

"That's the best part," Patrick said. "That document is the operating contract that will tie all ten companies together. It can't be overturned. Now, I want you to listen to me," he ordered. "Stop thinking like a union man and start acting like a strategist. Fight for what you want from *inside* the company. Strike a deal with Oscar Blackstone to demand a seat on the board of directors of U.S. Steel. You could help run the new company. You'll be more powerful than any labor leader ever dreamed."

The truth of that dawned on Liam, who looked dumbfounded by the prospect. He wandered to the window, gaping at the glittering skyline of New York City as the implications sank in.

"My grandfather is leery of the deal," Liam said. "So is Natalia. Making a deal with Mrs. Carnegie would be doublecrossing them."

It might seem that way, but they were playing a high-stakes game, and the fate of the college hung in the balance.

"You never vowed automatic loyalty to Frederick. Your motives aren't selfish. You will be using your God-given intelligence to vote on behalf of what you believe is right. Let me haggle with Oscar to get you a seat on the board of U.S. Steel. Oscar doesn't want you out on the streets, adding your name to the rabble-rousers picketing the new company, because he knows you can stoke up their anger more than anyone else in the world. He needs your cooperation. If we can pull this off, you will be helping direct the largest steel company ever created."

Liam still looked a little overwhelmed, but he straightened his shoulders. "I never thought I'd say this, but I'm willing to shake on the deal with Mrs. Carnegie."

34

They caught the ferry back to Cormorant Island the following day, and Gwen's spirits were over the moon. Mrs. Carnegie had agreed to permanent funding for the college, meaning that her father's dream was going to endure.

Today was the lobster bake, a time when everyone relaxed and enjoyed the beachside simplicity of the annual event, and hopefully Patrick could finally see her family at their best. Frederick hadn't been on the terrace when Patrick and Liam were accused of theft, but his support of them would silence Poppy's wagging tongue.

"The lobster bake is my favorite event of the year," she told Patrick and Liam as they stood at the railing of the ferry. "In the morning, the men dig a trench on the beach, and I take the children to gather seaweed and driftwood for the firepit. We shuck corn, and Bertie brings down a big galvanized washtub that he carries over his head while he marches up and down the beach singing patriotic songs. The children think it's hysterical."

Liam remained sullen. He had wanted to stay in Manhattan rather than face Frederick's wrath over his shocking about-face on the steel vote, and his anxiety spiraled higher as the ferry drew nearer to the boathouse.

"Please don't bite your fingernails," she said.

Liam jerked his hand away from his mouth. "I don't know how to confess what I plan to do," he said in a worried voice.

"Don't say anything," Patrick said. "The vote is still weeks away, and voting on behalf of the workers isn't a sin."

For once, Patrick's counsel didn't ease Liam's qualms, but they'd arrived and had no more time to discuss it. The entire clan was already on the beach by the time they disembarked. The breeze carried the aroma of seafood and laughter as children played in the surf. Red-checkered cloths covered the tables, which were filled with baskets of corn bread, tubs of butter, and plenty of iced tea. Most of the adults were at the picnic tables, but Oscar and Poppy sat on padded wicker chairs placed a few yards away because Poppy didn't like the scent of seafood.

Her grandfather lifted his straw hat in greeting. His face was flushed with good cheer, and a half-empty bottle of white wine graced the table. "There's still some lobster," he called out. "Come quickly, before Bertie finishes it off."

"I've only had three," Bertie defended. He met Gwen's gaze as they approached the table. "We didn't expect you back for a few more days. Did Mrs. Carnegie send you packing?"

Gwen glanced at Aunt Martha, whose sheepish look made it clear she'd spilled the beans about where they went and why.

Liam nodded. "She knows how to make her intentions clear."

"Ha!" Bertie chortled. "That's why I let Oscar do the talking for us. No wonder you look so glum."

Her cousin Joshua gave Liam a condescending smile. "Serve an apprenticeship in San Francisco like Grandfather recommends. It's better to fail in a small pond than in the big city."

Uncle Oscar's gaze had the cautious laziness of a panther watching from afar. "Well?" he asked.

"Mrs. Carnegie proved firm in her position about the steel merger," Gwen said in a deliberately casual tone. "We couldn't budge her off it."

Oscar nodded graciously. He raised a wineglass and sent a polite nod to Liam. "That was as expected, but you are to be commended for trying. As my father suggests, a few years in San Francisco might be a better starting place for you."

Liam didn't need to hide in San Francisco to learn the ropes. The plan was to get him on the board of directors for U.S. Steel, and Gwen couldn't be prouder of him. Happiness as pure as the blue sky above them made her almost giddy with joy.

"Although Mrs. Carnegie won't budge on the steel merger, she has authorized the college's continued financial support," she said. "In conjunction with Grandfather and Count Sokolov, we have enough votes to continue funding the college in perpetuity."

Uncle Oscar set down his wineglass, all traces of humor gone. "No," he in disbelief.

"*Yes*," Patrick countered.

Oscar silently fumed, but all Gwen cared about was Frederick. Her grandfather stood to his full height and doffed his hat, his eyes beaming in pride.

"Well done, Gwendolyn. Well done."

She turned to the men beside her. "I couldn't have done it without Liam and Patrick. I'd say it was a group effort."

"And I'd say this is cause for celebration," Frederick said. "Not so much for the college's survival as for the return of my grandson. And granddaughter! I may have underestimated the pair of you. Liam, you are proving to be a true Blackstone. Well done, sir!"

"Well done?" Oscar demanded. "He's following in Theodore's misguided footsteps. The biggest danger on Wall Street is a powerful man with an easily manipulated heart." He turned his ire on Patrick. "This is your doing," he said bitterly. "That lummox with an eighth-grade education couldn't argue his way out of a paper bag. Now the two of you have gone and stabbed us in the back."

Liam bristled. "I don't stab people in the back," he retorted. "If I want to cross you, I'll go ahead and stab you in the front."

"Pipe down," Patrick ordered, stepping between the two men and sending a warning look at Liam.

Gwen's spirit plummeted, dismayed at how quickly Liam let himself be provoked by her uncle. Oscar knew exactly what he was doing when he began taunting Liam, and now Frederick had seen as well.

Frederick's voice was calm but stern. "Liam, you need to master your temper if you're going to play the game on Wall Street. Don't blazon your intentions to your opponent."

Good advice, especially since Liam was keeping silent on his real prize, the U.S. Steel agreement.

"Don't get used to this," Oscar said, his voice quietly seething. He turned his back on them and stalked toward the staircase leading back up to the house, kicking up sprays of sand behind him.

"Pay him no mind," Frederick said as he sat back down in his chair. "Oscar isn't used to having competition, and the three of you are giving it to him. That's all to the good."

"How is it good?" Poppy asked. "It seems like the bank just lost millions of dollars in a hopeless cause."

"Begging your pardon, ma'am," Patrick said. "The college has done a world of good for people all over the country by curing diseases and educating the next generation of scientists. You can't put a price tag on that."

Poppy smirked. "But there's a price tag on *you*, isn't there?" She turned her attention to Frederick. "Patrick dances attendance on Gwen because he owes her $15,000 for some medicine, and she's paying him off at an allowance of $250 a week. The butler says she wires the money each week to his bank account."

Gwen stepped forward. "That's nonsense. Patrick is here because he believes in this cause."

Poppy remained unmoved. "Gwen, I think it's precious that you've found a new man to take Jasper's place, but that doesn't mean you need to flaunt him around in polite company."

Liam shoved her aside to confront Poppy. "You're a nasty piece of work, aren't you?" Liam snarled, but all Gwen could see was the mortification on Patrick's face.

He didn't look at her as he turned to Frederick. "Forgive me," he said to her grandfather. "The annual lobster bake is a family event you all look forward to, and I regret seeing it ruined. I will catch the ferry back to the mainland."

"Patrick, don't go," Gwen said, tugging on his arm. He whirled to face her, and she flinched at the anger on his face. He jerked away and continued heading toward the staircase.

She tried to follow, but Liam caught her arm.

"Let him go," he said quietly. "The last thing a man wants after being publicly humiliated is to have a woman fussing over him."

"But he knows I don't think like that."

"Which is why he doesn't need you to soothe his ego. Let him have his pride."

She couldn't. When someone was hurting, she needed to offer comfort. Poppy had identified Patrick's deepest wound, split it wide open, and poured in a gallon of salt in front of the entire family.

She needed to make it right.

Patrick flung his traveling bag on the bed and dumped his clothes inside. These people were despicable. He wouldn't want his future children exposed to them or thinking that this was the way life ought to be. Walking away from Gwen was going to hurt, but marriage was more than joining two people together. It meant joining two families. He didn't want his children to be like the hideous Penelope-Arabella or look up to people like Poppy and Oscar Blackstone.

"You aren't really leaving, are you?"

Gwen stood in the open doorway, looking like a wounded doe. He didn't want to hurt her, but they'd been foolish to imagine there could be anything lasting between them.

"We both know I don't belong here," he said.

"Is it just Poppy who's driving you away? I'm sorry she spoke as she did, but the rest of the family doesn't feel as she does."

Maybe they were better at hiding it, but Patrick knew exactly how the rest of the family felt. He snapped the clasp shut and tugged the heavy bag off the bed. "Poppy is the ringleader, but she's got a loyal following."

"We don't have to see her," Gwen said quietly. "I've got a lovely house on campus. You've seen it. It isn't grand or fancy, but it's big enough for us . . . if someday there is going to be an us."

He turned away, uncomfortable with her pleading. She'd done the same while trying to win her unworthy husband away from his mistress, and Gwen was better than that. She shouldn't grovel for any man.

Footsteps pounded downstairs and a voice called up from below. "Gwen, it's time for horseshoes!"

She made no move to leave, and they watched each other from opposite sides of the room. This was it. This was the end. This fleeting summer interlude was over, and he wished there was another way, but it was better to get out now before they hurt each other even more.

"I'll be in touch with Liam to lead him through the July board meeting," he said. "If you need me to show him the ropes in Manhattan, just holler. I'll help however I can."

"Is there anything I can say to make you stay?" she asked. "Tell me, and I'll say it."

His spirit sagged. "Don't ever beg, Gwen. You're too good for that."

He left the room without saying anything else, but the pain on her face haunted him long after he left the estate.

Gwen was too ill to eat after Patrick's departure. The ferry wouldn't leave until tomorrow morning, but Mr. Smitty rented rooms over the general store where Patrick could stay the night.

She ignored the horseshoe game on the beach and joined Liam at the picnic table. It was amazing how quickly conversation returned to normal after Patrick left. Chester went back to discussing a racehorse he wanted to buy, and Bertie pestered Edwin about a pricey antique he'd ordered.

"When am I going to see it?" Bertie asked. "I paid six hundred dollars for it."

Edwin preened as he described the rare find for the group. "It's a fifteenth-century flask from the Ming dynasty. It's made of jade and very rare."

"When can I see it?" Bertie pressed.

"Come by my townhouse when we're back in the city," Edwin said. "Maybe I can interest you in a Han dynasty funerary urn." Edwin launched into a monologue about Chinese antiquities, but Poppy was bored and pulled an exaggerated stretch as she rose from the table.

"I shall go for a little stroll," she said, cradling her belly. "The doctor says I must walk for twenty minutes a day before the little one arrives. And, Edwin, if you say one more word about the Han dynasty or any other, we are all in danger of falling into a catatonic stupor."

Everyone except Liam laughed at the comment. Poppy was an undiluted snob, but her influence in the family would only become stronger once she gave birth to Oscar's long-awaited heir. If Patrick was ever to marry into the Blackstone family, Poppy needed to be neutralized.

Gwen stood and put a hand on Liam's shoulder. "Liam, would you like to see the eggs of a nesting sandpiper I found yesterday?"

He glanced at her. "Not really."

She nudged him. "Are you sure? It's quite interesting."

He must have understood her intent, for he pushed away from the table and headed out after her. Poppy was a speck of pale pink muslin in the distance as she meandered on the path leading into a cluster of scrubby oaks.

"I can't stand that woman," Liam seethed.

"I can't either, but we need to see that she is declawed."

Liam snorted. "She'll grow a new set within the hour."

"I intend to appeal to her better nature. She can help smooth

the way for you and Patrick to join the family. We need to persuade her to stop lobbing bombs at you both."

Liam folded his arms across his chest. "Let her come after
me. I don't care that she's a woman. I'll return fire and blast
that smug look off her face."

"No, you won't. That's not the right way to handle this situation."

Liam glowered. "It's how I handle things."

"Then you need to grow up," Gwen said, turning to face
him. "From the moment you arrived on my doorstep, half-
dead, angry, and mistrustful, I accepted you. Now I need
your help declawing Poppy, and to do that, we need to flatter
her. I want you to appeal to her better nature and ask for her
advice."

He cursed and looked heavenward, but she wasn't having it.

"I won't let Poppy drive Patrick away. We need to get Poppy
on our side, and frankly, it won't be that hard. Ask for her help
learning croquet. Praise her skills. She'll like that."

"I'd rather beat her with a croquet mallet than ask for her
help with it."

"Too bad. We both owe Patrick, and it's time to start delivering."

They cut across the dunes on their way toward Poppy. Trudg-
ing across the sandy dunes was slowgoing because Liam still
had to move gingerly. In the past few days, it had been easy to
forget how far he'd come in healing from the stab wound, but
it was still tender. Even with Poppy's slow, ponderous gait, it
took them a while to catch up to her.

"Yo! Poppy, wait up," Liam called as they drew close.

Poppy turned to look at them. With her wide-brimmed straw
bonnet, she looked like a Gainsborough portrait as she watched
them approach on the path through the long grasses. The cattails were chest high and swayed in the stiff breeze, brushing
against Gwen's skirts as they walked.

The path was only wide enough for two people, so Gwen
dropped behind, watching in approval how Liam offered his

arm to Poppy, letting the pregnant woman accept his help as they walked along the scrabbly path.

"I liked the way you beat Edwin at croquet," Liam said, and Poppy preened.

"I won five dollars from him, and that's not easy," Poppy said. "Edwin takes sports very seriously."

"I was hoping maybe you could give me some advice on the game. I hear you're a champ when it comes to croquet."

"You came to the right place," Poppy said in satisfaction.

"Maybe you can help Patrick too," Liam said. "Patrick is a good man, and you were pretty tough on him back there."

"I had to be," Poppy said. "Gwen is consorting with the help, and it's tacky. I can't imagine why Frederick doesn't put his foot down."

"You know that I can hear every word you say," Gwen called.

Poppy tossed her a condescending glance over her shoulder. "Darling, I'm saying it for your own good. Patrick isn't comfortable here. Everyone can see it. Poor Liam can't help what happened to him, but he's one of us and will blend into the fold eventually. Patrick never will. Oh look, wild blackberries." She stepped in front of Liam toward a tangle of blackberry vines.

A loud crack and a bang echoed across the dunes. Gwen startled at the noise. "That sounded like a gunshot!"

Liam cursed. Poppy had fallen and started screaming.

"Hit the dirt," Liam yelled. He grabbed Gwen's arm, tugging her down.

It *was* a gunshot. Blood was all over Poppy's bodice, and she continued a ghastly wail.

"Shut up, Poppy," Liam ordered. "Tell me where you're hit."

The edges of Gwen's vision dimmed in shock as another loud crack echoed over the dunes. Poppy clutched her upper arm, where blood pulsed from between her fingers. Liam grabbed a handkerchief and mashed it onto her wound, making Poppy scream.

Had a hunter accidentally shot at them? Sometimes men hunted wild turkeys on the island, but it would be hard to mistake them for turkeys.

Liam peeked above the cattails for a split second. "Stop that blasted shooting," he hollered. "There are people walking here!"

A third shot rang out, triggering another round of screams from Poppy, but Liam clamped a hand over her mouth.

"Shut up," he hissed. "They meant to shoot us, and screaming is giving our location away. Be quiet, and let's move."

Gwen cowered beneath the screen of cattails, and Liam helped Poppy roll onto her knees to crawl toward a cluster of oak trees, where they could take shelter. It was hard to stay low enough to remain hidden by the cattails. Sand kicked into her face from Liam's boots as they crawled.

"Are you okay?" she whispered to Liam.

"I'm fine. You?"

"Fine."

Except for the terror streaking through her. Whoever was shooting at them had probably aimed for Liam but accidentally hit Poppy when she stepped in front of him for the blackberries.

Poppy continued whimpering, but Liam was surprisingly kind.

"Hang in there, Pops. We're going to have to ride it out here." Another blast from the gun ricocheted through the scrub.

Suddenly, Gwen heard Joshua calling out in an annoyed voice. "Is one of you idiots firing a gun?" he asked as he strode through the cattails toward them.

"No," Liam bellowed. "Someone is shooting at me, but they hit Poppy instead. Get down, you fool!"

Joshua's eyes grew horrified at the sight of blood all over Poppy. He dove for cover, but not before another blast from the gun hit the trunk of a nearby oak tree, spraying chunks of wood and bark that hit him in the face. He scrambled through the underbrush, blood dribbling from the nicks on his face as he reached them.

"Who's shooting at us?" he asked in appalled wonder. "And why?"

"Probably whoever stabbed Liam last month," Gwen whispered.

Poppy tried to speak, but Liam's hand clamped over her mouth made it impossible to understand.

"Let her talk," Gwen urged, and Liam hesitantly lifted his hand.

"My water broke," Poppy said.

"Oh, for pity's sake," Liam muttered. "We need to keep moving, then. As soon as we get to the trees, we'll be safer. We're sitting ducks out here."

As a group, the four of them inched their way through the tall grass, desperately trying to avoid brushing against the cattails and revealing their location. They barely made any progress, but a full minute had passed and there had been no more shots.

"Maybe we should make a run for it," Liam said, nodding toward the thick screen of trees ahead.

"I can't run," Poppy said. "I can't even walk. *I've been shot!*"

"I can't carry you," Liam said. "I've got a healing stab wound in my belly, and I'm not ripping it open for you, Pops."

"Stop calling me Pops. I've been shot!"

"I'll carry her," Joshua said, scooting forward. Gwen moved aside, amazed at his courage, but Joshua didn't hesitate as he reached Poppy and wiggled his arms beneath her.

In the distance came the sounds of shouting and clanging. Was that Bertie's voice? He was yelling orders, and Gwen risked a glance, spotting a pair of the old aunts banging pots together. Aunt Martha scolded the foolish hunters to stop shooting. Even ancient Uncle Herbert waved a red-checkered tablecloth for attention.

Joshua gaped at the old people heading their way through the cattails and choked out a relieved laugh. "Here comes the cavalry." He still looked terrified, his complexion a ghastly white against the streaks of blood dribbling down his face. He tentatively raised a hand above the cattails, and there were no more shots.

Bertie came tromping through the scrub, his face red with

exertion. "Who on God's green earth is hunting turkeys while there's a beach party going on?"

Gwen reached for Liam's hand, and for once he didn't tease her because he seemed as unnerved as she was. Soon a group of the aunts with their banging pans and checkered tablecloths had arrived, and the octogenarian cavalry surrounded them.

They were safe.

35

Gwen experienced a strangely unreal feeling after the shooting. The entire family was forced to congregate in the gathering room. No one had confessed to shooting a weapon, and Frederick didn't want anyone wandering off to hide a recently fired gun until he knew who'd done it. The main room was large, with plenty of upholstered furniture on one end and a massively long dining table on the other, but it felt crowded with three dozen people crammed inside. The elderly aunts and their husbands took the upholstered seats, while the second and third generations filled the dining chairs or sat on the fireplace hearth. The children crawled on the floor or sat on nervous mothers' laps.

Uncle Oscar had watched in horror as Joshua carried Poppy to the only bedroom on the first floor. Everyone fell silent at the sight of Poppy's blood-spattered gown, and Aunt Martha went to assist with preparing for the birth. There was no doctor on the island, nor was there any form of law enforcement. Oscar wanted both.

"I'm sending the *Black Rose* back to the city to fetch a doctor immediately," he insisted, his voice tense with agitation. The crew had been living aboard the yacht and could reach the mainland within an hour.

"It's starting to get dark," Bertie said. "It's not safe to send a yacht off at night like this."

"And it's not safe for my wife to deliver a child without a doctor!" Oscar roared.

Frederick held up a hand. "No arguing," he said in a voice of command. "The *Black Rose* leaves in ten minutes, and I want Liam aboard."

"What?" Liam asked, sitting on the hearth, exhaustion on his face. "I can stay. You might need help."

Frederick whirled, his face iron-hard. "I already lost you once. I won't tolerate it happening a second time. I want you off this island until we figure out who is trying to kill you."

Gwen scanned the room. Nobody admitted to shooting a gun, and the only people from the estate who weren't here right now were Patrick and Aunt Martha's husband, Milton. Patrick still hadn't returned from wherever he'd stormed off to after Poppy's insults, and Milton had been fishing for saltwater bass all day.

"Could it have been Milton?" someone asked. "Does he hunt?"

Aunt Martha was tending Poppy and couldn't be asked, but Aunt Helen refused to believe it. "Don't be ridiculous," she said, her pin curls bobbing. "The only person who was nearby for both attacks on Liam is that lawyer fellow."

"Patrick didn't do it," Liam snapped.

"How can you be so sure?" Aunt Helen asked.

"Because I'm the one who got stabbed in the gut, and I'd already be dead if Patrick hadn't saved my life."

Edwin rose, leaning heavily on his cane. "I'd like to head back to the city too. Liam will need someone who knows Manhattan to get him to a safe place."

"Absolutely not," Frederick said. "We don't know who fired those shots, and until we do, I want Liam protected. Bertie was with me when the shots rang out, so we know it wasn't him. Bertie will accompany Liam home."

Edwin looked appalled. "It wasn't me either. I am an excellent shot and wouldn't have missed an easy target *six times*."

"Sit down, Edwin," Uncle Oscar ordered. "Natalia, I need you to ride into town and send a telegram to Poppy's doctor so he can be waiting at the port when the *Black Rose* arrives. Promise him a fortune if he gets here before Poppy delivers."

Natalia stood. "Of course."

Liam looked grim as he shrugged into a jacket, preparing to board the *Black Rose*. None of the crew had been on land when the shots were fired, so it was safe to send Liam on the yacht.

Before he left, Liam crossed the room to Gwen, and she stood. Regret covered his face.

"Stand by Patrick," he said. "No matter what, don't let these harpies bring him down. He's my brother in every way a man can be." He leaned down to hug her, and she squeezed him tightly. He'd been annoying from the moment she met him, but everything was different now, and how intensely she regretted parting from him on this terrible night.

"Take care," she whispered. "Please don't let yourself get killed. It would bother me."

"It would?" Liam looked partly amused, partly touched.

"It appears miracles really do happen," she said fondly. "Yes, it would bother me a great deal."

A blister formed on the back of Patrick's heel before he arrived at Mr. Smitty's general store on the other side of the island. He'd been furious when he left the estate, but the long walk had cooled him down. He still had no intention of going back. He would rent one of the rooms above the store and take the ferry back to the city in the morning. His work here was done. He would help Liam during the July board meeting, after which he would cut ties with the entire Blackstone family. A clean break would be best. There was a squeezing in his chest at the thought of never seeing Gwen again, but he would get over it.

Eventually.

A bell dinged when he entered the store. Mr. Smitty was jawboning with a customer up at the soda fountain. The customer turned at the sound of the bell, and Patrick was surprised to see old Milton Abernathy, Aunt Martha's husband.

"I thought you'd gone fishing," Patrick said as he took the stool beside Milton.

The older man nodded to a bucket on the floor, where several dead sea bass were covered in ice. "I caught those a few hours ago, then headed over here to relax."

That was a surprise. Gwen had given him the impression that the annual lobster bake was a tradition the entire family looked forward to each summer.

"You weren't enjoying the lobster bake?" Patrick asked.

"Did you?" Milton asked with a hint of amusement.

"Not particularly."

Milton clapped him on the back. "Not a surprise, lad! I always escape to town whenever I'm on the island. Martha thinks I'm fishing, but I'm just looking for a little fresh air."

"It seems you've been looking for a little fresh air for the past forty-five years," Mr. Smitty said, and Milton nodded in concession.

Over the next hour, Patrick got a lesson in Blackstone family dynamics, and it wasn't pretty.

"Martha warned me about them, but I didn't take it seriously," Milton said. "I figured I would be accepted because I'm a self-made man like Frederick. A shoelace factory isn't as glamorous as banking, but I made a good living and didn't need Blackstone money to support my wife. Plenty of them look down their noses at me anyway."

Milton went on to say that he once had grand plans for expanding his business beyond shoelaces. The cording machines in his factory could easily produce corsets and undergarments, but the Blackstones discouraged it. Shoelaces were bad enough, but they certainly didn't want to be associated with underwear, so he set his plans aside.

After his son was born, Martha persuaded Milton to accept her family's money to buy a nicer house and send Bertie to private schools. Milton never felt good about accepting Blackstone money, but Bertie took to it like a duck to water.

"Bertie likes the finer things in life, and we don't see any harm in it. He sings in a barbershop quartet and is very talented. Dedicating his life to that quartet isn't what I'd have wanted for a child of mine, but Bertie enjoys it. I suppose that's the main thing."

Patrick refrained from comment. Bertie was fun at a party and he seemed like an intelligent man, but unlimited access to money was a corrupting force. It could blot out the drive and ambition necessary to realize a man's God-given potential.

The hours dragged by, interrupted only by the arrival of the ferry and mail from the mainland. An envelope was addressed to Gwen, and Uncle Milton promised to deliver it to her. By the time the sun went down, they had switched from drinking soda to bottles of cold beer. Milton seemed delighted to have found a comrade to join him in playing hooky from the Blackstone festivities. They'd been sitting at this counter for six hours, and it was a typical day for Milton. He put in a few hours fishing, then hid at the soda fountain for the rest of the day to avoid Martha's relatives.

Milton clapped Patrick on the back and tried to persuade him not to leave on the ferry when it would return to the mainland tomorrow. "It's not so bad," he said. "I could use a partner in crime. Tomorrow I'll take you fishing in the morning, then we can come back here and do it again."

The prospect of following in Milton's footsteps was unthinkable. Patrick didn't want to spend his days at a soda fountain to hide from Gwen's family. She had been so convinced he would adore them, but she couldn't have been more wrong. Like Uncle Milton, he didn't belong here.

The bell dinged over the door, and Natalia came racing into the store, her normally pristine hair a scraggly mess.

"Smitty, I need to send a telegram," she panted.

Patrick stood, alarmed by the panic in her voice. "What's wrong?"

"Somebody shot Poppy. She's gone into labor, and we need a doctor right away."

Mr. Smitty pulled the cover off the telegraph machine, but Patrick could barely absorb what she'd just said. "*Poppy?*" he asked in disbelief. "What about Gwen. Is she all right?"

Natalia gave an impatient nod, then turned her back on him to dictate a message to the mainland. Her father's yacht had already left for New York, and she wanted a doctor to be waiting at the port for a return trip to Cormorant Island tonight.

After the telegram had been sent, Natalia relayed the entire story of an unknown assailant who unloaded a six-shooter at Liam but hit Poppy instead while Gwen cowered in the underbrush.

Patrick's mind reeled. While he'd been drinking with Milton, Gwen had been dodging bullets. "I've got to get back right away," he said.

He only hoped Gwen would be able to forgive him for sulking during her hour of need.

It was dark when Patrick arrived at the house, where the Blackstone clan remained crammed into the main gathering room. Everyone looked exhausted, but Frederick wouldn't let anyone leave until police officers from the mainland arrived, which probably wouldn't be for a few more hours.

Edwin played cards on the dining table and looked bored out of his mind. "Now that Liam is gone, we're all safe," he muttered.

"No one is leaving," Frederick insisted. "If any evidence remains about who was firing that gun, I won't provide an opportunity to hide it."

The windows were open, but it was still sweltering with all these people crammed inside. Patrick felt smothered. Gwen sat on the floor, singing to the five-year-old twins, who gaped at her like she was a goddess. He grabbed a stool to sit beside her.

"You survived intact?" he asked, his churning stomach a sick reminder that while he'd been grousing about the Blackstones at the soda counter, she could have been killed.

Gwen didn't go out of her way to make it easy on him. She glanced at her cousin Joshua, the useless one from Yale, who was playing cards with Edwin. The younger man's face was riddled with ugly scratches.

"Joshua's face took a hit when a bullet exploded a tree next to him. He was very brave as he carried Poppy to safety. We're all quite proud of him."

Gwen wouldn't even look at him as she continued playing with the twins. It could have been Gwen's face that was injured by flying shrapnel. While Patrick sulked, Gwen had been alone and vulnerable.

"I'm sorry," he said. "I should have been here to protect you."

"Don't worry, I survived without you." There was no thaw in Gwen's frosty demeanor, but perhaps it would only take some time.

Uncle Milton came over to deliver the letter that had arrived at Smitty's store. The envelope was on college stationery, and she flipped it open without much interest, but her shoulders sagged as she read the contents.

"Bad news?"

"The Spanish monks turned down our request to send us the old date seeds."

"Are they the same Spanish monks who own a piece of the bank?"

She nodded. "They're rich, so they can't be tempted by money."

Gwen had once told him that if she ever pursued a doctorate in botany, she wanted to use those seeds as the focus of her research. She seemed unusually disappointed, but Patrick couldn't get worked up over old seeds. The date seeds were three hundred years old, and if it took her a few more years to get her hands on them, it wouldn't matter. She would never tear herself away from Blackstone College long enough to pursue a doctorate anyway.

Some of the younger children dropped off to sleep, and Patrick carried them to the far side of the room, where pallets had been laid out for them. He returned to Gwen, who looked exhausted and uncomfortable as she shifted to a new position on the floor.

"Why don't you head up to bed?" Patrick prompted. "Everyone knows you had nothing to do with this."

Frederick's iron-hard voice cracked across the room. "No one is to leave this room until the police arrive."

Patrick stood. Gwen had been through a lot today, and the old ladies looked worn out and miserable. Maybe no one else had the backbone to stand up to Frederick, but Patrick did. "Under the laws of New York procedure, you can't issue a blanket order to detain us without specific probable cause."

"My house, my rules," Frederick said. "I want to know who is trying to prevent Liam from rejoining the family."

Edwin turned away from the card game to face the others. "What if the real target was Poppy all along? You have to admit, she can be annoying."

"Don't be ridiculous," Natalia said.

Edwin bristled. "It could have been you," he snapped. "You've always been jealous of Poppy and probably want to take her out before she can give birth to a male heir."

"Edwin, you can't possibly be as stupid as you sound right now," Natalia said, fanning herself with a bamboo fan.

No one in the room was going to defy Frederick Blackstone, and Patrick couldn't force them to disperse. He sighed and took a seat on the floor alongside Gwen. It was going to be a long night.

36

A small but healthy baby boy was born shortly after the doctor arrived at two o'clock in the morning. Oscar opened a bottle of champagne, but Patrick and the others wanted only to stagger to bed. Now that half a dozen police officers from the mainland had arrived, Frederick allowed everyone to return to their bedrooms while guards were posted throughout the grounds. A search of the island would begin once the sun rose, but Patrick would no longer be here. He wanted to get off this island and away from these people as soon as possible.

In the morning, the police found a recently fired varmint gun in the shed, but the only ammunition on the island was for skeet shooting. No wonder the shots had gone wild.

Oscar wanted Poppy and his newborn child in the safety of his mansion back home and ordered the *Black Rose* to set sail shortly after sunrise. Transporting Poppy down the long set of stairs to the boathouse was a challenge. Milton suggested that the canoe he used to fish on the nearby lagoon could be lined with blankets and used to carry her down, so Patrick found himself gingerly scooping Poppy up from her bed. He didn't like her, but she was frightened and exhausted and had just given birth. He gently carried her to the padded canoe and lowered her inside. He and Joshua were the strongest men here, and they each held one end of the canoe as they carefully navigated the stairs to the boathouse.

Oscar carried his newborn son. He, Poppy, and the baby would be the only passengers on the first tender to the yacht because it was filled with trunks, hatboxes, and pillows for Poppy's comfort. It would return shortly for anyone else who wished to return to Manhattan.

As soon as the tender pulled away from the dock, Patrick and Gwen were alone in the boathouse.

"I'm going back with Oscar," she said. She set her hand on his arm, and it was trembling. "There is room on the yacht for you, if you want to join us."

"I'll take the ferry back later this morning," he said, avoiding the wounded look in her eyes.

"But why?"

"I can't be trapped alongside those people any longer. I'll jump out of my skin."

Her expression tightened. "And by *those people*, I assume you are referring to my family?"

"Yes, Gwen. I am." He turned away to pace, his footsteps making dull thuds on the planks of the boathouse. He dragged a hand through his hair as he struggled to find the right words, but there was no way to express how he felt without hurting her. "I know you think highly of them, but I've had my limit. We come from different worlds, Gwen."

"You don't have to live in their world," she said in exasperation. "I have a beautiful house. There's room enough for your mother and a yard where children could play."

"I'm not going to be a kept man, Gwen."

"That's ridiculous. If you won't move into my house, then I could move to the Five Points."

"And be a martyr for the rest of your life? You hate my place in the Five Points and always complained about the noise. The lousy plumbing."

"I could have the plumbing fixed. It's a health hazard."

"You see? You haven't even moved in and you want to rip out

the plumbing and begin anew. The plumbing in my building is good enough. It's what I can afford. I don't want to wake up some morning years from now and find out I've turned into your uncle Milton, who has shrunken into a shell of the man he should have been. Did you know he pretends to go fishing so he can hide from your family?"

"That's ridiculous."

"It's true. If your family was embarrassed by Milton's shoe-laces or underwear, how will they feel about my job defending people for drunkenness or bounced checks or dallying with prostitutes? That's what I do, Gwen. I am called to help down-trodden people who have fallen off the path and need a hand back up in the world."

Worry replaced her anger as she held up both palms in appeal. "Slow down. We always knew we would encounter bumpy times, but you can't just walk away. I can change. I can move to the Five Points."

She had tried to change for her first husband, and it had been a disaster. His anger drained away, replaced by aching poignancy.

"I don't want you to change," he said. "You're perfect just as you are. I may not think much of your family, but as I watched you on the beach, playing with the children and spreading optimism and beauty wherever you went . . . it would be a crime to change that."

"I can be that way in the Five Points."

He shook his head. "Your house has a two-acre garden where you hold soirees and grow healing herbs and heirloom roses. In the Five Points, the best I could offer you is a windowsill."

Tears pooled in her eyes, and her voice was so soft he could barely hear it. "I would make it a beautiful windowsill."

He touched the side of her face. "I have no doubt of that, but we should cut our losses now and go our separate ways."

Gwen rallied, a spark of energy straightening her spine and strengthening her voice. "You're letting pride stand in the way of what we could have. Since we met, I have felt more alive, more driven, and more excited to face each day. Don't throw away what we could be together."

"I'm sorry," he said. "A thousand times, I'm sorry. It was my fault for leading you to believe that I could fit into this world. I'm sorry that I can't. And I think we need to end things before I hurt you even more."

She winced but didn't look away. "Jasper hurt me. He let me down, but I didn't curl up into a ball and stop living. Not then, and not now. I want to build a life with you. What if we try and the worst happens? If it all collapses, I will be hurt and wounded like never before . . . but guess what? I'll survive. I did before, and I can do it again. Patrick! If we join forces, we can strengthen and nurture each other and do something great with our lives. Save a college? Cure a disease? Rescue people on the verge of eviction and give them hope for another day? I don't know what the future holds for us, but I don't want to lose the chance to find out because you're afraid of Poppy Blackstone's sharp tongue."

He bristled. "I'm not afraid of anything."

"Prove it," she said. She glanced toward the water, where the tender was returning. Her look was pointed, challenging him to get on board and sail back to New York with her.

He couldn't. It would only prolong the inevitable.

"It's not going to work," he said as gently as he could.

Her look of disappointment was hard to bear, but there was no bitterness in her voice, just a hint of resignation. "Sometimes the greatest strength a man can have is not letting his pride stand in the way of moving in the right direction."

The barb landed exactly where she intended, but he didn't flinch. The boat arrived, and he stood motionless as she boarded without looking at him again. He watched Gwen sail away, taking a piece of his heart with her.

37

Gwen returned to her house on its quiet, shady street bordering campus a little battered and a lot sadder than when she left, but she would survive. Her life went back to normal as she worked in her garden, hosted the Friday evening soirees, and gave the good news to President Matthews about the restored funding for the college.

As the days went by, her thoughts constantly strayed to Patrick. He would fit in perfectly at Blackstone College. She could get him a job as an attorney for the college, except he wouldn't take it. His pride wouldn't let him accept help from her, and maybe that was for the best.

Did he think about her? Did he hurt even a little over what they had lost?

One thing she didn't need to wonder about was what Liam was doing, for her brother kept her informed through daily messages about his progress consulting with labor union leaders and learning the finer points of the steel industry. Patrick was by his side the entire time, and soon they would approach Uncle Oscar with their plan to put Liam on the board of directors for the new company in exchange for Liam's promise to deliver union support for the merger.

As promised, Gwen had hired an attorney to transfer half of

what she inherited from her father into Liam's name. It didn't take long. Within two weeks, the necessary accounts had been set up and funded. Liam's world would never be the same, but Gwen's life continued as it always had. She was proud of Liam but didn't participate in his journey. Her life would always be here at the college.

As June turned into July, her days were spent preparing for fall classes and managing the greenhouse. This morning she was showing Mimi how to propagate goldenseal. Behind her thick glasses, Mimi had rich brown eyes the same shade as Jasper's, and she watched the process in fascination. They were at the worktable out in the garden, with the roots of the goldenseal plant laid out before them.

"These are the rhizomes," Gwen said, pointing out the little nodes. "These are what we will use to propagate new growth. I think we can get four or five new plants from this one."

Mimi carefully followed Gwen's instructions by clipping a notch beside each node. The girl had to lock her braces to stand long enough to get the job done, but she never once complained.

Spending time with Mimi was a balm on Gwen's wounded soul. Frankly, a broken heart was nothing compared to the lifetime of challenges Mimi had before her.

"What kind of medicine can you make from this plant?" the girl asked.

"Goldenseal roots can be brewed into a nice tea for digestive disorders."

Mimi nodded. "I've always wanted to make a nice tea for digestive disorders," she said with utmost seriousness, and Gwen hid her smile. Mimi was such a bright little girl and might someday become a scientist herself. Maybe even a doctor. If Mimi wanted to attend Blackstone College, Gwen would move heaven and earth to be sure it happened regardless of her physical challenges.

Her musings were interrupted by the clang of the telephone. Gwen dried her hands on a rag and hurried inside, suspecting what the call might be.

She was right. It was Liam with news.

"Uncle Oscar has taken the bait," Liam said, his voice tense with excitement. "Patrick and I are going to his place tomorrow to let him know that the labor unions are supporting my lead. I can't stop the deal, but I can make things tough in the press unless Oscar agrees to put me on the board of U.S. Steel."

She clenched the earpiece and leaned against the wall in silent exaltation. The news was not unexpected but still amazing. Who could have imagined that the crude, ill-mannered man she met a few months ago was primed to be appointed to the board of directors for the largest company in the world?

"Good luck, Liam," she said, proud beyond belief of her older brother.

Her gaze strayed to the painting of Hansel and Gretel as they wandered out of the dark and dangerous wood. Gwen had her brother back. He was on his way to becoming a man who would fulfill their father's wishes to protect the longevity of Blackstone College.

It would probably be an ugly battle at Uncle Oscar's house, but Gwen had no desire to attend. Her home was at the college, and she would trust Patrick to help Liam through the labyrinth ahead.

Patrick walked alongside Liam as they approached Oscar's Fifth Avenue home. It was three houses down from Frederick's mansion and even more grand.

"Do you really think this is going to work?" Liam asked as he adjusted the starched collar on one of his new, custom-tailored suits. Gwen had been right about the suit. Liam looked like any other sharply dressed man of the city. Patrick's best suit looked like a potato sack in comparison, but their clothes didn't matter today. All that mattered was the set of legal documents Patrick had been working on for the past two weeks.

"You've got all the cards in your hand," he said as they mounted the flight of marble steps. "Appointing you to the board of directors is a huge concession, but Oscar knows you have the unions in your back pocket. We won't settle for anything less."

Patrick's biggest fear about the meeting was Liam himself. Dealing with him was like trying to tame a whirlwind because Liam still couldn't control his impulses.

Patrick stopped directly in front of Liam and looked him in the eye. "Don't you dare go off on a tangent. Stick to the script."

"I'll follow your lead," Liam assured him, but Patrick still worried.

A butler answered the door and led them through several corridors lined with gilt-framed paintings and Roman busts on pedestals before they arrived in Oscar's private office.

Oscar stood as they entered. Unlike the rest of the showpiece mansion, this was a working office filled with dark wood paneling and practical equipment like a telephone, file cabinets, and reference manuals. A separate table held a ticker-tape machine that tracked movement on the New York Stock Exchange.

Patrick reached across Oscar's desk to shake his hand. "I trust Poppy and the little one are doing well?"

"Alexander is thriving," Oscar said with pride. "He arrived in the world three weeks early, but the doctor reports he is as strong as any full-term child."

They got down to business, and Patrick laid out their plans as concisely as possible. "Your father has had a change of heart about the creation of U.S. Steel. He fears sinking too much of the bank's capital into a single entity and intends to vote against it."

Oscar's lips thinned. "My father may vote his thirty-percent share however he chooses, but he can't scuttle the deal."

Patrick kept up the pressure. "If Liam uses his ten percent to vote against the merger, it will be a black eye for the bank. A vote that close is guaranteed to fire up the labor unions."

Oscar leaned back in his chair, his eyes hard. "You still don't have a majority, and you don't want to make an enemy of me."

"That's right, I don't," Liam agreed. "But I want a little something for my ten-percent vote."

Oscar raised a single brow. "Proceed."

"I want a seat on the board of directors of the new company. I know the steel business from the ground up, and I can make the mills a better place for every man toiling on the line."

Patrick watched Oscar carefully while Liam spoke. A hint of a smile hovered on Oscar's face.

"I could be persuaded," Oscar said. "But it would come at a cost. My father has the power to award you that ten-percent share in perpetuity, but you aren't ready to take them over. Not yet, and maybe not ever. If you sign a legally binding agreement to surrender those votes back to me, I'll see that you have a seat on the board of U.S. Steel."

Patrick and Liam had already discussed this. It was exactly what they expected of Oscar, and they were prepared to settle for it. Liam didn't have the perspective to understand other aspects of the bank's business, and all he truly wanted was control in the new steel company. All Patrick wanted was to save Gwen's college. The college cost the bank three million dollars a year. U.S. Steel would make that much in a day.

Patrick met Oscar's gaze across the desk and laid down his terms. "We want Liam on the board of directors and a clause guaranteeing the annual funding of Blackstone College in perpetuity. If you give us those two things, Liam will surrender his shares back to you."

"We have a deal," Oscar said, standing to extend his hand.

Patrick grinned and shook Oscar's hand. This was *exactly* what they had hoped. Oscar had probably known what they would be asking, because he had given in too easily for this to be a surprise.

Patrick was ready to proceed to signing on the deal when Liam threw a wrench into the works.

"There's one more thing I want," Liam said.

A stone landed in the pit of Patrick's belly. Why, why, *why* couldn't Liam ever control himself? All Patrick's senses went on alert, and he shot a warning glare at Liam, praying he wasn't going to ruin this entire deal with an irrational demand.

Oscar looked just as guarded. "Well?" he asked, a hint of menace in that single word.

"I want the *Black Rose*."

Oscar stiffened. "Out of the question."

"Gwen said it belonged to my father and that she inherited it from him," Liam said. "She gave it to you for nothing. I want it back."

Oscar didn't budge. "That yacht is important to me. I take my family out every weekend. I intend to do the same with my son as he comes of age."

"Don't ask me to cry over your poor deprived kids," Liam said. "I had a miserable childhood without any doting fathers or weekend yacht rides. Crocket Malone pounded me into a man with his fists. I grew up in a freezing cold tenement because he was too cheap to buy coal, and when most kids were in school, I sweltered in a steel mill tending the furnaces. I only have *one* happy memory from my childhood." He leaned forward in his chair as he locked eyes with Oscar. "I remember being on a boat with my real father. I remember facing into the wind and laughing with him as we threw crusts of bread up to the sea gulls wheeling above us. That boat was the *Black Rose,* and I want it back."

Uncomfortable seconds ticked by, and Oscar narrowed his eyes in a glare. "I think you're bluffing."

"Try me," Liam said. "If the U.S. Steel deal flies without opposition, you will be rich beyond all imagination. You can buy another yacht, but there's only one *Black Rose*. I can't get my childhood or my father back, but I can get the *Black Rose* back."

The challenge hung in the air, and Patrick wanted to strangle Liam. This was precisely the sort of tangent he'd warned Liam against because it endangered the real prize, but the gamble paid off. Oscar caved, and Liam signed over his ten percent of the vote in exchange for a seat on the board of directors for U.S. Steel. The agreement would make Liam one of the most powerful men in the steel industry.

As they walked out of the mansion, Liam carried the title to the *Black Rose* in his back pocket.

38

Gwen arrived at the college's greenhouse on Wednesday morning with a couple of students to add an extra layer of insulation to the north side of the structure. Little Mimi sat inside the greenhouse, charged with potting the goldenseal roots they'd prepared the other day. Mimi stared dully at a bowl of potting soil sitting in front of her. It was early, and she was probably sleepy, given the way she stared with limp interest at the bowl.

Gwen helped Hiram and Jake lay a roll of foil into the trench they'd dug around the north end of the building. It took almost an hour, and when they returned inside, Mimi still sat slumped before the bowl of potting soil. She hadn't touched it yet.

"You're not going to let us down by neglecting those plants, are you, Mimi?" Gwen teased.

To her horror, Mimi's expression crumpled, and she curled over, hiding her face.

Gwen gasped, racing to hunker down beside the girl. "Sweetheart, what's wrong?" she asked, but Mimi just shook her head and didn't speak.

Hiram and Jake both dropped what they were doing to stand nearby, looking on in concern.

"You can tell me anything," Gwen whispered. Mimi was always so cheerful and optimistic. It was awful to see her battling tears. Gwen rubbed Mimi's back. "Please tell me how I can make it better."

Mimi lifted her head. Her lower lip trembled furiously, but she was finally able to stammer out a reply. "My walker got broken."

Gwen glanced at the metal frame with wheels that Mimi depended on to walk. It looked all right from here, but Jake was inspecting it.

"Yup, Miss Mimi, it looks like the bracket on this wheel got bent. How did that happen?"

Mimi's lip started wobbling again, and tears spilled over. "Some boys on my street took it away from me. They put it up in a tree, and I couldn't stop them because I couldn't walk. They left it up there, and when my mama came to get it down, it fell, and the wheel broke."

Gwen stared, aghast.

"What are their names?" Hiram demanded.

"I don't know who they were, but they were mean," Mimi said. "They laughed at how I got stuck on the ground and couldn't even stand up without my walker."

"Okay, so what did they look like?" Hiram pressed.

Gwen pulled Mimi tighter in her arms. "Don't make her re-live it," she murmured to him, but Hiram was just as adamant.

"I'm going to find out who they are," he whispered fiercely. "No bratty kids are going to gang up on Mimi and get away with it."

But they *would* get away with it. Even if Hiram figured out who those boys were and scared the daylights out of them, children could be cruel, and there would be more who would find an easy target in Mimi's thick glasses and malformed legs. Mimi was only just beginning to understand that she was different, and the coming years were going to be hard for her.

Jake was more pragmatic as he examined the damaged wheel. He cautiously rolled the walker forward. It still worked, but the wheel made a knocking sound as it rotated. "I'll bet Professor Jenkins can fix this in short order. He's an engineer and can probably have it repaired before lunchtime."

"I don't think it will ever be the same again," Mimi whispered, and Gwen's heart split wide open because it wasn't the walker Mimi spoke about. She scrambled for a way to make the girl feel better.

"Why don't we go over to my house for a snack?" she suggested. "I have a pan of brownies, and I can't eat them all myself. I think the three of you deserve a treat."

Hiram carried Mimi piggyback-style on the short walk to Gwen's house. Jake dropped off the walker with Professor Jenkins and joined them for brownies with milk in the garden. Word about what had happened spread quickly on campus, and soon the students who worked in the library came over to help cheer up Mimi.

The girl ate part of a brownie, then became engrossed by the fish swimming in the pond. She asked permission to feed them, and Gwen fetched her a slice of bread. Within an hour, Professor Jenkins showed up, wheeling the repaired walker, which had been decked out with ribbons and a bouquet of carnations tied to the handle.

Mimi beamed when she saw it. Even more professors and a couple of graduate students accompanied Professor Jenkins. The garden was full, and Gwen raced inside to assemble a platter of fruit and cheese for the impromptu party.

It was bittersweet. She loved this garden and the parties that had been held here over the years. She loved that Mimi felt safe here, and that the people of the college came out in support of this much-loved little girl. There would come a time when the staff and students of Blackstone College could no longer protect Mimi from the cruelty of others, but it would be better for the girl to have a few more years to grow strong and confident before facing the harsh realities of the world.

Gwen pulled Hiram aside. "Can you stay with Mimi for a few minutes? I have an errand I need to do."

He looked a little befuddled but readily agreed. "Sure thing, Mrs. Kellerman."

Tears blurred her vision as she closed the door of her house and began walking toward the heart of campus. Each block was laden with memories. She passed the president's house, where she had been born and raised. She passed the biology building, where she earned her degree, and the quadrangle, where endless summer days had been spent learning, growing, and making lifelong friendships. She walked beneath the elm trees and silver maples that shaded campus. They were tall now, but she remembered when they were newly planted saplings during the early years of the college.

It had been a wonderful place to grow up. She had been surrounded by adults who were as protective of her as they were of Mimi. This college was a cocoon of learning and a celebration of the world around them. Gwen would be forever grateful for her years here, but she didn't need the safety of a cocoon anymore.

Mimi did.

It was cool inside the administration building as she headed toward the accounting office. Vivian sat at the front counter, her fingers clicking on an adding machine. Her face cooled when she saw Gwen, but she didn't move.

"The house is yours," Gwen said. "You and Mimi can move in at the end of the month."

It was time to say good-bye to Jasper and the life they once shared. She was ready to move out into the real world and discover who she could become if she had never hidden herself away in an ivory tower.

It was the morning of the vote to buy Carnegie Steel and merge it with ten other mills to form the United States Steel Corporation. Patrick expected it to be a stressful day, but he hadn't realized he'd spend the final hour before the meeting in the men's washroom of Blackstone Bank, helping Liam battle the nerves that were getting the better of him. Liam was sweating so badly he'd had to wash his face, and he was now leaning over the green marble washbasin with gold-plated taps.

"Don't be so nervous," Patrick counseled Liam. "The vote is a foregone conclusion."

Liam closed the taps and blotted his face with a towel handed to him by a uniformed attendant. What sort of place had staff in the washrooms to hand out towels? Whenever Patrick thought he'd gotten used to the foibles of the Blackstones, something like this rose up to smack him in the face.

"Yeah, but I'm not used to double-crossing people," Liam said. "I'm scared to death about what Frederick is going to say when he finds out I've flipped to Oscar's side. I feel sick to my guts about it. Andrew Carnegie is going to be here. J.P. Morgan too."

For the past hour Patrick had been using kind, priestly counsel to gently build Liam's confidence, but none of it had worked. Perhaps it was time to change tactics. He grabbed Liam's shoulders to jerk him upright and toughened his voice.

"If you want to serve on the board of directors, these are the kind of men you'll be working with every day. Stand up straight, look them in the eye, and treat them like equals."

Liam glared. "They're not equals; they're the enemy."

"Knock it off," Patrick ordered, his voice loud enough to echo off the tile. "As of today, they are your business partners. Start acting like it."

Liam took a bracing breath, then blew it out and stood up straight. "You're right." He adjusted his collar and tugged down the vest of his insanely expensive suit.

Just before leaving, he tipped the washroom attendant. "You didn't hear anything, right?" Liam said to the man.

"Of course not." The attendant flashed Liam a wink. "Good luck, sir."

They rode in an elevator with turquoise and jade inlaid on the marble floor. Patrick watched the brass dial above the door rotate with each floor they climbed until they arrived at the top level and the attendant cranked the doors open.

A dozen men mingled in the lobby outside the boardroom. Patrick immediately homed in on the only woman in the group.

Natalia stood beside her father, wearing a sharply tailored emerald-green ensemble with a vest, tie, and jacket that still managed to look remarkably feminine. It was good to see a familiar face.

"I didn't expect to see you here," Patrick said, reaching out to shake her hand.

"I've got Count Sokolov's shares to vote," she said. "I'll never have a vote of my own, but Father lets me sit in on the meetings and vote the count's shares. Hello, Liam."

"Natalia," Liam acknowledged, but he was staring across the lobby toward where Andrew Carnegie stood alongside J.P. Morgan. "I didn't realize he was so short," he whispered. Andrew Carnegie was a colossus in the business world but only stood a few inches over five feet.

Before Patrick could reply, the doors to the boardroom were opened, and everyone began funneling inside.

The longest table Patrick had ever seen dominated the center of the room. It was so glossy it could be used as a mirror, and each seat had a nameplate before it. The owners of ten steel companies were here today. Frederick Blackstone took the seat at one end of the table, and J.P. Morgan sat at the opposite end. Between the two men, they were about to finance the creation of U.S. Steel.

"Gentlemen, please have a seat," Frederick said.

Introductions were made, for these steel magnates had come from across the nation and some had never met before. Frederick went out of his way to welcome "my grandson William" to the table.

J.P. Morgan had complete control over his bank, and recording his shares was a simple matter. The Blackstone shares were a little more complicated, with Oscar representing most of the votes that had been submitted to him via proxy, and Natalia voting the count's shares. Then it came to Liam, who stood.

"I expected to vote alongside my grandfather, but after careful consideration of the operating agreement, I believe the unions can get a fair shake from this company. I want to acknowledge my support of that agreement by voting in favor of it."

Frederick looked stunned as he gaped at Liam, but Liam kept his gaze on Andrew Carnegie.

"I will make it my mission in life to ensure this new company thrives, both for the workers and the health of the company as a whole. Neither side can prosper without the other, and I hope to be a trusted go-between for both sides." Liam swallowed hard and looked directly at Frederick. "I hope this doesn't disappoint you."

Liam sat, looking a little less confident.

Frederick leaned back in his chair, an inscrutable expression on his face as he spoke. "Since the moment you walked back into our lives, I wondered if you would take after Oscar or your father. Now I know. You are split straight down the middle. You are a man ruled by his heart but who uses cold, hard logic to get there. I won't underestimate you again."

It was impossible to know if Frederick approved or was furious, but the rest of the votes proceeded without incident, and by four o'clock the world's largest corporation had been born.

39

*G*wen spent the afternoon packing books to be moved to her new home. For two years she had avoided sorting through her library, unable to throw out Jasper's old books. Now it was easy. She was preparing for a new life, and that meant shedding the old. Most of the coming changes were going to be daunting, but discarding Jasper's books wasn't.

In September her new life would begin. She would leave this house to pursue a doctorate in botany, something she had always longed for but lacked the courage to do because it meant leaving Blackstone College. She hadn't been ready before.

Now she was. Someday she would like to return to Blackstone College and become a full-fledged botany professor, but first she had to earn that privilege by proving herself at New York University. It meant moving to downtown Manhattan and starting a completely new life, but she could never get where she truly wanted to be without embarking on the challenge.

Time got away from her as she worked, and she was running late for the grand party to celebrate the creation of U.S. Steel that Liam was hosting aboard the *Black Rose*. Aunt Martha had telephoned earlier in the day to ask for a ride because Milton had taken their carriage to go fishing.

Gwen was happy to oblige. Martha's son, Bertie, was always

fun, and he kept them entertained during the twenty-minute ride to the marina.

"Who could have imagined that Liam would nab the *Black Rose* away from Oscar, eh?" Bertie asked as the carriage set off. "You know anything about that, Gwen?"

She shook her head. "I haven't seen much of Liam in the past few weeks." She'd spoken with him by telephone almost every day but only learned he'd acquired the yacht when the announcement of tonight's party arrived.

It was going to be the first time she would see Patrick since that humiliating morning three weeks earlier when she begged him to stay with her. She would be calm and dignified. She didn't *need* Patrick, even though she ached from the loss of his companionship and teasing humor.

"Let's just hope Liam can throw a party as fine as Oscar always did," Bertie said.

"I heard Liam is keeping the same crew," Aunt Martha said. "I'm sure they have a well-oiled routine for entertaining. He'll probably even have the same string quartet Oscar always used for his yacht parties."

The carriage finally arrived at the designated yacht slip. The rigging of the *Black Rose* had been strung with celebratory lights, and most of the family was already on deck, laughing and mingling. And the music! This was no string quartet. It sounded like a ragtime band, with banjos, clarinets, and a piano.

Aunt Martha looked at the ship with a hint of appalled nostalgia. "Somehow I don't think things are ever going to be the same."

Gwen beamed. Oh yes, change was certainly coming to the *Black Rose*, and Gwen couldn't be prouder of Liam, who stood at the top of the gangway, waving her aboard. Wearing a simple white shirt with an open collar, he looked happier than she'd ever seen him.

"You're late!" he called down. He looked completely at home on the *Black Rose*, and she impulsively hiked up her skirts to run up the gangway. She was out of breath but delighted as she flung herself into his arms.

"Congratulations." She laughed as he hoisted her off her toes. This was what she had missed all these years. She finally had a real brother, even though he wasn't at all what she'd expected. Liam could be crass, rude, and perfectly awful, but perhaps that wasn't very different from most older brothers.

"We're still waiting on Natalia, but then we're off," he said.

She gazed over the deck of the yacht, crammed with family members and guests. Oscar and Frederick were here, along with plenty of businessmen she didn't know but suspected were major players in the new company that had just been formed.

"So the *Black Rose* is now yours," she said to Liam in amazement, and he nodded in satisfaction.

"I'm planning on living aboard. I've always been happiest on a ship, and it's plenty big enough. It will save on rent."

"Will you dock it here or in Philadelphia?"

"Here," Liam said. "This is where U.S. Steel is going to be headquartered, so it's where I need to be."

Living aboard a ship sounded horrible to Gwen, but Bertie had finally lumbered up the gangway and interjected himself into the conversation.

"Liam, my lad!" he said, giving her brother a jovial clap on the back. "Where's the caviar? I'm famished."

Liam grinned and shook his head. "None of that fancy food tonight. We've got biscuits, pulled pork, and spareribs coming up as soon as we set sail."

Bertie seemed to approve of the changes, as his eyes grew wide. "Excellent choice," he said, then hollered across the deck to the other side of the yacht. "Edwin! Liam says we're having spareribs as soon as we sail."

Her cousin Edwin limped over, a cane in one hand and an empty martini glass in the other. "Sounds good," he said to Liam. "I like the changes you're making. I never could stand caviar, but Poppy isn't happy about losing it. She thinks pork is lowbrow."

Poppy sat at the stern of the ship, swathed in robes and accepting congratulations on the birth of her son, who was safely ensconced in his grim nursery back home. She was surrounded by the elderly aunts and boasting of little Alexander's astonishing accomplishments in communicating when he was hungry.

"Next thing you know, Poppy will say he is fluent in Greek," Bertie said and turned back to Edwin. "Say, did you bring that antique vase you owe me?"

Edwin looked momentarily annoyed, but it vanished quickly. "Sorry, old man, I forgot it back at my place. Next week, I promise." He turned his attention to Liam with a huge smile. "I must congratulate you on the U.S. Steel appointment. You've taken us all by surprise."

"A good one, I hope," Liam said.

"Good, indeed!" Edwin threw a friendly arm around Liam's shoulder. "Say, how about we put together a group of people to go bet on the horse races? There's a fine little racetrack nearby, and I can show you the ropes."

A hint of irritation flashed across Liam's face, but it came and went so quickly that Gwen thought she might have imagined it.

A waiter emerged onto the deck with flutes of champagne, drawing Bertie and Edwin to him like a lodestone. Liam watched them leave with a pensive look on his face.

"You were right," he said once they stood alone at the railing.

"Right about what?"

"The way people treat me is different since I got rich. The wife of the guy who runs the marina keeps throwing herself at me. A *married* woman, and she never misses a chance to lob a proposition at me. The girls at the diner where I get lunch come after me too. Everyone wants to be my friend now. Edwin wants me to join his racing club, but he's all full of fake smiles and backslapping. It kind of makes me appreciate Poppy. She's a horror on wheels, but at least she's honest."

Gwen's heart softened with a tangle of bittersweet sympathy. While it was far better to be rich than poor, money brought a unique set of challenges. Liam would never again be able to automatically trust anyone who tried to befriend him. Every person he met for the rest of his life would know he possessed a fortune, and it would change things. She witnessed it even now as she stood at the railing with him. Cousins came over to congratulate him, far warmer than they'd been on the island. Some wanted details of the meeting this afternoon, while others wanted to know when to expect their first infusion of dividend payments.

A pair of tough-looking strangers loitered near the catering area.

"Who are those men?" she asked.

Liam followed her gaze. "I hired a couple of bodyguards. I figure it's better to be safe than sorry."

She had to agree, especially since they had never figured out who was trying to kill him. How ironic that just as she was feeling ready to step outside of her safe, protected bubble, Liam was being forced into one of his own. She glanced at the bodyguards again just in time to see Patrick emerging from the lower deck.

Her heart caught at the sight of his tall form and the way the light highlighted the planes in his kind, friendly face. His eyes found hers across the crowded deck, and his smile was wistful.

She would handle this with cool dignity. The anguish blooming in her heart could be ignored, and she crossed the deck to meet him beneath the awning of the portside door.

"Hello, Patrick," she said, managing a smile.

"Gwen." He looked like he was trying to be as civilized and dignified as possible.

"I suppose congratulations are in order," she said.

He nodded with a little laugh. "It was a bigger job than I could have imagined. Liam and I were holed up in my office until ten o'clock every night going over all the details. It was hard, but we had a grand time of it."

A hint of jealousy gnawed at her. She'd never expected that Patrick would become closer to Liam than to her. His help spiffing Liam up was supposed to have been a business arrangement, not a real friendship.

"What will you do now?" she asked.

"I'll go back to the Five Points," he said. "That's the sort of law I was meant to do. All this corporate law and rubbing shoulders with the rich was a bit of a stretch for me. I'm glad it's over."

He shifted in discomfort, scanning the assembled guests. Only about half the people here were Blackstones. The others were leaders from the smaller steel companies and financiers from J.P. Morgan's bank. The one thing they had in common was that they were all rich. None of them were salt of the earth like Patrick.

"Do you still look down your nose at us?"

Patrick crossed his arms over his chest and looked away, almost as if she'd hurt him. When he spoke, his voice was quiet. "I can see the good in some of you." He swallowed and continued. "I'm sorry about the way things worked out. I don't want to fight with you."

He was right. She came here determined to be dignified, and yet she'd just thrown the first dart. She needed to walk it back.

"Forgive me," she said. "I'm just tense and nervous over all the changes in my life, and I shouldn't have taken it out on you."

His eyes softened in concern. "What changes?"

"Liam didn't tell you?"

"Tell me what? All we've had time for is corporate business."

She couldn't help the smile that broke out across her face. "I'm starting classes at New York University next month. With luck, I'll have my doctorate in three years, focusing on botanical medicine."

"Good for you!" he said, genuine happiness lighting up his face. He opened his arms as though about to embrace her, then remembered. He dropped his arms and withdrew a step. "I'm proud of you," he said a little awkwardly.

She nodded, feeling equally uncomfortable. What was she supposed to say?

She was spared a response when Liam's strong voice bellowed across the water. "Natalia! Hurry up and get on board. We've been waiting for you!"

People began applauding as Natalia hurried up the gangway. The moment she boarded, two deckhands pulled up the ramp and prepared the ship for departure.

Natalia came immediately to Gwen's side, looking flushed and embarrassed. "I'm sorry to be late," she said. "I didn't realize I was the last to arrive. I was delayed by wiring Count Sokolov about the vote."

"Couldn't you have sent him a telegram tomorrow?" Patrick asked.

"Of course not!" Natalia said. "He knew the vote was today, and he always wants to know every detail as soon as possible. He's fussy that way."

"But the vote was four hours ago!" Patrick said.

Natalia laughed. "Do I need to remind you how difficult it is to contact a man in Siberia? Or how he enjoys nattering on over the silliest things? Oh, Gwen, he's completed his juniper perfume and named it in your honor. He says it's a masterpiece, but don't get your hopes up, because he tends to exaggerate."

Natalia continued speaking about Count Sokolov, whose hungry mind was always searching for distractions while stuck in his lonely Siberian outpost. The yacht had begun moving, sailing down the river toward the Upper Bay, but Gwen's mind was far away. At this very moment she was surrounded by friends and family yet still felt desperately alone. It was like a physical ache inside, filling her chest and weighing her spirits.

"I envy you," she said to Natalia.

"Really?" Natalia asked. "Why?"

Gwen struggled to find an explanation for this strange emotion. "I'm jealous," she admitted. "Your friendship with Count Sokolov is charming."

Natalia leaned forward and kissed Gwen's cheek. "It is indeed," she said, then flitted away to greet Oscar and the other bankers.

"It's not real," Patrick said.

"What's not real?"

"Her supposed friendship with Count Sokolov. It's just rich people wasting money on expensive telegrams."

Her whimsical musing about Natalia and her lonely Russian count evaporated. Just because Natalia's friendship was unlikely didn't mean it wasn't real. Sometimes love and friendship blossomed despite barriers of time and distance and class. Patrick might refuse to believe it, but that was his shortcoming, not hers. Frustrated annoyance with him boiled over.

"Patrick, you are the biggest snob on this yacht, and considering Poppy is aboard, that's saying a lot."

She walked away before she said something even more unkind.

Patrick watched in astonishment as Gwen stormed away. He was a man of the people! He didn't have an ounce of snobbery or entitlement and had dedicated his life to serving the poor. Temptation to follow Gwen and demand an explanation clawed at him, but Liam foiled his chance.

"Yo, Patrick!" Liam called from the stern of the ship, where he was clustered with some of Gwen's pretentious cousins. "We need your saintly wisdom to settle a legal argument."

Patrick shoved his frustrations aside to join Liam and several of the Blackstone cousins from the third generation. Joshua, whose face had fully healed from his brush with the wild gunshots, seemed much friendlier today than he'd been before.

"Three percent of the bank's shares are owned by a bunch of monks in Spain," Joshua said. "How do priestly vows of poverty reconcile with the riches they're likely to start earning from U.S. Steel?"

"I've got no insight for you," Patrick admitted. Aside from the fact that they had been tightfisted about the seeds Gwen wanted, he didn't know a single thing about those Spanish monks. "Monastic finance isn't something I have experience with."

"Really?" Joshua asked. "I thought you were an expert on church finances. That you holed up with Father Murry's church in Pittsburgh every night to set up a special accounting system."

It took a moment for Patrick to digest that statement. Everything Joshua said was true, but the details of those long afternoons with Father Murry weren't something he'd shared with anyone aside from Liam. Patrick's heart rate picked up a notch, but he kept the tension from his voice as he spoke directly to Joshua.

"How do you know about my work with that church in Pittsburgh?"

Joshua looked uneasy, shifting his weight while struggling for a laugh. "Well, you know . . . there was that newspaper article about it. About how you helped yourself to the till. Not that we believe it, of course! You remember, Poppy was talking about it at the lobster bake. She had a newspaper from Pittsburgh that she was showing everybody."

Patrick tried to remember exactly what was in the article Poppy had been showing around, but Liam cut straight to the chase.

"That article was from the Pittsburgh police blotter," Liam said. "It never mentioned the priest's name or what Patrick was working on for him, so how do you know it?"

"Poppy told me," Joshua said simply.

Poppy was only ten yards away, holding court with the elderly aunts. Patrick needed to pin this down, because Father Murry's name hadn't been printed in that article, which meant someone knew a lot more about the incident than had appeared in the newspaper.

He strode toward Poppy, and the others followed. Liam snapped his fingers, summoning his bodyguards, who had been posted near the stern of the ship. Soon all of them were standing next to Poppy, who sat enthroned on a wicker chair with a huge rounded back.

"Poppy, what do you know about the crime I was accused of in Pittsburgh?" Patrick asked bluntly.

All five aunts swiveled to gape at him, while Poppy looked offended. "Excuse me, I was having a civilized conversation with my husband's aunts about the birth of my child."

"And I need to know how you got your hands on that newspaper from Pittsburgh." Figuring out how that newspaper got to the island might reveal who was behind the trumped-up charges at Father Murry's church.

Aunt Martha pushed herself to her feet to soothe the troubled waters. "I hope you know that none of us believe that nonsense," she said, but Patrick wouldn't let the subject drop.

He leaned in closer to Poppy. "I want to know how you got your hands on that newspaper."

By now, plenty of others had gathered around, all of them awaiting Poppy's answer.

"Edwin gave it to me," she said. "He subscribes to all the major newspapers on the East Coast so he can buy antiques that get listed for sale."

"Edwin doesn't have two dimes to rub together," Liam said. "Just last week he asked me for a loan. He ought to get a real job instead of trying to make a go of it buying old junk."

"Junk?" Bertie asked. "I paid him six hundred dollars for an antique flask, and I still haven't seen it yet."

Patrick spoke directly to Liam. "Being broke isn't a crime, but it's awfully convenient that Edwin was reading the Pittsburgh police blotter. Someone tried to frame us in Pittsburgh and probably pulled some strings to get it reported in the paper. I wonder if Edwin was in Pittsburgh this summer."

Liam's expression turned fierce. "Let's go ask him." He gestured for the bodyguards to follow him to the far side of the ship where Edwin was playing deck shuffleboard with some of the younger cousins. Even Poppy rose to follow.

"Edwin, when was the last time you were in Pittsburgh?" Patrick asked.

Edwin straightened and leaned casually on his shuffleboard cue. "I've never been to Pittsburgh."

"But you subscribe to the Pittsburgh newspaper," Liam asserted.

"No, I don't," Edwin said, beginning to glance nervously at the people suddenly gathered around him.

"Yes, you do," Poppy insisted. "You said you monitor it for antique sales and that's why you had a copy on the island."

Edwin shook his head, smiling condescendingly at Poppy. "You brought that newspaper to the island. Don't you remember? You said you wanted to follow the Pittsburgh golfing league."

Poppy looked confused. "No. The only time I heard mention of the Pittsburgh golf league was when that redheaded fellow mentioned it during the croquet game last weekend. He's such a crass fellow. I don't care that he is your hunting partner. I don't like him and wish you would stop bringing him to my croquet parties."

The only assailant who'd gotten away the night of Liam's attack was a redheaded man with a long, crooked nose.

"Tell me more about this redheaded fellow," Patrick asked, striving for a calm tone so Poppy would cooperate, but Liam was more aggressive.

"Did he have a long nose and carry a hunting knife with deer antlers carved into the handle?"

"I have no idea," Poppy said defensively. "He's Edwin's friend, not mine, and I've asked Edwin to stop bringing him around because I can't tolerate the smell of garlic on a man's breath."

Edwin looked sick, but he still managed a nonchalant laugh. "Poppy's got it wrong," he said, looking at Liam. "She brought the newspaper to the island, and she was the one who showed me the article about Patrick stealing from some kind of church fund."

Poppy bristled. "That's a lie. You brought the newspaper to the island, and now you're trying to blame me."

"You probably shot at us too," Joshua said, staring straight at Edwin in appalled wonder. "None of the Blackstones even know how to load a gun except you."

"But I'm an excellent shot," Edwin defended. "If I wanted to shoot someone, I wouldn't have missed."

"That was because the gun was loaded with the wrong ammunition," Joshua said. "Of course the shots went wild. You ruined the best weekend of the year."

"And I've got a scar on my arm I'm going to have for the rest of my life," Poppy yelled, giving a two-handed shove to Edwin, who stumbled back. The cast on his leg made him clumsy, but he caught himself before falling.

Patrick reeled as the implications sank in. The redheaded man was the lead assassin, and it looked like he and Edwin were hunting partners. Edwin had been short of cash lately.

"Where's Bertie's jade flask?" Patrick asked. "He's been asking about it for weeks."

"What's the redheaded guy's name?" Liam demanded. "He almost killed me in front of my mother, and if I have to beat his name out of you, I will."

Liam and Patrick stood shoulder to shoulder as they closed in on Edwin, who continued retreating until his back was against the railing of the yacht. His nervous glance darted around the others who congregated around them, but no pity was to be found.

One of the bodyguards looked at Liam. "Do you want us to take him down?"

The color dropped from Edwin's face as the semicircle of men closed around him. He swallowed hard, turned around, then dove into the bay.

Edwin's mother screamed. "Somebody save him! My poor boy, he's got a broken leg and won't be able to swim!"

A pair of deckhands scrambled to lower a tender to the water below.

"Bring along plenty of men," Oscar ordered. "Desperate men do desperate things."

"I'll go," Liam said, his voice a combination of anger and anticipation.

"Not you," Patrick said. Given Liam's furious mood, Edwin

might not survive the rescue, and they needed him alive. He glanced at Joshua, a healthy man who looked keen on getting to the bottom of this. "Joshua? Care to join me?"

Joshua nodded and shucked off his coat.

Edwin was making progress swimming toward shore despite the cast on his leg. He swam toward the Jersey coast in long, overhand strokes.

Patrick, Joshua, and three crew members boarded the tender, then the deckhands began lowering the boat. Patrick looked up at the people clustered along the railing and spotted Gwen watching Edwin in shocked surprise. She liked Edwin. She bragged about his world travels and knowledge of antiques. This was going to hit her hard, but she had to learn that her wonderful, eccentric family had at least one truly rotten apple.

The boat wobbled as it hit the water. Crew members detached the ropes, and Patrick took his place beside Joshua, both of them rowing after Edwin. It didn't take them long to pull alongside him. Edwin had resorted to a breaststroke, still heading for shore but barely making any progress as his strength faded.

Patrick leaned over to talk to him. "We can take you aboard now or do it on shore. Either way, you're not going to escape."

Edwin spit out a mouthful of water and kept struggling toward shore. "I was broke," he said, panting and barely able to keep his head above water. The cast on his leg was probably getting heavier by the second.

"You ordered a hit on Liam because you were broke?"

"I didn't want to do it," Edwin panted, still swimming. "There's a price on my head. If you get in too deep with the moneylenders, they play tough."

"The kind of tough that ends up with a broken leg?"

"Yeah. Atlantic City . . . the cardroom."

Edwin's need for a plentiful stream of revenue might explain why Liam's sudden arrival back in the family was such a threat. Liam was outspoken in his hostility to the steel merger. He could have stoked up the unions and delayed the creation of U.S.

Steel. After getting control of his father's shares, Liam might even have scuttled the deal for good, meaning that the lucrative dividends Edwin expected to earn from the deal would vanish. He'd made a preemptive strike to eliminate the possibility of Liam ever returning to the family.

Patrick released the oars, as did the other men in the boat. Edwin was no longer making any progress. A weak dog paddle was all he could manage, and he finally reached up to grasp the side of the boat, wheezing, his face sick.

"I don't want to go back to the *Black Rose*," he panted. "I don't want to face them."

It was understandable. They were only a few hundred yards from the shoreline, but Patrick didn't feel like spending the rest of the evening traveling back to Manhattan from Jersey City. Sometimes a person didn't have many choices in life, but Edwin had dug himself into this hole all by himself, and the people around him had suffered enough for it.

A crew member clamped a boarding ladder onto the side of the boat. Edwin still hesitated to take it.

"I can't force you to climb aboard," Patrick said. "I don't want to watch you drown trying to swim to shore, but that's your choice, not mine."

Edwin climbed aboard, and the crew members scrambled to turn the boat around. The world's most awkward family reunion on the *Black Rose* was about to occur.

40

After Edwin's shameful fall from grace, Gwen did her best to look forward to her new life. She moved out of her house and onto the *Black Rose* to live with Liam until renovations to the apartment she'd purchased could be completed, and in September her new life would officially begin.

Liam teased her mercilessly. To his eyes, she had merely changed one college for another. She tried to explain that the safe, cozy world of Blackstone College was a very different place than the intimidating urban environment of New York University, but he wasn't convinced.

"They're all just rich college kids," he said dismissively.

Maybe so, but she was about to embark on a doctorate in botany, something she had always longed for but lacked the courage to get because it meant leaving Blackstone College. She hadn't been ready before.

Now she was. Someone else would take over her botany class at Blackstone College while she embarked on the challenges of original research, publication, and laboratory work. Someday she would like to return to Blackstone College as a botany professor, but first she had to earn that privilege by proving herself at New York University.

School started next month, and today her only task was to

help Liam toilet train his dog. One of the first things Liam did after taking ownership of the *Black Rose* was to send for his beloved, slobbery bulldog, who was going to be living on the yacht with them. A box of gravel was set out near the stern of the ship, and they walked laps around the deck while waiting for the dog to do its business.

They rounded the bow of the ship, where the view overlooked the marina. The sun was just beginning to set, and Gwen spotted a familiar figure loping across the pier toward them.

"Tell me that isn't who I think it is," she said.

"Uncle Mick," Liam confirmed in a grim voice. "That's his wife walking beside him. Guard your wallet. They're both crooks and desperate for cash."

The publication of Mick's memoir had been canceled. Since Liam's return, it was obvious the memoir was a pack of lies. There were no Italians who'd kidnapped little Willy Blackstone. There was no unjust prosecution. Mick had kidnapped Willy Blackstone, then passed him off to his cousin when the police closed in on the Five Points. Crocket hated the Blackstones enough to hold on to the boy, raising him in the same dingy conditions the rest of the workers in the steel industry endured.

"Don't even let them onboard," Gwen advised. "You're a respectable man of business now, and consorting with shady people can ruin your reputation."

Liam ignored her pleas and lowered the gangway. Five minutes later, Mick and his blowsy wife were onboard, craning their necks to admire the fine brass fittings and elegant deck furnishings. Mick was rail-thin, his wife a little plump and bedraggled, and they both lugged overstuffed canvas satchels.

"We heard you'd moved aboard," Mick said. "It seems to me you'll be lonely here. Do you suppose you've got a room for me and Ruby?"

Liam folded his arms across his chest. "Forget it. No room at the inn."

"You can't just turn us away," Mick protested. "We're family. You owe us."

Liam's eyes narrowed. "I don't owe you anything. You and Crocket ruined most of my life, but no more. From this day forward, my name is Liam Blackstone. And if you ever try to come near me or touch anything else I own, I'll set the law on you."

Mick sputtered in outrage. "We don't have anything left! They canceled my book."

"Am I'm supposed to feel sorry for you? Get off my ship." Liam grabbed Mick's satchel and threw it onto the pier below, where it landed with a splat, scattering Mick's paltry belongings over the planking. He reached for Ruby's sack next, but she clutched it to her chest and started heading toward the gangway.

Mick reluctantly followed, spewing obscenities that echoed across the harbor. Gwen recoiled at the vile tone, but it was a terrible peek into the crude world her brother came from. Liam's knuckles were white as he clutched the railing, but his face was emotionless as he watched Mick and Ruby walk out of his life.

"Does it hurt?" she asked.

Liam took a while to respond as he stared into the darkened marina. "Yeah, it hurts. It shouldn't, but it does."

She understood. The crime Mick perpetrated against her entire family was going to be hard to forgive, but it would be hardest for Liam. He was probably right in making a clean break with the Malones. Like her, Liam was going to have to cut ties with the past before stepping into a new future.

41

Patrick spent the two weeks after the steel merger dealing with a flurry of cases from his regular clients. He fended off evictions, helped a man charged with illegal dumping, and defended a woman arrested for jaywalking while drunk. He visited men in jail to arrange for bail and filed lawsuits against insurance companies who refused to pay on their claims. None of it was glamorous or involved massive corporate mergers, but these cases meant the world to the people he served, and he burned the midnight oil chipping away at the backlog of paperwork.

His mother had returned to her job at the bakery. It was as if she'd never been sick. She still made him dinner each evening, pestered him to get married, and played pinochle with Mrs. O'Shea on the weekends.

One evening she brought home a special cake. The vanilla layer cake featured the shield and motto of Blackstone College.

"I'd like to thank Mrs. Kellerman," Birdie said. "We can't afford to pay her for the serum, but I want her to know I'm grateful, and a cake is the only thing I can offer."

"It's a nice gesture," Patrick said, but guilt gnawed at him. A cake seemed embarrassingly paltry compared to what Gwen had done for them. He could never repay her for the serum, and then he'd made things worse by leading her to believe they might have a future together. They both got carried away building castles in the air, and it was his fault for letting it go too far.

"You'll take it over to her, then?" Birdie didn't look at him as she diced carrots for a stew.

He scrambled for an excuse. "Don't you think it would look better coming from you?"

She shook her head. "I'm cooking dinner, Patrick. She knows who baked that cake, but I think you should take it over."

He sighed. His mother was matchmaking and he didn't like it, but he'd look like a coward if he wormed out of it. Besides, he probably needed to settle things with Gwen. The last time he'd seen her had been during the disastrous party on the yacht when he fished her cousin out of the water. He owed her the respect of a proper farewell, even though it wasn't going to be easy on either of them. He loved her, but nothing could ever come of it.

He put the glass cover over the cake and set off for the streetcar stop. It took forty minutes to get to Blackstone College, all the while awkwardly holding a cake on his lap, but soon he was walking down the tree-shaded avenue to her house. The leaves were just beginning to turn, the sun was setting, and it looked as pretty as a postcard as he headed up the walk to her front door.

Gwen's artistic flair could be seen everywhere. Chrysanthemums bloomed in the garden, and lovely ironwork scrolls framed the door. He swallowed hard and rapped the iron knocker, feeling a little foolish holding a cake in front of him.

After a moment, a beautiful blond woman answered the door. "Can I help you?" she asked.

He was taken aback. "I'm looking for Gwen Kellerman."

"She doesn't live here anymore," the blond woman said, her voice cool.

He couldn't believe it. He angled his head to look past the woman and down the hallway of Gwen's house. The furniture was different, and a little girl with braces on her legs read a book in the front parlor.

"Are you Vivian?" he asked, and his stomach sank when she

replied in the affirmative. Unbelievable! How many times had he nagged Gwen to get moving on that unenforceable will her scoundrel of a husband had scrawled? She obviously hadn't, and now she'd lost her house because of it. "Where has she gone?"

Vivian crossed her arms. "Who are you? Are you from the college?"

He shook his head. "I'm her lawyer. Where has she gone?"

"She's gone to live on some sort of boat. I have no idea where it is."

The *Black Rose*. It had to be. It wasn't right that Gwen should be ousted from her home because she couldn't stand up to her faithless husband's mistress. She deserved better than that.

"Here," he said, thrusting the cake into Vivian's hands. He couldn't be saddled with a cake when he had work to do.

Each evening Gwen read from botany journals in the privacy of her cabin on the *Black Rose,* and it was her favorite part of the day. Her mind had been parched for knowledge, and now she was being drenched with a flood of insight and discovery. Why had she waited so long to do this? Her fingers literally trembled as she turned the pages, because soon she wouldn't just be listening to other scientists talk about their work, she was going to have a chance to actually *do* it.

She had just started another article on the hardiness of wheat seeds exposed to frigid temperatures when a deckhand knocked on her door, announcing a visitor.

"Who is it?" she asked in confusion.

"I don't know, but he's down on the pier, shouting up to see you. Shall I tell him to go away?"

She shook her head. It could be someone from the college, and it might be important. She pulled on a robe to cover her nightgown and headed up to the deck.

It was dark outside, but Patrick's tall form was easy to spot on the pier below. He was illuminated by the harbor lights that glinted on the water and lit the angry planes of his face.

"Why did you let that woman take your house?" he yelled up at her.

Seeing him again hurt. She'd been doing her best to move on from the anguish of their split, and until thirty seconds ago she had been succeeding admirably. Now he was back and wanted to talk about *Vivian*, of all things.

"I gave it to her," she called down.

Patrick let out a stream of curse words that echoed over the marina. "Why?" he finally roared. "You love that house. It's yours. Let me get it back for you."

She stifled a laugh. "I don't need you to get it back for me. I gave it away."

He held up both arms in frustration. "This can't be what you want. I'll call down the stars and blast through every legal roadblock to get that house back for you. I'll build a case like no one's ever seen before. Woman, I will go to *war* for you. I'll fight to the ends of the earth for you. Just tell me what you need."

Oh, Patrick, always trying to be a savior. But that wasn't what she needed.

"I need a man who is strong enough to stand beside a Blackstone woman without wilting," she yelled down, and Patrick flinched. His chest caved in, and his shoulders sagged.

When he finally spoke, all the swagger was drained from his voice. "Now you're hitting where it hurts," he said.

"You asked; I answered."

His shoulders straightened again. "It's not that I'm afraid of your family. And it's not that I don't love you, because I do."

She looked heavenward in exasperation. Down in her stateroom she had a stack of botanical literature she was itching to get back to, and ripping the bandage off this wound seemed needlessly painful if all Patrick wanted to do was count the reasons he was too proud to be a part of her world.

"What good does that do if you're too stubborn to believe we can be together?"

He glowered at her. "Yes, I'm stubborn, and I want to use that to help you. Gwen, don't you know that I want to give you the world? I don't have much to offer. The only thing I've got is my strength and my brain and my ability to clear obstacles out of the way. Let me fight this battle for you. I'll get your house back."

She sighed. She didn't want her house back, she only wanted his heart. They needed to talk, but hollering this conversation so that everyone in the marina could hear was too embarrassing, even for her.

"Stay right there," she said. "I'm coming down."

It took a while for a crew member to lower the gangway. She didn't realize until she picked her way down the steeply angled ramp that she was still barefoot and wore only a robe over her nightgown. The planks were rough beneath her bare feet, but she scurried across them until she stood before Patrick.

He looked tired and sick at heart. "Why did you give away your house?" he asked. "You can't tell me that you wanted to, because I won't believe it."

She touched the side of his face. "There is a little girl I love very much. I want her to have a happy childhood, and she will have one there. I was glad to give her the house. That house isn't what I need. It never was."

He clasped her hand to his cheek. "You once said that I was letting my pride stand in the way of doing what's right."

"I remember." She took her hand back and withdrew a few steps. She would have made any sacrifice for him, and the fact that he wasn't willing to bend even a little for her would probably always hurt.

"I don't feel very proud right now," he said on a ragged breath. "I feel humbled by the fact that you had the strength to walk into a new world. Unafraid. Fearless."

She choked on a laugh. "Does it look that way? I'm not. I've had butterflies in my stomach ever since I decided to go back to school. I bought a new place to live on Boulanger Avenue and will move in as soon as the plumbers are finished."

His eyes narrowed in disapproval. "Mrs. K, that's not exactly a safe neighborhood."

Her new apartment was midway between Wall Street and the Five Points, and it was walking distance to New York University. It was a middling neighborhood, but hundreds of people lived there, and she could too.

"Nothing in this world is safe," she said. "Marrying Jasper wasn't safe. Trusting Liam wasn't safe. Sometimes our gambles work, but not always. I'm strong enough to survive, even if the worst happens. I'm going back to college. I'm scared but happy and excited too. I'm determined to make a wonderful life in my cozy little Boulanger Avenue apartment, even if I live alone for the rest of my life."

He swallowed hard. "You being alone would be a crime."

Patrick always said that when he was nervous, his Irish accent came on strong, and it was strong enough to cripple a horse right now.

"Mrs. K, I let you down," he said. "I got too caught up in worrying what people thought of me when I should have been counting my blessings for the miracle that brought you into my life. By rights, you and I should never have met, but we did, and maybe the hand of God had something to do with that."

His voice stumbled to a halt, and to her stunned surprise, he went down on one knee. He looked as surprised as she felt.

"Gwen, I love you very much, and it's not going away." He swallowed hard and looked terrified. "I would be honored if you would be willing to be my wife."

This was going too fast. It was coming out of the blue for both of them, and that wasn't the way to start a marriage.

"Oh, Patrick, please stand up, and let's not do anything impulsive. You didn't come here because of a desperate urge to marry me. You came over to evict Vivian."

He got back up on his feet. "Can't I do both?"

A burst of laughter escaped her, and she stepped into his arms. Being wrapped in his embrace again was like coming home. Through their clothes, Gwen could feel his heart pounding so fast she feared for his health.

"I appreciate the gesture, but this is too important to rush."

He pulled back to look down at her in surprise. "Are you saying no?"

Was she going to regret this? Possibly, but no woman who had suffered through a bad marriage wanted to repeat the experience. She had worked hard to create a life of purpose. In her heart, she hoped Patrick could someday be a part of it, but she didn't need him to have that life.

"I'm saying *not yet*. Go home, Patrick."

The shock on his face was almost comical, but it would be awful to become engaged in a rush of sentimentality and regret it later. Someday he might come to her with an offer of marriage without misgivings or that panicked look in his eyes, but until that day, she would build a strong and meaningful life on her own.

42

*P*atrick was stunned when Gwen turned down his proposal.

Stunned and *humbled*. It was embarrassing, but he'd expected Gwen to fall on his offer, not go about her new life without him. In September she began classes at New York University, creating a new circle of friends among her fellow students and the teaching faculty. She had the nicest apartment of any of the graduate students, and her home on Boulanger Avenue became the natural gathering spot for study sessions after class. Her famous Friday night soirees continued with resounding success.

Patrick had to *ask* to be invited. The gatherings were a wonderful mix of people from the university, artists who made their living in the city, and the occasional Blackstone relative. Bertie kept everyone in stitches whenever he came, and Patrick had even befriended Joshua, who attended Gwen's parties whenever he came to the city to exhibit his paintings at a Manhattan gallery. The home Gwen created on Boulanger Avenue was one of spiritual vibrancy that naturally attracted people to her.

With each passing week, Patrick fell more in love with her, and his fears about marrying into the Blackstone family diminished. It was Gwen he would marry, not her cousins or uncles or the people who drifted in and out of her world. Gwen brought out the best in people. The best in *him*. He wanted to create a warm, joyous, faith-filled home with Gwen at the heart of it.

Except he wasn't entirely certain she would have him. As the weeks passed, she never gave any hint she wanted to rush to the altar. It was to be expected that her studies would keep her busy, but there were times when he only got to see her on Sundays, when they went to church together and then had lunch at his apartment with Birdie and Mrs. O'Shea.

In hindsight, he was embarrassed by his impulsive and clumsy proposal on the pier. A marriage should start with a strong foundation and a gift to symbolize his commitment. He couldn't afford a fancy diamond ring or anything else extravagant, but he could offer her something better. Something to prove that he had the heart, mind, and desire to support her deepest dreams and share her world.

He met with her cousin Joshua at the library of Saint Boniface College to begin planning a strategy. The librarian had pulled several research books, and they were open on the table before them.

"You want a painting?" Joshua asked curiously.

"Like the kind you painted for Frederick's summer house," Patrick confirmed, gesturing to the photographs in the books. "Except instead of a house, it's a sixteenth-century monastery perched on a hilltop. You'll have to guess at the colors, but it's in the southern part of Spain where the climate is dry and arid."

The book before them had a grainy photograph of the monastery, and Patrick pointed at the hillside below the old stone walls. "Leave out those houses and the goat farm because they're all new. I'd like you to cover the hillside with groves of date palms instead. That's where the monks once had their groves before they cut them down in favor of grazing land."

A librarian showed them some botanical drawings of date

palms, so Joshua had everything he needed to re-create the image of what the monastery probably looked like centuries ago when they supported themselves through growing dates. Joshua's face held a spark of enthusiasm as he studied the various images.

"I can have it done within a week," he said.

The painting was only one part of Patrick's carefully planned proposal of marriage. The biggest part had taken Father Doyle's help. Those Spanish monks had been unmoved by Gwen's offer to buy the ancient date seeds she wanted so badly. They were getting rich off their three-percent stake in the Blackstone Bank and were impervious to monetary temptation. The academic appeal from professors at Blackstone College had failed too. Patrick and Father Doyle put their heads together to think about what the monks truly wanted, and after a few weeks of transatlantic cables, a bargain was struck.

The monks wanted converts. Their denomination had recently founded a new monastery in Kentucky, and they needed students who were willing to consider embarking on the unconventional life of holy orders in a rural monastery. Father Doyle couldn't promise them new disciples, but he agreed to alert students preparing for holy orders at Saint Boniface of the chance to spend a season of contemplative prayer at the new monastery. It might ultimately lead to new converts who wished to join their community.

And with that, the monks promised twelve of the rare date seeds on the next ship. A sack of three-hundred-year-old seeds arrived the last week in November. To Patrick's eye, they looked so dark and shriveled that it was hard to imagine they could be resurrected, but if anyone could do it, Gwen could.

Patrick appealed to Aunt Martha for advice on creating the perfect evening for Gwen, even though Martha was horrified by Patrick's idea to propose on a fire escape. He remained firm on the location but took her advice about what sort of flowers Gwen liked best. Not only were peonies a classic symbol of love and marriage, but they had a heady fragrance, and the fire escape overlooking the Five Points could benefit from a flowery scent.

His mother helped prepare the apartment. She covered the dining table with a white linen cloth and arranged the peonies in a pitcher for a centerpiece, but the main attraction was an elaborate three-tier cake featuring dates and walnuts. Joshua's watercolor of the monastery was on an easel beside the cake. The painting would help Gwen imagine what the monastery looked like hundreds of years ago when the date seeds Patrick had in his pocket had been created. Perhaps someday soon those seeds would be coaxed back to life in the carefully controlled environment of the Blackstone College greenhouse.

Gwen was due to arrive at seven o'clock. Ten minutes ahead of time, his mother helped him light a dozen votive candles that he placed around the fire escape. Inside, he'd dimmed the kerosene lantern so she wouldn't get distracted by the display on the dining table before he could get her outside.

Everything was ready, and it was time for Birdie to leave. "Hurry, Ma," he urged. "Mrs. O'Shea will be waiting for you next door."

Having his mother in the main room while he was trying to propose right outside on the fire escape would be awful. He was going to do his proposal right this time.

Birdie took her own sweet time as she gathered a shawl and headed next door. Patrick locked the door behind her, then went outside to wait on the fire escape. The amber tones of the sunset made the humble neighborhood look almost romantic. The matchbox containing the seeds was in his pocket.

Soon he spotted Gwen heading his way. She no longer traveled with bodyguards or feared the inner city, and she made the half-mile walk between their apartments regularly.

"Hello there, Mrs. K!" he called down to her.

Gwen looked up, a bright smile on her face as she waved up at him, but a scolding voice came from next door.

"Call her by her given name, Patrick," Mrs. O'Shea said.

"Hush," his mother whispered. "He's not supposed to hear us."

Patrick sighed. "Close the window, Ma."

There was some grumbling from the ladies next door, but he heard the rasp of the sash being pushed down.

"All the way," he ordered.

Birdie quibbled a little, saying they needed the fresh air, but he pressed until he heard the definitive thud of the casement hitting the windowsill. He really didn't want any help from his mother as he proposed to the love of his life.

He hurried back through the window and reached the front door just as Gwen arrived.

"How lovely," she said, taking in the candlelit apartment and drifting toward the gorgeous bouquet of flowers on the table. He steered her shoulders toward the fire escape instead.

"First I thought we could head outside for a little toast," he said.

"Your mother isn't here?"

"It's just you and me tonight. It will be like old times out on the fire escape."

Gwen smiled agreeably. "I have fond memories of evenings on the fire escape. What's the occasion?"

He was suddenly tongue-tied and ducked out the window first, then turned to help her navigate through. She had done this so many times that she didn't need his help, but she still took his hand and demonstrated surprising grace as she emerged on the other side.

"My goodness," she said, gazing at the votive candles and the cluster of flowers decorating the plain metal platform. Her face flushed a gorgeous shade as the implications of the romantically transformed fire escape started to penetrate. The champagne had already been uncorked, and he poured her a glass.

"To us," he said as he raised a glass to her.

She smiled and took a sip but set it down quickly. "Patrick, what's this all about?"

He swallowed hard and stood up straight. This was it.

"I may be a big Irish lunk, but I learn from my mistakes," he said. "I love you very much. I'm sorry it took me so long to get off my high horse and see that you and I could be perfect together despite all the differences between us."

He was about to launch into the rest of his prepared speech, but Gwen's attention had wandered across the lane.

"Good heavens, that looks like my cousin Joshua," she said in amazement.

He followed her gaze, where Joshua sat on one of the benches outside the pub across the street. Father Doyle sat beside him, with Aunt Martha and Uncle Milton on the other side.

"I really didn't want an audience for this," Patrick muttered.

Gwen leaned over the railing, squinting through the gathering twilight. "Liam is watching us through the pub window," she said.

Patrick scowled. Sure enough, Liam, Natalia, and Bertie were all crowded inside the pub, looking up at them. The entire pub was probably crawling with Blackstones.

"My mother never could keep a secret," he said in frustration.

Birdie's voice rang out from next door. "I heard that! It was Martha who rounded everyone up."

Down below, Joshua stood up and hollered, "Did she say yes?"

"I haven't asked her yet," Patrick bellowed down. "Too many people keep butting in."

"Oh!" Joshua looked suitably embarrassed as he sat back down beside Father Doyle. "Don't mind us. Carry on."

Heat engulfed Patrick as he sighed and turned to Gwen. Her eyes glowed with laughter and affection. By now, all element of surprise had been blown to smithereens.

"It looks like you've figured out why I asked you up here tonight," he said. "I'm sorry. I wanted this to be a lot more romantic."

"Oh, Patrick, there are worse things than having a loving family and community coming out to support you."

No doubt, but he refused to propose in front of them. He slipped through the window and helped her back inside, shutting the window behind them. They were finally alone. He stole a quick kiss, then guided her to the table. His mother's artistry made it look perfect. The candlelight, the flowers. Birdie had even bought little jars of fancy imported dates to set beside the cake.

"Josh painted a picture of that monastery in Spain," he said. "The ones who were so stubborn about the date seeds you wanted, even though they've grown rich as Croesus from their percentage of shares in the Blackstone Bank."

She picked up the watercolor that was mounted in a simple brass frame. "This is what it looks like? I've never seen it before."

"That was what it probably looked like a few hundred years ago, back before they plowed the date palms under in favor of grazing land. I wanted you to see what it looked like when they tended an orchard."

He reached into his pocket for the matchbox and set it in her hands. "Most men probably propose to a woman with a nice ring, but I thought you might like this better. I wanted to give you something to prove that I understand what you need to be happy. I want us to love and support each other forever. I want to be your husband and the father to any children God blesses us with. If you'll have me, I'd like to build a family with you. Gwen, will you marry me?"

Her eyes looked luminous in the candlelight, and her voice was confident. "You don't look terrified anymore," she said. "I'll happily marry you."

He was the luckiest man on earth. Finding the right woman had taken longer than he imagined, but as he held her in his arms, he knew they had made the right choice. A solid home involved family and community, but it was mostly the responsibility of the two people at the helm to nurture, provide, and inspire.

"Can I open this box?" she asked against his shoulder.

He stepped back and held his breath as she slid the matchbox open, revealing the shrunken, shriveled seeds inside. She glanced up at him, her face full of wonder as she asked if these were what she thought they were.

He nodded. "The Spanish monks finally agreed to let us have a go at making them germinate. I figure you'll know what sort of tending it will take to give them a healthy start."

"I do," she confirmed. "I don't know if these are past hope, but I'll provide them with the ideal conditions to give them a chance."

It was the best they could do, and the rest would be in God's hands. It was the same with raising a family. There were no guarantees in life, but he and Gwen would build the foundation of a loving, faith-filled home that welcomed friends, family, and community.

He hopped out onto the fire escape and cupped his hands around his mouth to bellow out the good news to the people in the street. "She said yes!"

His mother's shrieks of delight came from next door, while people from the pub raised their glasses in a toast.

He grinned and stepped back inside. "I figure we have about two minutes before they all come charging in here," he said as he took her into his arms.

"More like thirty seconds, since your mother is next door."

"Let's not waste it, then," he said, leaning down for a long and deep kiss.

Gwen returned it, and he lifted her off the ground, loving every moment of this. Only seconds later, Birdie and Mrs. O'Shea were rattling the doorknob, pestering to be let inside, but he wanted this moment to last forever. He set Gwen down and cradled her face between his hands, smiling down into her eyes.

"You're the best thing that ever happened to me, Mrs. K, but I think we're out of time."

Soon Liam was pounding on the door too, wanting to congratulate his new brother. Gwen gave him a radiant smile, then unlocked the bolt and threw the door open. The apartment flooded with friends and family, both from his side and from hers. Father Doyle said a blessing, and the rejoicing began.

337

Historical Note

*O*scar Blackstone is a fictional character loosely based on J.P. Morgan, the financier famous for his ability to merge companies into huge corporations. Morgan cooperated with several New York banks to buy Carnegie Steel and merge it with other large steel companies to create the United States Steel Corporation. When U.S. Steel was listed on the New York Stock Exchange in March of 1901, it was valued at 1.4 billion dollars, the first company in the world to be valued at more than a billion dollars. During its first year, U.S. Steel produced almost seventy percent of the steel in the United States, eventually leading to charges that it violated the Sherman Antitrust Act, which prohibited unfair monopolies. By the time the case reached the U.S. Supreme Court, the company's market share had decreased, and the court sided with U.S. Steel, allowing it to continue in its present form.

Louise Carnegie did indeed play a role in convincing her husband to sell his company in order to retire to Scotland. Thereafter, the Carnegies split their time between Scotland and New York, devoting themselves to philanthropic activities such as Carnegie Hall and the Carnegie Technical School, which is now called Carnegie Mellon University.

Gwen's old date seeds could probably be resurrected if she treated them well. In 2005 botanists succeeded in reviving a two-thousand-year-old date seed found in the ancient fortress of Masada, the site of the famous siege in AD 74. The first date palm that sprouted was named Methuselah and was identified as a Judean date palm, a tree that had been extinct for hundreds of years. Other date seeds found at Masada have also sprouted, and the palms were named Adam, Jonah, Uriel, Boaz, Judith, and Hannah. Date palms have long been known for their medicinal qualities, and as these ancient palms grow and are propagated, it is hoped they may offer new insight into herbal remedies that were lost to history.

Questions for Discussion

1. Gwen and Liam get off to a rocky start, but Patrick cautions, "*The two of you are very different, but people of good character can disagree and still be admirable.*" What does he mean by that, and do you agree?

2. What do you think of the way Gwen tried to win Jasper back from Vivian? Could it ever have worked? How would you have counseled her during this time?

3. Do you think Liam will ever be able to forgive his mother? Should he?

4. Gwen struggles to accept Liam upon his return because he does not fit her preconceived expectations of what an older brother should be like. Have you seen preconceived expectations cause difficulties among people in your own life?

5. Patrick prides himself on being "a man of the people," so what did Gwen mean when she accused him of being a snob? Is snobbery always a one-way street?

6. The extraordinary marble mansions of Gwen's family are quite different from the craftsman-style home she designed for herself. If money were no option, would you choose to live in gilded splendor, or would you choose a home that reflects a more traditional style?

7. Patrick says, "*Sometimes the Lord sends us into the valley for a reason, even if we don't understand why.*" Can you see examples of this in the novel or in your own life?

8. Gwen's comfortable life at Blackstone College led her into complacency about pursuing her ambition to earn a doctorate in botany. What caused her to develop the strength to pursue it near the end?

9. Liam partners with Uncle Oscar at the end of the novel. How do you predict that alliance will play out?

10. Some of the Blackstones are admirable people, but some are not. Penelope-Arabella is only eight years old but already behaves in an entitled and rude fashion. What role, if any, should the extended family play in trying to correct such behavior?

11. When was the last time you had a tetanus booster? They should happen every ten years. What are some of the dangers of living in an era where medical miracles have become commonplace?

In 2022, look for Natalia Blackstone's story in

Written on the Wind

Book Two of The Blackstone Legacy series

Natalia Blackstone is a rarity in Gilded-Age America. As a trusted analyst for her father's bank, she is helping finance the legendary Trans-Siberian Railway. From her office in New York City, Natalia relies on a charming Russian aristocrat to oversee the construction of the railroad on the other side of the world.

Count Dimitri Sokolov witnessed an incident during his work on the Trans-Siberian that threatens the Russian monarchy. In an effort to silence him, the czar has stripped Dimitri of his title, his lands, and his freedom. But Dimitri has one asset the czar knows nothing about: his deep and abiding friendship with Natalia Blackstone.

After Dimitri and Natalia join forces, their friendship deepens into a turbulent romance as they embark on a quest to protect the railroad from political catastrophe. From the steppes of Russia to the corridors of power in Washington, DC, Natalia and Dimitri will fight against all odds to save the railroad, but can their newfound love survive the ordeal?

Elizabeth Camden is best known for her historical novels set in Gilded Age America, featuring clever heroines and richly layered story lines. Before she was a writer, she was an academic librarian at some of the largest and smallest libraries in America, but her favorite is the continually growing library in her own home. Her novels have won the RITA and Christy Awards and have appeared on the CBA bestsellers list. She lives in Orlando, Florida, with her husband, who graciously tolerates her intimidating stockpile of books. Learn more online at www.elizabethcamden.com.

Sign Up for Elizabeth's Newsletter

Keep up to date with Elizabeth's news on book releases and events by signing up for her email list at elizabethcamden.com.

More from Elizabeth Camden

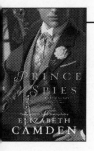

Luke Delacroix's hidden past as a spy has him carrying out an ambitious agenda—thwarting the reelection of his only real enemy. But trouble begins when he falls for Marianne Magruder, the congressman's daughter. Can their newfound love survive a political firestorm, or will three generations of family rivalry drive them apart forever?

The Prince of Spies • HOPE AND GLORY #3

You May Also Like . . .

Secretary to the first lady of the United States, Caroline Delacroix is at the pinnacle of high society—but is hiding a terrible secret. Immediately suspicious of Caroline but also attracted to her, secret service agent Nathaniel Trask must battle his growing love for her as the threat to the president rises and they face adventure, heartbreak, and danger.

A Gilded Lady by Elizabeth Camden
HOPE AND GLORY #2
elizabethcamden.com

Gray Delacroix has dedicated his life to building a successful global spice empire, but it has come at a cost. Tasked with gaining access to the private Delacroix plant collection, Smithsonian botanist Annabelle Larkin unwittingly steps into a web of dangerous political intrigue and will be forced to choose between her heart and her loyalty to her country.

The Spice King by Elizabeth Camden
HOPE AND GLORY #1
elizabethcamden.com

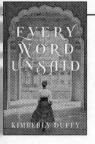

As the nation's most fearless travel columnist, Augusta Travers explores the country, spinning stories for women unable to leave hearth and home. Suddenly caught in a scandal, she escapes to India to visit old friends, promising great tales of boldness. But instead she encounters a plague, new affections, and the realization that she can't outrun her past.

Every Word Unsaid by Kimberly Duffy
kimberlyduffy.com

BETHANYHOUSE

More from Bethany House

After Pearl Harbor, sweethearts Gordon Hooper and Dorie Armitage were broken up by their convictions. As a conscientious objector, he went west to fight fires as a smokejumper, while she joined the Army Corps. When a tragic accident raises suspicions, they're forced to work together, but the truth they uncover may lead to an impossible—and dangerous—choice.

The Lines Between Us by Amy Lynn Green
amygreenbooks.com

After a deadly explosion at the Chilwell factory, munitions worker Rosalind Graham leaves the painful life she's dreamt of escaping by assuming the identity of her deceased friend. When RAF Captain Alex Baird is ordered to surveil her for suspected sabotage, the danger of her deception intensifies. Will Rose's daring bid for freedom be her greatest undoing?

As Dawn Breaks by Kate Breslin
katebreslin.com

After an abusive relationship derailed her plans, Adri Rivera struggles to regain her independence and achieve her dream of becoming an MMA fighter. She gets a second chance, but the man who offers it to her is Max Lyons—her former training partner, whom she left heartbroken years before. As she fights for her future, will she be able to confront her past?

After She Falls by Carmen Schober
carmenschober.com

BETHANYHOUSE

Printed in the United States
by Baker & Taylor Publisher Services

12/2021